COMPROMISING
AGREEMENTS

ANNIE DYER

Compromising Agreements

ABOUT THE AUTHOR

Annie Dyer lives in Manchester, England. She spends her time finding ways to procrastinate from tidying up, usually through creating characters. Staple foods include chocolate, Pad Thai and whatever hasn't gone off in the fridge.

You can find out more about Annie's upcoming books and the inspiration behind them through her newsletter and Facebook group, Annie's London Lovers.

https://www.facebook.com/groups/AnniesLondonLovers

Visit her website to sign up for the newsletter and received access to bonus epilogues!

https://www.writeranniedyer.com

For my Great-Great Auntie Marian, who loved books almost more than me, and apparently liked the steamy ones too! I'm sure you'd have approved!

———

ALSO BY ANNIE DYER

Simone Wood is a restaurant owner who loves to dance, she's just never found the right partner until her head chef Jack starts to teach her his rhythm. Problem is, someone's not happy with Simone, and their dance could be over before they've learned the steps.

Mythical Creatures

The enigmatic Callum Callaghan heads to Africa with the only woman who came close to taming his heart, in this steamy second-chance romance. Contains a beautifully broken alpha and some divinely gorgeous scenery in this tale that will make you both cry and laugh. HEA guaranteed.

Melted Hearts

Hot rock star? Enemies to lovers? Fake engagement? All of these ingredients are in this Callaghan Green novel. Sophie Slater is a businesswoman through and through but makes a pact with the devil – also known as Liam Rossi, newly retired Rockstar – to get the property she wants - one that just happens to be in Iceland. Northern lights, a Callaghan bachelor party, and a quickly picked engagement ring are key notes in this hot springs heated romance.

Evergreen

Christmas wouldn't be Christmas without any presents, and that's what's going to happen if Seph Callaghan doesn't get his act together. The Callaghan clan are together for Christmas, along with a positive pregnancy test from someone and several more surprises!

The Partnership

Seph Callaghan finally gets his HEA in this office romance. Babies, exes and a whole lot of smoulder!

The English Gent Romances

The Wedding Agreement

Imogen Green doesn't do anything without thinking it through, and that includes offering to marry her old - very attractive - school friend, Noah Soames, who needs a wedding. The only problem is, their fauxmance might not be so fake, after all…

The Atelier Assignment

Dealing with musty paintings is Catrin Green's job. Dealing with a hot Lord who happens to be grumpy AF isn't. But that's what she's stuck with for three months. Zeke's daughter is the only light in her days, until she finds a way to make Zeke smile. Only this wasn't part of the assignment.

The Romance Rehearsal

Maven Green has managed to avoid her childhood sweetheart for more than a decade, but now he's cast as her leading man in the play she's directing. Anthony was the boy who had all her firsts; will he be her last as well?

The Imperfect Proposal

Shay Green doesn't expect his new colleague to walk in on him when he's mid-kiss in a stockroom. He also doesn't expect his new colleague to be his wife. The wife he married over a decade ago in Vegas and hasn't seen since

Puffin Bay Series

Puffin Bay

Amelie started a new life on a small Welsh island, finding peace and new beginnings. What wasn't in the plan was the man buying the building over the road. She was used to dealing with arrogant tourists, but this city boy was enough to have her want to put her hands around his neck, on his chest, and maybe somewhere else too...

Wild Tides

Being a runaway bride and escaping her wedding wasn't what Fleur intended when she said yes to the dress. That dress is now sodden in the water of the Menai Strait and she needs saving - by none other than lighthouse keeper Thane. She needs a man to get under to get over the one she left at the altar - but that might come with a little surprise in a few months time…

Lovers Heights

Serious gin distiller Finn Holland needs a distraction from what he's trying to leave behind in the city. That distraction comes in the form of Ruby, who's moved to the island to escape drama of her own. Neither planned on a fake relationship, especially one that led to a marriage that might not be that fake at all…

Manchester Athletic FC

Penalty Kiss

Manchester Athletic's bad boy needs taming, else his football career could be on the line. Pitched with women's football's role model pin up, he has pre-season to sort out his game - on and off the field.

Hollywood Ball

One night. It didn't matter who she was, or who he was, because tomorrow they'd both go back to their lives. Only hers wasn't that ordinary.

What she didn't know, was neither was his.

Heart Keeper

Single dad. Recent widow. Star goal keeper.

Manchester Athletic's physio should keep her hands to herself outside of her treatment room, but that's proving tough. What else is tough is finding two lines on that pregnancy test…

Target Man

Jesse Sullivan is Manchester Athletic's Captain Marvel. He keeps his private life handcuffed to his bed, locked behind a non-disclosure agreement. Jesse doesn't do relationships – not until he meets his teammate's – and best friend's – sister.

Red Heart Card

She wants a baby. He's offering. The trouble is, he's soccer's golden boy and he's ten years younger. The last time they tried this, she broke is heart. Will hearts be left intact this time around?

Severton Search and Rescue

Sleighed

Have a change of scenery and take a trip to a small town. Visit Severton, in Sleighed; this friends-to-lovers romantic suspense will capture your heart as much as Sorrell Slater steals Zack Maynard's.

Stirred

If enemies-to-lovers is your manna, then you'll want to stay in Severton for Stirred. Keren Leigh and Scott Maynard have been at daggers drawn for years, until their one-night ceasefire changes the course of their lives forever.

Smoldered

Want to be saved by a hot firefighter? Rayah Maynard's lusted over Jonny Graham ever since she came back to town. Jonny's prioritised his three children over his own love life since his wife died, but now Rayah's teaching more than just his daughter – she's teaching him just how hot their flames can burn.

Shaken

Abby Walker doesn't exist. Hiding from a gang she suspects is involved in the disappearance of her sister, Severton is where she's taken refuge. Along with her secrets, she's hiding her huge crush on local cop, Alex Maynard. But she isn't the only one with secrets. Alex can keep her safe, but can he also take care of her heart?

Sweetened

Enemies? Friends? Could be lovers? All Jake Maynard knows is that Lainey Green is driving him mad, and he really doesn't like that she managed to buy the farm he coveted from under his nose. All's fair in love and war, until events in Severton take a sinister turn.

Standalone Romance

Love Rises

Two broken souls, one hot summer. Anya returns to her childhood island home after experiencing a painful loss. Gabe escapes to the same place, needing to leave his life behind, drowning in guilt. Neither are planning on meeting the other, but when they do, from their grief, love rises. Only can it be more than a summer long?

Bartender

The White Island, home of hedonism, heat and holidays. Jameson returns to her family's holiday home on Ibiza, but doesn't expect to charmed by a a bartender, a man with an agenda other than just seduction.

Tarnished Crowns Trilogy

Lovers. Liars. Traitors. Thieves. We were all of these. Political intrigue, suspense and seduction mingle together in this intricate and steamy royal romance trilogy.

Chandelier

Grenade

Emeralds

Crime Fiction

We Were Never Alone

How Far Away the Stars (Novella)

COMPROMISING AGREEMENTS

Compromise Agreement: A **compromise agreement** is an **agreement** to settle a previously existing claim with a substituted performance. A valid **compromise** and settlement bars all right of recovery on the previously existing claim. This is so because the **compromise agreement** is substituted for the claim, and the rights and liabilities of the parties are measured and limited by the terms of the **agreement**. The previously existing claim is extinguished by the **compromise** and settlement and, as a result, any subsequent litigation based upon it is barred. A **compromise agreement** is a contract and, as such, there must be mutual assent of the parties and consideration.

CHAPTER 1
MAXWELL

"I'm sorry, but that room is already taken for the duration of the semester."

Those were not the words I expected to hear. My hand immediately went to stroke my jaw and I tried to concentrate on the fact that my beard needed a trim in order to cease and desist the tantrum that was building. I wasn't a spoiled brat, although my upbringing and bank balance would give evidence otherwise, but I was impatient and had no time for people who didn't read their emails.

"Look," I said to the dark brown head of hair that was half hidden by the biggest computer monitor I had ever seen. "I used that room for all my seminars last year. It's close to my offices which means I get there on time for my students and it's steeped in history. It gives more credence when trying to get undergraduates to understand the legacy of what they're studying…"

"I understand that, Professor Callaghan—"

"It's Mr Callaghan. I don't use professor," I interrupted, this time rubbing my jaw in a firmer manner. I had been lecturing at King's College, one of London's top universities, for three years, writing articles and contributing to the odd publication. I didn't grow an ego on purpose but the office staff knew me and generally made sure any new employees knew me too. It stopped time wasting conversations like this when I needed to get back to my desk to prep for court tomorrow.

"Apologies, Mr Callaghan, but the room is scheduled for someone else to teach in, and while I'm aware that puts you to some inconvenience, it can't be altered. Maybe we can find an alternative time, or maybe another room in that building?" Her tone was flat, almost as if I was listening to a pre-recorded response.

I didn't think I was that *predictable*.

"I've already worked my meeting schedule around that time and not needing more than five minutes to get to the venue," I said, my hand flecking through my hair which also needed a cut. I'd been too busy. Even though summer was only just ending my desk was swamped; I'd just received a huge class action case and had two new solicitors working for me that needed training in the very basics despite allegedly being at least three years qualified.

The brown head sighed. "Leave it with me. I'll see what I can do around the use of the other rooms in that building."

"Can't you just ask the other class to move times or elsewhere? If my seminars can't be accommodated there I'll have to rethink lecturing and teaching this year." Which might be a good thing given how heavy my workload already was, although teaching was something I enjoyed immensely. I thrived from the buzz I got when students understood some of the complexities of law and became engaged with it, seeing it as being a real life embodiment of our society. And I liked the interaction that wasn't just with my family and work colleagues, which rather sadly summed up my life.

The door to the back office swung open and a slight, white-haired woman walked in, looking somewhat startled as she caught my last words. "Victoria will sort it, Max," she said, squinting at the huge monitor.

Carol Sommers was the Dean of Law and her mere presence made Victoria sit up a little straighter. "One of the other rooms will have to be freed up." Carol pointed to something on the screen.

"The history department are using it at that time. They can move." She squinted and stared at Victoria. "The room next door is being used by the Assassins' Guild. They can also shift."

"I'm not sure…" Victoria began. I caught sight of thick rimmed glasses but the rest of the side of her face was shielded by long hair that was almost black.

"They were struggling for a space—there aren't many departments that will let them use a room."

"With good reason," Carol said. "It's the Assassins' Guild. Surely you're not that far removed from your undergraduate years to have forgotten the amount of havoc they cause. If their meetings are located near to you when you're teaching, at some point you're going to be interrupted." She looked half angry, half amused. "I'm sure Max won't mind the Assassins' Guild going homeless."

She beamed at me, just as she had in court once, when I was newly qualified and had a case against her. I lost. I'd hated her beam ever since, which she knew. Carol Sommers was the best in her field.

"My youngest brother was in the Assassins' Guild when he was here," I said, thinking of Seph with what could almost be described as affection. "Unfortunately, he wasn't shot often enough or hard enough. If they're stuck for a room, I'm sure Seph can sort something with his friend who runs a bar near Borough Market." I rubbed my chin again. The Assassins' Guild had been a pain; a society of students who were given targets to 'kill' before they were killed themselves, usually with a nerf gun or a water pistol. The last person standing won. Seph had managed to win three consecutive times, which was probably the result of the skills he'd picked up from escaping me, Jackson and Callum when he was younger and we wanted someone to torment that wasn't our sisters.

"That will solve the problem," Victoria said. "Can you ask your brother for that favour? I'd try to sort it myself but I'm struggling for time."

Wasn't that her job as an administrator? I felt my heart rate climb up with irritation and knew I needed to get to the gym tonight and box a few rounds in the ring. "Sure. Seph's in court all day but I'll ask him. I'd prefer the other room if possible. It does have significance for one of topics I'll be delivering. Would the history professor mind swapping?"

"I think that could be arranged. Don't you, Victoria?" Carol said, opening a drawer and taking a sweet.

"That particular room has some historical significance for the seminars taking place there too. The war memorial…" she said, her voice sounding tense. "I think the person teaching would also like to use that room."

I didn't have time for these arguments; not when I'd sent a detailed email about three months ago outlining what I'd need and why. Most professors had a certain degree of eccentricity: Niall McInnery, who'd written the book on Torts when I'd been a student, demanded a fresh pot of coffee and two apple Danishes at the start of each lecture he gave; Ruth Reece would only use lecture theatres with an odd number. My choice of time and location was, to be fair, rather rational. "I sent an email requesting that room some months ago. I don't mean to act like a dick, but I don't ask for much and it's not my fault if someone hasn't checked their email."

I heard another sharp intake of breath from Victoria, admin extraordinaire. She was clearly pissed off with me. "If you emailed it to Michelle directly rather than the admin account then it won't have been picked up. Michelle's taken extended leave. I've been brought in to cover for her. I don't think the person delivering the history seminars will want to swap. Maybe you could do the hour after?"

"How do you know the history faculty won't switch? Isn't it worth contacting the person teaching rather than just speaking for them?" My fingers tapped on the desk, peering over at the brown head and spying her hands flattening either side of the keyboard with a slight thud.

Then she stood up and I heard Carol laugh quietly at my mouth gaping open. The computer screen had masked a woman who would now star in my fantasies for at least the next few weeks: tall, slender, wearing a high-necked, sleeveless shirt that showed off more than a handful of breasts, large doe-like eyes and lips that my cock now wanted to meet up close.

"Because I'm leading the seminars there. And I'm going to use that room!"

———

My oldest younger brother took a long swig of his beer, sat back in his chair and eyed me as someone would do a rabid bear. "So, exactly how did you lose your shit?" he said. "Because if it's anything like you've done in the office you could be looking at her pressing charges."

I rolled my eyes. "I'm not that bad."

Jackson raised his brows.

I shook my head. This year I had been through four secretaries until Claire, one of my sisters who also worked for our law firm, had found me Jean, a wonderful woman who had raised five boys and scared the shit out of me. She was also bloody good at being a legal secretary, one who dealt with medical malpractice and didn't get the basics wrong. We were going to have a hopefully long and happy relationship where I brought her coffee and croissants every morning.

"I didn't raise my voice too much. I just mentioned about her using her position as an administrator to serve her best interests rather than the department she was taking a salary from."

"Oh," Jackson said mildly, rolling up his shirt sleeves as if suspecting we were in for the long haul. "And how did she take that comment?"

I shrugged, turning away to glance around the bar. I hadn't made it to the gym. My altercation with Victoria the administrator had slowed my day down considerably; plus, one of my team had forgotten to file documents at court, which resulted in various phone calls and calling in favours from the judge. I had agreed to meet Jackson at our usual after work bar. "As you would expect, I suppose."

"What was her reaction?"

"Feisty. It was feisty." Feisty enough to give me a raging hard on and have to fight the urge to fuck the sass out of her temporarily, because that would've resulted in a lawsuit.

Jackson laughed quietly, finishing the rest of his beer. "Who won?"

I rested my elbows on my knees and held my head in my hands. "Neither. She won't change rooms or her time."

"So she's won?"

"No. I didn't say that."

My brother smirked. "But you haven't got the room. Therefore, you have lost. To a history lecturer. I think this could be the highlight of my day. Tell me, was she attractive?"

I groaned, shaking my head. "That's irrelevant. She works in the admin department and lectures in history. And she has my room."

"It's not your room. And it's already booked." Jackson's eyes flickered over to the door, probably looking for Vanessa, his fiancée. They'd been together for just over six months or so and had the wedding booked for next May. My brother had changed, becoming less work-obsessed and more Vanessa-obsessed instead. Thankfully, she'd felt the same way, else we'd have been looking at a restraining order. "Therefore there is nothing you can do. Get Seph to sort a room for the Assassins' Guild and hopefully they'll adopt him, we'll no longer have to see the fucker on a daily basis and you get a room in the building you want at the time you want, so your schedule remains unsullied."

"But I sent an email requesting that room months ago. It's not my fault the admin person was on leave and it wasn't picked up. Someone should've been checking her emails." I paused, finishing the rest of my beer. I didn't often drink, not always liking how it made me feel, however, today was an exception.

"Yes, they should. But that's not Victoria's fault either. Why is a history lecturer working as an admin in the law department anyway?" Jackson sat up straighter and I figured Vanessa had arrived. "I didn't think lecturing was that poorly paid."

"I have no idea. Nor do I care. Another beer?" I stood up, feeling a soft hand grasp my arm. "Hey, favourite sister-in-law to be." I leant into her and kissed her cheek. "How are you? Seen the light and changed your mind about which brother to marry yet?"

She laughed softly. "It depends on whether he lightens up over the space I need in the bathroom."

Jackson shifted to his feet and pulled Vanessa into him. "You can have as much space as you need. Ignore Maxwell. He has nothing to offer."

She kissed him on the stubble he called a beard. "I'll get the drinks. Same again?" She gestured to the glasses and we both nodded.

"Stop trying to pretend you can steal my woman," Jackson said, and I realised he was almost serious.

I spluttered. "Chill the fuck out, Jacks. You know I just trying to wind you up because it works. Besides, I don't think she even realises anyone else exists. Can't you bring the wedding forward or something?"

He shook his head. "It's all booked and it's exactly what she wants, so that's what we're having. She likes you and Seph way too much. She actually mentioned having everyone over for Sunday lunch this weekend."

"You're not up for that, I take it?" I said, very much amused with Jackson. He had been terminally single until Vanessa was contracted to rebrand Callaghan Green, our law firm. Our father had been the senior partner up until his retirement earlier in the year; now, Jackson and myself were the senior partners, with Jackson managing the day to day running of the firm and running a few litigation files. His love was for business, second only to Vanessa. Mine was for the law and had been since I was a kid and old enough to go into work with our father and—before he retired—my grandfather too. My grandfather had a fascination with law and its history; how it changed and how it would reflect societal values at the time. I suppose it was that fascination that was passed onto me and, thankfully, Jackson was keen to run the business side of things, leaving me to the academic and messy legalities. My specialism was mainly medical negligence cases, but I kept on top of most areas and ended up advising my siblings and colleagues when necessary. It left me with little time to spend arguing with history lecturers, however pretty they were.

"I see enough of you lot during the week and not enough of her," Jackson said, his eyes fixed on Vanessa who was at the bar. "But she really wants everyone over. Even Seph."

"Give me a time and I'll be there. I'll even come over earlier and give Van a hand in the kitchen," I said, grinning at my brother.

"Fuck off. It's bad enough how she tries to look after Seph—who is round at our house far too often, by the way—without her being nice to you too. You need to find you a girlfriend and then she'll stop worrying about you being 'lonely'," Jackson said. "Maybe you could bring one of your stable with you and she'll stop fretting."

"I'm not seeing anyone at the moment," I said, pushing away the image of Victoria with her long brown hair and oversized glasses from my memory. "Too busy."

"You mean you haven't been to a university social yet and met the new science professors? Or was science last year? Geography this time maybe?" Jackson said, his eyes still flickering towards Vanessa.

"You make it sound like I was dating half the university faculty," I said. "I went out with two women who lectured there. How many other lawyers have you dated?" For some reason my family thought I would only date women who had a doctorate.

Jackson shrugged. "Fair enough. But you're tense and more irritable than usual. Maybe you need to get laid. Have you met Vanessa's friend Sophie?"

"Yes and I'm not going anywhere near a friend of your fiancée's as that's just a recipe for disaster. Although I suppose Van would stop speaking to me and that would make you happy," I said as a pint of beer was deposited in front of me. "Thank you."

"You're welcome. Did Jackson mention Sunday lunch?" Vanessa said, squeezing onto the seat next to Jackson. "Callum's said he can make it."

I glanced at my brother. Since Callum had returned from doing veterinarian work abroad we had seen very little of him. "I'm available. Is there anything you want me to bring?"

"I'll text you and let you know. Jackson mentioned something about you having a run in with a history lecturer. Do I need to prepare a statement for the media in case she presses charges?" Vanessa said, clutching a glass of red wine like it was her life blood. It was a Thursday and she generally looked frazzled by this point of the week.

"Is nothing a secret between the two of you?" I said before

swigging the beer. This would be my last one of the evening. I'd head off home and hit the new case I'd been given today to familiarise myself with the medical reports before meeting with the claimant next week.

"Some things," Vanessa said coyly. "My wedding dress, for example. Do you still have a half empty room at your apartment?"

I raised a brow. "Why?"

She smiled. Jackson rolled his eyes and looked away. "I need somewhere to store wedding stuff. The sort of things Jackson can't see."

"You're finally showing me your underwear?" I couldn't resist.

"I'll see if one of your sisters has space," Vanessa said. "Comments like that turn him into a caveman later."

"I thought that was a good thing," Jackson said, his arm slipping around her waist.

I looked away, not needing that visual. I let them carry on their conversation while I attempted to enjoy my beer and tried not to think about the history lecturer with the body wet dreams were made of, trying to dismiss the thought that I'd be spending two hours each week in the room next to hers.

CHAPTER 2
VICTORIA

While I had the patience to study historical documents and sources in a greater depth than most other people I'd ever met, I had none for insufferable males who had larger egos than Jupiter and assumed that they could have everything their own way. Maxwell Callaghan had managed to push every nerve laden button in my body and two weeks in a nunnery where men were not allowed to even breathe within a twenty-mile radius was becoming necessary.

Although totally not happening.

"That expression looks unbecoming."

I looked up from my gloom to see James Jacob Howell III staring at me as if I was covered in pustules, or worse. I tried to smile.

"Fucking stupid men. I'm going to sign up for a nunnery," I declared. "Fuckwits the lot of them. Thinking they can have everything their own way."

"Your brother being a dickwad again?" Jacob, as he was known to everyone he was bothered about, sat down opposite me and immediately caught the attention of the waitress.

"Two margaritas please," he said. "The large ones you do that look like they should come with a free goldfish swimming in the glass."

The waitress beamed a smile at him that bordered on flirtatious and gave me a sour glance. Pity she'd be disappointed if she thought she would get anywhere with Jacob, given that his last partner had been six foot two, with eyes of blue and biceps bigger than my purse. He'd also been called Shane and Jacob had likened him to a cowboy for more than just his name.

"So why do you look like someone has urinated all over your well thought-out and carefully considered parade?" he said, leaning forward, his eyes like two pole dancers on speed.

I made a noise that sounded like a gorilla growling.

"You're going to need to be more specific than that," he said. "Let's start with who, to be followed by where and when. And possibly how, but we'll see how the first few go before more complex sentences are required."

"Maxwell Callaghan," I spat. "Dick of the year winner."

Jacob's eyes grew wider.

"Do you know him?" I asked, leaning in towards the table as if Jacob was about to confide some deep secret. I didn't think Maxwell was gay, that wasn't the vibe I got when I caught him assessing my boobs, but then not many people would think Jacob was.

Until they saw him during Pride wearing a feather boa and very little else.

"He's a top lawyer. Of course I've heard of him. I've met him a couple of times too." Jacob's father was a judge and although Jacob had swerved anything to do with law as a career in favour of publishing, he'd been to several law-themed functions. "He's all broody and mysterious. I remember seeing him at a law society ball once; he barely said a word all night then went home with some blonde. They must've communicated through hot looks alone. Although that's all I would've needed. What's he done to you? I can have him taken out, if you wish."

I cracked a smile. Jacob was fiercely protective and when he wasn't in dramatic mode could appear fairly menacing—as long as no one got him on the subject of the theatre, musicals or tweed. "He's a professor at King's and I've booked his room for my seminars. Not on purpose, I hasten to add."

Jacob looked mildly confused. "First come, first served. Or doesn't that apply to him?"

I shook my head. "He'd emailed the woman I'm covering for, but no one's thought to check her mail. It's sorted, but he's in the room next to mine as opposed to the one he wants."

"And he expected you to give in and let him have the room?"

"Correct."

Jacob sat back and laughed loudly as our cocktails were brought over. "Sweetie, you won. Why be so mad?"

"Because he's yet another man who thinks he has the God-given-right to have his way and I'm fed up of it. History is littered with them: cockwombles who think only of themselves," I said, stuffing the slim straws in my mouth and sucking violently. I needed alcohol.

"And history is also full of decent men who thought about plenty other than themselves. Why was the room so important to Mr Maxwell Callaghan, or should it be Professor?" Jacob swiped some of the salt from the rim of his glass and licked his finger.

I wrinkled my nose. "Too salty," I said.

"A bit of salt's good for you," Jacob said, delicately nibbling a finger. "Maybe you should try a bit of salt more frequently. Sweeten you up."

"Fucker," I said, giving him the finger and causing a middle-aged woman to raise her eyebrows in horror. I smiled apologetically, giving her the same gesture once she had turned her head. "He said the room was important as it was where some law or other was decided or discussed or something and it made it real for his students. He needed that room and time so it fitted in with the rest of his very important schedule, otherwise he said he couldn't teach. Carol—the dean—almost had a heart attack when she heard that. I'm sure he uses her tongue as toilet paper."

Jacob wrinkled his nose. "That's a disgusting analogy, Victoria. You could be less uncouth. However, back to the cock-womble aspect: why exactly do you need that room at that time?"

I took a long gulp of my margarita. "Because the room has historical significance which will be useful to my students and it fits in with my schedule. Your point?"

"Would you have expected him to swap with you, if his email had been read when it should have been and the room booked as he asked?" Jacob lounged on his chair, margarita in hand. He looked like a male model; chiselled cheekbones and blonde hair, the iciest blue eyes that had never been photo-shopped. I grabbed my phone and snapped a quick photo as he gave me his best blue steel gaze. He'd been my best friend for over a decade and we'd never had a cross word or a disagreement that we'd hadn't solved before bedtime. I'd been his first and last kiss with a female when we were eighteen and that had been enough to solidify a friendship that was already older than most marriages I knew.

"Would I have expected him to swap with me?" I stuttered briefly, knowing exactly the answer. "Of course not!"

"I call bullshit."

"Well, that room is more pertinent to what I'm teaching. And just because he's some hotshot professor-lawyer doesn't mean he's worth more than me. Or that his subject is more valuable than mine," I said, hearing the tinge of sulkiness in my voice.

"I'd say law is infinitely more valuable than history, sweetie. What are you earning compared to him?"

"I have no idea. I can pay my rent. And my fees. And scrape

by on bread and beans." Unfortunately, it wasn't that far from the truth.

Jacob frowned. "Have you heard from your solicitors recently?"

"Nada," I said, slurping more margarita, the alcohol going straight to my head. "I need to chase them. Again."

"You need to find new solicitors," Jacob said, gesturing to the waitress for two more drinks.

"I can't. I'd have to pay the costs so far before my case could be transferred and I haven't got the money." It had kind of become a moot point by now. I was destined to plough my way through life without the inheritance my grandfather had wanted me to have. My half-brother had contested the will and tied it in enough strings to ensure that finishing my doctorate was going to drown me in student loans.

"I've already said I'll lend you the money. For crying out loud, Victoria, I'd pay the fees for you if you'd accept. Or get a favour from a friend of my father's who'd do a proper job and get you what you're entitled to. You're living in poverty and working for that law department when you don't have to. It's ridiculous. You should be completing your doctorate and starting your career properly as an academic." He scratched his baby soft chin, so different to the beard-covered one Maxwell had sported in the office. My mind drifted back to the infuriating man I'd almost jumped over the counter to throttle and I suppressed another growl. "He's really pissed you off, hasn't he?"

I drained my glass of the remaining margarita and glared at my friend. "I think that might be stating the obvious." It was possible that I had overreacted slightly in the office to Maxwell's suggestion. It was possible that a calmer and more rational approach would've been more appropriate. It was also possible that I needed to smooth things over with the man in question as I would more than likely be working there until the end of the academic year, or until I had a job lecturing at a university, if I ever finished my doctorate. "It's possible I should've been calmer."

"Really, Victoria? You surprise me. Let's consider this further: hot man enters, hot intelligent man. He asks for his teaching room to be the one he requested some months previously. Admin girl he has never met before refuses room, is completely uncooperative and what else might you have called him?" Jacob smiled, taking off his cufflinks and depositing them on the table.

I made a mental note to pick them up later and put them in my handbag as there was no way he would remember them.

"A typical male filled with his own self-importance."

"And?"

"An obnoxious twat. But that was after he said history was an inconsequential subject unless it was being used to further understand a subject with more importance such as law or litera-ture or even art." I noticed I had clenched my fists. It was a good job Maxwell 'don't call me professor' Callaghan wasn't there, or else they'd have been pummelling his face.

"Apart from adding art into that equation, I think I agree with him, but that's not the point. Victoria, sweetie, you know you have a rather instantaneous temper—did the dean hear all of this?" Jacob suddenly looked concerned. He knew I was suffering with a more than part-time admin role in order to make ends meet and complete my PhD.

I nodded. "She stayed outside up until I called Maxwell a clusterfuck of a person—in my defence he had referred to me as an over-polished-librarian at this point—and then she retreated into her office. I heard her laughing. After Maxwell had cleared off she came out and offered me a glass of wine." I pushed my glasses back up my nose. I had a very low prescription just for reading but was accustomed to wearing them most of the time. Jacob pointed out on many occasions that I hid behind them, to which I usually just smiled. He wasn't wrong.

"So she wasn't pissed off that you were insulting one of her star professors and probably one of the biggest pulls to students studying there?" Jacob said as a different waitress returned with two more overly large margaritas: if there was any such thing.

I pulled my hair together and twisted it up into a bun before letting it drop down my back. It was thick and heavy and straight, and very, very sellable should I ever need an extra source of income to pay for rent or buy food. "She enjoys a good drama. I've heard more gossip from her in the past couple of weeks than I did during the whole of my master's degree."

"She didn't mention Maxwell Callaghan?" Jacob looked dubious.

"No. Nothing. He only teaches two modules: a second year undergraduate module on medical negligence and a module on the taught master's course. He guest lectures sometimes for the medical undergrads on clinical negligence but he's nowhere near being anything like part time." This margarita was stronger. If I went anywhere near a third there would be a good chance I'd end up at whichever palace Maxwell lived in to launch some more well-deserved abuse at him.

"Google him when you get home later. And I don't just mean look at the pretty images. Read about him. He's from a legal dynasty—and one that's got a future, not just a pretty history. Then look at the pictures with your vibrator close to hand. Did you get the one I recommended?" Jacob looked uncomfortably happy about the direction this conversation was taking.

I strongly debated the third margarita in order to simply survive the day. "No, Jay. I didn't buy the vibrator you recom-mended as I needed to pay the subscription for some online jour-nals and buy food. And I will google Maxwell 'the prick' Callaghan so I have more ammunition with which to assassinate him, but he has no place in any erotic fantasies." That was possibly not entirely true. There was nothing I loved more than a good argument with someone who wasn't scared of arguing back. The problem was that I looked every part of the delicate librarian who should be sitting quietly by a window, reading romances from before they got graphic and dreaming of a gentle alpha male who could take care of me and rid me of my virginity. As much as the said alpha male would be quite welcome, especially on evenings and weekends when I was too broke to go out, I certainly didn't need taking care of and my virginity had been disposed of some time ago by a Spanish teenager called Miguel on a sun lounger in the Canary Islands when I was sixteen.

Maxwell had been stunningly and broodingly gorgeous. Dark, messy, slightly curly hair that was in need of a cut; deep, dark chocolate eyes, chiselled cheekbones and a beard that I'd like to get messier than it already was. He'd filled his suit in such a way that suggested it had needed to be tailored: broad shoulders, bulging biceps but unfortunately I didn't get the opportunity to check out how well his trousers had been cut because by that time I'd seen red and was filling the room with insults. But Max had argued back, with heat and passion too, and at no point had I felt he was holding back. That had been a turn on.

Jacob looked disappointed. "I'll treat you to one. The anal stimulator is like no other. It'll open up a whole new world. Especially while you're having a barren spell. You know, sweetie, it wouldn't kill you to have a one-night stand. Lose the glasses, curl your hair, pop on those leather trousers and a halter neck and take home some stud-muffin for the night. Scratch an itch and all that."

The glare I sent him should've pierced a lung at the very least. "I'm done with all that. Been down the pretty boy route but they inevitably either have a small dick or are secretly gay and lose the capacity to perform. Besides, I'd actually like someone I can have a discussion with."

"Wouldn't that be classed as a relationship?" Jacob once

again looked concerned. He didn't do relationships, just repeats of one-night stands where sex was the only item on the agenda.

"It's not a fate worse than death, Jay. Besides, I'm way into my thirties. My biological clock is starting to gently tick every so often." I took a very long slurp of my margarita and debated naming my first daughter after my drink.

Jacob shook his head. "You can adopt. Or have a sperm donor. I have several gay friends who would like to co-parent and your genes are shit-hot. Besides, you've got years left in you yet. I read about a woman in her fifties giving birth a few days ago."

"Not. Something. I. Want. To. Do," I said. "I'd like to look like the child's parent when I pick them up from school and not be mistaken for their grandmother. Now's not the right time to be thinking about this anyway."

"You still thinking about America?" he said, frowning enough so that a faint line appeared on his head. Clearly the Botox was due for a top-up.

"Jerry's mentioned there would be an opening at Johns Hopkins in September next year, as their World War One specialist is taking retirement. There's no guarantee I'd get it, but it's an option," I said, confiding in him with something I'd been keeping as a small hope, a wish for some good luck, finally.

"A lot can happen between now and then," Jacob said. "You might finally see sense and change solicitors, getting this inheritance that is yours and not your God-awful brother's."

He referred back to the small matter of a few hundred thousand sitting in a bank account while my brother continued to throw reasons for ignoring my grandfather's wishes that it should go to me. Unfortunately, my brother also had a hideous wife who had some money of her own and was determined to add to it. Secretly, I thought the only reason she'd married Francis was because of the promise of his inheritance. I couldn't think of any other reason why a woman would've touched him, even wearing surgical gloves.

"You're right; I might. In the meantime, I suppose I need to smooth things over with Maxwell Callaghan," I said with a sigh.

Jacob looked at me, his head cocked to one side. "You've run out of insults. You didn't give him a middle name."

"I'm trying to be professional."

He laughed loudly. I joined him.

CHAPTER 3
MAXWELL

No one else was in the office, which given that it was just after five on a Tuesday morning, was unsurprising. Sometimes Jackson would be here this early, although he seemed to opt for spending a longer breakfast with Vanessa rather than cracking open the emails before seven since she had moved in.

I shifted the ice pack onto my right shoulder and booted up the iMac I'd insisted on, as I hated PC's. I'd spent the evening before at the gym, boxing with Mikey, an ex pro who wouldn't shy away from hitting you hard to make you better. My concentration had lapsed and I'd taken a hard punch to my shoulder which was going to bruise like a beast, despite all the ice and arnica I'd applied. The aim was not to wince when I moved my arm in front of my sister, Claire, else I'd be getting another lecture about giving up boxing that would take too much time from my day.

My emails opened automatically, all unread, some flagged to return to now I was in the office. I clicked on the most pressing, leaving it open while I went to make coffee. Like most of my siblings except Payton, and I wasn't sure about Callum, I didn't function without at least a pot of caffeine in my bloodstream before I had to speak to anyone. If it could've been offered intravenously, I'd have declined. I enjoyed good coffee, liked the taste, the burn of the hot liquid and smell of the beans as they were ground.

Ten minutes later, I was back at my desk, an espresso inhaled and a large mug of the best Fairtrade Kenyan coffee I'd found, topped with a small splash of cream. I looked at my screen, expecting to see an empty inbox given that it wasn't even five-thirty, but one unopened mail sat there, looking ominous, especially when I looked at the sender.

Victoria Esme Davies.

There was only one Victoria whose surname I didn't know that would be emailing me: the admin Historian woman with the long brown hair. Fuck.

I debated not opening it, especially if she'd set up a read report, but I'd never been a patient man. Taking a long mouthful of coffee, I clicked it open, half expecting a virus, or at least some porn to appear.

From: Victoria Esme Davies
    To: Maxwell Callaghan
    Re: Rooms
    Today at 5.21am
    Dear Mr Callaghan,

    Firstly, I'd like to apologise for losing my temper last week. I'm very passionate about teaching my subject, as, I can tell, are you. As we both want that particular room for the benefit of our students can I make a compromise of each using it on alternate weeks. I feel this would make the best of an unfortunate situation.

    Also, can I confirm that your brother has secured use of a function room for the Assassins' Guild meetings?

    Kind regards

Victoria Davies BA(Hons), MA, PGCE

————

Checking the time on my watch, which hadn't yet been replaced by my phone for that purpose, I debated whether it was too early to phone my youngest brother, Seph, or Joseph as he was known when I wanted to piss him off. The minute hand hit six and I figured the lazy ass should be out of bed by now anyway. He worked for us at Callaghan Green, specialising in employment law and he was damned good, although I would never tell him that. He was also the biggest pain in the backside Jackson and I had as he lacked common sense, was ridiculously intelligent and far too reliant on his twin sister to regulate him. He was also my littlest brother, despite not being far off thirty, which gave me the right to bully him as I saw fit.

Including waking him up half an hour earlier than usual.

"What the fuck?" Seph moaned into the phone after it had rang out for what felt like half a day. "What's up? Is someone ill?"

I almost felt bad, as he wasn't a bad kid, and I didn't want to worry him. Much. "Yeah, do you remember that girl you pulled back in June? The one from The Ivy?"

"No. What? Who?" He became suddenly clearer, probably having sat up. "Can't really talk about her—*it*—now. Got company." I heard a woman's voice in the background. "Shhh, it's only my brother. Go back to sleep. Hang on a sec, Max."

There was rustling, the sound of footsteps and then coffee beans being ground. "What about that girl?" he said quietly.

"Just checked the post from yesterday. She's claiming she's pregnant."

There was silence. I struggled to keep from laughing.

"You're fucking shitting me." He finally spoke.

Laughter escaped me.

"You're a bastard, Maxwell. You're a fucking bastard. An absolute tool. What the fuck did I do to deserve you as a brother. Fucking dick. You're an ass," Seph said. I heard him slamming a cup down and laughed louder. "What the fuck do you want then? It had better be good."

"The Assassins' Guild at Kings need a place to meet once a week and I said you could sort them out with the room above The Grapes," I said once I'd managed to stop laughing.

"Oh, offering my services, are you? I should tell you to fuck right off. Why? Is this something to do with you losing your shit at the university last week?" Seph said, and I debated the wisdom of pranking him when I needed a favour.

"Yep," I said. "The other room needs freeing up and the guild are in it. They'd be better in the pub anyway. It's a Thursday evening, six till seven."

I heard more things being moved about and the sound of a woman's voice again, followed by a suggestive giggle and Seph murmuring unintelligibly. I figured my little brother was about to get lucky.

"Fortunately for you, I'm with Mia now, so I'll ask and get back to you. I might be able to pull some strings," he said. "That's it, babe."

"I assume I'm not the babe you're referring to. Text me." I hung up before I heard anything else that would require bleach to cleanse my brain and began to check the flagged emails.

Fifteen minutes later my phone pinged with a text.

Seph: The room's free and there's no charge. I paid for it in kind.

Me: You didn't last long.

Seph: You're welcome. And don't worry—I haven't got your problems.

• • •

I opted to not take the bait and opened Victoria's email again, considering a response. I didn't quite trust her intentions; she'd given in far too easily to a compromise that hadn't been asked for, and it was a fair compromise too. It wasn't her fault that the email I'd sent hadn't been checked, or that I could be a complete and utter ass when I had to expend energy on something that should've been sorted if systems were run competently. I pulled at my beard, debating what to put.

From: Maxwell Callaghan
  To: Victoria Esme Davies
  Re: Re: Rooms
  Today at 5.54am

Good morning Victoria,

Should I be concerned that you're sending work emails this early from the university? I wasn't aware they required admin staff to be in before eight am. Thank you for the compromise on sharing the room. Given that neither of us are at fault for the mix up, I consider this a very fair agreement.

Having spoken to my brother this morning, he has confirmed that the room above The Grapes is available for the Assassins' Guild on Thursdays between six and seven pm. Please inform the chief assassin (if that's what they're still calling themselves) that they need to confirm arrangements with Mia.

Kindest regards,
Maxwell Callaghan
Callaghan Green Solicitors

• • •

Reading through an email three times was usually something only newly qualifieds did, or should do, but I had to check it for content and grammar, having a feeling that Victoria Esme Davies would be on me like my sisters on a shoe sale if there was the slightest mistake. I had thought about adding the letters after my own name but decided it would irritate her more if I didn't. She was expecting me to be an ass; I didn't have to give her the satisfaction of knowing she was right for at least a few more encounters.

My door opened and Jackson stuck his head round, peering at me like he could see into my skull. He'd had that look since he'd been about three; it had unnerved me even then.

"Oi, dick, what've you done to Seph?" he said, staying at the doorway. "He's properly on it this morning, and he's got that meeting with Tudors at nine."

I chuckled. "Last time I spoke to him he had Mia from The Grapes about to give him head. Then he texted me about fifteen minutes later, so draw your own conclusions."

Jackson's face broke into a grin. "Gold. Fucking gold. Coffee's on."

I glanced at my diary that was on my screen. "Am I missing something?" We had no meeting scheduled and as far as I was aware, nothing urgent had come in.

"Have you not heard from Claire?" Jackson said, looking serious. "Shit. I thought she'd text everyone." He entered my office and closed the door.

I pushed my chair away from my desk, needing room in case I wanted to stand up and move suddenly. Claire was the next eldest after Jackson, and was a senior partner, taking mainly complex family law cases.

"The case she's working—the messy divorce," Jackson said, resting his back to the door. "She's staying elsewhere for the next few weeks."

"Why? What's happened?" I stood up, pushing the chair away with my foot. My fist was clenched and I tried to relax it.

"Calm the fuck down because nothing's happened. Not to her anyway." Jackson took a long breath and stared at me. "The idiot working for the other side and the same guy who broke into Mum and Dad's cottage were in her apartment last night. They were caught."

I nodded, thinking rapidly before I spoke. Claire had taken on a case representing a woman wanting to divorce her wealthy and prominent husband. She'd alleged he'd been abusive and she had evidence that would damage his reputation, if not put him in trouble with the law. While Claire worked on the case, we'd added a security detail, thinking something like this would happen. The husband was a nasty piece of work and held far too much power. "Where was Claire last night?"

"Staying with Killian," Jackson said.

Killian was my best friend, my roommate from university. He was ex-Navy and now ran a security firm with his brother. He was also my sister's boyfriend.

"I'm just getting everyone together to divide up a couple of files she's working on. There's nothing extra for you, but I want you to have the head's up on who's doing what," Jackson said, studying me like he always had.

"Okay. Is Killian staying with her?"

"Yes. Everything's taken care of and you don't need to panic or go into beast mode." He came in closer to me, his eyes almost on the same level as mine, just half an inch difference. Half an inch and a year between us. "I need you to keep everyone calm and stop the inevitable gossip."

My head nodded of its own accord. "I can do that. I'm in court later…"

"Yep. Business as usual."

I followed him into the meeting room, grabbed a cup of

coffee that Jean handed to me and sat down with my game face on.

———

My brothers and sister were all smiling as we left the room half an hour later. Order was resumed; Claire's cases were being handled by other fee earners and our stepmother, Marie—who knew the cases thanks to Claire's over-organised manner and determination to forge a team as opposed to being competitive, which could be a negative feature in our industry. I sat back down at my computer and saw my inbox with ten unread messages.

Opening it, I knew there was only one sender I was looking for and she didn't disappoint. I clicked to open and started to read.

From: Victoria Esme Davies
  To: Maxwell Callaghan
  Re: Re: Re: Rooms
  Today at 8.01am

Good morning Max/Maxwell/Mr Callaghan,

Just in case you decide to investigate the department for slave labour (which it almost is, so feel free) I was in early to work on my PhD thesis as my internet at home has decided not to work. Plus, it's warmer and I can't afford heating, being a poor student and all.

My seminars begin the week before yours, so if I start in the desired room for my first one, and you use it for your first, we should work together quite seamlessly. I would just like to apologise for the multitude of insults I may have called you, cockwomble being my favourite. None of these were meant in the long term, just in that moment, so please don't take too much offence.

Please thank your brother for me for organising the room for the

Assassins' Guild. They've asked if he would like to be an honorary member this year but can't promise not to assassinate him whilst he's in court, so you may wish to consider whether or not to pass on this message.

Kindest regards also and have a good day,

Ms Davies/Victoria BA(Hons), MA, PGCE and soon a f@*cking PhD if I ever finish my research.

I found myself rereading it and laughing quietly, causing Jean to look at me as if I was going slightly insane when she came in with letters for me to check and sign. As I read through the other emails that were starting to mount up, I debated whether or not to respond. There was no need, except to confirm the dates for the use of the room and to try to make her laugh like she'd made me.

From: Maxwell Callaghan
   To: Victoria Esme Davies
   Re: Re: Re: Re: Rooms
   Today at 8.32am

Dear Ms Soon to Have a PhD,

The schedule for the desired room use sounds logical. There is a cupboard in there where I usually keep handouts etc. I usually use one shelf, leaving plenty of room for yourself. I hope this will be agreeable.

I sympathise with the lack of internet at your apartment but agree that using the university resources is financially efficient, although your fees will technically be covering what you use, so don't feel too guilty.

I thought the use of cockwomble was very imaginative. In turn, I would like to apologise for calling you a glorified coffee maker with atti-

tude. However, I do not rescind my comment that history is a pointless subject unless studied in conjunction with something else, such as law. Given how well you argue, you could perhaps have a change of heart about where your future could lie. I am happy to provide careers advice free of charge.

I have taken on board your advice and shall not be telling Joseph about the invitation to join the Assassins' Guild on this occasion. It was a complete f@*cking nuisance when he was an undergrad and I can only foresee it being ten times worse now he is almost an adult.

Have a wondrous day,
Max

Nerves at sending an email weren't something I was used to and I didn't think about analysing why. I wanted her to reply: I needed a distraction from worrying about Claire and something other than work-related emails floating into my inbox, usually with a sting in the tail. And when I was lying in bed for the past few nights I'd thought about her; how she'd almost launched herself across the desk to physically tear me a new one, her quick words and answers for everything and that fucking glorious hair. I'd noticed her tits immediately—along with legs they were usually my favourite part of a woman—but behind her glasses she'd had the biggest brown eyes, like milk chocolate. It had been a good few weeks since I'd last hooked up with someone and that had been a casual but careful one-night stand with another lawyer from a firm in Manchester when I was there on business. I was busy shifting between considering possibilities and starting to dictate an advice to a client when my inbox pinged with her name.

From: Victoria Esme Davies
To: Maxwell Callaghan

Re: Re: Re: Re: Re: Rooms
Today at 8.42am

Let me know when you have a spare half an hour and I'll inform you of exactly why you're wrong about history.

I think I know your brother.

Vic.

My first thought was bullshit and the second, fuck. I did not like the idea of her knowing Seph and didn't want to think about how she might've known him, or his friends. Nor did I want to consider the possibility that she might've met Callum who was the biggest manwhore in London.

"Joseph!" I yelled out of my door, down the corridor to his office, which wasn't much more than a glorified broom cupboard with an ancient desk that he'd taken a liking to.

"You politely called," he said, sticking his head out. "Make it quick; I've got this meeting."

I resisted the urge to tell him not to fuck it up, but I'd already messed with him enough for one morning. "Do you remember a Victoria Davies? History student, has a PGCE? About Payton's height, really long brown hair?"

His expression remained stoic. "Decent tits?"

"For fuck's sake, you can't say that when other people can hear. At least try to be politically correct."

He shrugged. "There's no one to hear apart from Jackson. Yeah, I remember her. She was at a law ball years ago with a friend or her boyfriend or someone. His dad was a judge. We talked about King's and she knew Cassie." His ex-girlfriend was rarely mentioned for fear of him dwindling back into the pit he'd landed in when she'd finished with him a few months ago.

"Who was her friend's dad?" It hadn't occurred to me that she might not be single. It was bothering me that she might be attached, which was new.

Seph shrugged. "I was plastered. It was a law ball. I only remember her because she was telling me about Cass before she realised she was my girlfriend." Seph's eyes darkened.

"What did she say about her?"

"Just that she'd seen her coming out of one of the rooms. It doesn't matter, does it? It was years ago. Why are you asking? Is she the admin girl?" Seph said, his expression changing like magic.

"She might be," I said cautiously. "When's your meeting?"

He checked his watch. "Shit. Better go. Don't think I've forgotten about this!"

———

Another email was waiting for me when I got back to my desk. In fact, several were, but the first one I opened had nothing to do with work.

From: Victoria Esme Davies
To: Maxwell Callaghan
Re: Re: Re: Re: Re: Re: Rooms
Today at 8.47am

If I'm right, which I usually am, you've just gone to ask Seph how he knows me. If he remembers, it was from a law ball years ago when I went with my best friend. I dropped his girlfriend in it—I knew her from one of the seminars I was teaching.

Carol says Professor McInery is having a 'soiree' at his house on Friday evening. Your attendance is required. As is some decent whisky in order to survive the evening.

Pants are optional.

Vic

. . .

From: Victoria Esme Davies
  To: Maxwell Callaghan
  Re: Re: Re: Re: Re: Re: Re: Rooms
  Today at 8.57am

Couple of notes to that email. Carol made me put that pants are optional and then snuck off laughing to herself. I'm wondering if psychiatric help is required—possibly for me if I continue to work here much longer.

And I hope you don't mind the smiley face. I felt we were at that point. Plus, your emails sound like you have a huge stick up your ass, so I thought I'd start to try to remove it.

Have a spiffing one. I'm now updating student databases. The joy!

Vic :)

From: Maxwell Callaghan
  To: Victoria Esme Davies
  Re: Re: Re: Re: Re: Re: Re: Re: Rooms
  Today at 9.05am

:) :) :)

Carol has always sailed close to the far side of insanity. Has she offered you wine before midday yet? If not, wait till Freshers' Week. In fact, I'd recommend stocking up on something harder beforehand. I can recommend an excellent single malt that might just take the edge off your mornings.

Please tell Carol and Niall that I have no reasonable excuse to get out of attending Niall's 'soiree' on Friday. Has he moved house yet, as he's been threatening to for about four years? Are you going? If so, I'll mark you off for half an hour on my dance card and you can try to sell me history. I wish you luck.

Seph told me he knew you through a wild party where you were all swinging around naked and offering bodily fluids to the Roman gods. I refrained from asking for any further details. You know, with the stick and all.

Hope the student databases are as riveting as the advice I'm meant to be dictating.

Max :)

From: Victoria Esme Davies

To: Maxwell Callaghan

Re: Re: Re: Re: Re: Re: Re: Re: Re: Rooms

Today at 9.35am

What the hell were law balls like when you were a trainee? I've clearly missed out?

She offered me wine last Thursday after you stormed out like a teenage girl who had just been told she was grounded.

We have a variety of interesting first names this year. Clearly names such as ours are now outdated and preference is given to countries, cities, nineties' celebrities and granny names. And food.

Vic :)

From: Maxwell Callaghan

To: Victoria Esme Davies

Re: Re: Re: Re: Re: Re: Re: Re: Re: Re: Rooms

Today at 10.45am

Law balls were mainly fuelled by tequila and cheap fizzy wine. There may have been nakedness but not usually in public, although I think my other lawyer brother—Jackson—did once expose himself by accident. There are pictures somewhere. Should you ever meet him, please feel free to ask and also mention it to his fiancée.

I did not storm out like a teenage girl. I'm far too manly for that. I left the room in a dignified and masculine manner.

Name wise—Esme?

Max ;)

. . .

From: Victoria Esme Davies
To: Maxwell Callaghan
Re: Re: Re: Re: Re: Re: Re: Re: Re: Re: Re: Rooms
Today at 12.05pm

Law balls sound a lot more fun than history balls. Not as wrinkled and saggy. Although we do get the good wine. I bet you like a good wine. In fact, I know you do—I've heard you whine.

How's your definition of dignified and manly? I think your parting words were 'I'm too busy and have more important things to do than sort out the mess that someone else has created.' To be fair, you had a certain swagger when you left the room that could be termed manly. I'll let you have that.

Esme was my great-grandmother's name. She was a nurse in the First World War and spent several months at a casualty clearance station just outside of Ypres. That was where she met my great-grand-father. My grandad told me stories of the war and how they met when I was little and that's why I fell in love with history.

By the way, Carol has reiterated that pants are optional on Friday. I sense the wine is out.

I note the upgraded emoticon. Way-hey! The stick is loosening!

Vic (.)(.)

At which point Jean ran into my office with a glass of water, mistaking my laughter for a choking fit. I tried to muster some dignity, failed miserably and went in search of coffee, needing to take my mind off a history lecturer with far too much banter and knowledge of inappropriate emoticons.

CHAPTER 4
VICTORIA

My mission had become to make him smile via email at least four times a day, and so far I was winning. He received copious notes on the comings and goings of the office, including the odd historical fact and various concerns about Carol's liquid consumption, which was, in all honesty, mainly tea and coffee. In return, I learned about his siblings: Jackson, Claire, Payton, Callum, Ava and of course, Seph, mostly Seph. By Friday evening, I felt as if I knew them personally having been told about—amongst other things—how Jackson lost his virginity; Claire's past irrational hatred of Max's best friend Killian but now they were together; Payton's no gender preference in relationships in the past; Ava's ridiculously stupid comments and enough about Seph to fill a novella. There was very little about Callum and I had wondered why, but for once my filters had been working and I hadn't asked.

I sat on my bed, facing what would be called my wardrobe (except there were no doors or top to it), wearing just a bra and matching panties. I was debating Carol's statement that pants were optional as I literally had nothing to wear. There had been a couple of heavy downpours during the week, summer ending with a bang rather than a whimper, and the roof had leaked, soaking half of what I owned. The half that I would've chosen to wear to a 'soiree'. Generally, I would've also chosen to not give a shit, cobble something semi decent together and had a story to tell, but tonight I actually wanted to make a slight effort to look attractive and it had nothing to do with a certain medical negligence lawyer that I had emailed for most of the week.

Nothing at all.

I picked up my phone and dialled Jacob. His sister was staying with him and she was a similar size to me, so there was potentially something I could borrow there.

"How's the drowned rat?" he said, the background noise suggesting his Friday had already started.

"Clothesless," I said. "I need a fairy godmother."

"Well, my father called me a fairy a couple of times when he found out I had boyfriends," he said.

I laughed. I knew for a fact his father had called him no such thing as he didn't particularly care what sort of relationships Jacob had, as long as he was discreet and careful.

"Drawers. Black leather pants, black bra and the semi-sheer top that tucks into the trousers and makes your waist look tiny and your butt look *bazinga*. Stick a smoky eye on, contour like I taught you and the pink nude lipstick—I think it's called Confession—and wear the heels that should be classified as a weapon and he won't know what's hit him."

"Why do you know my wardrobe better than me?" I groaned, opening the drawer and finding the trousers. I hoped they still fit: I hadn't worn them for months and the gym had been an expense that wasn't on the essential list. "And I'm not trying to impress him."

"Don't try and bullshit me, Victoria. I've seen the emails. Now get dressed and take a selfie." I heard a loud cheer, followed by an obscenity and the line went dead.

———

Professor Niall McInery's house was a ten-minute walk away from my rundown apartment, but the neighbourhood was far more upmarket. I'd managed to find a decent bottle of red wine that Jacob had brought round one night but we'd never drank, so I wasn't empty-handed. One of my colleagues answered the door and relieved me of the bottle, passed me a glass of something sparkly and I started to mingle, aware of the difference in how I looked given the glances I was receiving.

Most of the law faculty were there, plus a couple from the history department and a guy I recognised from the economics staff. But there was no Max. I tried to quell the feeling of disappointment in my stomach and focus on having a good time with people I was coming to genuinely like. There were egos in the department—why wouldn't there be, given the wealth and success that some had accumulated—but most were kind and interesting and as my grandad had always told me, I struggled to dislike someone as much as I struggled not to argue.

"Wine, dear?" Carol said, brandishing a bottle of something that had a layer of dust coating it. "Niall's actually cracked open the good stuff, although I'm hoping Maxwell is still bringing the whisky."

A pixie in my stomach started to do a happy dance. "Is he still coming? I noticed he wasn't here."

She smiled. "He's had to visit one of his sisters somewhere, so he's running late, but he is coming. I'm surprised you noticed his absence, given your exchange of words last week."

"We've been emailing since to sort the rooms out. I think we've moved past some of our differences. Maybe," I said, sipping at the wine and trying to pace myself. Alcohol would only induce me to call someone else a cockwomble at some point.

"That's good. I'd like Max to take on another few lectures, as

David's had to go back to Harvard, but I know his schedule's rammed. If you're on his good side try and persuade him for me. He's a good man, but rather intense. Had a difficult childhood." She tipped back her glass, drinking what was left and then topped it up with the bottle she still had hold of.

"I thought his family were well-off," I said, puzzled. I had googled Max Callaghan and read his bio, a few articles on his family and a rather breath-taking feature in a magazine from a few months ago which had some rather well-taken photos.

"They are. Doesn't mean his childhood was happy though, especially with him being the oldest. Keep an eye on how patient he is with the undergrads. He can be a bit passionate with what he teaches and if they aren't well-motivated he becomes a tad agitated," she said. "This wine's delicious. Want some more?"

I held out my glass although I had barely drank any.

"You're a bad influence, Carol."

I turned around and nearly left Carol pouring onto the carpet. I'd only heard Max's voice once and we'd been shouting towards the end, or using raised voices at least, but I recognised it.

"Maxwell! I'm glad you made it!" She flung her arms round him, glass in one hand, wine in the other. "How's your sister? Did you help her sort the issue?"

He nodded and smiled, although it didn't reach his eyes. "To a certain extent. She's in court next week on a big case. I'll be glad for her sake when it's over."

"You remember Victoria, don't you? Our history lecturer who's covering admin so she can support her studies," Carol said, backing out of the way so she wasn't standing in between us.

Max's eyes seemed to drink me in like a long glass of iced tea. His hair was neater and his beard was trimmed; the suit replaced with a pair of Levi's and a white shirt. I took a sip of wine in the hope of covering any drool that had escaped. As irritating as he had proven himself he was one damned fine male specimen.

"She's been the highlight of my week," he said, not taking his eyes away from mine. "I've had a thorough education in emoticons and the soap opera that is the law faculty. Would you mind passing me a glass, Carol? I've left some whisky on the table in the kitchen."

"Super!" Carol said. "Back in a sec!"

He nodded at her and then focused back on me. "You look nothing like a librarian," he said, his eyes flicking down to my chest.

It was one look, just one look, and I was glad the trousers were leather rather than cotton as my panties had been incinerated. That was clearly Maxwell Callaghan's super power: melting panties. "That's because I'm not a librarian. I'm a historian."

"Same difference." His eyes shone like polished toffee. "It's all stories."

"History has huge relevance on how we live today, from the history of the country where we live to our family's history. You can't dismiss it as stories. Look at your own subject: what's gone before has led to what's relevant and important now…" He took my arm and guided me over to a chaise longue, covered in fabric that looked like it had been spewed up by a fifties housewife. "This chaise, for example. It's a living piece of history. The fabric, its quality and colours tells us about… You're fucking with me, aren't you?"

The bastard folded to the side of the chaise, laughing silently, his face creased with mirth. I smacked his arm. "Fucker. I was just about to give you the whole history of this sort of furniture. You really are a git, aren't you?"

He managed to sit up, still laughing. Carol passed him a glass of wine, tapped his shoulder and moved on, as if seeing Maxwell Callaghan having a laughing fit was an everyday occurrence.

"I'm sorry," he managed to stutter. "But you were so sincere and genuine." His gaze locked on mine, suppressing more laughter. "Now I feel bad. Really bad. You look like someone just told you they'd bought you a whole new wardrobe of clothes but they were two sizes too big."

I sighed and my shoulders dropped and his laughing stopped for real.

"Victoria, shit. What did I say? You can tell me about the chaise. I didn't mean to make you sad." He rubbed his chin, which I'd figured was his go to nervous tic.

"It's not what you said. You were a bastard for the chaise, by the way. I'll make you listen to my speech at some point. I need to practice it for my first lecture anyway. The roof in my apartment leaked and ruined most of my clothes. This is pretty much all I have left to wear for going out until I get paid," I said, cursing myself for bringing it up. "I'm sorry. I don't mean to dampen the evening. Fuck knows my week's been damp enough."

His arm slipped around my shoulders and pulled me in. "Why didn't you tell me? We've been emailing all week."

I shook my head. "Because it's one of those things and I'm used to coping with those things by now. I'm claiming on my insurance, but it'll take a few weeks to come through, if I'm lucky."

I wanted to lean my head on his chest, take on some of the heat that was radiating from him, but thirty-two years of life told me now and here was not the right time or place.

"Yet you still managed to look beautiful," he said. "No glasses tonight?"

"I only need them for reading. Or computer work."

"So most of the time, then?" He smiled, his hand still on my shoulder, arm still around my back.

I notice Leanne, one of the law lecturers, giving us a curious look. Niall came by and started to chat, discussing a recent change in law that I was semi-aware of. All the time we were talking, Max stayed close by; a hand around my waist, a gentle graze of my shoulder, a smile.

His words were generally brief, to the point and without unnecessary descriptive detail. He answered questions, talked about his father and siblings and a couple of cases that had completed, and enquired after his colleagues. The egotistical bastard from last week had taken a break for the night, it seemed.

But I wasn't in the market for a man. A temporary fix, maybe, but nothing with the potential to last. I didn't know where I would be in twelve months' time—I had to go where a good position was, at a university where I could continue studying and writing, working towards becoming a professor with tenure and a reputation that would mean something to me, and to my grandfather. For a moment, my thoughts drifted to my brother, Francis, and his determination to keep my grandfather's inheritance to himself. I knew I should push the solicitors. With the money my grandfather had meant for me, I wouldn't be struggling to complete my doctorate or living somewhere damp climbed up the walls and the lock didn't quite work. He'd have hated the predicament I was in at the moment.

"Hey. Where've you gone?" Max said, and I realised we were standing together, just the two of us. "Back in that wardrobe?"

I looked up into eyes I could happily drown in and then argue into a rough, but exciting ocean. Taking a deep breath, I decided not to consider what I was about to say next. Sometimes I figured it was best to just jump straight in.

CHAPTER 5
MAXWELL

Callaghan
GREEN

The Mount Street Social had been open just a few months, owned and managed by Simone Wood, a Michelin starred chef who had been a client of Vanessa's marketing company. Simone had recently added a conservatory for drinks and bar snacks only, and by bar snacks, I meant posh ones that Seph couldn't pronounce.

I'd become friends with Simone through Vanessa and I was fairly confident when I sent her a text that she'd find a quiet table for us in the conservatory, so I could get the bottom of Victoria's issue with her half-brother over her inheritance. So far, what I had gathered between interruptions at Niall's house, was that she was being stalled and overcharged by her own solicitor, so I'd stopped drinking, made our excuses and taken a cab to Simone's.

"So your grandad's house has been sold. The funds from that are being held by your solicitor while your brother contests the will, along with his savings. Some money has been released to your half-brother but not to you as your half-brother is already claiming you've had your share?" I said, confirming everything with baby steps as she'd gulped a couple of glasses of wine as she was telling me the story.

"Which I know can't be right. My grandfather paid my university fees throughout and was going to pay off the tuition and living expenses for my PhD. I put that on hold to care for him three and a bit years ago and looked after him until he died. Francis immediately contested the will, saying that there was another, held by his solicitor and that's where I've been stuck since," she said, fingers toying with the coffee cup.

It was a fucking good job I was focusing on what she was telling me as it was stopping me toying with her fingers myself. Since I'd seen her when I'd first walked into Niall's, I hadn't been able to take my eyes off her.

Even in heels she was petite, almost a foot shorted than I was, and she was slender with a curvy ass and tits I struggled not to stare at, although she had caught me a few times. Her lips were full, pinked up by lipstick, and her eyes told me everything she was thinking. She gave off both strength and vulnerability and I was finding the combination intoxicating, along with how quickly her brain worked. She had kept up with me whether it had been via email or this evening, completely nonplussed by the letters after my name, my family or my wealth, and I liked that. More than I knew what to do with.

"Okay," I said. "None of that sounds remotely like what should be happening. What's the name of the firm you're using and your brother's?"

She gave me the names. "The solicitor my brother's using is his brother-in-law."

I typed the names into my phone and checked their websites, frowning. Something wasn't sitting right. "Okay, Miss Feisty, I'm going to call Jackson. He's going to take your case on."

"No!" she said, almost knocking over her coffee. "I can't afford the fees I've run up to pay my solicitor and he won't let me transfer the case to someone else without…"

"This is what I do for a living and I do it very well, so shut up and trust me." My brother answered the phone fairly quickly, the background noise sounding similar to where we were. I was thankful I hadn't interrupted him and Vanessa. Their penchant for having sex at every given opportunity was becoming notorious, to the extent where Seph had refused to phone Jackson outside of office hours. "Jackson, you good?" Victoria glared at me and I debated ordering a bottle of wine to see if it would make her compliant to me taking on her case.

"Fucking amazing. Why are you phoning me at this time on a Friday? Shouldn't you be in bed with one of your university groupies?"

I thanked whichever deity was on duty that Victoria couldn't hear him.

"Fuck you. I'm at Simone's with Victoria. Can you come over? There's an inheritance case she's involved with and I want your opinion. It's urgent." It wasn't urgent. Nothing could be done until Monday at the soonest, but she was urgent. There was something about her that made me want to prove myself in a way I hadn't needed to since I was the best student in my class just to show my father.

Jackson laughed. "I'm coming over. We're round the corner at Cicero's. Not that there's anything I can do now, but I need to see this girl." I heard Vanessa asking him what was going on and Jackson still laughing, then he hung up.

Victoria pouted at me. "It isn't urgent. My brother is a complete bastard, Max. His wife's loaded and she'll keep funding their solicitor until I give up."

I ignored her. "Have you seen this will?"

She shook her head. "Only the one that I thought was the more recent."

"Has your solicitor asked to see the will your brother has?"

She thought for a moment. "I think so. He's not told me

anything in detail about it, just that there's a more recent will where my grandfather left everything to Francis."

"Do you believe that your grandfather would've done that?"

Her eyes caught the waiter's. "Can I have a large glass of merlot, please?" she said. "Actually, make it the bottle, and don't let this man pay."

"Do you believe that your grandfather would've done that?"

"Are you going to keep asking me the same question?"

"Until I get an answer that's truthful, yes."

Her stare was agonising. "No. My grandfather despised Francis and the woman he married. He gave him money towards a deposit on a house and after that he refused him anything. Francis was an egotistical, assuming bastard who thought he deserved everything without working for it."

"Don't hold back on your opinion."

She smiled and I felt like the king of a very large country. "However, I don't know much, if anything, about how the law works and my solicitor seemed to think that my grandad had done that."

"What if I was to tell you that your brother's solicitor and your grandfather's were related?" I said, half holding my breath. She hadn't researched the companies; if she had it was as clear as a fresh tattoo on a virgin back, and a huge conflict of interest.

"Then I would assume that someone was being paid off, but I may have read too many conspiracy theories." Her expression was interested and alert, but I couldn't read her eyes.

"Okay. Here's my thoughts: your brother has filed a caveat that your solicitor is supporting, for whatever reason. He's waiting for you to run out of money and stop contesting his argument so the inheritance falls to him. I want Jackson here so he can look into it—he's the best person I know for rationalising what's right and wrong," I said. Going off my gut instincts, she was being had and whoever was acting for her and her brother was due a windfall when she gave up. "How much is your grandfather's estate worth?"

"I think it's 4.5 million."

My coffee cup tipped over, almost knocking into her wine glass.

"Pounds?"

"No, fucking roubles. What do you think?"

I laughed loudly and she started to join in. "Why weren't you contesting your brother's claim?" I said, trying to keep us real.

"I thought I was. My lawyer told me it took time and he was dealing with it and I kept getting the bill for his fees. I ended up not being able to pay for a couple of months and he said he couldn't proceed any further until I was up to date with my payments." She met my eyes and held my gaze. "Judging by your expression, I was stupid."

I paused, wondering if I should sugarcoat my answer. "I'm not sure stupid is the right adjective. You should've questioned the advice, but most people in your position would've trusted what they were told. Drink your wine. I'll let Jackson explain what we're going to do."

"How do you know what he's going to say?" she said, her eyes wide and pleading and god knows how I resisted sweeping her up and carrying her to the nearest private area where I could start to consume her.

"Because he's my brother and we've worked together a long time. And from what I'm hearing, we're looking at reporting your lawyer to the Solicitors' Regulatory Authority at the very least. We'll take your case from them and go after your brother, but you need to hear that from Jackson and not me," I said, filling the glass that had been left for me with the wine the waiter had left at our table.

Victoria nodded, sipping quickly at her own. "I don't care about the money," she said. "I know that sounds ridiculous, but I always set out to make my own way with studying and lecturing and then writing. But I know my grandfather wanted me to use his money to support me with that, as it was what he had wanted to do."

"Why didn't he do it?" I said, persuading myself to not find out her brother's address and pay him a visit in the morning.

"Because Grandad couldn't afford to when he was young enough. His money came from compensation from my grand-mother and an accident she had at work that left her an invalid. Then he had to look after her. Davies versus McHammond Homes. I suspect you've heard of it."

I had. It was a textbook case: life changing injury on an industrial site that would ultimately lead to death. She was the main earner for the family, with two children to support. The compensation had been unprecedented and deserved, the lawyer doing a thorough job. It had clearly been well-invested by Victoria's grandfather to have that as a legacy though.

"Yes. I studied it."

"Studied what?" Jackson appeared, Vanessa immediately taking the seat next to Victoria and finding an empty wine glass.

I gave him the case and date and he nodded. No matter how much alcohol they had consumed my siblings always knew their shit.

———

Forty minutes later, he knew as much as he needed to know right now. The bottle of red wine was empty, Victoria was gulping back a pint of water and Vanessa was half asleep leaning against Jackson's shoulder.

"I think it's time I got you home," Jackson said, moving hair from Vanessa's face. "Walk or cab?"

Vanessa mumbled something unintelligible.

"Cab," Jackson said. "My shoulder's too sore to carry you."

There was another mumble from Vanessa.

"I should head home too," Victoria said. "I still feel bad about Max hijacking your night." She looked at my brother and Vanessa, who now had her eyes open.

I scowled.

"No hijacking involved. I'll get your file transferred to us on Monday and oversee it. Make sure that Maxwell has your contact details and I'll speak to you Monday afternoon," Jackson said, his hands massaging Vanessa's shoulders. My own hands itched to touch Victoria; something about the four of us sitting there together felt right. I rarely introduced a woman to my family as I had no intention of settling down. Having a wife and children wasn't something I thought was for me, so I didn't want to lead any woman I was seeing on by letting her think it was something more. But nothing was going on with me and Victoria. We'd only ever met twice, although we had communicated a lot via email. I'd had my arm around her, I'd touched her and maybe not entirely platonically, but we hadn't kissed. I wasn't even sure she wanted to kiss me.

"It was good to meet you. Max doesn't always introduce us to his colleagues from the university," Jackson said.

She smiled sweetly at my brother, sweetly with a touch of sass. "Given that I'm sure you've met Niall and Carol before, is it just females in their late twenties and early thirties he doesn't introduce you to?"

Jackson and Vanessa both laughed. I rolled my eyes and looked heavenwards. "I rarely have time to introduce anyone to anyone. Plus, I could jeopardise my job at the university if the administration questioned the sanity of my family."

"All the best people are mad," Victoria said, her eyes meeting mine, her smile now sweet with a hint of sex.

My cock twitched in my jeans and my eyes dropped to her tits, her bra just visible through a semi-sheer shirt.

"It's a good job you think that," Jackson said, standing then pulling Vanessa up to her feet gently. "Because we're definitely certifiable. Have a good weekend; I'll probably see you next week."

Vanessa leaned in and gave Victoria a quick hug. "It's been lovely to meet you. Hopefully I'll see you again soon."

"You too," Victoria said, hugging her back. "I should head off myself."

"I'll drop you off," I said, slapping Jackson on the back as he headed out.

"You don't know where I live," she said. "And I'd rather you didn't find out."

I froze, studying her. "I'm not stalker material," I eventually said. "You've nothing to worry about from me."

Victoria reddened slightly. "Sorry—I didn't mean it like that. It's just where I live is a bit of a dump. And I wouldn't have put you down as a stalker type."

I felt my shoulders relax. "You said the roof was leaking. Is your landlord getting it sorted?"

Throwing her coat around her shoulders, she headed to the door and into the night outside. "It's the cheapest accommodation I could find close to the university, so it saves me time and money for tube fares. The landlord isn't bothered about fixing stuff because if I don't like it, I can move out and he'd easily get someone else in instead."

I stamped on the urge to fix everything for her because she didn't need that from me. "What about university accommodation? Is there nothing available?"

"There's an apartment coming vacant in January through May, as one of the history professors is going on a secondment to Durham. I'm subletting and it should get me through to the end of my doctorate. So I can put up with the city's worst landlord and a flat that smells of mildew," she said, looking up at me with a smile. "I have to pick my battles, Max. Otherwise I'd spend my whole life fighting."

I didn't smile back. "Don't you think you're doing a disservice to whoever rents that flat next by not reporting the landlord to the council? And if the damp's that bad, it's not good for your health."

After our mother died—mine, Jackson's, Claire's and Callum's—I'd taken over the role of protector, given that my father was completely absorbed by work and had no idea how to relate to children. By the time Dad married our stepmother, Marie, who was the best thing to ever happen to us, I'd had a few sharp lessons in helping other people to look after themselves, rather than doing it for them, although I still found it hard.

She stopped walking and faced me. "Maxwell, I appreciate you trying to look out for me, but honestly, I'm okay. And I'm not sure if you're going in the right direction."

"I'm walking you home. It's late. Or I'm getting in a cab with you so you get home safe," I said, although it sounded more like a growl.

Victoria poked me in the stomach. "Ouch! You have abs. I think you've just broken my nail!"

"Then you shouldn't have poked me." I eyed her, trying to judge her mood. "Unless you'd like me to poke you somewhere?"

This time she used her knuckle to dig me in the stomach. "I'm rarely at my apartment. I sleep with the windows open so it's well ventilated and I can walk home by myself, but if it makes you feel better, it's about another fifteen minutes from here." She turned and started to walk, faster than anyone in high heels should be able to. "We'll have the poking conversation when I'm more sober than I am right now."

I followed, as if I would've done anything else, catching her up easily. "If we can get some of your inheritance released, would you look for a better place to stay?"

"Yes. I'm not a martyr. But given what my brother is like, I'm not expecting anything. I get that you're good and your brother seems even better," she eyed me, tempting me to take the bait, "but you're not miracle workers. I know my grandfather wanted me to have his money and the house but with Francis saying there's another will—"

"Which no one has seen," I interrupted. "We'll be asking to view the will within five working days. When it's not produced, Jackson will start various proceedings that will scare the shit out of them professionally. He'll go after your brother for attempt to fraud and look to sue him for damages because of how you've had to live, paying for your doctorate when it was your grandfather's wish for it to be paid by him, and other circumstances that you've suffered."

She looked up at me, words about to spew out that I already knew.

"Victoria, it's one point two million. It is a life changing amount of money. Even if you don't change your lifestyle, it leaves you free to pursue an academic career without having to worry about your finances," I said before she could deny wanting the cash.

Her lips closed and I dug my hands into my pockets so I didn't try to touch her.

"I know. I don't want it to change me. How much are you worth?"

I almost stopped walking in surprise. No one had ever asked me that before, although I'd had plenty of girlfriends who had been interested in finding out how well-provided for their shopping habits could be. "More than one point two million," I said. "I couldn't tell you exactly how much because it fluctuates with investments, but I don't have to worry about money."

"Do you think you would've been a different person if you hadn't been so wealthy?" she said, heels clicking on the pavement.

"Yes," I said without having to think. "I would've been more concerned with making money rather than doing what was necessarily right for my clients. I wouldn't be working at the university as my time's more valuable spent on cases."

She stopped walking suddenly and stooped down, taking off her shoes. "These fucking things are killing my feet. Why they can't design them to be comfortable, I don't know." She stood up, shoes in hand.

"You're going to walk the rest of the way in bare feet?" I said. "Jump on." I stopped and squatted down.

"What?"

"I'll give you a piggy back."

"I'm okay. I've walked home barefoot before."

"I've no doubt you have, but not when you're with me. Jump on."

"I'm heavy."

Like fuck she was. "I can squat two hundred ten kilograms without sweating. Jump on."

I expected her to continue to refuse, but instead I heard her laugh and felt a hand on my shoulder, then her legs wrapped round my waist, those glorious tits pushed against my back. Immediately, I knew it was a bad idea. My body reacted exactly as it should to a gorgeous woman being so close to me, smelling of musk and flowers.

"You're a gentleman," she murmured into my ear as I set off in the general direction.

"Need to know where I'm going, Miss Feisty," I said, ignoring her comment. "We'll discuss my fee when we get there."

"Maybe not so much of a gentleman." She ran a hand through my hair, pulling lightly and I wondered how she'd pull it if my head was between her thighs, eating her out.

"What plans do you have this weekend? Not that I'm trying to encroach on them or anything."

"I'm seeing my dad and stepmum at their house in Oxfordshire. We're all going," I said, finding my stride and managing to cope with the semi I had going on in my trousers.

"It sounds good. It must be nice to have a big family you can hang out with," she said, sounding sad. Taking her with me was an option: my parents were used to us bringing friends or partners with us for weekends up at the big house, but we had a lot going on with Claire right now and throwing someone into the mix wouldn't necessarily be the right call. And I always made the right call.

"It is. As much as they irritate the shit out of me, I quite like them. What are you doing?" I said and she pointed to take a left turn.

"Research for the dissertation. I have a meeting with my mentor on Monday so I need to be a bit further on than where I am. I'll be pretty much living at the law admin block for the next couple of days. I'm seriously debating taking a sleeping bag," she said, her hands resting on my shoulders. "You give a good ride."

"That's what all the pretty girls tell me," I said, my fingers on her leather covered legs. "If you want somewhere with decent Wi-Fi and a better kitchen than what's at the department then you can use my apartment. I think you're trustworthy enough to have my keys for a couple of days."

"We're taking the next left," she said, pointing down a quiet side street. "Thank you for the offer. I'm okay working at, well, work, this weekend as I can use the internal systems to check out some online journals, but another time that would be useful. This is me."

We stopped outside a run-down terrace whose window frames looked rotten and crumbling. The front door opened and a man with a large belly and stained t-shirt appeared, eyeing Victoria greedily.

"I know exactly what you're thinking and you don't need to

say anything because I agree with you. However, this is only temporary and I'm very careful. Thank you for a lovely evening and you can put me down now."

I stalled, debating keeping hold of her, turning around and installing her in my apartment, or better still my bed.

"Maxwell," she said.

I bent my knees and felt her weight change to the ground.

Barefoot, she was almost a foot shorter than me, her long hair stopping at her waist. "Sorry. I wouldn't have my sisters live here."

"I know. That's why I didn't want you to take me home as I knew what your reaction would be. But I don't have your sisters' money."

Doe eyes looked up at me and if she wouldn't come to mine I wondered about staying here with her. Then I remembered the temper and fire I had seen just over a week ago; she could look after herself and to offer my protective services would insult her.

"If you can manage to get some of my grandfather's money, that will be a huge help."

Nodding was about the only thing I could trust myself to do.

"Maxwell," she said quietly. "Are you seeing anyone?"

"No."

She cupped my face with her hands and stood on tiptoes to reach me, pressing her lips to mine. No tongue, no depth, just the sweetest kiss; full of promise like the first page of a book.

"I thought not," she said, returning her heels to the floor, her arms back by her sides. "You can't keep your eyes off my boobs."

I should've attempted to look embarrassed but opted instead to look at her tits. I could make out hard nipples through the thin material of her shirt and bra, which wasn't padded. I hoped I had been the cause of them hardening. "You've got the best pair of tits I've ever seen," I said, biting my lip immediately after.

That wasn't something you should say to someone you worked with and were now acting for, even if it was the goddamn truth. "Sorry, I shouldn't have said that."

Her hands moved to her chest and she gently cupped them through her clothes. The semi I'd had became a full-on erection and if she looked at my crotch it it would be obvious to her the effect she was having on me.

"Why? If it's the truth, then why not say it? And you're right. They are pretty great. I get to see them naked at least twice on a daily basis." She grinned at me, giving her tits another squeeze before letting them go. Her nipples were hard bullets now and I felt my cock pulse against the zipper of my jeans.

"Fuck," I said. "If we're being honest, then know that all I'm going to be able to think about for the rest of the night, and probably the weekend, is what they'd look like with my mouth on them. Shit, Vic. This isn't a conversation we should be having."

She stood on her tiptoes again, her arms wrapping around my neck and bringing me into a hug. Her breasts pressed against my chest and my hands went to her ass, pulling her against me so she could feel exactly how hard she had made me. I shifted so I could kiss her, a mirror kiss to the one she had given me. Her lips were soft and I could taste red wine and something that was just her. "I'll stand here until I see your light come on and I know you're in okay."

She nodded. "Have a good weekend and I'll see you next week. You have my number?"

"It's in my phone," I'd programmed it in earlier. "I'll text you so you have mine."

"Goodnight, Max."

I watched her enter through the door that was half off its hinges, her ass swaying in the tight leather trousers. A minute or two later a light came on, then a silhouette at the window. It was Victoria, standing at the glass two storeys up, long hair down over her tits that were no long restrained by clothes or a bra. Her hair concealed her nipples and most of her flesh, but that didn't matter. She'd given me even more to think about, and probably become frustrated over. And given the slight wave she gave me before she turned away, baring the flesh of her back, she knew it.

CHAPTER 6
VICTORIA

Maxwell: You're a tease.

Me: (.)(.)

Maxwell: Still a tease. And anyone could've seen.

Me: That's part of the fun. They didn't though: there was only you out there. And you didn't see anything either. One of the benefits of long hair.

Maxwell: It's long enough. And what it was hiding is all I can think about.

Thinking before acting had never been something I was particularly consistent with, so taking a quick photo of the side of my boob and sending it to Max wasn't a considered move.

The dancing dots appeared and then went. Five minutes, then they were back again.

. . .

Me: Stuck for words?

Maxwell: Had to do something.

Me: Did it involve your hand?

Maxwell: You have no idea what you're doing
to me.

Me: Would you like to know what I'm doing
to me?

Maxwell: FFS, if you carry on, I'll have to come
back over to yours and you won't get any of
your work done this weekend.

I pulled my hair over a nipple, letting a little bit of pink slip
through, changed my phone to selfie mode and snapped a
picture. I edited it straight away, adding horns and a tail to my
boob. I didn't make it a habit to send pictures of my anatomy to
anyone, but the vibe I had received from Max so far was that
pretty much anything was safe with him, although I had a
feeling he had a side that would come out differently when he
was in the bedroom.

I liked sex; I liked it rough and hot and gentle and long. I
liked a good fuck up against a wall or being taken quickly in a
bathroom. I loved the feel of a man and what my body could do
to him. I liked to experiment and role play, and I liked someone
who knew what he was doing with a woman. I did have an exhi-
bitionist streak and I liked my body being looked at. Standing at
the window with just my hair covering my nipples, knowing
that Max was looking even though we'd barely even kissed was
exhilarating.

My curtains were now closed, the lights dim. I lay naked on my bed, eyes on my phone, waiting for his response. My other hand slipped between my legs where I was wet to the point of dripping and I began to stroke my clit in circular motions, imagining Max was there with me, pinching my nipples, biting at them, fingering me.

My orgasm happened quickly and violently, hips lifting off the bed and I cried out involuntarily as my body shook. Once the earthquake had subsided, I lifted my hand and looked at my fingers that were coated with my juices. I took a photo and saved it. Maybe at some point I'd send it Max. Maybe.

> Maxwell: I don't want any more photos until I've seen them for real. And had my hands on them. Licked them. Sucked them. I want to make you orgasm just by touching your tits and then I want to come all over them. Then take a photo.
>
> Maxwell: When can I take you out? Properly. On a date?

My heart pounded, overtaking the fact that I was insanely turned on again by his words. I wasn't sure about dating. A good fuck was more than welcome, and I had no doubt that Max would be good—what I had felt through his jeans was bigger than my favourite vibrator—but I knew already that he would be good at the whole dating scene.

My finger hovered ready to type a response. I knew what I wanted to say, it could just change things. There was a chance that after I'd completed my PhD I wouldn't be staying in London. Opportunities could lie elsewhere and having a steady boyfriend would create complications. But I wanted to spend time with Max, to get to know him, to see if he lived up to his dirty talk.

> Me: Lunch on Tuesday? Or any other day apart from Monday.

Maxwell: I'm in court on Tuesday. Wednesday?

> Me: Wednesday's good. I'm giving a lecture at 12, so do you want to meet me after that?

Maxwell: What's the lecture on? Are you making up stories about posh kings and queens?

> Me: Kind of. It's on King Arthur and the legend of Camelot—introductory lecture. So your attempt at demeaning my subject hasn't really worked! *evil laugh*

Maxwell: I shall continue to attempt to demean your subject. Lunch on Wednesday then?

> Me: It'll be the highlight of my week.

The banter we'd been exchanging via email spilled into our text messages over the weekend. I took to sending him useless history facts; he sent me comments on what his siblings were doing, including a few photographs usually of Seph in inevitably stupid poses. By Monday morning, I'd achieved a hell of a lot of work to support my dissertation, arranged to meet a historian in Ypres in November and had decided that a date with Max wasn't going to be that scary.

Jackson called me shortly after lunch on Monday to ask me to go into his office to see him regarding some paperwork that needed signing and to have a quick chat over what he had done so far. I was surprised by how quickly he had got around to contacting my grandfather's lawyers, given the other cases I knew he must have on, and I wondered if Max had pulled strings to get his brother to start it so fast.

The offices of Callaghan Green were set in one of the older buildings near Borough Market and I was met by a tidy and well organised reception and a smiling woman.

"I'm here to see Jackson Callaghan," I said confidently. Although I didn't have a clue about the intricacies of law, except for some of its history, I was very rarely intimidated by places or situations or people. If Jackson managed to send some of my grandfather's inheritance my way, he would take a fee, so I didn't feel indebted towards him or overawed by his reputation.

"He's expecting you. Take a seat and I'll let him know you're here."

I smiled and sat down, picking up a legal magazine that had the recognisable face of Maxwell Callaghan on the front. I kept my laughter to myself and started reading through the article on him, listing his achievements, his formidable presence in court, the major cases he'd won and the small section on his personal life where he refuted having a girlfriend and insinuated that he was married to his job.

"I'm more fun than what that article makes out," a voice whispered into my ear and I jumped in surprise, almost hitting the ceiling. "I think I am anyway."

"I'd say so. I take it the journalist didn't know about your liking for dirty talk?"

His eyes shone wickedly. "She didn't send me cleavage shots first thing on a Monday morning," he said quietly so he couldn't be overheard.

I wanted to touch him, to bring his face to mine and let his tongue in my mouth, but the receptionist was watching us in amusement and this was where he worked.

"Jackson asked me to come in," I said, fighting the urges.

"I know. Follow me." He led me through the building, passed a dark wood staircase with intricate carvings and original tiles on the floor to a dark wood door with Jackson's name on it.

Jackson was sitting behind a desk, his phone stuffed between his ear and shoulder, both hands full of paperwork. "I know Van, but they can't start until next week, so you'll have to get the delivery put back. It's one of those things." He looked up at us and scowled at Max who was doing some sort of action with his thumb. "I have to go; Max is here with Victoria. Love you. See you tonight. Yes, wear that." There was a dirty laugh. "Seriously. People in my office."

"How fucking under the thumb can you be?" Max said, taking a seat. I now understood the gesture.

Jackson didn't look fazed. "One day you'll understand. Ignore my brother, Victoria. He has some issues that he's been working through for a while."

I heard Max swear under his breath.

"I've spoken to your brother's solicitor this morning and asked to see the will they claim they have in their possession. I mentioned to them that once any such document materialised I would be having an independent expert look at it to ensure it wasn't fraudulent as part of our due diligence. They're getting back to me," Max said.

"You didn't have issue getting my grandfather's solicitor to pass the case to you?" I said, surprised already. I'd been telling myself for months that I'd rather keep my sanity than have a fight with my brother over the money.

"None whatsoever. Your fees should've been paid out of your grandfather's estate from the start, so all the bills you received from them and the refusal to do any work until you were up to date with costs were completely bogus and seem to be a stalling tactic, which I've claimed. I've also told them I'm reporting them to the solicitors' regulation authority, so to put it in layman's terms, they're fucking shitting themselves. That's as far as we've got." He gestured to a file on his desk. "I need you to have a look through those and sign where I've starred. I don't think you'll have any trouble understanding what's there, but Max has offered to go through it with you anyway."

"Thank you. Thank you so much for this," I said, picking up the file. "What should I tell my brother when he contacts me. He won't be happy about this so he will be in touch."

"That's easy," Max said. "You tell him to fuck off and that if he needs to contact you he does so through your solicitors. Unless you have a good relationship and you do want to talk to him."

I shook my head. My half-brother was several years older than me. He hadn't got along with my father, who my mother had married after her first husband—Francis' father—died. After my parents were killed in a car accident he'd hated me even more. I was the apple of my grandparents' eye and although they'd treated him fairly, he'd been inexplicably jealous. "I'd rather not speak to him again. If he gets in contact I'll tell him that. Thank you."

Jackson nodded as his phone began ringing. Max gestured to follow him out and he led me to another office, slightly larger, messier, with an old antique looking table near the window. "My room," he said, almost proudly. "I think I spend most of my life here."

"I think that about my computer. I spend most of the time at it. Is there anything in here that you don't think I'll understand?"

He shook his head and pulled a chair over to me, taking me through each page one at a time, adding in comments about the history behind the legalities and where certain terms stemmed from. He was patient and animated, clearly in love with his subject, as I had expected him to be.

"You never told me you taught history," I said, my leg

pressed against his, the warmth being passed through going straight to my centre.

"Don't insult me, Victoria," he said, his voice deep and melodious. "You know I don't have time for pointless subjects." He was teasing, his smile broad.

"You were loving all those history facts I sent you over the weekend," I said, weakly punching his upper arm.

"I loved the photos more." His gaze dropped from my eyes to my chest and lingered long enough for desire to bubble in me. I dug in my back pocket for my phone. Keeping the screen hidden from him I sent him the picture of my fingers.

His phone pinged, the photo thankfully not coming up on screen. "I changed the settings to protect your modesty," he said, unlocking the screen. "Fuck, Vic. Is this what I think it is?"

I sent him another, one I'd taken this morning as I was getting ready, a mirror selfie where I was wearing a black lace bra and matching panties, my nipples visible through the fine lace. My face was out of the picture; not that I didn't trust Max. You just never knew who might end up with his phone or mine.

"Is this what you're wearing now?" he said, his voice low and gruff.

"Yes," I said. "Do you like it?"

He groaned, burying his head in his hands. "What am I going to do with you?" he said, more to himself that to me. "I lasted less than thirty seconds jacking off to that photo you sent last night! I'm seriously concerned that should I ever get the opportunity to be inside you, I'd be a massive disappointment. You've turned me into the teenage boy I never was, Victoria."

I stood up and pushed my chair away, turning him around so I was facing him. I cupped his chin with one hand and made him look at me. "We have a date on Wednesday. If we still like each other after that, let's go out Friday. Then we have the weekend."

He shook his head. "I can do Friday but I'm going to see my sister on Saturday." He lost some of his swarthy colouring;

clearly something there was bothering him. "Friday and Sunday. That'll be three dates."

"You have a three date rule?"

He looked at me, puzzled.

"No sex until after the third date?"

Max laughed, his hands holding my hips. "I want you to know that I'm attracted to you for you and not just the best pair of tits I've ever seen parts of."

"I get that," I said, perching my ass on his desk. My fingers went to the buttons on my shirt and started to undo them slowly. His eyes stared, transfixed. My bra became exposed and his hands froze, still on my hips. Between my legs, my pussy burned and I yearned for some friction to ease the ache, but the waiting would make it sweeter and clearly both Max and I were happy with delayed gratification.

The bra had a front fastening and came undone easily, pinging back and letting my breasts spill out. I was big for my frame and they were perky. An ex-boyfriend had once suggested that I could always fall back on being an erotic model if I ever fell short. The idea had turned me on, but I was too aware of the pitfalls it could've caused professionally and my heart was in history and making a name for myself as an academic.

I pinched my nipples, making them harder still and Max's breath became deeper, faster.

"Is your door locked?" I said. We were side on to the door and large bay window which had privacy glass installed.

"No," he said. "And my brothers and Payton will walk in." He kept eye contact with me whilst speaking which softened me further towards him.

"I shouldn't stay like this for too long then," I said, taking hold of his hands in mine and guiding them to my breasts.

His touch was light, reverent, a finger on each hand tracing over the skin in concentric circles, making their way to my nipples which were puckered and hard enough to cut glass. He pinched sharply, sending an electric current straight through to my pussy. I knew I was soaked already. And then his mouth was on my left nipple, nipping and sucking. He switched to the right, leaving the left shiny and cooling from his mouth, his hand caressing the flesh.

"How wet are you?" he said, his fingers now working magic, pinching and stroking and massaging.

"You wouldn't need to do anything else to be inside me," I said honestly. I didn't know how I was going to get back home without having to bring myself to orgasm somewhere.

"I don't want you to touch yourself until I make you come," he said, then kissed each nipple.

"When will that be?" I wasn't sure I could keep such a promise.

"After Sunday. I'll do the same too. And I want more pictures of your underwear. And of these." He tugged and I gasped. I was close to orgasm and he knew it. A hand slipped down my body and up my skirt. His fingers stopped at the top of my thighs. "You're so wet your panties are soaked through.

He pushed his chair back and pushed my skirt up. At first I thought he was going to go down on me, but instead he started to devour my juices from my thighs, completely ignoring where I needed it most. He bit the soft flesh, then licked and kissed it, leaving my breasts exposed.

A knock sounded at the door and I jumped. He laughed and stilled me with his hands. "Come back in five," he shouted gruffly, reminding me of the man who I had met nearly two weeks ago. Then he gave one quick kiss to my clit and moved back, staring into my eyes and holding my breasts with his hands. "You taste like my every favourite thing."

I was passed coherent speech, only capable of thrusting my breasts into his hands and causing him to laugh.

"I could have you right here, over my desk and pound into your pussy like the world was ending around us. I want you coming on my cock so hard that the only name you know is mine and then I'm going to do it to you all over again, so when you walk everyone knows what you've been doing and everyone knows who you belong to." His eyes were dark and wild. He let go of my breasts, leaving me exposed to his gaze.

"The only person I belong to is myself," I managed to hiss, broadening my chest and spreading my legs, keeping the power with me because he couldn't tear his gaze away.

He didn't smile. Instead his hand went to his trousers, undoing the zip and pulling out his cock. He was large and thick and I couldn't stop the quiet moan that fell from my mouth when I saw it. He stroked himself and my chest began to rise and fall, my breathing laboured.

A knock at the door sounded again. "Max, your client's here."

"Make them a coffee and I'll see them in room three," he said, his hand still on his cock.

"Maxwell," I said, quietly, not wanting to be heard. "We need to come. I want you to fuck me, but if you're not going to, let me get myself off while you come on my tits."

I pulled my skirt up round my waist and slid off my panties, deciding to leave them there for Max—they were too sodden to put back on. My hand went to my centre and I pushed a finger inside me, watching him watching me. His hand on his cock began to move faster as he watched, drawing closer. I saw pre-come glistening at the tip and licked my lips, wanting him in my mouth, then between my tits.

"You're so fucking beautiful," he said, his voice a low whisper. "Everything about you is so fucking beautiful. Your pussy, your tits, your fucking legs. But it's your feistiness that gets me, your independence and your intellect. You don't stop captivating me."

My fingers moved around my clit and I felt my orgasm running up at pace. He came closer, one hand still touching his cock, the other on me, two fingers pushing into my tight cunt. I came immediately, his fingers skilled and demanding, trying to hold in my cries. Hot lines of come spurted from him onto my breasts and he let loose a low call of my name, his fingers still inside me.

"Fuck," he groaned. "*Fuck.*" I watched his face; he was mesmerised with his semen coating my chest.

I grabbed my phone and took a picture, keeping my head out of the frame. "There," I said. "An important occasion forever captured in digital." We looked at each other and started to laugh, the thick sexual tension lightening.

Max pulled his fingers out and cupped my sex as if trying to provide comfort. "You're amazing," he said. "I'll get you cleaned up. I think your underwear's out of commission though."

"I can walk home pantyless."

His look was one of pure protective male. "Only if I'm walking with you and I have to see a client. I'll get you a car. And some new underwear. And I need to kiss you. I've had my fingers in you and I've come all over you, but I haven't kissed you properly yet." His hands left me, leaving me cold and went to cupboard, pulling out a towel. "I should wash you down, but I like the idea of still being on you."

"I'm going to need another orgasm if you carry on talking like that," I said.

He started to gently wipe away his come from my breasts.

"I know the feeling. I want to pick you up and take you to a cave somewhere so I can fuck us into oblivion." He put the towel down and with fingers that shook slightly, did the clasp on my bra and then started to button up my shirt, struggling to match the buttons correctly.

"Let me finish," I said, lifting one his hands and bringing it to my lips to kiss. He let me complete the task, watching and then leaned down and kissed me, my mouth opening for his and letting his tongue in. The kiss was deep and slow, more tender than I'd expected and I didn't want to go back to the office or home afterwards. I wanted to stay with him, for more of those kisses.

"I have to see a couple of clients," he said, apologetically. His gave me a hand to help me off the desk and then kept hold of me. "I'd rather be going somewhere with you, but I will see you Wednesday."

"You will. And I'll text you later. Or phone you," I said, feeling my face heat. We hadn't spoken on the phone yet.

"I'd like that. I'll call you a car. We have a guy we use if we need to give people lifts. I trust him with you."

I saw that his hands were still fidgety and that although I certainly didn't feel as if he was panicking after the level of intimacy we'd shared, his brain was overthinking something.

Ten minutes later and I was sitting in the back of a limo, my saturated panties tucked inside Max's desk drawer, wondering why I wasn't feeling panicked and where this strange sense of calm had come from, and how long, exactly, it would last.

CHAPTER 7
MAXWELL

"The only other person who checks their phone more than you is Jackson, and that's because he's pussy-whipped," my most irritating sibling told me, trying to peer around my hand to see what was on the screen.

I moved my phone away, having no intention of letting him read any of the conversation between me and Victoria.

"It's work," I said, still looking at my phone. "If you ever took your life seriously, you'd be doing work stuff on your phone." I had no issue with lying my ass off to Seph.

"I got the contract, by the way," he said. "The one with Tudors."

"Well done," I muttered, typing a reply back to Victoria. "Remind me to buy you a big shiny medal."

"This is why I prefer Jackson to you. He actually listens to me!" Seph reached his hand out and grabbed my phone.

"What the... Give me that back, now!" I tried to take it from him, but he stuffed it into his jacket pocket. "Bastard."

"We're having coffee in public. There are small children present who don't need to learn bad words just yet and you can have your phone back later." Seph said, sipping almost delicately at an espresso. He'd spent a holiday in Rome over the summer and had come back thinking he was the king of Italian etiquette when in fact he just looked like a twat. I'd told him just as much, several times.

"I think your first word was 'fuck'," I said, trying not to let the withdrawal symptoms from my phone show too much.

Seph laughed. "It is mum's favourite word, so I'm not surprised. What was Payton's? Shit or fucking cunt?"

Marie was my stepmum; Payton and Seph were her eldest children with my dad. Marie was worshipped by all of us and should've been given mother of the year multiple times, even if it was just for taking on four motherless kids—and fatherless to a large extent—without blinking an eye. I remembered when she came over to England from New York after a whirlwind romance with my father and started to take on the role of mum. She'd sat there one evening when Jackson, Claire and Callum had gone to bed and looked at me while she paired socks. "I have absolutely no clue what the fuck I'm doing, Maxwell," she'd said. "So if I swear a lot and throw the odd thing I apologise now." She had sworn a lot, sometimes at us, sometimes at my father, on one occasion at my teacher, but she'd been everything else we'd needed and more.

"More," I said. "And that's not a joke. Well done on the Tudor contract. Jackson told me last night. You must've impressed them as I know they were thinking of going with Cole Alexander."

"Thanks," Seph said, almost preening. "I've mentioned to Jackson about expanding the department at some point—if we get another couple of contracts similar to Tudors."

Seph specialised in employment law and was unfortunately very good at it. He had also inherited Marie's charm and personality and if on the off-chance he didn't know the answer to something, he could bullshit his way through it and scatter rainbows at the same time.

"That's Jackson's call, not mine. He does the figures," I said, thankful again that I had a sibling with business acumen and an interest in running the firm. "But if you get one more client half the size of Tudors you'll need another fee earner for sure."

Seph pulled my phone from his pocket and stared at it. "It's been like having a vibrator in my pocket. Who's texting you?" He stared at the screen. "Victoria. Isn't that the girl from the university?"

"The one who's grandfather's will we're looking at, yes." I felt no shame in telling a half-lie. "I'm meeting her in an hour for lunch."

"Even though it's Jackson handling the case," Seph said pointedly. "I wondered why you weren't rushing back to the office. And you've put that suit on that tapers at your waist."

"Coincidence," I said, reading the messages and smiling. She was telling me about the lecture she was about to give. I was close enough to the lecture theatre to catch the last half of it but I wasn't sure how keen that would make me look, or how I felt about wanting to go.

I looked up to see Seph staring at me curiously. "Tell me about her. Because she's not your client and you're trying to bullshit me. You first tried to bullshit me when you told me I'd get chocolate if I put my hand in a bag full of cow shit and I didn't believe you then, so I'm not going to fall for it now."

It had nearly worked and probably would've done if Payton hadn't refused first. "She's a history lecturer, studying for her PhD and she works at the law faculty in the admin," I said, telling him nothing he couldn't have found from google.

"Another professor?"

My siblings had a standing joke that I only dated women with PhDs. It was almost true—by coincidence and not résumé filtering. I'd been out with several lawyers since qualifying, as work was naturally where I was going to meet people. There'd never been anyone who captivated me and after a night in bed, all we'd had to talk about was law. Working at the university meant I'd met different women and they had doctorates or master's degrees. "She will be."

"Age?"

"What's this? A fact hunting mission for mum?"

Seph shrugged. "It's nice to know stuff before Claire for a change."

"She's thirty-two."

"Is she hot?"

I put my head in my hands. "You know, sometimes you're like this amazing prodigy, securing this huge contract and wowing clients with your knowledge. Other times, you're just a complete and utter dick. She's lecturing at the Mason Hall around the corner. Why don't you come with me and maybe learn something that's not about Star Wars for a change?"

"She's hot, isn't she? Have you got a picture?" he said, making a grab for my phone and succeeding.

"Seph, don't open the photos…" I started, but it was too late. My phone was already unlocked and my brother was staring at Victoria's perfect breasts.

He passed me the phone but only after he'd had a good enough look to make his eyes widen. "I'm going to need to pretend I haven't seen that, aren't I?"

"Yep," I said.

My phone rang and I took the call as we walked: a new client whose story was similar to mine. It was a brief conversation, just to confirm I had received copies of medical reports and the log showing the times and details about when his late wife was checked on. She's been suffering from post-natal depression, just as my mother had been, and had been admitted to a ward after making threats against her life. Unfortunately, it hadn't been enough to stop her and now the family were making a claim of negligence, that she should've been continuously monitored as opposed to twenty minute checks.

"You okay?" Seph said.

He'd heard enough of my side of the phone call to know what it was about. All my siblings would know about the case. All of them would be keeping an eye on me while I was working on it. This was why I'd specialised in medical malpractice and clinical negligence and I knew enough about my own psychology to understand that I was continuously avenging my mother's death.

"I've done this before, Seph, but your concern is noted and will be remembered when I'm Christmas shopping on Christmas Eve," I said, thankful for him being there even if it wasn't needed. "Please try not to embarrass me if you speak to Victoria and for fuck's sake, don't tell her you've seen her—"

"Tits," Seph interrupted as we went into the building. "I'll try not to. They were fucking amazing though."

"Wipe the image from your head else I'll have to hit you very hard," I growled, not sure how to deal with the nasty feeling in my stomach that my little brother had seen something that was not his. And by not his, I did mean that it was mine.

"Forgotten. Shit. She is hot. Like librarian hot. As in the librarian you'd fantasise about when you were at school and it was the main reason for going to the library," Seph started to verbally crap himself at the back of the lecture theatre, only collecting one glare from a student who looked serious enough to be studying law.

Victoria was stood at the front, a large screen behind her, displaying an array of pictures that she would zoom into and discuss. Her hair was tied up in a huge messy bun, loose bits around her face. The oversized glasses were perched on her nose and she wore wide legged trousers that gathered tightly at the ankles, a white shirt with a low neckline that was tucked into the waistline and a pair of ridiculously high heeled black shoes.

"You do not fantasise about her," I said quietly to Seph. "You do not think about her in any way, shape or form unless it's like you would one of your sisters. Do you understand?"

"Does she have a sister?"

I sighed loudly, hoping he was just after a reaction from me, but I realised he was serious. Instead of continuing to be annoyed by the walking hormone, I focused on what she was lecturing and found myself interested. It was an introductory lecture to first year undergrads who were in their first week at university. Most of them would have hangovers and had more than likely just scrambled out of bed in time to get there, but all were captivated as she discussed the legend of King Arthur and Camelot and what was historically factual.

The lecture concluded, a smattering of applause resonating. Then students started to vacate, passing me and Seph, a couple of girls giving us appraising glances. I started to make my way down the stairs to the dais where Victoria was lingering, explaining something to a student who was way too close to her for my liking.

"You've visited Tintagel? So you'd have seen the importance it has had on the tourist industry there?" she said, her face lighting up with enthusiasm.

I stayed a few feet away, aware that I was perfectly capable of knocking this young man's head off his shoulders should he place a finger anywhere on her.

"Yes, I spent a few holidays there when I was a teenager. I think it's what really started my interest in history. It certainly wasn't the teaching at my school—that was really dull compared to your lecture," the kid continued to ramble.

I elbowed Seph who was standing with his arms folded over his chest, looking a cross between a bodyguard and an over-dressed student. "Were you that dumb when you came here?" I said, quietly enough so that the kid wouldn't hear.

"Probably," Seph said. "I was better at it though."

"Better at what?"

"Having game."

I groaned. It was loud enough to attract Victoria's attention. She looked over and smiled. "Hey," she said. "I thought I was meeting you at Romano's?"

The kid looked over at us, his expression saddening. Surely he didn't think he had a chance?

"I decided to try to get some extra education for my brother." I elbowed Seph again a little harder. This time he played along and winced loudly.

Victoria turned back to the kid and bestowed a smile upon him. "I have a lunch date. Have a good Freshers' week and I'll see you in lectures next week."

"Will I be in your seminar?" he asked, a little too quickly.

"I'm not sure. Lists go up tomorrow." She gave him another smile, picked up a pile of papers and headed towards us.

"You can go now," I said to Seph. "You're no longer required."

Victoria laughed, her eyes softening as she looked at Seph. "That's not fair, Max. You've just made him sit through a history lecture. The least you can do is buy him a drink."

Seph's chest puffed out and he gave her his most charming smile. "I'm Joseph, Maxwell's younger brother." He held out a hand and I hoped to fuck he wasn't going to take her hand and kiss it.

Instead, Victoria stepped in closer and gave Seph a quick hug. I messed with my beard, watching where his hands went.

"It's good to meet the ex-president of the Assassins' Guild," she said, beaming at him. "Thank you for sorting the room out for them. There was a mix up with where your brother was taking his Thursday evening seminar."

"There are always mix ups where my brother's concerned," Seph said. "If you hang around him enough you'll realise that."

Victoria lifted her brows.

I shrugged. "Possibly. But we're not hanging round Seph today. I thought you had a meeting at one?"

"Why do you know my diary better than I do," Seph said, checking his phone, probably looking at the calendar and seeing that I was right.

"Because I bother to make an effort to know what other partners in my law firm are doing. I'll see you later," I said as he began to shift towards the exit. I knew my brother too well; he'd have checked the timing to see if he could pick up a sandwich from Gertie's and get back to the office in time. The answer to that was yes, he could, if he left now.

"Good to meet you, Victoria, but I do need to go. Hopefully see you soon. Join us for drinks on Friday." Seph shot her a grin and started to hotfoot it out of the lecture hall.

I stayed standing next to her, knowing that my diary was clear for another couple of hours, although I had a shit ton of work to get through that would now take me late into the evening.

For a moment, I wondered what the fuck I was doing, taking this edible woman to lunch. I didn't do this. I didn't set myself up to be distracted all day when I had a big case that I needed to be consumed by. I loved my job; I'd long ago made a decision to focus on law and my practice, along with the lecturing rather than pursuing a relationship like what Jackson now had. I didn't take three hour breaks during the course of a working day. It was only because my friend Amelie owned the coffee shop near the offices that I actually managed to remember to feed and water myself, as she sent occasional texts reminding me.

"I've only got half an hour or so myself," I said, telling myself I wasn't technically lying.

"Let's grab some soup or a sandwich then. There's a really cute café round the corner where I sometimes grab lunch," she said without reprimand in her expression. "I've got some points to finalise with my tutor for my dissertation by the end of the day so I could do with getting back early. Plus, there's the small matter of sorting out the lists for the seminars as they need to go up tomorrow."

I followed her outside, feeling like a dick. I didn't want to spend just ninety minutes with her: I wanted the whole of the afternoon, then the evening and the night too. "How did your meeting with your tutor go?"

She nodded. "Good. I thought it would as I'd prepared pretty well for it. My old tutor is at Johns Hopkins now so I could run some things by him beforehand. I'm just hoping I can get it all done relatively quickly."

The café was less than two minutes away, tucked down a side street and looked nothing from the front. "This is it?"

"Yes. The food's great, especially for something quick." I followed her inside and we sat at a table towards the back and again I felt like an utter bastard. This was meant to be a date, partly to make up for what happened in my office where I still felt like I'd taken advantage of her and partly to get to know her.

"Look," I said. "I want to do this properly. When I'm not thinking about work and getting back to the office and what I should be doing."

"I understand."

"I don't take much time out of work and this feels completely out of my comfort zone…"

"I understand. I've hardly spoken to anyone unless it's been to do with work, my studies or my friend Jacob in the last twelve months."

"What happened in my office—"

"Was a mistake."

I closed my mouth and rubbed my shirt, wondering if something from my jacket had just stabbed me. "A mistake?"

"A mistake. We kind of work together. We're both really busy and I'm probably moving to the States, or I'm hoping to, once I've finished my PhD, so seeing someone, however casually, is probably a bad idea," she said. "And that doesn't mean texting you and seeing you in your office hasn't been the highlight of my year, because it really has, but I need to focus and you're a distraction."

"Can I take your order?" A girl who looked just about old enough to be allowed out on her own came to our table.

"The soup of the day and a pastrami sandwich, plus a macchiato. Thanks, Elise," Victoria said, looking and sounding a hell of a lot calmer than I had.

"The same," I said. I hadn't even looked at the menu.

"Sure. Be five minutes." Elise disappeared. I looked at Victoria, trying to read her, but her soft brown eyes gave nothing away.

"I don't think I've been called a distraction before," I half mumbled. "In my office, I wasn't..."

"Maxwell." She reached for my hand and linked her fingers with mine. "I took a selfie of your come all over my tits and texted it to you. I don't think I have any problem with anything that happened, except not having had an orgasm since." There was a coy smile.

I managed to nod, swallowing whatever weird shit I was feeling and talked to her about the fucking weather.

CHAPTER 8
VICTORIA

"And why in the name of god and all that is holy did you tell him that?" Jacob looked up from what appeared to be half a bottle of red wine in a very large glass and simmered at me. "He's got the cock of a horse, a mouth dirtier than a sewer, looks like a Greek god and you've told him you don't even want anything casual. Are you mad?"

"Quite possibly," I said, taking a mouthful of the red nectar. I'd seen the fear and worry on Max's face on Tuesday and it had immediately raised all the concerns I'd tried to bury. "I might have made a mistake."

"You think?" Jacob said, almost knocking over the bottle— that was probably almost empty anyway—with a sudden hand gesture. "Have you heard from him since?"

The wine tasted so good, especially after a day spent studying and finishing posting the lists for the seminars that started next week. "He's texted a few times. Kind of similar stuff to before about his family and work, some stupid legal history facts." I had been surprised, thinking he'd probably have distanced himself. He rarely had to come into the admin block at the university, most stuff being dealt with online and it was Jackson who was in touch about my grandfather's will.

"And you haven't sent him anymore photos?"

"Yes. Just not of me." I'd messaged him a few pictures; a disaster of a dinner I'd cooked, my knee-high socks, the office at midnight with a strange shadow and my lunch from the café yesterday.

"I'm not sure what your problem is," Jacob said, the wine magically disappearing. "He's confessed to being married to his work so he's not going to want anything long term or serious and you really could do with a good fuck. Can't you think of it as therapy and maybe even offer to pay him?"

"I'm not sure he'd be totally cool with being a male escort."

"I don't mean on a contractual basis: just as a token gesture so that no feelings were involved. You don't kiss or exchange gifts, that sort of thing," Jacob said. "But you both get to scratch an itch, otherwise known as having mutual orgasms. It could be a no lose situation." He sprawled a bit further down one of his sofas.

Jacob's apartment was luxurious and warm. Mainly white with the odd splash of pastel colours, it shouldn't have suited him, given that he was, in his words, a show pony, but he was also the kindest person I knew. We were spending Saturday night in, drinking wine and polishing off a very large Chinese takeaway, both bemoaning our busy weeks and impending doom at the sword of work. The conversation had taken a turn towards sex, and then Maxwell.

"It'd be too complicated."

He sat up. "That's because you actually like him, don't you?"

"No. He's an ass. An egotistical, driven workaholic ass."

"That was what you thought originally. Since then you've seen his dick. And had conversations. You like him," Jacob said, looking triumphantly at me. "I think you should send him a picture of your underwear with it still on."

"I don't have time to like someone like that, and besides, I just want to focus on my doctorate and writing a few more articles. This opportunity at Johns Hopkins will be huge if it comes off and I want to make sure I'm in with the best chance of getting it," I said, refocusing my eyes on the prize I'd set myself when I was a little girl, listening to stories from my grandfather about my great-grandparents and the war.

"You don't have to work in America, you know. There will still be universities over here once you've finished your ridiculously long essay. I'd much prefer it if you stayed," Jacob said, his expression now serious.

I knew he wanted me to stay, but I had to go where the best opportunity would be. My grandfather had talked about it at length and it had been his suggestion that I looked further afield if necessary, in order to do the best I could.

"And if the right position comes up, I'll look at it. I promise you. Now, pour me some wine," I held my glass out and he drained the rest of the bottle into it, the rich smell making my mouth water.

"I still think you're mad," he said.

I sipped the wine and silently agreed with him.

―――――

Autumn in London was a multi-faceted gem: some days the sun would still polish the pavements, shining on paths of gold for the tourists; other days the sky would be as grim as the Thames, the steps down to the tube slippery with the rain from wet feet. Monday was the latter; wet and dreary, making me dream of warmer climates with sunnier skies and maybe a beach where I could sit and drink cocktails, waited on by some charming man with a beard and tattoos.

If any money materialised from my grandfather's legacy, after paying off various student loans and credit cards I had promised myself a holiday somewhere warm where I could luxuriate on a beach and disappear into a good book.

"Sorry," a voice pulled me out of my fantasy where the waiter had taken on Max's face and build. "I need to find out where to go."

I sat up and tried to look awake. "Where are looking for?"

"I'm not sure. I missed the library induction and I could do with someone showing me how to log in and find the books I need." He looked confused and uncertain, his hair unbrushed and overlong.

"I can show you how to log in to the library online," I said. "You can then reserve what you need and collect that day. Are you a first year student?"

He shook his head. "Second. I transferred from Cambridge."

"Peter Coffey. I added your details to the student database a few days ago. I'm Victoria Davies; admin here and a history student." I walked around my desk to a computer that we kept for the purpose of helping students either with logging into various accounts or printing the odd essay that just wouldn't email or upload onto the system.

"Thanks for helping me," he said awkwardly. I noticed that he was clenching his fists and figured that he was seriously nervous.

"You're welcome. I know it's difficult getting used to new systems. I've been there myself." I started to help with his log in, showing him how to navigate onto the library database from the intranet. He said very little and made hardly any eye contact, something I'd been used to in my time at university, but not in the law department. Aspiring lawyers had to have a certain level of confidence, arrogance almost. "So if you click there, they should be reserved for you. I recommend that book also, as it's on the reading list for Maxwell Callaghan's module."

He clicked it, the only acknowledgment that I'd spoken.

"It's a good book, if you're looking for something to help you sleep." I looked across the desk and saw the man himself, glad I was sitting down as my legs suddenly didn't feel strong enough.

Peter looked as if someone had just told him he was expected to perform on stage with no rehearsals and no plan.

"Hi, Maxwell," I said, trying to lessen the awkwardness emanating from Peter. "There's some post for you in your pigeon hole." I breathed deeply, regulating and rationalising the array of feelings that were fluttering around my head and stomach. It was far easier to concentrate on Peter and practicalities than it was on the six feet two of sheer maleness that was dominating the office. "Peter, do you want me to show you how to use your student area? You can check that the information about your first year has been transferred correctly for a start and I can show you how to download the lecture notes or watch the video if it's been uploaded."

Peter looked at me, forced a smile and nodded, so I started to talk him through the various aspects of the virtual learning environment, wondering how similar it was to what he had been used to at Cambridge and also wondering why Max was standing behind us, watching everything from over our shoulders.

"I think that's everything," I said to Peter, when I had tried to bore Max into leaving the office by going through the most tedious and unnecessary shortcuts to upload documents. But he was still there; hands in pockets, smirk on his handsome face. "Is there anything else I can show you?"

Peter shook his head. "I think I'm good. Can I get you a coffee to say thank you?"

Max seemed to choke and then cough from behind us. I ignored him. "I have to catch up on some stuff here but thank you for the offer. I hope you enjoy the rest of Freshers' Week."

Peter gave that awkward smile, sent Max a strange look and scarpered out of the office, leaving me with my tormentor.

"Can I take you for a coffee?" he said. "Because I'm pretty

sure you don't have stuff to catch up on and you probably need something to drink after that tutorial. You realise he wasn't concentrating on what you were trying to tell him?"

"He was just nervous. I suspect he doesn't engage much with women," I said, logging off the computer. I wanted to go for a coffee; I definitely needed a break and a change of scenery but sitting opposite Max for any length of time would be tantamount to the torture of my willpower.

Since Saturday, or really since Thursday, I had reconsidered my suggestion to him that we stayed platonic. If neither of us were interested in anything serious, if it could just be fun, then what was the harm in having a few dates, maybe the odd sleep-over? Jacob had joked about me needing a new vibrator and he wasn't wrong. I wasn't actually convinced my lady parts would know what to do with a real penis, given how long it had been.

"Coffee," he said, or rather demanded. He seemed taller today, wearing a blue suit that set off his dark hair and beard that looked neater today. "Let's grab half an hour. I need to hear some tales of the law office or something to get my mind off a case."

It was a strange request from a self-confessed workaholic and I rarely turned down any plea of help, no matter how well disguised. "Let me put the phones on lunch mode. Kate should be here in a minute anyway for the afternoon shift." I technically wasn't full time at the law department office, but this time of year when students were enrolling and lectures and seminars were being arranged was always busy. The overtime would come in handy, should Jackson Callaghan's genius not be enough to wrangle my grandfather's inheritance from my brother.

"My friend has a café come speakeasy a few streets away. Let's go there. Her soup will be as good as your place." He looked at me oddly, as if I was wearing a tin foil blanket at the end of a marathon.

"Sure. I'll let you pay," I said, grabbing my leather jacket as today was not a day when the sun was baking the tourists with September smiles.

He led me to a bijou looking place that was almost full. Golden Age reproductions hung from the walls and there were a large row of cakes on the counter that were far more interesting than soup.

"I recommend everything," he said. "The cakes are homemade. The coffee's all Fairtrade."

"Hey, sugar." An elfin blonde appeared, her smile broader than the Thames. "You've brought a friend. Good to know I'm still good enough to recommend."

"Amy," he said, sitting down at a now empty table. "How are things?"

"Good," she said. "But you knew that. You didn't need to sort everything for me, Maxwell. You've already done enough."

"It's only what you would've done for me," Max said, removing his suit jacket. "This is Victoria. Vic, this is Amelie, one of my oldest childhood friends."

"Notice how he says oldest meaning 'not young'. I'll add rat poison to your coffee for that. What can I get you lovely people? It's great to meet you, by the way, Victoria. It's not often Max brings anybody here apart from his work."

I caught his eye and kicked his shin under the table. He shrugged.

"I'll have the soup and a flat white coffee. Plus, a piece of the red velvet cake I noticed. A large piece."

"Sure, sugar," she said. "Maxwell?"

"Soup, coffee, sandwich," he said. "The usual."

She beamed at him. "I get to experiment. Super. Be a few minutes but I'll send Del over with your coffees as soon as I can." She touched him on the shoulder, her hand lingering as she gently squeezed, and I averted my eyes, not wanting to see his response.

"Thanks for coming with me," he said as Amelie scooted into the kitchen. "I really did need to get away from work and I wasn't sure how else to do it."

"Thanks for treating me, even if you didn't offer and I demanded it instead." I wanted to keep the tone light and try to take his mind off whatever was bothering him.

He smiled, his eyes crinkling at the sides and something in my chest boomed a little wider for a moment. "I don't ever mind treating a friend," he said, and I swore his eyes dropped momentarily to my chest.

"How do you know Amelie?" I asked as Del brought over our coffees.

"I've known her for as long as I can remember. She grew up in the house next to ours and me and my brothers and sister would play with her and her brothers all summer long. We've always kept in touch since she moved out," he said, his hand gripping the mug.

"I thought you had more than one sister," I said. My hair had a mind of its own today and I found myself myself messing with it more, something that looked like a nervous habit.

He laughed. "I have two half-sisters, Payton and Ava. Payton is Seph's twin, Ava's the afterthought. There's seven years between me and the twins and nine between me and Ava, so they were too young to play with Amelie and her brothers. We got stuck with baby-sitting duty though. Some days it still feels like that with Seph," he said with a dramatic roll of his eyes.

"I don't believe that. You seem to be very fond of each other. I don't have that relationship with my half-brother so you're lucky," I said. "When you don't get along and there's resentment it's very difficult."

He eyed me curiously. "Why don't you get along?"

I shrugged. "His mum died when he was eight. His dad then married my mum a couple of years later and they had me. I don't think Francis was very keen on the whole idea of a stepmum and a half-sister to share the attention and he resented me from the start. My parents died when I was seventeen. I moved in with my dad's dad—something else Francis wasn't happy with, as he was after Grandad to downsize and with me there, he wouldn't. It was definitely about the money at that point and that's how it still is."

"Jackson mentioned he'd had correspondence from his solicitors earlier. There's no other will. They wanted to go to probate, but Jackson has asked on what terms. He thinks they'll retract their claim soon and the money will be released," Max said.

My heart doubly thumped now.

"I'll expect another phone call from Francis then."

"He's been in touch?" Max looked concerned, a bit like a guard dog when it hears a noise.

"He's rang five times but I haven't answered and my voicemail is switched off as I knew he'd leave me some ranting, insulting messages that I wouldn't listen to anyway. At some point he'll come to find me to have 'words'," I said, shrugging my shoulders. My brother had only ever taken one stance with me: that he was older and therefore wiser. His advice was usually just to benefit him though; any grief or sadness he caused was simply an additional perk.

"Are you worried about it?" Max said after a pause, during which I figured he was probably giving thought as to what to say.

"No," I said. "He just gets cross with me and tells me what I must do. He's no threat although this is really going to piss him off. Once it's settle though, there's no reason for us to have any more contact. Not that we ever had much beyond his 'advice'."

"What family do you have then?"

It was my turn to laugh. "I don't. My mum wasn't close to her family so I wouldn't know them if I sat next to them on the tube. My dad was an only child. I'm close to my tutor from my masters, Lance Reyes. He's at Johns Hopkins now but we're close."

"Were you in a relationship with him?" The question was quick and almost choked him.

"No. Lance actually had a fling with my friend Jacob. I'm not his type. Part of the reason he took the job in the States was because that's where his now partner lives. I've got Jacob and a couple of other very close friends. I got lucky in some ways: I got to choose my family." I had to look at it like that; I didn't have the fall back of sisters and brothers so I'd become adept at making good friends and sustaining those relationships.

"You almost make me glad I've got my siblings," he said. "And that none of them are like your half-brother. My dad struggled with us four eldest from when we were born. After my mum died he was pretty much clueless and just worked even harder than before. I suppose he stuck to what he was good at."

"What was it like after your stepmum joined you?"

"I found it hard at first. It wasn't my mum and I missed her, but Marie was different and she made us—me especially—into children again, as we didn't have to worry about Callum anymore. He was just a baby when our mum died. But Marie didn't try to replace her: she was just Marie. A lot crazy, very American, very sweary and very stubborn. She stood up to my dad something amazing and made him be a father, even though he was terrified," Max said, the expression on his face crossing between sadness and sheer appreciation.

"Marie sounds amazing. I'm not sure there are many people who could take on four kids, especially ones so young."

"I know. I think I thought at first that she wouldn't stay, so I was horrible to her. I didn't speak to her for weeks because I figured that she wouldn't handle us." He eyed me, as if assessing a temperamental horse. "How did you lose your parents?"

"Car crash," I said. "Wet road. They were likely going too fast as my dad was a bit of petrol head in all honesty. No one else was involved. They'd spent a lot of time working abroad as research scientists so I wasn't especially close to them. That didn't mean I wasn't upset or sad, and I still miss them, but they were often away for big occasions like birthdays and Christmas so I was never used to having a big family like yours."

"I'm sorry that you don't have them though," he said. "Or your grandfather."

I nodded. "He was a huge loss but he was very poorly. I miss him and I'm sad he's not here, but he was in so much pain at the end it couldn't have continued." His eyes asked me what the matter was. "It was a brain tumour. We had a year from diagnosis until the end and we spent it together, travelling to various historical sites and visiting Ypres and the Somme, until he became too ill to travel. What about your mother?"

Amelie arrived with our food and had a large grin for both of us. "Soup and a Mediterranean panini for you." She popped a plate in front of Max. "And soup and cake for the lady my teenage customers keep staring at. Please don't scare them off as they keep ordering more food so they can stay and look. In fact, sugar, I'll need a life-size cut out of you before you leave."

Max turned around and glared at the group of boys who looked about seventeen or eighteen, not quite college age. "Haven't they learnt manners?" he said, his eyes darkening.

"Like I said, don't scare them off. Enjoy your lunch and don't rush to give me the table back," she said, smiling at the boys before going on to the next customer.

"They're not doing any harm," I said, catching the eye of one of the boys, who went extremely red and looked at his phone.

"I'm not sure about that," Max said, stirring the soup. "I don't trust them."

"You don't need to. It's daylight, we're in a busy area and I'm with you who looks like a professional boxer, just a bit taller and without a squashed nose. Besides, I think I could handle most of them," I said, gently kicking his leg under the table. I wouldn't quite call it playing footsie, but it was definitely physical contact. Later I'd have words with myself about wanting physical contact as it should be completely off my agenda.

"My mum committed suicide," he said, almost suddenly. "She had postnatal depression and was being treated for it. It got worse after Callum was born but my dad didn't notice as he was working so much."

"Do you blame your father?" I knew my filters should have been on, but my gut told me direct, honest questions were appreciated by the brooding, great man in front of me.

He shook his head. "Not now. It's more complex than assigning blame. But it's part of the reason I specialised in medical negligence—mental health in particular."

"And it's why you advise on law making too. And write articles." He made sense.

"Yes. I know none of us four are to blame, although with hindsight, you look back and think 'what if'. It's taken a long time though."

"I think it takes forever," I said, pinching his sandwich to take a bite.

"Do you want your own?" he said, taking it back as soon as my mouth was full.

I shook my head, chewing madly.

"You just want mine?"

I shrugged. "Other people's food tastes better. I'll share my cake." I said, smiling hopefully.

"After. I'll sample it."

And I wanted to be sampling him again. Regret was firmly sitting in my loin area that I'd stopped what was happening between us before I'd had him inside me. But the more I got to know him, the more I liked him. The more I saw him and talked to him, the more I was attracted.

"I'm guessing that's what your new case is about—postnatal depression."

Max nodded. "Yes."

"You want the latest office gossip?"

"Yes. If you tell me the latest chapter in the chronicles of Carol, I'll let you have another bite of my panini."

"That sounds rude."

"Good."

CHAPTER 9
MAXWELL

"If he doesn't start checking letters before they're sent, we need to start disciplinary procedures. Same with phone calls: we've had three complaints from different clients about his manner with them in two months. He needs some intense mentoring, or a new job. Most likely a change of career."

The rest of the scalding coffee hit the back of my throat and I reached for the jug for some more. One of the new qualifieds we had employed potentially needed to go back to law college or find himself at the end of my very stretched wrath.

"I'm going to ask Michael to supervise him and his caseload for a couple of months. He can fucking assist. If he doesn't pick up from Michael how to deal with clients we'll be parting ways," Jackson said, making a note in what must've been his eightieth notebook of the year. "We've had a very successful week, even with David's cock-ups. I propose setting up a bar tab for drinks after work. I might even see if the room upstairs in The Bear's Den is available. Make sure all staff know about it—it'll do us good to celebrate. We work fucking hard enough."

"Are you asking Vanessa?" Seph asked.

I assumed the question wasn't worth asking as aside from

working hours, my brother was wherever his fiancée was. I was pleased for him, rather surprised at first as Jackson was as much of a workaholic as I was, and I had accepted the change in our relationship as easily as I could. Jackson had always been my best friend, but Vanessa meant his time was shared. I liked her a lot; she was intelligent and as much of a workaholic as he was. She also put up with our drunken poker nights and looked after Seph when he couldn't find his way home. But things were different and that had meant Seph and I had become closer—Victoria had been right.

"Van's coming. Sophie too," Jackson said.

He mentioned Vanessa's best friend who was the most prolific man-eater I'd ever met, which was saying something when compared with a couple of the women from the science department. And one of the men.

"So it's fine that I asked Victoria?"

I was on my feet before I spoke, coffee covering Jackson's notebook. "What the fuck? Why are you contacting my…" I searched for the correct adjective and couldn't find the appropriate one. "Friend." It was lame, fucking lame.

Seph glared at me over his glasses that I was pretty sure were just for show. We'd been interviewed for an article in a legal magazine a few months ago—something Vanessa had organised for our rebrand—and Seph had ended up with a following of fans on his social media. The photographer had styled him with glasses for a few pictures and they seemed to have stayed as an accessory. Quite possibly an accessory to murder.

"We share friends, Maxwell. Victoria is my friend too. I thought she'd appreciate a chance to meet some new people," Seph said, his tone purposefully patronising.

"Do you need to take this outside?" Claire asked, just back a couple of days ago from her hideaway and in a much better mood than she had been for months. "Or even better, a boxing ring. Knock some sense into each other."

I sat back down. "No, Seph's right. Let's move on."

"Let's not," Seph said, passing some paper towels to Jackson to mop up his notebook. "Let's talk about Victoria. Maybe mention the photos she sends you."

"Fucker," I said. "I told you to forget that. Don't ever mention it. To anyone." My fist was clenched and waving at him. It had been awhile since I'd hit Seph, and even then it had been under controlled conditions with pads and boxing gloves.

"I give permission for Seph to enlighten the rest of us," Jackson said, chucking the paper towels at my head. "Because something's got your ball sac in a twist."

"There's absolutely nothing to tell," I said, feeling a bit too warm. I knew why I was feeling slightly odd; Victoria had altered the course of my trajectory. However, this wasn't something I wanted to analyse with my siblings.

There was a general wave of laughter.

We met like this once a week, usually early on a Friday morning to evaluate the past few days. It didn't always happen; leave, a New York office, a Manchester branch—the possibilities of one of us being absent on a Friday were endless—but when it did it was priceless. Except today; today was a bad time to be a Callaghan.

"Max, you've been weird for a couple of weeks. We know something's changed and from what Seph's said it's this Victoria," Claire said, looking a little too victorious.

"We're just friends. She's a really nice girl, but she's looking at moving to America once she's finished her dissertation so she doesn't want to get involved." I knew the words sounded false as in the past that would've been ideal for me and still should've been, but Victoria had been very clear she didn't want anything more than to be friends. I hadn't thought too much about how I felt about this, instead just trying to accept it and keep the can of worms closed. Tightly.

"So why the reaction at Seph asking her out tonight?" Claire said, phrasing her words right to annoy the shit out of me.

"I wasn't aware that she and Seph were friends," I said, deciding at that moment to be as honest as I could without losing face. "Seph knows me and Victoria weren't just friends, so if he's making a play I think that's wrong. Anyway, can we get back to business?"

I felt Seph's eyes pierce through my skull and tried to ignore them.

"I've asked her as a friend, Max. That's all. I figured she might fancy a night out with someone different. Nothing more, especially because I've seen the way you look at her." Seph poured himself some more coffee, his expression triumphant.

My thighs didn't ache as I stood, as legs' day at the gym hadn't happened for too long. I needed to get back into my routine.

"If there's no other business to conclude I have things to do." And that was the truth: I had a backlog of work to get through that was unheard of for me, as I'd either spent the time messaging or speaking to Victoria or thinking about her which had meant my work rate had been slowed. Rather than being resentful of this, as I would've been previously, I was mournful.

I left the room, seriously conscious of the amount I had to get through. Victoria needed to be elsewhere than my mind and not at the forefront of it while I got the shit done that I was paid to do.

"Hey, big brother," Claire said. I hadn't realised she'd followed me out. "Don't be pissed off at Seph. He's trying to do a good thing. Tell me about Victoria."

"There's nothing to tell." Just that she was intelligent, feisty, beautiful and had a pair of tits I'd jacked off to at least twice a day since I'd seen them. I liked talking to her and looking at her and I figured she thought the same about me. Sharing stuff with her about my mother hadn't been hard like it had been in the past with other people. She'd accepted it and not tried to analyse me or the situation.

"That's total shit, Maxwell. You like her."

As far as sisters went, Claire was the least annoying except when it came to our love lives. She liked to matchmake. She said she wanted to see us happy and settled, but why that had to involve a relationship I was completely unsure.

"I like her. She's a good person, but like I said, nothing is going to come of it." I headed to my office.

"So you're fine if Seph does ask her out?"

I held the door still, knowing that fine was the last way to describe how I'd be. "He's too young for her. He'd drive her mad."

"He's not going to. I think he likes the idea of you seeing someone."

"He'll lose his man card if he thinks things like that."

"Seph doesn't have a man card. He just borrows mine occasionally," Claire said. "But he has mentioned about you dodging relationships."

"Does he know why?"

"He figured it out but he doesn't understand it. He asked me last night why you were so scared of losing someone you loved when me and Jackson had our heads around it. And he made a fair point about Marie and Dad; as much of a dick as Dad was when we were younger, he and Marie have done a decent job of having a solid marriage."

"I know," and I did. I'd seen a couple of counsellors, both as a child and as an adult and they'd helped rid me of the guilt I'd felt that I didn't stop our mother from taking her own life. I'd also learnt that I wasn't my siblings' keeper, and that being the oldest didn't mean I had to be the most responsible. Jackson running the firm instead of me gave me the first taste of freedom I'd properly had since being a kid. "But I'm not husband and father material, Claire."

"Why?" she said softly. "You were an amazing big brother when I was a kid and you know how good you were with Payton, Seph and Ava. If your wife or girlfriend struggled with depression after having kids you'd know how to deal with it, Maxwell. You need to stop thinking you're like Dad."

"Yeah, well, I've got work to do." My office was in its usual state of organised insanity, which meant I had a lot of excuses to not think about Victoria—not that I'd achieve that.

The door creaked open. "Max, you've been different since you met this woman. I don't think you've noticed it but you've been lighter. You've smiled more."

"You've been tucked away in the wilds of Cornwall for the past couple of weeks: how would you know?"

"Jean told me," Claire said, grinning.

"When are you telling everyone about Killian?" Firing Jean wasn't an option, no matter how much she snitched on me to my sister.

Claire shook her head. "Not yet: it's too early. We need to just be us for a bit longer before everyone goes hysterical over it. But we won't leave it too long. People need to be used to it before Jackson's wedding."

"I'm pleased for you. Killian needs to understand I'm not going to beat him up for sleeping with my sister both now and when you were eighteen," I said, meaning it. I knew they'd had a relationship while they were at university and one they thought had been secret. Since Killian had left the Navy, they'd done nothing but goad and attack each other.

"I don't think he's worried, Max," she said..

Killian was ex-Navy, slightly taller than me and a wall of sheer muscle.

"I'm looking forward to meeting Victoria. Even if you say she's no more than a friend." Her words were intended to rile me.

The papers on my desk became infinitely more interesting

than they actually were. "Sure. See you later." I sat down waiting for her to leave. She watched me for another few seconds before clearing off, just long enough to be more than mildly irritating.

———

New clients always took that bit of extra time at first as you found out what they were like and the best way to handle them. Some needed clear boundaries as to how often and when to correspond, others needed everything broken down for them, a few needed this to be their therapy. My newest client was the last: missing his wife and now the sole parent of a thankfully happy and healthy daughter, he was having to rehash the worst days of his life. I knew he would win his case, that there would be a good financial payout which would go some way to looking after his daughter, but it would never replace the loss of his wife and the little girl's mother. The negligence shown by the hospital was obvious: mix ups with staff rotas, a lack of communication and organisation with medical notes and the failure of staff to spot the errors timely enough to prevent Jenna Hughes from taking her life were undisputed. Technically, it would be an easy case. Emotionally, it would not.

At five past five, I started to shut down my computer, deciding that I wouldn't work this weekend and instead would visit my dad and Marie for a break. Usually, I would have a couple of drinks with my colleagues, wait for the traffic to die down and then head over to Oxford but as Victoria was allegedly coming out, I didn't want to depart too early and leave her with Seph.

The tapping sound at my door registered only partially as I was too engrossed in thinking about the new case.

"I don't want to disturb you," a quiet voice said. "But you look so lost in thought."

She looked stunning: her hair was loose, her lips painted

pink and she was wearing a tight top tucked into a pair of skin tight jeans, highlighting all those curves.

"You've rescued me." I closed the file and turned to her, trying to keep my reaction at a respectable level of perv.

"You don't mind me joining you tonight?" she said, her expression concerned. "I don't want to gatecrash. Seph mentioned it when I was in to see Jackson on Wednesday and I could do with a night out." Her smile was watery.

"Bad week? You should've told me." We'd spoken every day and texted several times.

Her smile was a little stronger. "My brother paid me a visit at work. It went exactly as you'd imagine."

"Why didn't you tell me. I could've done something." I stood up and undid my tie. There wasn't enough time to have a shower and I didn't want to leave Victoria to Seph, even briefly.

"You'd have gone round and growled at him," she said, leaning against the door. "Am I getting a striptease? Can I film it?"

Her eyes followed my fingers as I started to undo the buttons of my shirt. I'd seen most of her naked, but she'd seen very little of me and I was keen to see her reaction, even if this was just friends. I worked out a lot. I lifted and boxed. I kept myself fit and healthy.

"Sure. As long as it's for your use only. Seph gets jealous when I get more fan mail than him."

She smiled, her eyes flickering over my chest. "How many tattoos do you have?"

Ignoring the last few buttons I pulled the shirt over my head. "I don't know. I've been having them done for about eight years and just building them up. It's the best therapy I've ever had." I had sleeves on both arms, my pecs were pretty much covered and my upper back. Nothing on my lower half.

"They're amazing." Her stare followed the black lines reading the words and pictures that told the story of my life. She stepped away from the door and came closer, and I felt her heat and presence cause something in me to bubble.

A finger lifted and she started to lightly trace the tree that formed the main part of the sleeve on my left arm. "Whoever did it is really talented."

"Rachel," I said. "She's an artist. Do you have any?"

She nodded. "On my back. I love them and I'm planning another when I can afford it, which may be sooner rather than later. I may get her number from you."

The physical connection between us was slight, just the tip of her finger but my dick was hard and my body was blazing with some all-consuming heat. "I'll take you to see her. I want to listen to what you want."

Her laugh was breathy and then the palm of her hand was flat on my chest. "Your body's amazing," she said. "We should have you stuffed and mounted."

I put my hand on top of hers and kept her touch, not wanting to lose it. "You can look any time you want." Her eyes caught mine and I wanted to spin her round onto my desk and bury myself deep inside her. "Crap, Victoria. I thought we were just being friends."

"I know," she said and I thought her expression was regretful. I hoped it was. "I don't want to be just friends."

My door flew open, both Jackson and Seph walking into my office ready to go for drinks. Seph's eyebrows rose tellingly, his head nodding. Jackson stared, forcing himself to look bored.

"I'm sorry, we're clearly interrupting," Seph said. "How you doing, Vic?"

She turned, her hand still held onto my chest by mine. "I'm good. Just feeling up your brother. Hope you don't mind."

I started to laugh at her openness and lack of embarrassment. "There's not much I can say to that."

Jackson shook his head. "Feel him up all you like, but I'd rather not see it; that's not my kink."

"Nor mine," Seph said. "Clearly you're still getting him dressed, so we'll see you over there. If you get round to it."

They left and I reluctantly let her hand go, walking to the closet where I kept spare shirts.

"Sorry," she said. "For groping you in front of your brothers. I can be a bit forward sometimes."

"You can grope me whenever you like," I pulled a shirt off its hanger aware that my trousers were rather tented. I hoped my brothers hadn't noticed as that would be something they wouldn't pass up the opportunity to bring up. "And wherever you like."

Her laughter lifted the remains of a grim day away from me. "I'll keep that in mind for when I'm in the mood to grope a man. You don't need to wear a shirt on my account. And I still haven't taken my video."

"We'll make it a project for later. Let's go, else… never mind."

"Never mind what?"

I put my hand on the small of her back and guided her out of my office, saying goodnight to Kevin who supervised the cleaners and locked up most nights. "Else we won't leave."

"Oh. This friends' thing's quite hard, isn't it?" I caught her glancing down at my trousers.

"It's very hard. I need it to stop being hard else there are going to be some very uncomfortable questions," I half muttered.

"I'll try to make it as easy as I can," she said. "And seriously, if me being here isn't a good idea then just say."

"I want you here," I said, feeling the truth to the statement everywhere. I wanted her with me: underneath me, on top of me, on her knees in front of me. "We just need to keep it friendly."

———

By half past ten, I was in pain in more than one place. I'd spent a third of the night on high alert for any men who spent more than thirty seconds talking to Victoria. Her hair and curves and downright prettiness, plus the vibrancy she seemed to ooze captured more than my attention. My sisters and Vanessa monopolised her, working their way through the cocktail menu and Seph kept bringing her water. I kept to the bar, drinking lime and soda and pretending I was interested in what my office manager had to say about the weekend's rugby fixtures.

"I think I've had too much to drink," Victoria said, her legs looking like a newborn deer's. "Your sisters can drink."

"It's how they find shit out. Especially Claire," I said. "You want to head off for a coffee? Escape the alcohol?"

She shook her head and I felt half disappointed. "I could do with some fresh air. And five minutes of no noise."

"I'll come out with you," I said as I knew there were at least three blokes who were eagerly waiting for the chance to chat to her alone, myself not included. I felt her hand on my back and wrapped an arm around her waist. She wasn't unsteady and I'd figured she could handle her drink pretty well, but her heels were high and the flooring wasn't the best.

I led her out of the bar and down the side of the building, the sounds of people laughing and the faint thud of music still audible. "I love nights like this," she said. "When it's still slightly warm in the evening and everyone's in a good mood like tonight." She leaned back against the wall, taking a deep breath. Her cheeks were flushed, eyes bright. I stepped in closer to her.

"It's been a good evening."

"It has." She smiled at me. "Except I've hardly spoken to you since the strip show in your office. That was the highlight of the evening."

"Like I said, I'm happy to repeat it anytime."

"This friends thing is really shitty."

"Tell me about it. I've had to watch at least five guys hit on you."

"They weren't going to get anywhere. You didn't have to worry. I've seen at least three girls try to give you their number."

"They weren't my type."

"What is?"

I stepped in closer, one hand on the wall next to her. "Petite and curvy. Long thick hair. Intelligent and argumentative and the best pair of tits I've ever seen. Fuck it." I moved into her, my other hand now on the opposite side of her, boxing her in. She leaned forward, her mouth meeting mine and her arms going around my neck. The kiss was hungry and desperate. I could taste the tequila from her margaritas and mint. The scent of her hair pulled me in further and she wrapped a leg around my waist, pulling my crotch against hers.

My hands left the wall and went to her waist, seeking the soft skin under her top. She pressed her tits against me and all the blood in my body went south. My hand crept further up her top, over her bra to her nipple. She moaned into my mouth as I ran a rough thumb over it.

"Fuck," I said, pausing the kiss.

"I would right now, here," she said, tilting her hips into me. I wondered how wet she was. "But I don't want your family or employees to catch you."

I chuckled. "You're protecting my honour?" I pinched her nipple making her sigh and squirm.

"Something like that."

I took her mouth with mine again and the kissing became heavier, our hands greedily searching each other. The alleyway didn't offer much in the way of privacy, something I was conscious of as I unbuttoned her top to her chest and dropped my mouth, desperate to take a nipple in my mouth and find out how sensitive she was. Her bra was black lace, her nipples dark and dusky through the material. I moved my head back so I could see. "You're perfect."

Her chest heaved. "If we plan this better, I won't wear a bra next time."

"Then I'm not letting you out." I pinched both her nipples at the same time, just about aware of footsteps nearby.

"Max."

I pressed myself close to Victoria so no one could see. Seph stood nearby, keeping enough distance so it was clear he couldn't see anything, although what we were doing was obvious. "We're heading to get something to eat. Are you, um, coming?"

Victoria started to laugh, her arms around my back. "We are. To get food, that is."

"Cool," Seph said and I could tell even in the darkness that he was shuffling his feet. "I'll leave you to sort yourselves out."

I groaned and stepped back enough that I could do up her buttons. "We're not just friends. I want you too goddamn much to be just friends. I can be your friend as well as the person who gets to worship your body and make you come."

She stood on her tiptoes and nipped my chin. "You haven't made me come yet, Maxwell. So yes, I think you need to work on that."

CHAPTER 10
VICTORIA

Almost a week had passed without seeing Max, although I heard from him through several mediums. Friday night had ended with Max and Jackson helping a very drunk Seph find his way home and Max staying over there, before they both headed to their parents for the rest of the weekend. I'd spent the weekend somewhere between the university, Jacob's and trying to encourage my landlord to fix yet another leak in the roof. It was old water too and contained a certain smell that was both unpleasant and concerning. Jackson had suggested I may well receive an interim payment in the next week or two and if that was the case, I'd definitely be moving apartments.

"There's a core chapter to read on the conversion of the Danelaw," I said to my small bunch of first year history students, who were still all bright and shiny with their new stationery and youthful expressions. "We won't be discussing it for the next couple of weeks, but it might be worth reading ahead, especially if you need to get the textbook from the library." It was our second seminar and I was enjoying teaching again. I'd done a couple of years delivering the A-Level syllabus at a private college before starting my master's degree and as much as I'd liked it, I preferred to lecture and lead seminars with undergrads.

"When do we start with tutorials?" one of the more confident students asked.

"In a couple of weeks. I'll post a list of times on the forum and you can sign up to one that suits you. In the meantime, have a good evening." I swept up my papers from the long table that took up the middle of the room and offered a smile. Sometimes students would want to talk after a seminar, to discuss aspects they'd found interesting or needed some help getting their heads around. This evening, most seemed keener to get to one of the nearby bars where some band was playing.

"Will we be in this room next week?" Jemima, a quieter, mousy looking student asked.

"No, the one next door. We're alternating with one of the law faculty," I said. "Long story."

"Damn right."

I turned to the doorway where Maxwell was standing, hands in his pockets. The man was sex personified as far as I was concerned and I wondered how obvious my reaction was.

"Has your seminar finished?" I said, glancing at the clock on the wall and realising that I'd overran by nearly half an hour.

"Some time ago. I decided to wait for you and when no one left I came and enjoyed the last twenty minutes of some historical shit."

"That's a very disparaging remark!" my mousy student said, almost out of the door herself. "And one that completely typifies lawyers." She turned and walked and I figured she probably wasn't going to listen to the band.

The rest of my students had gone; the building falling silent. "Busy week?" I said, knowing it was. He'd called me last night at ten thirty, still at his desk.

"Long. Productive. Tiring," he said. "Better for seeing you. I wanted to see you earlier in the week but I knew what my diary was like."

I nodded. "I haven't stopped. I've covered two lectures and taken on another three seminars, plus one of the admin systems wasn't playing so I've had to re-enter a job lot of data. It's good to see you now though."

"Are you busy for the rest of the evening?" he said, drawing a little closer. "Can I take you out for dinner?"

Despite over two weeks of communicating, we had yet to go out on a proper date. Some of that was arguably down to my decision that we should just be friends—and his agreement—so actually being out together for a planned meal, without his work colleagues or siblings, seemed like a huge step. One that made me slightly nervous. "I've nothing planned. Maybe somewhere casual though, otherwise I'll need to go home to get changed."

He eyed me a bit like a large cat would a small, already trapped and powerless mouse. "I need to take you to one of the balls at the law society and see what you look like properly dressed up," he said. "Because right now, I'd be happy to be with you anywhere."

I grinned, unpinning my hair partly for the effect but also because the pins were digging in my scalp. I wasn't wearing anything other than office clothes; a pencil skirt and fitted sweater, with a pair of patent leather stilettoed court shoes and sheer black stockings. I tried not to look like a conventional history professor, liking clothes and fashion almost to the extreme, just one that was cheaply found in charity stores. I had a decent designer wardrobe—when it wasn't being wrecked by rain—most of it being sourced from rich people's charitable donations. "That's kind of you, but I'm also starving and eating somewhere my nicest table manners aren't required would be good."

"There's a good pasta place near my office. We can probably get a table there?" he said.

I wanted to drown in his eyes.

Nodding, I took the few steps I needed to be able to put my hands on his shoulders, feeling the taut muscle beneath his shirt. "Sounds good," I said, his hands coming to my waist.

Footsteps, loud and impatient ones, broke the silence that hung in the building. We both turned towards the door as my half-brother attempted to strut in and I stifled a groan. I never needed my brother and his bossy attempts to control the aspects of my life he was concerned about: in this case, money.

"Victoria, this is absolutely abominable," he said, finishing his strut just two feet away from where we stood. Max's hand remained on the small of my waist. "I don't know which shysters you've appointed as solicitors, but you have to see that this is both unfair and completely wrong of you." He finally glanced at Max and rolled his eyes. "As your older brother I should warn you to look out for men who are simply after your money too."

"I'm pretty sure that Max isn't interested in my pitiful inheritance,' I said, unable to stop a grin. "But thank you for warning me because some men would certainly be put off a relationship with me given your strangely protective approach."

He clearly got the sarcasm in my tone, which was unusual so I did wonder if I'd laid it on a bit too thick.

"I think we should speak in private. God knows who you get yourself involved with nowadays."

The slight shake I felt from Max's hand told me he was fighting laughter, which was definitely the best response. "This is Maxwell Callaghan," I said. "His brother, Jackson, is my solicitor. Max, this is my brother, Francis Davies-West." My brother's expression was one I wished I could photograph. "As you may have now worked out, Max isn't interested in any money I may inherit."

"*Will* inherit," Max corrected. "Your solicitors confirmed today that there is no other will so the one that stands means Victoria inherits your grandfather's estate in full. Given that you've already been paid money from the estate, the suggestion is that you don't contest it else charges of fraud will be brought."

His tone was relaxed and non-confrontational, but still my brother's face drained of all colour.

"I don't think here and now is the right place for you to be discussing it with me," Francis said. "This is hardly proper—"

"Then why did you come here to find me?" I said, stepping forward from Max. "You knew I'd be here; my guess is that you contacted the history office this afternoon and fed them some story about needing me to sign something. If you think you're going to guilt me into letting you have what Grandad left me, it isn't going to happen and if you continue hounding me, I will get a restraining order against you."

"I'm the only family you have left—"

"I'm not entirely sure you can call yourself family, seeing as you were trying to defraud me of rather a lot of money. You sold my grandfather's house without my permission, something that should not have been done as that's probably where I would've lived. The only times you've wanted to have anything to do with me is when it's been of benefit to you," I said, the words flying out of my mouth like mud from under a tractor's wheels. Mud with a hell of a lot of cow shit in it.

"I can see there's no use in reasoning with you," Francis said, his usual ignore-everything-that-I-don't-agree-with tone making an appearance. "I'm sure my solicitors will agree that the will needs to be taken to probate. I was his grandchild too and he would want to see me just as much supported as you have been. With all your tuition and the money you've saved living with him, it's only fair that I should benefit just as much."

"And you should consider the four hundred thousand and the fact that we're not pressing charges for fraud what you benefit from," Max said.

He stayed in situ, not even taking half a step towards Francis or trying to intimidate him in anyway, which made me shudder with something that was anything but fear.

"This isn't the time or the place to discuss this, although you seem certain to do just that. You will leave and from now on, the only contact you have with Victoria will be through your solicitor. No more seeking her out, no more phone calls and no more messages. Everything has been logged and if it continues there will be a restraining order. Are we clear?"

Francis looked at me. "Are you really going to let him talk to me like that?"

"He's being nothing but clear and polite, Francis, and for the final time, I am not discussing this with you," I said, feeling waves of anger start to fire through me. I had a temper, as Max had discovered and it was being stoked more thoroughly than a steam engine's fire. "I'm more than happy to pretend you don't exist. You've been nothing but a gold digger for years. When Grandad was diagnosed the first thing you asked me was whether or not I knew if he had a will. Then you asked him the same thing. Where were you when he needed taking to the hospital for treatment? Where were you at the end?" The red mist started to descend and I knew that this wasn't what was needed right now.

"I had a family to look after, Victoria. I didn't have time to see to Grandfather as well," Francis said, looking agitatedly at the door.

He couldn't cope when I made him feel in the wrong.

"Grandad was your family and you have the time to deal with solicitors and make up wills, so why didn't you have the time to make a phone call or pop in to see him once in a while? Maybe because you weren't being paid for it, because let's face it, all you've ever been concerned with is money. So, Francis, fuck you, because if you so much as come anywhere near me I will file a restraining order and if it wasn't for the fact that I'm not obsessed with how much money I have, I'd be instructing my lawyer to have a fucking good look at what shit you've tried to tangle everything in to ensure you got what he left, even if he didn't want to leave you a penny. He saw you for exactly what you are: a classless fuckwit who needed cash to keep his wife because his dick issn't big enough!"

Francis gave me one last half-scared look and took off, heavy feet slapping the tiled floor outside the room. The solid wooden door slammed shut in what was hopefully a final ending to the altercation, to all the altercations.

Me and Max looked at each other, my final words still hovering in the now silent room.

"'A classless fuckwit who needed cash to keep his wife because his dick isn't big enough,'" Max said, his mouth twitching. "Did you really just call your brother that?"

"I've thought worse," I said. "I really shouldn't have said that to him, should I?"

"Why not?"

"Because of the will and everything," I said, cursing my temper. Although it felt good when I let everything out, afterwards there was always the regret, the hangover of words spoken in the heat of the moment.

"And there's a lot he shouldn't be saying. You've nothing to worry about. He has plenty. You're right, he really is a fuckwit, and you're hot when you're angry."

His eyes burned into me causing goosebumps to erupt on my skin.

I laughed and shook my head. "Maxwell Callaghan, you have some weird fetishes clearly."

His chuckle was deep and throaty. "You have no idea." He put his hands back onto my waist, drawing me closer into him. "Are you okay? I know you're like steel, but you shouldn't have to put up with that from a fuckwit you're related to."

Resting the palms of my hands on his chest, I looked up at him: dark eyes, dark beard, mussed hair. The tops of his chest tattoos were just visible at the above his shirt. "I'm fine. You're right with what you say, but I'm fine. I've dealt with him being worse than that without anyone to support me, so I'm glad you were here."

His head dropped to the top of mine and I felt him nuzzle my hair. "You're beautiful, you know that?"

"Sometimes," I said with a smile. "Sometimes I'm sweatpants and no make-up with a tub of ice cream and Chinese takeaway. I'm not beautiful then."

"I'd have to see it to make an assessment." His fingers started to explore my waist, creeping under my sweater. When I looked up at him he caught my lips with his, softly at first. I nipped gently, the fight still not dimmed, which made him growl. "I can never decide if you're a gentleman or an animal," I said, as his hands cupped my ass and then moved round to the front.

"If I was a gentleman I'd move my hands away like this." He shifted them back to his sides. "Then I'd take you out to dinner. Then maybe back to mine for a glass of wine before taking you home." He clenched his fists and then relaxed them, looking as if he was battling with himself as to which he wanted to do.

My hands stayed on him, running up and down his arms, committing the route of his muscles to memory in case this didn't happen again. "I like the idea of you taking me," I said, pulling his head down to mine and bringing him to my mouth. Our teeth clashed and he fought me for possession. His fingers went into my hair, before moving down my back and then under my sweater.

"Off," he demanded, pulling away from me as he pulled my sweater up and over my head, leaving me in just a blue lace bra that pushed up my breasts and barely covered my nipples.

He didn't excuse his gaze on my chest, bring his hands up to gently cup them, thumbs running over my already erect nipples. I moaned, my eyelids feeling heavy with desire. "I like you touching me," I said. "I like you looking at me."

"Good," he almost whispered. "Because I'm going to do more of both."

I expected him to drop his head and take a nipple in his mouth, but he didn't. Instead, he slowed the action down and simply touched me through the lace, gently pinching, softly massaging. I was sensitive anyway and could almost orgasm through my breasts being played with and watching a man's reaction to them. Watching his expression, hearing his breathing change made the wetness between my legs start to soak through my panties and I wondered if he could smell my arousal.

"Fuck, Victoria. I've never seen anything like you," he said, his hands shifting to my back and unclipping my bra. I pulled it to the floor and watched him look, my own hands now occupied with undoing his shirt, exposing his chest and those tattoos.

He didn't rush me, letting me look and touch and taste as I traced my tongue from his pecs down the centre line of his body to the top of his jeans where I pulled away, undoing his button and zipper, feeling his erection straining beneath the fabric.

"Your skirt," he said,

My articulate lawyer was now reduced to fragmented sentences. Standing up and pushing my breasts forward slightly, I moved my hands around my back and unzipped the skirt which dropped immediately, leaving me in panties and stockings. Again, we allowed time to keep us, looking our fill.

I slid off my panties, kicking them and my skirt out of the way. I was bare and knew that my pussy was glistening with my juices. "I need you to fuck me, Max. Here. Now. Then we can fight over who gets this room instead."

"Is this just your plan to get the other room on a full-time basis?"

"I'll settle for this every other week. The table's firmer."

He dropped his trousers and underwear, stepping out of them and towards me naked, pre-cum like a diamond at the top of his cock. My legs separated and I backed myself towards the table where my students had been sitting less than half an hour ago, the notion of it arousing in itself.

"The front door's still unlocked," I said. "Someone could come in."

"Then they'd get a show," he said, reaching down to his jeans and taking out his wallet. "But they'll know they can't touch. That's just me who does that."

I rested my ass against the table, watching him put on the condom he'd taken from his wallet. "You need to start touching, Maxwell." My hands cupped my breasts and I squeezed my nipples, my eyes closing. I would come quickly, the anticipation almost too much.

He was as close as he could be to me without touching when I opened my eyes.

"Is all this wetness for me?" he said, one finger trailing down my stomach to my clit.

"Yes," I said, meeting his eyes. "You. I hope you're going to make good use of it."

His finger moved away abruptly and I crushed my thighs together, trying to create some relief for the desperation I now felt.

The laugh he gave was deep and throaty and full of sex and all the feels. "Lie back," he said, one hand gently pushing me down, leaving my legs dangling. He kissed one nipple softly and moved over to nip the other. My fingertips dug into his back and he copied the trail his tongue had taken but this time continued to between my legs.

It took two flicks of his tongue on my clit and I came like thunder, deep and wild. He pushed inside me with his cock before my orgasm had finished, fully inside me in one thrust.

My cry was loud, partly with the sweet pain, partly at finally being filled.

"You good?" He stilled, letting me feel all of him on me.

"So good." I started to rock my hips, needing him to move. "Teaching in this room won't be the same."

"You shouldn't be thinking of teaching." One shift of his hips and I wasn't thinking of anything. He started slow, deep each time, his eyes moving between mine and my breasts which bounced as he thrust. "Pinch your nipples," he told me and it took all the wits I had left to comply. "Does it feel good? My cock inside you?"

"Yes."

I was rewarded with a deeper, slightly faster thrust.

"You look amazing under me like this," he said. "Your pussy is so tight and warm and all I want to do is fill you up."

"Do it," I said, as his rhythm changed in tempo to shorter, faster pulses. He pulled me further down the table, allowing him to fully possess me. I could hear my moans, the rest of my body liquid and pliant, ready to come again around him.

"Fucking you is everything I thought it would be," he said. "Once won't be enough. Going to need to fuck you again, see my cock in your mouth, my come on your tits again. Have you tied to my bed so I can make you come only when I want."

That was enough. My pussy clenched and my hips began to jerk. He held me steady, his face contorting as his own orgasm began and I wrapped my legs around his hips, pulling him deeper within me and wishing there wasn't a condom between us.

He called my name as he emptied himself, standing stretched and tall, our bodies conjoined. His eyes were on mine and his expression softened. When he relaxed he didn't pull away as I expected him to; instead he bent down to kiss me, helping me to a sitting position and bringing me on to his knee, removing the space between our bodies so he could hold me close.

"I need to take you home," he said. "To yours so you don't have to rush. Then we can order Chinese and recover and I can have you again before morning. Let me wake up with you tomorrow."

I rested my forehead against his chest, my breathing starting to settle, my body sated. "My place is a mess."

"Then pack your stuff and stay with me."

I wasn't sure whether he meant for the night or forever, and in the aftermath of the sex we'd had, I wasn't sure which I wanted.

———

We lay curled up in each other, which surprised me. Maxwell was all physicality and hard sex, his body primed to make a woman happy and his mouth full of dirty words. But now, now that we were both spent and tired, he'd wrapped me in his arms and shielded me from the rest of the world with him.

"I like how you smell," he said, a whisper against my ear.

"I smell of you, so you should," I muttered. His hand was on my hip, keeping my ass into his middle.

He chuckled, deeply and quietly. "Yeah, not lying, I like how you've just become my territory, but I like how you smell. It makes me feel happy."

I turned so I could see him in the faint light that seeped through the thin curtains. "What else makes you happy, Maxwell Callaghan?" I touched his lips, ones that I knew the talent of.

"Work," he said. "I really enjoy my job. Lecturing. My brothers and sisters. As much as they infuriate me, I wouldn't swap any of them, even Seph."

"What else? What do you like to do?"

"Lift weights, play rugby, take an intelligent woman out to dinner and listen to her talk. I'm not a complicated man," he said.

My fingers had moved down to his chest, tracing the trail of hair across his pecs. He was beautiful and delicious, a raunchy day-dream come true.

"I don't think you're as simple as you make out. Tell me about your parents. What are they like?"

He laughed, a deep, melodic sound that rumbled like thunder.

"Marie is my stepmother. She's amazing and the most foul-mouthed person I've ever met. My dad is like me: a workaholic who probably shouldn't have had such a large family—he's always been dedicated to his job."

"That doesn't mean he can't have both," I said. "Sometime it just takes a while to find that balance. You spend time with him now, don't you?"

Max's hand went up my back, cupping me towards him. "Yes. And more so when we were teenagers. But if we hadn't had Marie, I think I would' have screwed everyone up. I was changing Callum's nappies at six years old."

I moved my head and kissed his chest. "So you're nothing like your father in that regard. Although you may be as brilliant a lawyer as him."

"I could be terrible as a lawyer. How would you know?" he said.

"Google," I responded, enjoying the feel of having him so close to me, radiating in the heat from his body. "I searched your name."

His grin was of the shit-eating variety. "You were into me from the start, weren't you?"

My hands were taking in as much as they could of his skin, committing it to memory.

"I thought you were a cockwombling asshole, so yes, I googled you. Only when my friend Jacob told me to; he thought I needed to check you out a little more."

"Did I live up to your expectations?"

"You exceeded them," I admitted. "All three occasions. But I really need recovery time."

He shifted onto his back and pulled me on top, so I was using his chest as a pillow. "I'll take recovery time too," he said. "You good with me staying over?"

"More than," I told him honestly. "I like being with you."

"Good," he said, kissing the top of my head. "The feeling's mutual."

I drifted off to sleep, feeling happy and safe being held by a man who'd brought more passion and intensity out of me than I'd thought possible.

CHAPTER 11
MAXWELL

Her bed was a double as opposed to my king but it didn't matter because we would've taken up the same amount of space anyway. After grabbing takeaway on the way to her apartment, I was introduced to the space she called home: four rooms; kitchen, bathroom, living space and bedroom, all with mould in the corners and damp in the air. Water dripped through the ceiling in places and the heating system didn't work consistently. Intelligence defeated the animal and I didn't try to whisk her out of there with everything she owned to my apartment knowing that she didn't need a hero. She was able and willing to fight her own battles, so I ignored the state of the place, ate with her and then proceeded to eat her on her small bed in her damp room before burying myself in her. However, I put murdering her landlord on my to-do list for the following day.

Although I had almost avoided having a serious relationship throughout my thirty-five years, I wasn't averse to waking up with a woman. Another round of sex before falling asleep with Victoria wrapped in my arms, her ass tucked against my cock and there was no urge to run and leave her, although one part of my brain was waving a warning flag.

"Morning," I said as her eyes flickered open. She murmured something unintelligible and wriggled closer to me, my cock already at half-mast. "What time do you need to be in work?" I had a mountain to climb today but I would only move when she needed me to.

"Too early," she said. "No work till ten." Her hand moved behind her own body onto mine, grabbing the back of my thigh and pulling me closer.

I chuckled, nuzzling into her shoulder and softly nipping her skin. She was warm and soft, her hair sprawling across the sheets. As usual, I had a million and twelve things to do, but Victoria was at the top of the list.

She turned over, her head ending up on my chest, her leg and arm spidering across me.

"Comfy," she muttered and then her breathing settled and she was asleep. I eventually closed my eyes, knowing it was still early and although last night hadn't been stupidly late, it was after midnight before we finally went to sleep.

I was woken by the irritating chirp from my phone, by which time it was daylight outside. Fumbling on the cheap bedside table, I tried to silence it before it woke Victoria. It was a message, or a series of messages, from my siblings, something that usually presented itself with a healthy dose of fear.

Jackson: I've been knocking on Max's door for fifteen minutes. Does anyone know where he might be or am I calling the police?

Seph: It's 48 hours before you can report an adult missing.

Jackson: You just referred to Max as an adult. Has he passed that test yet?

Claire: You only passed that test, Jackson, because Vanessa agreed to coach you. Is she going with you to the law ball tonight?

Jackson: Yeah. It's cost me a new dress, new shoes and a purse.

Claire: You mean she borrowed your credit card, showed you what she bought and gave you a blow job?

Jackson: Pretty much. Don't tell her I told you.

Claire: Of course I will. If I don't, Seph will.

Claire: Max still hasn't read any of these, which is concerning as he's usually at work by now.

Seph: Maybe he's at the gym?

Jackson: That's where we were meant to be going this morning. Heavy weights session. I'm assuming he's been kidnapped by a harem of Victoria's Secret models and is being used for research purposes as that can be the only reason he's stood me up.

Seph: Or maybe just Victoria…

Seph: Although there are a shit ton of reasons to stand you up. All of them less appealing than Victoria.

Claire: Such as having a tooth out.

Seph: Or an ingrown toe nail removed.

Ava: Or not being woken up by a stream of ridiculous messages from your siblings who clearly have no life. Please keep me out of group texts this early. It's not human.

Seph: Why don't you put your phone on silent then, Ava, like normal humans do?

Jackson: I'll head to Victoria's. I might give Max a wakeup call, assuming he's there.

Seph: What if he's not there, and he's with someone else? It's Max the manwhore, remember.

Claire: Would you want to be interrupted while you were in bed with Vanessa, Jacks? Give him another hour at least and go to the gym by yourself. What's Vanessa wearing tonight? I don't know what to go for.

Jackson: A dress?

Claire: What colour dress?

Jackson: How the fuck would I know?

Claire: What's her new underwear like?

Jackson: White and barely there.

Claire: So you can describe that but not her dress?

Jackson: I'm getting married, not having my fucking man card removed.

Jackson: Maxwell, if you're reading this, it's now 6.42am. I'll be at Victoria's at 8am.

Jackson's message about timings wasn't the last in the series but it was the last one I read. It was seven forty-eight, twelve minutes before he'd threatened to arrive. Victoria stirred, still lying on my chest, her head positioned so that if I dropped my phone, she'd have a painful awakening.

"Have I missed work?" she said, her voice sultry with sleep.

"It's nearly eight," I said, wanting to either tell her to go back to sleep or to slowly wake her up in a way that involved my tongue and her orgasming, preferably more than once. However, Jackson had cockblocked me, certainly not for the first time, but definitely the last. "My brother's on his way round."

"Oh," she said, angling herself so she could look at me. Her doe eyes were full of questions yet still soft from sleep. Her lips were pink and slightly swollen and as my hand went to her hair I wondered how she would look in my bed and whether I could persuade her to be there tonight.

Shit. Law ball.

"I was meant to go to the gym with him, but worked out else-where," I said. "Are you okay with him coming in?"

She gave a sarcastic laugh. "To my five-star aparthotel? As long as he gives it a good rating on Trip Advisor."

"He won't judge you. That's not Jackson. But if you prefer I'll speak to him outside and send him away," I said. The sheet covering us had dropped lower, uncovering part of her tits.

Her lips pressed to my chest. "It's fine. I'm going to move out of here sooner than later."

"Good. I'll report the landlord when you've moved out," I said, pushing the sheet further down so I could see all of her.

She pulled the sheet back up. "Your brother's about to be here. I need to put some clothes on and you need to lose your wood."

I pulled the sheet back down and then moved my hand to her already hard nipple, rubbing it with my thumb. "There's a really good way to solve that problem," I said. "And my brother can wait."

———

Jackson phoned me half an hour later, informing me that he was downstairs and I needed to answer else he was breaking in. That wouldn't have been that difficult to do seeing as the door was about as secure as Seph's trousers around any female, but I tore myself away from what could've led to round two to let him in.

"Checking your phone is a common courtesy these days," he said. "Why the fuck are you only wearing jeans? Where are the rest of your clothes?" He eyed me suspiciously. "You've fucked Victoria."

"Do you have a problem with that?" I said, blocking the doorway with my build.

He shook his head slowly. "No, but I think you might have. Can I come in or is there incriminating evidence all over the place?"

There wasn't. Victoria was in the shower and the place was tidy apart from the bedroom that looked significantly used. "I'll put coffee on." I think I knew where everything was and it wasn't as if there were a dozen cupboards if it wasn't obvious.

Jackson followed me up, probably noticing all the things that broke regulations. "You need to get your girl out of here," he said. "This place is a hazard."

"She's said she's going to move out soon."

The mould around the windows was more noticeable in the daylight. "I'd get her staying with you while she finds something."

"Didn't you do that with Vanessa and she never moved out?"

"It worked out well for both of us," he said, grinning like a fucking idiot.

Victoria came into the living room wearing just a robe and a towel wrapped around her head. My first reaction was to hide her from Jackson's view, but my brother hadn't noticed anything else female other than his fiancée for months.

"Morning, Jackson," she said.

My eyes stayed fixed on her and I fought the urge to throw my brother out of the building and take her back to bed. Or to the sofa. Or anywhere that gave us enough privacy so she could come again on my cock.

"Kind of you to pay me a morning visit," Victoria said. "Is it going to be added to my bill?"

She headed to the coffee machine that I had just about managed to start up. It was an old model and needed replacing. Buying her a new one was something that had crossed my mind, but I wasn't sure how she'd take being given a gift like that. Maybe for a housewarming present.

"You can pay me in coffee. I see you stole my brother," Jackson said above the noise of the coffee machine.

"Kidnapping is a serious accusation, and I'm not sure Maxwell came against his will. He found the ropes and hand-cuffs to be very enjoyable," she said, those doe eyes serious, mouth unsmiling.

Jackson's eyes flicked to me and then to Victoria and back before he started to crack up. "You realise Max is nicknamed Mr Vanilla, don't you?"

Her eyes looked at me questioningly. "I hadn't heard that."

My brother continued to laugh loudly, enjoying himself, which was good as it might be the last thing he ever did.

"The first girl he slept with told Claire that Max only knew how to do it in the missionary position. We've never heard anything to disprove it." Jackson smirked at me then looked back at Victoria.

And I knew why: she was impulsive and would say the first thing that came into her mind if she felt passionately about it.

"Your brother's repertoire has expanded since then," she said, a smirk on her own face. "I'll share the details with Vanessa. Maybe then she can pass on some tips."

Now it was me smirking.

Jackson took the mug of coffee from Victoria, searching for something to say. "I'd say I taught my brother everything he knows, but that would be creepy and wrong so we'll leave this conversation here. Thank you for the coffee and for releasing my brother from the handcuffs, although I'm surprised it was that way round." Raised eyebrows greeted me when he turned my way.

"Like she said, you'll get the details from your fiancée. Something I'd be worried about. And for your information, it's me who does the tying down." I was watching Victoria when I said my last sentence and really wishing I'd disposed of my brother already.

Leaning back on the kitchen counter, Jackson gave me a look I recognised from when we were younger: the one that said he was about to drop me in the shit. "Victoria will have a chance to share your dirty secrets at the law ball tonight."

"And I expect I'll be hearing lots about your inadequacies too," I said, downing my coffee quickly. I had never taken a date to a Law Society ball, although I had been known to leave with one I'd found while being there. Jackson knew this and was being a dick, trying to put me in a position where for once, I could be said to have a girlfriend. When news of that got back to Marie, she would implode with excitement.

"What's Vanessa wearing?" Victoria asked.

If I was a better man, I'd have gone over to her, put an arm around her and pulled her into me. But I was still an ass. It was the perfect thing to ask Jackson though, judging by the look of death on his face.

"Did you tell her what Claire said in those messages?" he said, putting down his mug with a bit of a bang. "How the fuck do you describe a dress? It's a dress. It cost a lot and so did the shoes. I'm going to need a decent win at poker next week." He mentioned the poker nights we had at his place each week.

Victoria eyed him as she might to a rare specimen. "I bet you can describe her underwear though. When she tries dresses on for you, try to pay a bit of attention to it before getting down to her underwear."

"But the underwear's the best bit." My brother looked concerned.

I was enjoying this.

"For you, but not for her. She'll be spending more time in her dress than just her underwear. The underwear makes a statement for you, but the dress is for everyone, and you taking the time to notice and admire her, it will make her feel like she's wearing very expensive pearls, ones you don't need to buy," Victoria said with a stern expression that had me getting a semi.

Women like her weren't my usual type, apart from the intelligence. She was feisty and confident, upfront with her words and more than willing to give as much as she got.

I wondered what it would be like to let her have a little control at some point.

"Point taken," he said. 'And when you talk to her tonight, we never had this discussion."

She smiled sweetly, as if she had won the war and not just the battle.

"Don't you have a meeting first thing?" I asked my brother, impatiently. I wanted more time on my own with my girl and not just to ask her to the ball tonight.

"It's been rearranged," he said. "Why? Do you want me to go?"

"It's been lovely having you call in, Jackson, but I need to get ready. No doubt I'll see you tonight," Victoria said, the dressing gown coming apart to expose enough flesh to make me consider carrying my brother outside.

He made his way to the door before I had to. "See you at work, Max. Thanks for the coffee, Vic."

I followed him to the door, closed it firmly afterwards and put the catch on. "Are you wearing anything under that?" I tugged at the belt and she slapped my hand.

"Ball. What ball? Apart from your balls which are going to be hanging from the light fixture in about two seconds."

I winced. "I'd forgotten about it. Law society ball tonight. Three course meal, lots of pretentious idiots in tuxes, including myself. Plenty of alcohol and my siblings making idiots of themselves. Would you like to go with me?" I figured the pounding in my chest was my heart about to force its way through my rib cage.

"Were you going to ask me or is this just because your brother brought it up?" Her hands were on her hips, stretching the robe even further. I was absolutely convinced she was naked underneath.

"I had forgotten until I saw the messages this morning that the ball was even happening," I said, definitely not focusing on her face.

She pulled the robe closed and I looked up. "I know you're a lawyer but stop trying to evade my question."

"Honestly?" I said, remembering I wasn't a teenage boy anymore. "I don't know. I want to spend tonight with you. I'd prefer it if you packed a bag for the weekend now and stayed with me so I can show you where I live, take you for a proper date and then spend the rest of the weekend fucking you senseless. If you don't want to go to a ball, I won't go, because I'd rather spend more time with just you."

"You're still evading."

"I've never taken a date to a law ball before," I said, my hands in my pockets and trying not to feel like a child being told off.

"You don't have to take me. I can easily tell Jackson I already had plans. Or an emergency can come up. I'm good at those. And to be honest, if it rains again, there will probably be an emergency," she said, glancing towards the cornice. The wall was blackening near the roof, like it was in her bedroom. It looked like one heavy storm from flooding.

I thought about what she'd said to Jackson about dresses and how much Vanessa was looking forward to it and then I thought about what she'd look like on my arm and next to me. "If you think you'd enjoy it, I'd love you to come. If you don't want to, then we'll do something else."

My ribs had started to hurt and my stomach felt as if it was rejecting the coffee. I could stand up in court and speak in front of fuck knows how many people, but Victoria Esme Davies tied my intestines into a complex climbers' knot.

"Fuck," I said as she turned and left the room. My other brothers had been given the gift of being able to sweet talk, whereas I had taken after my father: a bumbling, crass idiot who was better off saying as little as possible.

Putting the mugs in the sink as the apartment was too tiny to have a dishwasher, I started to work out what to say to put right my stupidity at not being able to tell her that I did want her to go; I was just too fucking nervous at having something that could be labelled as a relationship.

"How's this?"

I turned around, not having realised she was back in the room. Her hair was damp and tied loosely on top of her head and she wore no make-up. She wore a blue dress, tight and fitted, with a plunging neckline that showed her cleavage. The bottom fishtailed out, reminding me of a mermaid that sailors knew would enchant them and make them leave their ship.

"Fucking amazing but you can't wear that." I knew the words were wrong as soon as they left my mouth.

"Why? Is there a dress code? Only I don't have any spare cash to buy anything new and I'm a little short on ball gowns," she said, looking down at herself and poking her cleavage.

"No, the dress code is cocktail, or it usually is. But you can't wear that as I'll be arrested for murdering every man that looks at you." This time my words seem to have been the right ones.

"Maxwell, they might look. It does make the girls look pretty outstanding, if I do say so myself. But no one but you gets to *touch*," she said, stepping towards me and putting her arms around my neck. Her tits pushed into my chest and I made a noise that sounded like a growl.

"How do you take it off?"

"You can find out tonight. But if you're wondering about underwear, there is none."

I was fucked. Well and truly.

CHAPTER 12
VICTORIA

rom: Victoria Esme Davies
To: Maxwell Callaghan
Ball(s)
Today at 11.26am
Dear Max,

I've packed as requested and have my bags with me. What's your address and when shall I meet you there? I'll need about an hour to get ready. If you'd rather me not clutter up your bathroom with girly shit then I can always meet you at the hotel.

See you later,

V x

From: Maxwell Callaghan
To: Victoria Esme Davies
Re: Ball(s)
Today at 11.35am
Vic,

I'll meet you at the law office, unless you're in the history depart-

ment today? I'll help you carry your stuff to mine. How much girly shit are we talking? I have two bathrooms.

Max

From: Victoria Esme Davies
   To: Maxwell Callaghan
   Re: Re: Ball(s)
   Today at 11.52am

Dear Max,

There's quite a bit as the lock on my door has broken so I wanted to take anything valuable. Am I okay to stay with you tonight and maybe tomorrow? I'm staying with Jacob on Sunday but he's 'entertaining' a 'friend' tomorrow. A second bathroom might be a good idea.

Hope you're feeling strong,

V x

From: Maxwell Callaghan
   To: Victoria Esme Davies
   Re: Re: Re: Ball(s)
   Today at 12.02pm

You can stay as long as you want. When did your landlord say it would be fixed by? Does Jacob have a second bathroom?

Max

From: Victoria Esme Davies
   To: Maxwell Callaghan
   Re: Re: Re: Re: Ball(s)
   Today at 11.52am

Dear Max,

Jacob has three bathrooms, but this isn't a bathroom owning competition. Landlord said his contractor was away till a week on Monday. There's nothing valuable in there, but I am laden like a packhorse.

V x

From: Maxwell Callaghan
  To: Victoria Esme Davies
  Re: Re: Re: Re: Re: Ball(s)
  Today at 12.02pm

Leave it at mine then, rather than move it again. If you want a night at your friend's just take what you need for that night. I'm more than happy to be your packhorse.

You can ride me any time.

:)

From: Victoria Esme Davies
  To: Maxwell Callaghan
  Re: Re: Re: Re: Re: Re: Ball(s)
  Today at 12.43pm

Dear Max,

I now have visions of your penis being dressed up like a dressage pony but I'll keep the finer details out of this email in case it gets screened by your secretary.

I don't want to impose. We've only known each other a couple of weeks so I could be a bunny boiling psychopath for all you know! Are you in the habit of offering temporary accommodation to random women you argue with? I approve of the emoticon, btw.

V x

· · ·

From: Maxwell Callaghan
   To: Victoria Esme Davies
   Re: Re: Re: Re: Re: Re: Re: Ball(s)
   Today at 12.49pm

I'm slightly disturbed at the thought of my penis having ribbons tied around it. There are other things that could be added to aid pleasure, but not ribbons. I'll save those for your wrists and my bed posts.

If you're there for anymore than a couple of weeks you won't be the only woman staying. My sister Ava is lodging with me while she renos her latest property.

Max 8====>

I laughed out loud at his cock emoticon and tried to focus on the pile of admin I needed to work through before I could crack on with my thesis, but last night and this morning was playing through my head like a video on repeat. I liked sex; I could enjoy it without having to have an emotional connection with the guy involved, although it was usually better if there was something there, and there was with Max. My fears about a relationship had been subsided by how we'd been in bed and out of it. There wasn't time for me to develop something serious with anyone if I was considering moving to the States, but Max had made it easy last night and this morning to think that having a little fun would be okay. A stress reliever while I was finishing my PhD and for him from his work.

The rest of the day dragged in between messages from Max. I hit a snag with my schoolwork, which set me back a couple of days as I'd need to supplement what I'd researched already with a bit more. By the time Max was at my office I was cross and annoyed and in need of a glass of something strong and red.

"Your packhorse is here," he said, looking at me over my computer screen. "Victoria?"

I looked up, pushing my glasses higher up my nose and semi-scowled at him. "I need to finish bookmarking this…" My gaze went back to the computer screen.

"Victoria, if you want the chance to have a glass of wine and get ready without rushing then we need to get your stuff over."

I looked at the clock on my computer screen and saw that it was nearing five-thirty. He'd probably finished early to come here and help me carry my stuff, although Uber might be a better idea. "Sure," I said, clicking on the last link I needed to save and jotting three words down on my notepad. "Sorry, I know you were probably in the middle of something too."

"It's fine. It can always wait. Where's your stuff?"

I pointed to the corridor off reception where Carol's office was. "I took a cab here. There is quite a bit. I can shift it to Jacob's though—he's been offering me one of his spare rooms for six months."

"I'm not surprised, given the state of where you've been living. Don't go back: the place is a health hazard and it's not safe," he said, heading through to collect some of my stuff. "Though looking at this, you're not planning on going back," he followed it with a chuckle, the deep, short laugh that suited him so much.

"I know, I'm sorry. I can leave most of it there over the weekend as no one will be in tomorrow—everyone will be hungover and Sunday really is a day of rest around here unless you're a third year," I said, switching my computer off at socket and heading to help him. "It's really just those three bags, the dress carrier and that suitcase. The rest I'll get to Jacob's tomorrow."

"We'll see," he said. The bags were now in in his hands. "Let me take that other bag. Your suitcase is on wheels. Is it too heavy for you to pull?"

"It's okay," I said. "I'm really sorry about this. I feel like I'm imposing terribly."

"Stop apologising else I will be annoyed. You're staying tonight and possibly tomorrow depending on whether you can put up with me for that length of time. I will need your landlord's contact details as you'll be due compensation for having to stay elsewhere while you're paying him rent," he said as we made our way outside, my suitcase wheels squeaking unhappily.

Max stopped abruptly, almost tripping me up. I managed to halt my feet and saw Peter Coffey, the ex-Cambridge student, lingering in a nearby doorway and watching me.

"Has he been hanging round a lot?" Max said, starting to walk, this time a little quicker.

"Maybe three times this week. I think he just lives nearby." I shrugged. He did seem a little odd but odd people weren't that unusual at a university.

"I don't like the way he was looking at you," Max said quietly.

It was a possessive thing to say, and although I suspected that once Max claimed a woman as his, he wasn't for sharing, but his tone suggested that it wasn't just possessiveness he was feeling but genuine concern.

Peter had bobbed in and out of the office all week, checking a few details of his course, looking to speak to a couple of the professors—all pretty much the norm. "He's a little strange," I said. "But he's nothing to worry about. I'm not sure he's cut out for law though."

"You can say that again," Max said.

We were at his apartment within ten minutes, just beating an autumn shower that began the moment he opened his door. It was a duplex and spacious, as I imagined it would be, filled with natural light. The biggest bonus was that there was no mould and no leaking roof, although the furnishings, which were a mixture of scandi-influenced dark wood and comfortable, sleep-able softness, were up there on the to-be-thankful list also.

I sat down on the corner sofa, a plush grey velvet that had to have been chosen by a female. "Who picked out this?" I said. "It's not leather, it doesn't recline and there's no beer holder."

Max passed me a glass of red wine and took one for himself, sitting down near to me but allowing us some space. "Good observation. My sister, Ava. The one who's staying."

"The renovator?"

"The one and only. I moved in here about three years ago and had barely any furniture. I managed like that for over a year until Ava got hold of my credit card and pin number when I was drunk. My bill that month was eye-watering."

The wine was good: smooth and full bodied. I wished we could just stay like this, maybe with a few less clothes, instead of having to head out to a ball. "She did a good job of it," I said. "It's gorgeous."

I watched him look around the room as if he was assessing it for the first time. "It is," he agreed. "But it needs bits, I suppose. I don't have the fiddly things that girls always know to get or pictures or anything like that. I wouldn't know where to start."

I thought about my grandfather's home where I had mostly grown up, the one that Francis had sold. It had been four storeys of walnut antique furniture, photos and relics from other ages that my grandfather had collected. Most of the larger items were in storage—I'd had them put away until I had somewhere more permanent to live, although my brother had auctioned some of the more valuable pieces. I'd been too upset to deal with the aftermath of his death, except to organise the funeral for which I'd held myself together. When Francis said he'd sort Grandad's belongings I'd been grateful, thinking he was finally trying to help me out, but once again it had been to his own end.

"Where did you go just then?" Max asked gently. He'd edged

closer, his arm around the back of where I was sitting, his fingers softly stroking my hair.

"I was thinking of the ornaments and knick-knacks I have in storage. There's an old globe from the eighteen hundreds that my grandfather told me belonged to Charles Dickens at one point. I doubt it did, but I like the idea."

"You still have lots of his stuff?"

"Plenty. I've nowhere to put it. We lived in a big house and you saw the size of my apartment." I gave him a broad smile. There was no need to be down tonight. We'd had a good time last night, and tonight was all about having fun too. I leaned over and kissed him slowly, keeping it PG rated else I knew I wouldn't have any time to get ready. "You'd better show me to the bathroom I can take over, otherwise we'll be late. What time are we meeting everyone?"

"Eight," he said and drew me into a kiss again, his hands holding me, thumbs caressing the skin he'd found. My body reacted automatically, wetness gathering between my legs. It had only been one night and one morning, but clearly I was already programmed with how to respond. "I've booked a cab for twenty to."

"Okay." My hands received the message that there was time for this, that it was needed and they started to undo his shirt buttons, managing not to pull any off or become impatient.

He let me have my time, let my lips leave his and kiss their way over tattooed skin and taut muscle. One of his hands combed the hair on my head, while the other clenched at his side.

His suit trousers were easier than jeans to undo, the fly slipping down effortlessly to expose his cock straining at the top of his boxer briefs. My mouth went there and between my legs got wetter, my breasts feeling heavy. I put my lips over his cock through the thin fabric and he moaned so quietly I could barely hear. Sliding his underwear down enough to release him, I began to lick the head, wrapping my mouth around the top. I sucked gently, the salty taste hitting my tongue. I liked men: I liked how I could make them respond and I enjoyed being physical. I hadn't had a huge amount of lovers—enough to count on two hands—but all had possessed a certain quality, Max possibly more so than any of them.

Max sat up further, his hands now pushing up my top, seeking my breasts. "Been thinking about these all day," he said. "I might have looked at your photos once or twice too." He pulled my thin jumper over my head, forcing me to move away from his cock. "Take your bra off."

Lounging back, he watched me, his eyes switching from mine to my tits, my nipples hard. "Take the rest off too. I want you naked in my home."

I obeyed, enjoying his response as his dick grew harder, his hand holding the base of it. "What if I told you that you can't touch?" I said.

Fire burned in his eyes. "I say you'd have to tie me up first. Come sit here." He gestured to his lap.

As I stepped nearer he pulled me to him, using his knees to spread my legs so I straddled over him, spread enough so that he could clearly see between my legs. "Close your eyes."

"Why?"

"Close your eyes. Trust me."

I did. And then I felt fingers finally travel down my arms to my waist and then up to my breasts, pinching nipples, stroking them until they were taut, like berries about to burst.

"So fucking beautiful," he said and I whimpered as I felt his mouth on a nipple, sucking it while he pinched the other in tandem. His other hand moved onto my ass, moving my centre closer to his erection. I ached, feeling needy and alive.

Then his hand moved between my legs and a finger brushed my clit, moving my wetness around. He gave my nipple a soft nip and pulled away.

"Open your eyes," he said. "I want to watch you while you come on my hand. Then I'll give you my cock so you can ride me like that pony you mentioned."

Electricity shot up me as he pinched my clit and nipple at the same time. I moved my hips, seeking more friction from his hand, making him laugh arrogantly. He was in control and he knew it but I didn't care. I wanted to come and I was chasing that orgasm.

"Let me come with your fingers in me," I said, desperate for something of his to fill my pussy.

"You can have my dick after. Then you can come again on that. And then I might fuck you again when you've got that dress on so everyone knows what we've been doing and they know you're mine."

I'd lost my words, incapable of anything apart from shifting my hips to heighten the pressure and watching the heated expression on his face. I came hard, gripping onto his shoulders and needing his free hand to steady my hips as I bucked against his hand. I'd barely finished the aftershocks before he had a condom in his hand from the side table. He tore it open and dressed his cock, his hands back on my hips and guiding me down onto his hip.

"You're tight so don't rush. Take it slow," he said, watching where our bodies joined. Sweet pain fractured me with the initial breach and I cried out, stopping and giving my body a moment to adjust. Then I took more of him and his hips started to move. I knew I was making him lose some of his control. My tits began to bounce as I found my rhythm and I altered my angle so he hit that sweet spot it had taken me so long to discover.

One of his hands left my hips and went to my breasts, holding, squeezing, pinching and then his mouth was there, sucking and nibbling. Our movements became more ferocious and I felt him push deeper into me and I tightened harder around him, my second orgasm coming closer.

"I'm going to come again," I breathed, my head going to rest on his. "Can you fuck me like this every day?"

His hands went to my hips, holding harder so he could take over the rhythm. "I'll fuck you like this every night and every morning if you want. And lunchtimes. I can always find a desk to bend you over. Make you come on my cock from behind." His words were said quietly, seriously. "So many things I want to do to you."

And then I came hard, possibly harder than I ever had before. I screamed loudly as it hit, losing all control of my body. He held me to him, his cock pounding me hard.

"I'm there," he said, giving one hard, deep thrust and groaning. He moved me up and down as he came and I managed to open my eyes to watch him, his body shuddering.

We stilled, him staying deep inside me. My chest heaved with my breathing and his hands left my hips to cup my breasts briefly then pull me towards him, nuzzling my neck with his nose.

"You good?" he said, his voice shaky.

"Yes," I said. "More than." He moved to be able to kiss me again, this time without the need. My body was still boneless, every muscle without stress. "You should be available on prescription."

"Just for you," he said. "While we're doing this, will it just be us?"

"I thought we could ask Jacob if he wanted to join in occasionally." I couldn't help myself.

He stiffened beneath me. "I thought you were just friends."

I tried to stop my smirk by biting my lips but I knew my eyes would give me away.

"Victoria Esme Davies." He lifted me up off him and slapped my ass as my feet hit the floor. "I'm a jealous man."

"I've noticed," I said, my ass stinging slightly. If he did it again I could be up for another round, but then I'd have no chance of being ready on time. "I find it quite endearing seeing you try to control it."

"You're avoiding answering my question."

"I should go and get ready." I walked towards the room where he had put my bags, grabbing my wine on the way.

It seemed to be the master bedroom; a faint scent of his cologne lingered in the air. There was a large ensuite with a walk-in shower and standalone bath which, if I'd had time, I'd have been in with a book and a glass of wine, and maybe Max to wash my back. Ignoring the rest of his belongings as time wasn't plentiful, I grabbed my shower gel and jumped into the shower.

By the time I came out, the bathroom was foggy with steam. Music played from a speaker somewhere and for a moment I dreamed that I had a place like this instead of a hovel with a leaking roof and a pervy landlord. I found a fluffy towel that I was certain hadn't been there before I got into the shower, having forgotten to check.

Wondering what mood Max was in since I hadn't given him a definite answer about us being exclusive, I stepped into the bedroom with interest. He was adding product to his beard, staring intently into the mirror.

"So you've thought about spending some quality time with Jacob then? He's keen on beards." Shifting the smile on my face was impossible.

He turned around, just a white towel hanging low on his hips. "That's a yes then. While we're seeing each other, you won't see anyone else?"

I let my towel drop so I could apply moisturiser. Eczema when I was younger had resulted in me having to use it every time I showered or took a bath. "I like being monogamous. It stops things from being messy. So you can return your jealous side to its cage."

He nodded, blatantly obvious about looking me up and down as I rubbed moisturiser into my skin.

"I'd offer to help but there's no way we'd be on time." The towel had started to become a tent.

"I'm liking the power I have over you."

"You're a witch," he said. "A beautiful, feisty witch."

I laughed, pulling my robe from my suitcase and throwing it on so I could begin the procedure of combing and drying my hair. It was long and thick and so straight, which meant apart from washing and drying it, I didn't need to do much more to make it stylable. If I'd have had prior warning about the ball, I'd have booked in somewhere for an up do, instead I'd have to make do with the YouTube tutorials I'd watched in the past.

Max sat on the bed and watched me get ready, peering over a book he was reading. The towel was still wrapped round him and I could make out the impression of his erection beneath it. The sight of it made my muscles clench and I was half tempted to pull the towel away and wrap my mouth around him again, but I needed to make sure I was ready first. Being late to meet his siblings would only mean receiving a lot of jokes about why and I got the impression Max wouldn't feel entirely comfortable about that. My guess was that he stayed away from relationships and although I didn't know why, at some point I would ask. Even if what we were had an expiration date on it, I hoped that we'd part with him able to have a longer relationship with the right person, and a family if he wanted it. I hoped the same for myself too.

I took myself into the bathroom to put my dress on, wanting him to see me finished rather than squeezing bits of flesh into what was a very form fitting gown. Lunch had been minimal because of the time, but that had done me a favour, helping to keep my stomach relatively flat.

My heels were higher than usual, keeping the fishtail just off the ground. I slipped them on and went to get a reaction from Max.

He glanced at me and then looked back at his book.

I glared. "Will I do?"

"Yeah, you look fine." His erection was still visible although he now had trousers and a shirt on, bowtie undone around his neck.

I picked up my lipstick and aimed it at the pillow, managing to hit him square in the face.

He clutched it and laughed, sitting up. "Not the reaction you were expecting, Feisty?" he said.

No words were available.

I chucked a pillow.

He laughed again, sitting up and looking at me with heavy eyes. "You look beautiful," he said, his words quiet, as if they would break if he said them loudly. "I think we should stay in."

I shot him a knowing glare. "Because you don't want any other man looking at me? Maxwell, really? Do you have to be such a Neanderthal?"

He nodded. "Although, I'll make sure they all know you're with me. The monogamy thing?"

"Yes?"

"We are v—monogamous? As in just us, even if it's only casual?"

His eyes were filled with something I hadn't seen before; an odd emotion that I couldn't pin down. His body was relaxed on the surface, but below there was a tension that ebbed and flowed into his eyes.

"We are. The only man I'll be thinking about touching me tonight is you. And if you play your cards right, Maxwell, it'll be the same tomorrow as well."

He shifted closer to the edge of the bed and put out his hands to hold my hips. "I'm glad you're a feisty ball of argumentative sass," he said. "And I'm glad you're with me tonight."

I stooped so I could kiss him. It wasn't a kiss that would induce another round of who could have the most powerful orgasm, but instead a sweet kiss, one with a tenderness I had forgotten I could possess. "You look hot," I said. "I need photos for future reference."

"I'll happily swap you later—photo for photo." He stood up and took hold of me, his touch everything I needed to feel right then.

My world was full right now and I was going to enjoy it.

CHAPTER 13
MAXWELL

I t was difficult to hold a conversation given that my whole attention was on the woman in the night sky blue dress and nowhere else. Thankfully, my sister Claire had opted for tonight to be the night when she and Killian came out as being more than friendly enemies to everyone who didn't already know, so the attention from Payton and Seph was taken away from my inability to hold a conversation.

I'd had women, more than my fair share, but this was the first time I'd been captivated. Earlier I'd caught my expression in a mirror and recognised it as the one I'd seen on Jackson's face after he and Vanessa had been together for a few weeks and it both terrified and enthralled me. Inviting her to stay with me while her landlord sorted out the lock on the door was making me freak out because I wasn't freaked out. It was only temporary; we'd spent time together on less than a dozen occasions and she was as independent as they came, but the idea of one day sharing space with her on a regular basis didn't make me want to run for the nearest exit, and that was unusual.

My hook ups were casual, with women who were after a decent fuck with a decent bloke who wasn't going to make them feel shit a day or even two days later. I knew that in this room there were at least three of my exes, all of whom had spotted me and the fact that I had brought a date, something I hadn't done before.

The rumour would soon be hitting the university treadmill that I was taken, and again I wasn't stirred by fear.

"Your girl looks good. I hope you've noticed her dress," Jackson said, arriving next to me with a glass of whisky.

"I've even examined underneath it," I said, intentionally crude.

He laughed. "Now I know you've not been taken over by aliens. You seem to really like her. I've not seen you even acknowledge anything else since we got here. You've not even tried to murder Killian."

Killian was my best friend and now my sister's boyfriend. "I'd known for a couple of weeks but she asked me not to say anything till they were sure."

"Turn up for the books," Jackson said.

I just nodded, there was more to the story but it wasn't mine to tell. "Where's Vanessa?"

"With Victoria."

I let my gaze slip away from Victoria for a second to notice that Vanessa was sitting next to her, slightly obscured by the man who had joined them. I recognised him as Judge Howell, her friend Jacob's father and one of the speakers at tonight's dinner. As far as I knew he was happily married so I figured steaming over there in a jealous rage would be pointless, plus it'd possibly cost me a case next time I got him in court.

"Is she still going to move to America?" Jackson said. "Is that the plan? She's going to get a lot more money than she thought."

"How much?" It didn't matter to me. I was one of the lucky ones who didn't have to worry about cash or even working, although I think my father would've hired a hitman if I'd ever suggested being a trust fund brat.

"Close to six million."

"Jesus." She wouldn't have a clue what to do with that. "Where did her grandfather get all of that from?"

"His wife's pay out from the accident at work which ultimately cost her her life; very astute investments; careful living and the sale of the house and some of the contents," Jackson said. "You can tell her if you like. I'll forward you the letter I'll be sending out on Monday. Her brother has no further claim. His solicitors have backed off completely."

"I'll leave it to you. I'd rather keep it separate. Out of interest, where was the house?"

"Mundania Road. It was bought by investors who are doing a big reno on it. Why, you thinking of buying her a present?"

I shook my head, staring at the whisky I had in my hand. "She doesn't know where she's going to be after she's finished her doctorate."

"So this is just a casual fling?"

Jackson's gaze was on Vanessa who was now headed towards us.

"Something like that," I told him as much as myself. I wasn't thinking much about her leaving, mainly because it was months away. The prospect of her moving away from London was possibly why I wasn't feeling the urge to keep her away from the staples of my life such as my family. It wouldn't turn into anything serious because she wasn't staying so I didn't have to commit or worry about hurting her, because it wasn't going to have longevity anyway.

"Not seen you look at anyone else like you do her," Jackson said, putting his arm around Vanessa as she came up to us.

"What's that?" my soon to be sister-in-law asked.

"The way Max looks at Victoria."

"Your fiancé's had too much to drink," I said. "I'd monitor what he has for the rest of the evening."

"He's right," she said to me, completely ignoring my

comment. "You do look at her differently. You're not usually so, well, watchful. Or tactile."

She had a point: if I brought a date or took a woman out I kept my hands to myself until we were in private. I'd been different tonight with Victoria but I'd needed to touch her, remind her that I was there and absorb her warmth.

"What do you think of her?" I asked Vanessa. They'd spoken last week and had been talking tonight, so I figured she'd have an opinion by now. I liked Vanessa a lot: she'd been good for my brother and the rest of us and her judgement of people was sound.

"Lovely. Outspoken and intelligent. To be honest, I would've thought she'd have eaten you for breakfast," Vanessa said, making Jackson snort.

I scowled at her. "Why?"

Vanessa laughed. "Because she's opinionated and completely unafraid of voicing what she thinks. The women I've seen you with have always been very bright but quieter whereas she's no shy, retiring type."

Victoria had started to walk over towards us, the judge with her. She hadn't worn her glasses and whatever she'd done with her make-up made her eyes stand out even more than usual. I swallowed loudly enough for my brother to cast me a concerned look and tried to peel my eyes away from her, but it was useless. She had completely captivated me.

"I believe you two know each other?" she said, gesturing between me and Judge Howell. "And you probably know Jackson too, Jim?"

Judge Howell nodded. "I've had the pleasure of seeing you both in court a few times. Well done on that clinical negligence case you had recently, Maxwell. The wrong ointment, I believe."

"Thank you. It was a tough one," I said. It hadn't been, not if you knew your stuff like I did, but arrogance with a judge was always a stupid path to take. "I hear you're thinking of retiring."

He nodded. "At some point next year. Have you thought about moving up in the future?"

"Maybe when I stop enjoying what I do. As it is, I'm finding my cases really worthwhile and the practice is growing significantly. It's an exciting time to work at Callaghan Green," I said, deferring a question that I'd been asked more than once. I was thirty-six but my career was that of someone much older than me.

"Your dad must be proud—of both of you," he said, looking between Jackson and myself.

We both nodded. "He is," I said, meaning it.

My relationship with my father had been strained. I blamed him for my mother's suicide, for not spotting the signs, for not stepping up to the plate of being a husband and father until Marie came along and taught him what to do. The time in between my mother dying and Marie arriving had seen me try to be what my little sister and brothers needed. I'd changed diapers, made up bottles, sorted out packed lunches and even though I was no older than six or seven, I'd done what I could to look after them. But I was my father. I knew I was success-driven and I'd inherited my skills and thirst for knowledge from him.

At first, my father had resented the four of us. If we hadn't been there, he'd have been free to pursue his career without the added hassle of having to sort out four young children. We'd also been a reminder of my mother, who he'd worshipped. But as I got older and became interested in what took him away from us so often, he'd started to take an interest in me, teaching me about torts and compromise agreements, land law and contracts. And I'd loved it.

The attention from him became a bonus. My motivation had not been to please him; I was too angry still for that. Instead, I'd fallen in love with law and wanted to be the best, and ultimately to change how things were done and what people were allowed to do.

"Is he enjoying retirement?" Judge Howell said. "I never thought I'd see the day when he stopped working."

"Neither did we," Jackson said. "We called the firm his eldest child. He's loving retirement but then Marie doesn't let him sit down. They've just bought a winery in Ontario so he's buried himself in business plans and marketing for that. Vanessa's had the pleasure of working with him this week on some branding ideas."

"Thankfully she managed not to brand him herself," I said. My arm was now around Victoria's waist, hand on her hip. She leaned into me, listening to the conversation. Judge Howell smiled at her. "When he's obsessed with something he's not the easiest person to work with."

"He's been a pussy cat," Vanessa interjected. "Jackson's worse when he's in full business mode. Your dad's been a lot of fun. And we get Christmas in Toronto which is exciting, if a little cold."

"And required a whole new wardrobe, or so Ava leads me to believe." Jackson pressed a kiss to her head. If I hadn't been pulling Victoria so closely I would've termed him pussy-whipped. Instead, I was being fucking pussy-whipped myself and a strangely warm feeling was running through me.

I put it down to the whisky.

"I told you, I have no suitable clothes for that temperature," Vanessa said, one hand touching the stubble he called a beard and I called a poor attempt.

"When do you two get married?" Judge Howell asked.

"April," Vanessa said. "I'm trying to keep it simple, but I don't think a wedding can ever be simple."

"My daughter aimed for the same thing and I think I ended up having to cash in a pension. You remember it, Vic?"

Victoria nodded. "It was lovely though. Probably my favourite wedding that I've been to."

"Hopefully mine will tie with that then," Vanessa said. "It's not the easiest thing to plan. I thought it would be straightforward but you have so many people trying to overcharge."

The conversation strayed down a path I had no experience of and little interest in. I caught Jackson's eye, then stepped away from Vanessa and Victoria, leaving them with the judge.

"Seph appears to have found himself a woman for the night," Jackson said, nodding towards the bar where our younger brother was standing. There was a tall blonde draped over him. I vaguely recognised her as a lawyer from another firm—these events were always filled with people you knew or recognised— and wondered how much intervention we'd need to provide.

"I think that's Nina Dewsberry," I said. "Works for Hawks Middleton."

"We're against them in a property dispute," Jackson said. "I think she does litigation though, if it is her. The last time I saw her she looked just about old enough to buy alcohol, let alone practice law."

"We're getting old, brother."

"We're not. Just wiser. Are you going to be my best man?"

He hadn't mentioned anything before. Vanessa's bridesmaids had been decided months ago, but Jackson had been quiet about his side. I'd thought that maybe he'd decided to leave that role, given that there were three brothers and a couple of very good friends to pick from.

"You realise I know more about how to embarrass you than anyone else?" It was the only response I could think of.

"And yet still I ask you."

"I have free range with the speech?"

"If you can take on the job of keeping me calm before and if she changes her mind getting me so drunk I don't wake up for a week then it's a deal," he said, his eyes on Vanessa.

"She's not going to change her mind, Jacks. For some reason beyond any level of intelligence she seems to like you," I said. "Just keep giving her your credit cards."

"Let's have another whisky to seal it then," Jackson said, heading to the bar.

Victoria was still deep in conversation with Judge Howell and the soft tap on the shoulder I gave her became my arms wrapping around her waist, as discretely as I could in front of a judge.

She looked behind to see me and smiled, her body relaxing into mine.

"I'm going to the bar. Do you want a drink?" Her hand had been empty for too long.

"A glass of rioja?"

"Anything," I said and pressed a kiss to her hair. "Vanessa, your husband-to-be forgot to ask."

"Just get a bottle of rioja. It'll save further trips to the bar," she said, grinning at Victoria.

"Judge?"

"A whisky, if you're buying, Maxwell," he said, smiling.

"It's Jackson's round, so I'll make it a double."

———

Victoria's head was against my shoulder as we sat in the cab on the way back to mine. The bottle of rioja had turned into two, and two intelligent, classy women had become two giggly females before two am had struck.

"I love your sister-in-law, she's just amazing," Victoria said, her words blurring into each other. "She's the composed, less volatile version of me. We're going out for cocktails next week with Claire. Do you mind?"

I loved the fact she could use the word volatile when she was off her face drunk. "Why would I mind?" She was as she'd described, only I would've worded it differently: feisty, passionate, original.

"Because this is just a casual fuck-fest and I'm having cocktails with your sister and sister-in-law."

Casual fuck-fest? I wasn't sure I'd had that term applied to what I'd been doing before. I didn't recognise how I felt right now, it was foreign and strange and not my usual. "I think you're amazing, they're going to think the same and they're pretty amazing too. Why wouldn't you want to meet up?"

She turned to me and gave me a sloppy kiss.

"You make me want to stay in London."

It was at that point I realised I was on the way to being well and truly fucked.

———

I woke for the second time in as many days with my body wrapped round the soft skin of a woman. Her scent was of peaches and morning dew and me; my aftershave coated her as I knew it should, even with the bleariness of gradual awakening.

When we arrived home, I'd persuaded her to drink water and eat grilled cheese. Of course, she'd demanded more wine and as much as I knew it was adding power to her hangover, I've given in. *Just one glass.* Who was I to say no?

Then she'd walked around the apartment, opening windows and destroying the air conditioning, complaining that it was too warm. The window in my bedroom was left wide open, the London noise filtering through. We drank more water and talked about politics and elections and leaving Europe and then she'd fallen asleep in my arms, muttering about history and how it's all part of the same thing.

It was Saturday morning and Victoria was sound asleep. I knew she'd spent most of the week working in the law depart-ment or on her thesis late into the evening and early into the morning. I'd received an email sent at three am one morning, outlining the law at the time around medical procedures during the First World War. I'd responded—it was something I could help her on at least, but even I'd not been awake at that time.

I slipped out of the bed, untangling myself from her limbs and hair and headed into my kitchen. My tablet was on the side near the coffee machine; the temptation to look at the house on Mundania Road was too much. It was a seven bedroom detached, the pictures illustrating the modernisation it needed. But it had been Victoria's home. When I looked closely at the photos I could see the ornaments and pictures she probably had in storage. There was a lot of dark wood furniture and one photograph showed a room that looked like it had been hers.

I closed the tab in my browser, needing to push this to the back of my head to think about later.

Coffee brewed as I opened the blinds, looking out on the London that surrounded me. It was Saturday and the world about us was awake and moving. From my vantage point I could see people heading towards The Shard or Borough Market, the Tate Modern beyond and I felt the pull of the city where I chose to live. I loved it here.

As kids, we'd spent our time between Oxfordshire and our schools and the city. My dad and Marie had kept the big house in the countryside and a large apartment in Southwark so my father could easily stay in London when he had a lot of work on.

The city had been my constant lover. The busyness and bustle appealed to me, the still and silence of the country gave me too much time to think. It was different now; I liked going to my parents' place and the peace it provided because the busyness I'd created had quelled any demons left inside me. But I couldn't trust myself to not be my father. How would I spot my partner's low mood if I was so immersed in my job? How could I ever step away from work if that was what I was.

"Good morning."

I turned around to see Victoria standing there, wearing just one of my oversized old Oxford university T-shirts. Her hair was curly from whatever she'd done with it the night before and her face was bare of make-up. She looked both tired and happy, her eyes sleepy and filled with what I thought was lust or at least attraction.

"You're awake. I didn't want to disturb you."

"You didn't," she said. "Well, you kind of did, but I don't mind. What time is it?"

"Nine-thirty," I said, unable to take my eyes away from her body, her full of legs and her breasts. "I like you in my clothes."

"Because they're yours or because they give a hint as to what's underneath?"

"Both," I said honestly. "But then I think you're the most beautiful creature I've ever seen no matter what you're wearing or what mood you're in."

She laughed and she was beautiful. "You don't know me well enough yet."

But I wanted to. "Coffee?"

"Hell, yeah. Do you have any plans today?"

There were a million ways to answer that question, all of which would've been honest, all of which would've brought immense pleasure to both of us, I hoped. But the rush of feelings I was having didn't mean there was any need for verbal diarrhoea. "No plans. It's been a busy week so I'm happy to chill."

She sat down on the sofa, pulling down a blanket that at some point Ava had artfully arranged. "Are you happy for me to chill here too?"

"More than. We don't have to leave the apartment."

"Don't say that. It's amazing. If I lived anywhere I could design I'd have it like this. Your shower and the space—it's perfect."

I added more coffee beans, intrigued by what else she'd tell me about the house where she'd pretty much grown up. "How would you have changed where you lived with your grandfather?"

"That's a hard question because when I think back to the house it was perfect. It had all of my grandfather's secrets, all the stories he'd found to tell me. It was old fashioned—the bathrooms and kitchen needed modernising and thinking about it, I'd have more open space, less wall between everyone. But there was this one room, like a snug, I suppose, with an old fireplace and a huge bay window with a willow tree out in front. I'd have that filled with huge bookcases and comfy sofas and throws and rugs. That's where I'd curl up on a cold day with the fire roaring." She looked wistful. "It was huge. Seven bedrooms. I hope a family bought it, or someone who wanted a family, with extra bedrooms for extended family to stay over."

"Do you want kids?"

She laughed. "We're a bit early for that conversation!" I laughed with her, unsure of what I felt. "But yes, I always imagined having at least a couple of kids so they could have a relationship more like what you have with your siblings than what I have with Francis. I'd like a family, but my plan's been delayed. In my ideal world, it'd be happening now."

"What's the plan?"

"Complete my PhD, get a lecturing position, write articles, books, whatnot. Then meet someone, have a family and take time out from teaching to raise them. I know it's old fashioned and I'm not exactly conventional, but I *was* the girl who played with dolls and pushed a pram. I coo over babies and I know it's not all talcum powder and baby smell, but I'd like to be a bit of stay at home mum. I suppose I want what I didn't have."

She looked sad and I figured I brought coffee at the right time, as I took a seat next to her and pulled her legs on to my lap.

"Does it have to be in that order?"

"My grandad talked about working in America and having that adventure. That's not something you can do with a two-year-old and a baby."

"It is if you have the right man."

"You volunteering for that position?"

My coffee sputtered around my mouth and she burst in to hysterical laughter.

"Two nights, Victoria, we've spent two nights together. Let's save the baby conversation for some way down the line."

She carried on laughing, sprawling over me and the sofa until I picked her up and carried her back to my bedroom.

"You're not hungover?" I said.

She shook her head. "I'm genetically programmed not to have them. My grandfather drank whisky as part of his medicine."

I put her on the bed, the daylight streaming through the window, curtains blowing open. "What are you thinking about right now?"

She laughed. "You. You being over me and what you can do. Staying in bed all day. Making you laugh and listening to you talk. Finding out about you."

I kissed her.

I think it was my first real kiss.

CHAPTER 14
VICTORIA

Because I was sensible and not a romantic I shifted between staying with Jacob and Maxwell for the next few days. The weekend had been spent curled up with Max, on his sofa, in his bed, on his cock and it was magical. We talked and touched and teased and all I could do was smile, but by Monday morning I knew I needed to preserve the smiles and give us some space.

He hadn't wanted me to stay elsewhere. Although he'd carried my bags, all set for me to spend a couple of days with my best friend—a male who happened to be gay and had absolutely no interest in my lady parts, scientifically proven—his expression was stoic and therefore betrayed the fact that he was revealing no emotion, which meant he was feeling it.

Because my man felt.

He hid it. Deep underneath everything, he covered what was going on in his heart for the sake of everyone else. Jackson asked him to be best man, but instead of being excited and nervous and delighted, he was cool and calm about it, as if it was just another thing to add to his list. It was because he didn't want to upset Seph and Callum, even though I knew Seph didn't mind; I couldn't speak for the brother I hadn't met.

Had I been a simpering, romantic sort of girl, I'd have embedded myself at Max's, made sure my scent and bodily fluid were all over every set of his sheets so the thought of me returning to the apartment from hell was unheard of.

It was unheard of. That was true. Jackson confirmed my inheritance on Monday, so Tuesday evening, Jacob and I went apartment hunting. I was looking for short term leases within walking distance from the college and therefore Max's place. Not that I admitted the latter to Jacob.

"You could just buy," he said as we finished viewing yet another overpriced hovel.

"I don't know where I'm going to be."

"You're going to be here. I can feel it in my water—and other bodily fluids. Vicky, if you leave it will be a disaster."

I stopped walking, hands on my hips and giving him the look I'd let my students have if they were telling me they were too heartbroken to complete an essay. "Jacob, my grandfather wanted me to have those experiences. I have to take this step while I don't have commitments like a house and bills and animals…"

"You can afford to buy back your house outright and not have to bother a bank. You could mothball it and work abroad and have a base back here. You can have it all, Vicky. Look at what you have going on right now: a decent man for the first time in forever and who knows what he's doing in bed, good colleagues and the promise of a friendship group," Jacob said. During the day, whilst he was at work, he was Mr Asexual, preferences non-disclosed. As soon as we were out of the public arena, his inner diva was let loose. He was also extremely romanticised.

"I've stayed at Max's twice. He's been at mine once," I started.

"Yes, that's true. But by stayed, you were there all day Saturday and Sunday and reluctant to leave on Monday. He lit your fires in bed and you're twitchy because you'd like some more of his cock sooner rather than later. Have you heard from him today?" Jacob's monologue shifted like it usually did. Most of the time it was useful as he could work himself away from topics rather than needing a full on intervention.

"We texted. And he called me at lunch. And after my tutorial." And while I walked to Jacob's. The conversation had been nothing meaningful, just general chatter about the day, politics, office politics, his PND case and my apartment. But it had filled a space I didn't know was there.

"You should go tomorrow," Jacob said, his hands on his hips. "Not that I'm throwing you out, but I am. And you need to decide on another apartment. Make some form of commitment for the next few months."

"Okay," I said, and I knew he was right. I had an inheritance —a rather large one—about to land in my bank account. I could quit my admin job and concentrate solely on my thesis and teaching and applying to wherever I wanted to be next September.

I wanted to be in bed with Max.

"I'll let this one," I said, gesturing around the ground floor apartment where we were standing. It was nothing special, except it was walking distance to the college and to Max's, not that being near him should be a deciding factor.

"Good," Jacob said. "You can have it on a nine month let, so you don't need to move again into shitty college accommodation."

"Excellent," I said. "I'll stay firmly put."

―――

For some reason I felt nervous. Not the sort of before-a-driving-test-nervous, or at an-interview-nervous, just plain old nervous. Which was bizarre as I wasn't a nervous person. I'd skydived; bungee-jumped; been arrested in Germany—long story; rode a camel; almost been exchanged for five camels; had a late period; all kinds of nervous, but meeting-a-specific-person-nervous? Never.

Vanessa Moore, soon to be Callaghan, remembered she had stored my number in her phone even after two, probably three, bottles of rather sublime rioja. I'd received a text on Sunday making plans for a coffee date, now a cocktail date on Wednesday. As lovely as she'd been and and friendly as her text had translated, I was nervous and that wasn't me.

Putting my finger on why I felt this way wasn't easy. There was nothing in mine and Victoria's short history that suggested we wouldn't get along: we'd had a couple of great evenings together; at the ball we'd been rather hysterical over something both brothers did—a point I couldn't quite remember but it concerned their penises—and the texts we'd exchanged had been humorous and self-deprecating in part.

The bar where we'd arrange to meet was busy, as was most of London at this time. I'd spent the day alternating between lecturing and teaching in seminars, so my dress wasn't quite office attire and more me—fitted, low cut with knee high boots, which the weather was now cool enough to let me wear.

A low whistle greeted me from a shaded table, away from the melee of the rest of the bar. "You look all kinds of fuckable, as my friend Sophie would say."

I turned and smiled, seeing Vanessa dressed in a cute three-piece suit, the shirt with a low neckline. "I feel all *studented*. By which, I mean talked to death and I have barely any words left."

"Then let's bring on the cocktails and see what they'll give back. I've promised Jackson I'll have three then meet him to go home. I hope you don't mind. Or if we're still drinking and it gets to seven, he's turning up. It's poker night at ours and a long story." She rolled her eyes. "Men. Actually, not even men. Just those brothers and Killian."

I nodded. "Max dropped off a key at my offices while I was in a lecture. He texted to say he might be late back."

"But I bet he said he'd try to be out quickly so he could get home?" she said, smiling knowingly. "I heard him grumbling this morning that he hadn't seen you since Monday morning."

"Really?" I tried to stop my heart from speeding up but quickly realised it was something I couldn't control. "I've been staying with my friend Jacob. It didn't seem fair to Max to impose for more than a couple of days, especially since I've only known him three weeks or so."

"Yeah to all that and he was referring to the same sort of thing when Jackson and Seph were teasing him, but he's been grumpier than normal since Monday so my guess is that he'd rather have you at his than you be at Jacob's," Vanessa said with a grin As two Long Island Iced Teas were deposited on our table. "It's two for one. This seemed like something no one could dislike and there's lots of alcohol."

I made an agreeable noise given that my lips were already on the straw and I was sucking up the drink like a porn star. "What about Claire?" I asked when I'd quenched my initial thirst.

"She's running a bit late. And she's on some no drinking kick. So where's the apartment you've rented?"

I gave her the address and a description of the place. It really was nothing amazing, but it meant I could move all my stuff into somewhere that wasn't full of mould and I wouldn't have to walk too far to work.

"You didn't consider staying with Max long term?" Vanessa said, a wicked smile growing.

I knew a comment like this would be brought up. She was digging for information and she was going to be disappointed.

"We're just having fun," I said. "And he got me out of a fix by letting me stay for a few nights. I don't have to go back to the hovel—my new place will be ready at the weekend as it came vacant suddenly. Max has been great."

She took a long drag of her cocktail, watching me with interest. "You do seem pretty keen on each other. At the ball on Friday you didn't seem like a couple who had just hooked up."

"It feels like we've known each other for longer than we have, but we've spent a lot of time texting and emailing. He's a good man." I felt a pull in my stomach as I spoke about him. Max was the cream in my coffee; he sweetened my day and made it more palatable. I'd had boyfriends and lovers before, but no one significant had ever rocked my world, or my bed. "But I'm not in the market for a long term relationship."

Heel clipped against the stone floor. "Does that translate to 'he's boring in bed and can't keep it up for more than three minutes?' I hope so, because I can't wait to share it next time we have dinner." Claire sat down next to me. "Please tell me the vanilla rumours are true?"

"You really want me to talk about what your brother's like in bed?" I said, turning to her. She was dressed immaculately: neat tailored suit, bobbed hair and make-up that was barely there. She glowed.

"I've been listening to stories about my brothers' sex lives since I was thirteen and Max's girlfriend at the time was my best friend's older sister. She described in the greatest detail just how boring my brother was in bed. I hope for your sake he's improved." Claire sat down, putting what looked like a glass of lime soda in front of her.

"How much detail do you want?" I threw out the challenge.

"If he's making your eyes roll to the back of your head on a regular basis then not much as there's no fun for me in that," she said, checking her phone.

"By the look on your face, I take it he's doing his job at hitting the spot," Vanessa said. "Jackson knows his way around my G-spot. If Max is anything like him, you'll never need to pay for another massage again. I swear my resting pulse rate dropped after we got together."

"I'd like to say Killian's had the same effect," Claire said, staring at her glass. "But since we got together it's been a bit of a rollercoaster. Not that I'm really complaining."

The conversation drifted into a discussion about weddings and business and men. I chipped in when I could, finding out about their close-knit world and separating myself from it. As much as I liked Vanessa and Claire—and could've quite happily been friends with them both—it didn't make sense to develop those sorts of ties when I wasn't sure where I'd be living in less than twelve months' time.

"I've discovered having a day off from Jackson doesn't work," Vanessa said. "He just ends up grumpy and I wonder why I'm depriving myself. I've also no idea for how long we'll be like this. Give us a couple of years of being married and maybe a kid and I doubt we'll manage once a month."

Claire's face looked concerned. "I'm not sure that always applies. Friends of mine ended up with ten months between their two, so one baby mustn't have put them off. I suppose it's down to the individuals."

"Another drink?" I said, looking to Vanessa first. I had my suspicions about why Claire wasn't drinking, the topic of conversation being a big clue.

She eyed her empty glass. "I'll have another one of these. Jackson texted to say he and Max are on their way here before poker night."

"I'm staying on my health kick. Trying to prove I can stop drinking when I'm not on a case," Claire said, sipping her drink and trying not to pull a face.

I headed to the bar, conflicting thoughts pinging around my head. I hadn't had a group of girl friends since my undergraduate degree, but I already felt uncomfortable enough about forming something on false pretences. I needed to feel comfortable with the situation to have any chance of being myself and if I didn't loosen up, they'd start to question why the hell Max was dating someone like me.

I clutched the bar for balance as warm hands grasped my waist and a familiar scent stopped me from turning around and kneeing my captor in the dick. Which, to be fair, he would've deserved but I had no intention of spoiling my own fun.

"You've survived my sister," Max said. "Who is drinking lime soda. That means she's at her least pleasant."

I turned around and he let one of his hands drop, seeming a little less possessive. "Any ideas why she's not having something alcoholic?"

"Some," he said, giving nothing else away. "I'm hoping you're staying with me tonight."

"If you're okay with that. I get the keys for my new apartment on Saturday, so if I can stay till then…"

"That's fine," he said, bending his head for a quick kiss. "I'll help you move and check it's safe."

"It even has a door that locks," I said, unable to take my eyes away from his.

"Added bonus," Max said. "Can we have three pints of Punk IPA? And I'll get whatever the lady's ordered."

I dug him in the ribs with my elbow. "I can afford a round of drinks, you know."

He chuckled. "I know. But I like feeling manly. Don't deprive me of it."

"I can think of other ways to help you feel manly." My hand slid to the front of his trousers and grazed his cock and he emitted a low rumble.

"Poker starts in half an hour," he said. "I'm usually grumpy. Do that again and I'll be even worse."

Smiling sweetly, I took my drink and stepped away from him. "I'll keep my hands to myself then. Maybe make good use of them while I cosy down in your bed and read a book, you know, one of those contemporary romance things."

Max groaned. "Maybe I'll miss poker."

———

There's a point when two cats, new to each other, make eye contact and the gaze between them seems like a fixed, unmovable point in time that even the distraction of a mouse or cheese or one of those red dot laser pens couldn't shift.

I was observing one of those stares now, but it wasn't one between two cats silently deciding whether one was going to submit to the other or they were going to have to yowl it out, probably loudly and with some demonstration of claws.

Only this wasn't cats or even tigers. This was two, allegedly grown, men.

"That table can just go here," I directed, hoping to break whatever silent conversation they were having. "Just here. It'll probably need the two of you to… Never mind."

Max lifted the table by himself in a blindingly obvious show of strength. Not to be defeated, Jacob picked up an antique wooden chair. "Where do you want this?"

"Well, I'd like it in one piece," I said under my breath. "Next to the bookcase. It's my reading chair." It was a piece of history, my history, the place where I'd sat on my grandad's knee while he told me stories of the Armada and Good Queen Bess and Mary Queen of Scots. If Jacob's take on the World's Strongest Man meant it was going to be damaged, I'd be showing him my strength in the area of batshit crazy.

"I'll just get my tool kit out of the car," Max said, looking slightly dishevelled after moving the table. "I'll start to put your bed together."

"I can do that after," Jacob said. "I dismantled it so I know where everything needs to go."

"Given that I'll be *sleeping* in it and you won't, I'd rather make sure it is as stable as possible..."

I turned around from emptying my books onto my bookcase and hands headed straight to my hips. Shakespeare's note about Hermia—'though she may be little, she is fierce'—was about to be defined by me not just losing the plot but rewriting the whole fucking thing and having it bound in leather.

"This. Stops. Now," I shouted. It was midday on a Saturday. If my neighbours were being disturbed, then good, they should be making the most of the weekend. "All goddamn morning both of you have been like a pair of cockerels just waiting for the farmer to turn his back so you can start trying to pull each other's feathers out and I'm fed up of it!

"Max—Jacob is gay. He would much rather have you naked in that bed than me, so stop trying to piss all over your territory. Jacob—back the fuck down. Just because I'm having sex with someone does not mean you have to act all possessive and jealous. I can be having sex with someone and still be your friend—although maybe not both at the same time because that would be a different level of kink than I'm used to."

Both men stood in front of me with their hands in their pockets, jaws slightly dropped.

"So can we please drop the alpha male urinating contest and maybe just concentrate on getting that van unloaded and my stuff in some kind of place so I can actually get on with unpacking and not having to oversee who's pissing where?"

They glanced at each other, the cat staring competition declared a draw. They would share territory, just not for the same purpose.

"Shall we bring the sideboard in?" Jacob said.

The sideboard had been one of my grandmother's prized possessions. When she was annoyed with my grandad, she would polish it until it glistened. When I had a second look around the apartment with Max two days ago, I'd realised I'd be able to take a bit of the furniture out of storage, as it was a bigger space than the hovel. The sideboard, bookcase and chair had been my less than practical selection.

"Good plan. We can get the bigger pieces set up then," Max said, hands still in his pockets.

"Excellent. You're playing nice. Keep it up for the next few hours."

As I emptied the boxes of books, the men brought in my furniture and then my suitcases full of clothes and shoes. Jacob passed stereotypical comments about me having more heels than a drag queen. I ignored him, my hands rediscovering treasured texts and novels. For some people, it was the smell of books; for me, it was how they felt, their weight, the texture of the pages against my fingers and smoothness of the covers.

"Feisty lady, come see how we've set up your bedroom."

I looked up to see Max, his T-shirt slightly sweaty, hair mussed. He looked serious and hopeful at the same time, as if he was worried I wouldn't like what they'd done.

I smiled, putting another book in its right place. "You've not murdered each other then?"

He dropped his head to one side, something I noticed he did when he was amused. "He's all right. Are you sure he's gay?"

"Very," I said. "I've met several of his one-night stands. Plus, I was his try out to see if he really didn't like girls when we were eighteen, and trust me, he doesn't know how to kiss a woman."

Max pulled his face. "You kissed him? Did you like him in that way?"

I laughed. "No. But we were drunk and he was curious. And I suppose I was too. I wanted to see if I could make him succumb to my female charms. He didn't. I was lacking a certain important part."

"Good. That you were lacking that part. You didn't feel bad because he didn't want to, you know?"

I tried to stop my smile at his uncomfortableness. "I've never lacked confidence with men, Max. One knock-back from someone who preferred bigger biceps and smaller pecs than mine didn't do me any lasting damage." For someone who was keen on the dirty talk, he was struggling with this. "Let's see what you've done to my boudoir."

The bed had been assembled, the wardrobe and a set of huge chest of drawers somehow guided through the door. My bed had been made and cushions arranged on it artfully, which had to have been Jacob's doing; Max didn't do cushions. One of the paintings I'd brought from storage had been hung exactly where I'd have chosen to put it and my standing mirror angled so it was away from direct light.

They stood like two schoolboys waiting to be praised and I wondered if they'd let me take a photo and send it to their families.

"It looks amazing. I don't know how you managed to get the drawers through the door. I thought they'd have to go in the hall or back in storage."

They grinned at each other and Jacob glanced at the window which had more finger marks on the glass than it had before. I decided not to ask any more questions, then I could deny all knowledge when I tried to get my deposit back.

"Teamwork," Max said, and I threw a cushion at him.

"I think I should buy you both a beer. I've done enough unpacking for now any way," I said, feeling the urge for a large glass of red wine or even a bottle.

Jacob shook his head. "I have to go and get showered. It's my monthly meal with the judge and I need to at least try to look presentable so he doesn't disinherit me. Besides, you probably want to check out the stability of the bed."

Max sniggered, maintaining the whole school boy vibe he was giving off.

I flung my arms around Jacob and thanked him profusely,

making him promise to come back the next day and help me sort my wardrobe.

"Now I'm convinced he's not interested in you," Max said when Jacob agreed, offering a makeover with my clothes.

I knew when I was packing that I was in need of losing a few of my previous favourite outfits as they were definitely past wearing in public.

"Too right," Jacob said. "You're far more my type. Let me know if you ever want an alternative experience."

Jacob gave him a flirtatious wink and dramatically exited, all signs of the alpha male well and truly buried. He enjoyed both roles: I suspected his affairs did too.

"Shall we go for a walk?" Max said, trying to neaten his hair that was stuck up in varying directions. "Isn't your grandfather's house near?"

I took the opportunity to put my arms around him, feeling muscles that had been used for lifting and carrying. "It's about a half-hour walk away. There are a couple of bars on the way though."

"I'd like to see it," he said, his arms around me, his hands on my ass. Apart from my boobs, my ass was definitely his favourite. I now had a bite mark or two there from Thursday night.

"I'll take you there."

We grabbed jackets as the weather was now feeling autumnal and headed off through the streets of south London, the Saturday tourists thinning out as we walked through the more residential areas.

My grandfather's house was a detached property, set back from the road with a large driveway. I hadn't been there since it had been sold, not having been ready to revisit some of most difficult days of my life when I was looking after him, knowing the inevitable end. Max made me braver. I wasn't a coward and common sense and practical actions were how I'd managed through a childhood that wasn't the most conventional, but he made me act instead of dwell.

The house had been bought by a company that renovated properties, flipping them and selling them for a profit. The builder's board was up outside but looked weathered. Half the windows had been replaced, the other half still looked like a pencil being poked at them would put them through.

My grandad had known that the house needed modernising: a new kitchen, bathrooms, windows, roof, but he'd never got around to it, a book or exhibition at a museum always being more important and in his last year it had been important to keep the house as he remembered it. My grandmother had still been in every room with its décor and furniture and neither of us had wanted those touches to be eradicated.

"How does it look?"

"Half finished. Do you think we can go inside?"

"Only if you know a way in that won't be locked," he said, looking only slightly concerned at breaking and entering.

"Through the cellars," I said. "Unless someone has replaced the doors down there they won't be locked." He looked hesitant. "If we get caught I'll talk us out of any trouble. Or flash them my boobs. That usually works."

I grabbed his arm and pulled him down the driveway while his mouth was still chewing on what words to say.

"Tell me you've never done that to get you out of trouble," he said, when speech finally returned.

We were finally at the outside steps that led down to the cellars, although they were almost covered with a garden that had been left to develop into a small, London jungle.

"If I did, I'd be lying," I told him, jiggling the door and yanking it up. There was a groan and it moved inwards, creaking ominously. "This was why I learned what WD40 was for. When I was a teenager and wanted to sneak outside at night I had to make sure this door was well oiled."

He studied me in the half darkness of the cellar. "If you ever have daughters you realise everything you did will be doubled by them."

"I look forward to them trying," I said. "It'll keep me young and quick-witted. These were the cellars. We would've converted them I suppose, or should've. A wine cellar and a cinema room."

"Or a gym," he said, using the torch on his phone to look around the room.

"Not something I've ever used. I get my exercise through other means."

Max's arm flicked around me and pulled me into his side. His fingers dipped down the waistband on my jeans and he nuzzled into my hair. "I'll help you out with that later. We need to test how sturdy that bed is."

"Want to try and break it? I wouldn't mind an excuse for a new one," I said, untangling myself and leading him through the antechambers to the stairs.

The first floor had been gutted, some rooms down to brick. A whole rewire had been completed, it seemed, but the plastering hadn't been finished. "This was the snug," I told Max. "That's where the chair I've got now used to be, with the bookcase next to it. This was my grandfather's—and my—favourite room."

We walked through and he listened to me telling stories of what had happened in each room: the day my grandad set fire to the kitchen and the black mark was still visible on the old tiles; the time I fell down the stairs when the tray I'd been trying to race down on had caught the carpet and sent me flying; the night I hid a boyfriend in the kitchen larder. He didn't like the latter, judging by the look on his face.

"How would you have it now. What would you change?"

I laughed. I would be able to afford to buy it back and redo it now, thanks to Max and his brother. "I'd knock through the dining room in to the kitchen and have it open plan. Extend out into the garden with Velux windows and bi-fold doors." I described my dream house as we walked through and he listened carefully.

"What about décor? Light fittings and wallpaper?"

"Wouldn't have a clue. I like greys and soft pinks. Other than that I'd have someone like your sister to advise. Then I'd have cushions. Lots of cushions."

"Why do you need lots of fucking cushions?" he said. "What is this female obsession with padded bits of material? My sister's got so many of them you can't sit on the fucking sofa."

I giggled, leaning in to him. "Makes it comfier," I said. "Especially when you consider spending time on your knees."

"Time on your knees doing what?" he said, looking about as innocent as a widow on her seventh husband.

"I could show you, but I need to ascertain you'll return the favour."

"I'm more than happy to, but why the cushions?"

"Keep your knees comfier. Increases staying power."

"If that's the case," he said. "I'm all for cushions in the future."

CHAPTER 15
MAXWELL

Standing in front of a half renovated detached monstrosity on a freezing cold Tuesday morning in November was not what I'd envisaged nearly three months ago when I'd been eyeing up houses to buy online. I'd expected a town house with a small, easily maintained garden, not something with an overgrown jungle where I could possibly find an odd village or two hiding away and minding their own business as they grew in size thanks to the orchard that had also taken over the fence at the bottom of the garden.

"So, this is it?" Ava stood next to me with her hands in her pockets. She was wearing a beanie hat pulled low on her head and a large scarf that covered most of her chin. She was my youngest sibling, the most spoilt and the smallest. I knew she still got asked for ID in bars, yet she wasn't afraid to have stand up rows using a lot of expletives with foremen on building sites. She scared most people.

This was possibly the most stupid idea I'd had to date.

Victoria didn't know I was here, looking at buying her child-hood home. If she knew, she'd probably put me straight into stalker territory and send my house key back to me via a bodyguard with the message to stay the fuck away. I didn't know why I was here, well, I did, but I wasn't ready to admit to all of it.

"This is it. I don't need your summary of my personal life, just your view on the renovation: what it will cost and what will be the potential sale value afterwards," I said, not looking at her. Instead, my eyes were on the solid wood front door with its stained-glass window. I'd been round twice since sneaking in with Victoria, both times with an agent who tried to sell the property with its period features and huge square footage. But what had persuaded me to come back with the keys were Victoria's stories. Even now, a couple of months after we'd broken in, she would tell me where certain items in her apartment had been at the house and the tale behind them.

We didn't spend every night together; both of us were busy and other commitments were regular occurrences in our diaries, but there had yet to be a night where I had opted to stay on my own rather than with her. It was effortless: we clicked.

So I was looking at her childhood home and wondering what the fuck I was doing.

"You're getting my summary of your personal life, Maxwell," Ava said, pushing me towards the door. "And then I'll tell you about this house and what I could do to it for you to either live in or sell on. I've always said you should start investing in flipping houses. Maybe not with your first one having such a big price tag though."

I unlocked the doors and we stepped into a dusty entrance way. Most of the walls lacked plaster, there were no light fixings and some floorboards were missing.

"You really like Victoria and you don't want her to move away. If you buy this house, you're hoping she'll choose to stay, which is the wrong reason," Ava said, starting to poke around at walls before she moved to lift a floorboard using some strange tool she had in her coat pocket.

"I'm not going to tell her if I do. If she decides to stay, I'll tell her then. If she goes, I'll probably sell it once it's finished." I looked at the banister and thought about her sliding down it. Given half the chance she'd probably do it again.

Ava stood up straight and looked at me in a semi-intimidating manner, which given there was over a foot difference in our height was quite comical. "Maxwell, the control freak and planner, is letting a woman dictate decisions about his future. That's a new one for all of us."

It was for me too. I woke up either with Victoria tucked around me or thinking about her being tucked around me. If she wasn't with me in the morning, I'd send her a message, or there'd be one from her. She had become the protein in my diet and I was aware that I was starting to put myself out on a very insecure and flammable line. "I like her. But maybe that's because she's more than likely moving away so it can't get serious."

Ava shrugged her shoulders. "Whatever. I'm here to drink whisky with you if she breaks your heart or babysit for you if you end up breeding. As long as you name your firstborn girl after me."

"I'm not having children," I said, now looking around the gutted kitchen. The old units had pretty much all been torn out with just some fucking awful green tiles left.

Ava shook her head. "Just because your mum had postnatal depression doesn't mean that the woman you marry or live with will have the same. And you are not our father. Out of everyone, it's you who knows when we're down or sad. There's no way you wouldn't support someone you loved."

My little sister had lived in almost awe of me since she was old enough to know who I was. I'd fed her as a baby, changed her, walked her to school, helped her with her homework, and because of the nine-year age difference had been more like an uncle than a big brother. Now, she was bigger and more confident, bossing men twice her size about and this was the first time she'd ever told me what she thought about me.

"It's more complicated than that," I said.

"Bullshit! You don't need to overcook the crap with me, Max. You've always been scared you're like Dad with everything, not just work. Don't do yourself out of being happy because of a little fear. Now, if you bought this, what would you think about knocking the fuck out of that wall and opening this up so you had an open plan kitchen-slash-diner? You could put a breakfast bar in and have an island in the middle, leaving you room for a fucking humongous dining table there." She pointed through the wall to the back of the house. "And still an area for a corner sofa and TV. If you wanted to go whole hog, I'd extend out into the garden—fuck knows there's enough space—and have Velux windows, bi-fold doors. Get wooden flooring down and a feature wall there. Actually, fuck that, I'd stick in a wood burning stove. Right, other rooms."

I followed her back into the hall as she tapped wooden panels, examined doors and swore a lot.

"This would be a great snug. Put a desk in here and book-cases, some comfy chairs and make the most of that fireplace. A big decorative mirror on that wall there. Fuck, I'd love this room." She continued upstairs, describing in graphic detail what she'd do to the bathroom, how she'd create a wet room down-stairs and add two en suites. The cellars were something else. Two hours later when we were locking the front door I felt as if I'd just spent five hours in a mediation.

"So, what's your overall verdict?"

"I think you need to buy me breakfast," Ava said. "I can give you some rough costings too. And I can also tell you if you don't buy it, I will."

———

The Star and Garter pub nearby did all day breakfasts and posh versions of classic London dishes, most of which I'd never tried. Jellied eels weren't my idea of a tasty snack, no matter how persuasive the waiter tried to be.

Ava downed her coffee before it had even had a chance to experience cool air. "I think you've made your mind up already," she said. "So part of what you want to talk about is null and void. The house is up for a steal, plus they have done some of the heavy work already with the rewiring and modernising the plumbing and heating systems. The roof needs replacing and the floorboards need a good looking over, but aside from that it's structurally sound. The remaining fixes are primarily cosmetic." She gave me a figure that didn't blow me away and added another few numbers for the interior decoration. "But that will need to be a conversation with Victoria."

"I'm not telling her. Once we've completed on the property, it's over to you and your team. You do what needs doing," I said, making the stupid mistake of checking my phone to see twenty-seven emails waiting for me.

"Max, if anyone else designed mum's kitchen, what would her response have been?"

I looked away from my phone. "She'd have skewered them and put them in the oven with a bit of sage."

"Correct."

"So what you're saying is that Victoria needs to have an input?"

"Well done. First prize for being astute."

The blank look I wore was probably the first since Marie had explained the menstrual cycle to me in defence of why Claire was being such a moody ass. As it turned out, it had nothing to do with Claire's menstrual cycle and everything to do with her being generally moody. Not much had changed.

"Maxwell, be smart. Finance this renovation for me. I can ask Victoria's opinion on things like bathrooms and the kitchen and the garden and then you're not outright lying to her," Ava said, gesturing wildly to the waiter for more coffee. I got the feeling that my little sister drank her bodyweight in caffeine on a daily basis.

"Even the windows. They need to be something more in keeping with the style of the house and the period when it was built."

"Slow down," I said. "Let me think about this."

"Has Victoria mentioned buying it herself?"

My phone vibrated with a call. I ignored it. "She thought about it, but because she doesn't know if she'll get a job in London or America after her PhD, she didn't want to commit."

"Then she won't be mad if I'm taking it on as a restoration project?"

"No, but I'll tell her. So temper down your enthusiasm."

"How quick can you get it bought?"

"Fairly. It's a cash buy." We'd been lucky financially to have trust funds from our parents that had grown with careful investments and savings from our drawings as partners in the company. But our money was old money: we didn't flash it around or brag, and big spends such as houses and cars were considered, not impulsive.

This wasn't impulsive. I'd thought about it while Vanessa curled around my side, her head on my chest, hair spread everywhere. I'd thought about it while she'd made breakfast and I'd ranted about the incompetence of the opposing lawyers in a current case. I'd thought about it while I had been buried balls deep inside her, feeling her muscles clench around my cock as she came.

Knowing why I was buying her childhood home was not neuroscience. The woman had me wrapped around whatever piece of her anatomy she wanted and I'd done what I'd always sworn not to.

"Tell her today," Ava said. "Get the ball rolling."

———

Air that was definitely wintery bit at our skin as we sat by the river, the familiar skyline towering over us and a sheet of stars above. Because I was cautious, and probably on the scared side of confident—although I'd never admit that to anyone—I'd left it until the sale on the sale had completed and the deeds were in my name before telling Victoria what I'd done. Ava had delegated her other projects to various employees that seemed to be joining her at a rate faster than the Thames in a thunderstorm and had started on the house that morning. The roof, plastering and floors were first, followed by ripping out a couple of walls and adding some more.

"I love mulled wine," Victoria said, her hands cupping a mug of the stuff through fingerless mittens. "It's my favourite thing about winter."

"Mulled wine?" I chuckled. She was sitting between my legs, my arms were wrapped around her, trying to keep her warm in the December chill. "There must be other reasons to love winter. Christmas?"

"I'm looking forward to seeing Lewis and visiting Johns Hopkins," she said. "And I like being wrapped up, although I'd give up my mulled wine for a real fire to sit by and read."

She'd made arrangements to visit her mentor and friend in America for Christmas. She had no family to spend it with and Jacob was going skiing with his father and brother. I was heading to Ontario and my parents' winery to spend Christmas in the house they had bought over there. We'd be on the same continent but still thousands of miles apart.

"Speaking of real fires." It seemed like a good way to start the topic of my new purchase, and it was potentially the opening as to why they'd later find my body in the river. "I've just bought a house for Ava to renovate."

"Really? You didn't say you were planning on doing that. Not that you needed to tell me."

I nuzzled between her scarf and coat and kissed the back of her neck. "You might not like this."

She swung around and eyed me.

"Maxwell Callaghan. If I'm going to be mad, aren't we best being in private for you know, afterwards?"

We were sitting outside a bar, on a large, wide wall. There were plenty of people passing by so she had a point. We argued, disagreed. I knew exactly what buttons to press to rile her but the aftermath was worth it. When she couldn't get her words out she used her body instead.

"But if we're in public you can't kill me."

"Tell me."

She'd never demanded anything of me before, apart from 'harder' and 'more'.

"It's your old house."

"Oh."

She turned back around to watch the river, the crests of waves catching the light. I inhaled the scent of her hair, my body reacting like it usually did but I kept my hands around her waist, giving her time to think about what I'd done.

"I'm glad it was you who bought it," she said quietly. "I worried that someone would buy it and not—not respect it. I know you'll make it a good family house for someone to live in."

"You don't think it's strange?"

She sighed, her body relaxing against mine. "Kind of. But you're a businessman and it was going for a song. With Ava renovating it, you'll make a good profit when it goes back on the market."

My hands were clammy even in the cool temperature and I felt my stomach turn. "Ava wants to ask you for ideas on a few bits. You know the house well and she thinks that will be important," I said, unsure as to how she would react. Victoria had been honest from the start about her goals and her ideals and dreams. Her passion and impulsiveness and honesty didn't just draw me to her, they had kept me hanging around like a bee needing more of her sweet nectar.

She leaned back into me. "I think I'd enjoy that. Tell her to text me when it's convenient to go round. I could dig out some old photos that were taken in the house and maybe put a scrapbook together so that the owners know of its history."

"Do you ever not think about history?" I said. "I'm beginning to think your grandad brainwashed you."

"Probably," she said. "There's something else I'm thinking about though." She turned herself around and pushed her lips to mine, moving her scarf out of the way. "Can you taste mulled wine?"

"I need to check again," I said, this time making the kiss deeper and tasting as much as I could of her. "Shall we go back to mine and we can see how long the taste lasts for?" I kissed her again, softly biting her bottom lip and hearing her moan. "And then I can see if the taste can be found elsewhere."

"I like that idea. And Max?"

I stood up, pulling her with me. "What, Feisty?"

"I'm not mad about the house. Maybe a little sad it's not me living there."

The only words I knew I could say would've landed me in unchartered waters without a compass or paddle, so I kissed her again and then took her home, using every shortcut I knew.

We were about five minutes from my apartment—three if I could rush her any more—when I figured someone was behind us, someone who wanted to stay unnoticed. My first thought was that it was her brother who, despite my threats and advice of his lawyer, was still contacting Victoria, although it was becoming less frequent.

I stopped, turning her round swiftly and backtracked until we came to a narrow alleyway.

It had a gate at the end of it, so there was nowhere for our follower to go and aside from someone breathing noisily, the darkness kept everything else hidden. Using my phone's torch— thank fuck for technology—I lit up the face of Peter Coffey.

He had recently moved into my seminar group, the Thursday night one, although that had finished now for the Christmas period. His coat was a thick and expensive down thing and the glasses he wore looked like the designer shit Seph wore when he didn't need to.

I kept an arm around Victoria's waist and stretched to my full six foot three. Somehow I was still finding time to visit the gym with Jackson; that and a bit of playing with my macros had meant I'd bulked out a bit more in the past few weeks and I knew I didn't look like you average law professor.

"Why are you following us?"

"Are you okay, Peter?" Victoria said.

I wished I could have some protective detail put on her. She'd broken up a fight last week between two very drunk idiots and the thought of her short ass being hurt by anyone had given me a slight aneurysm and caused an argument. Which had led to me fucking her brains out while her hands were tied to my bed. A good time had been had by all, several good times if you were Victoria.

His eyes lit up as she spoke to him and then focused solely on her. "I just wanting to speak to you."

I fucking bet he did. Carol had mentioned he was hanging around the law office a bit too much. "So if you wanted to speak to Victoria, why didn't you call her instead of following us like a creeper?"

Now his eyes flickered from side to side and then to the floor. Knowing my woman, she'd have picked up on this and would now be feeling sorry for him.

"It's okay, Peter. Max was just startled by someone following us. Is everything all right?" She put a hand on his arm and he fucking glowed, watching her bare fingers.

"Just wanted to check a deadline, but it's okay. I shouldn't have disturbed you, it being a Friday and you not being at work," he stuttered. "Can you let me go? I have a… I have an, err, date."

I shifted to the wall next to Victoria, keeping her pulled into me. Peter scuttled like a rabid rat and I waited until he was hopefully a good distance away before we headed off.

"Like fuck he has a date," I said, more to myself than Victoria.

"He might," she said, sliding her hand down to mine. "He's just a bit fragile, I think. And he worries about his essays and referencing things right."

Every muscle in me had tensed and I really hoped no fucker decided to surprise me right now. I'd had a similar instinct when I was younger and trying to look after Payton and Seph when we were in London one weekend and a strange man kept looking at them on the tube, only this time it was fierce and burning. It didn't take a genius to work out that it was directly connected to the woman who was starting to consume me. "Vic, he's finding excuses to come and see you. He finds you on a Friday evening and tells you it's about deadlines? Why the fuck not just send you an email or look it up online?"

"He barely knows anyone, he's transferred from probably his dream university and come here—cut him some slack. I know he's a bit too reliant on me, but I'm ten years older than him and probably more. He's looking for a friend." Her hand still clasped mine although she sounded frustrated with me.

I avoided telling her that she shouldn't be so friendly, determined to never be one of those men who told their woman what to do. "How often does he visit his *friend*?"

"Once every couple of days, maybe. He will pop in with a coffee or sweets for everyone."

"Everyone or just you?"

"Well, he gives them to me and I share them so…"

I unlocked the door to my apartment block, still holding onto her hand. I debated how to phrase my next few words, aware of the firework show I could be lighting. "Victoria, I think he likes you and I think he reckons you like him back if you're being nice to him and accepting his gifts."

She laughed as we went upstairs. "Maxwell," she said, pausing as I opened the door. Then her arms went around me and she pressed close. "Do you think you might be a bit jealous?"

I grabbed her ass. "I'm not jealous."

She laughed, pushing me back so she could start to unzip my coat. "I think you are."

"I'm worried."

"Because you're jealous!"

Her own coat was now on the floor of the entrance hall with her mittens and where her jeans and jumper would be shortly.

"I'm not jealous. Do you want me to show you what I do to people who call me jealous?"

Her pupils dilated and her centre pushed to mine, pressing her heat against my rapidly hardening cock.

"Will it hurt?'

"Only when I bite."

―――――

I had her safely tucked into my bed a while later, looking sated and happy and not thinking about that fuckwit of a student. We were lying face to face, a position we liked to start off in and then move, because it wasn't the most comfortable to sleep in. She was still naked, her smooth skin warm against mine, her tits pressed against my chest. They were my fucking obsession and I wasn't sure I'd ever get over it. She was slim and curvy, a ball of feistiness encapsulated in the most divine woman I'd ever met and I didn't want to let her go.

But I would have to at some point. I was my father's son and I couldn't do a relationship, not a serious one that would conclude with marriage and babies. I imagined myself and Victoria on holiday by the beach with a couple of kids, me teaching one to swim in the sea while she collected shells with the other. Or more likely, she'd be in the sea with all of us, ducking us under and telling tales of sharks and mermaids because she was full of energy and life.

Even asleep she looked as if she was somewhere exciting, that even her dreams contained as much joy as she usually felt in her job, her love of history and people.

I smoothed her hair back from her face and she muttered something before her eyes flickered opened.

"Max," she muttered, starting to turn over, still in my arms.

"Vic," I said, tucking her ass into me, spooning her and holding her.

"Stop staring at me and go the fuck to sleep."

I laughed quietly because that was my girl: astute even when asleep.

CHAPTER 16
VICTORIA

"There's the job here and I believe there's one at Stamford going too," Lewis said. "Maybe you should apply for both."

"And maybe," Clyde chastised, "you shouldn't talk about work over the Christmas period."

I smiled. Clyde, Lewis' partner, was the best I'd ever known at stopping Lewis from persistently researching or writing. We'd managed to make it through most of Christmas Day without getting on to our favourite topic. "Victoria needs to consider her options. Of course, you could stay in London. You sound like you're getting roots there now."

"What do you mean?" I said, sipping a glass of merlot. It had been a blissful two days. Lewis had instructed me to change my plane ticket to fly to New York instead, as he and Clyde had decided to have the holiday there, renting a suite in a hotel. Clyde did something in marketing—I had made a note to pass on his details to Vanessa—and had always wanted to spend Christmas in New York and New Year's in Times Square.

"You've talked a lot about Max, and Jackson who helped you with the will. And I know you're still friends with Jacob. Plus, your colleagues in the law department. It's the first time since I've known you that you've had a wider circle than Jacob and other history students," Lewis said, straightening the tie he'd insisted he wore.

We'd eaten Christmas dinner in a restaurant near the hotel and were now relaxing with our food comas.

"I have to look for the best options," I said. "That always looked like the States, at least for a couple of years." Although there were reasons to stay in London—a tall, muscular one in particular.

"Having you over here would be great, especially if it's Johns Hopkins. We could kick some historical ass together," Lewis said, a geeky look on his face. He'd been a great mentor and friend while I was studying and I had been devastated when he'd moved away. But as he'd reminded me, we had the internet and WiFi and text messages so there was no reason to not be as close as we'd become, but distance still changed things.

He and Clyde spoke of people I didn't know and referred to events I was unaware of and I'd started to wonder whether looking for tenure at Johns Hopkins was just a pipe dream that had helped me get through the worst of times with my grandad and then my brother. But my grandad had thought it was a wonderful idea: to work in a different country and study the subject he'd had such a passion for.

Clyde eyed him knowingly. "Then you have to be honest about everything," he said to Lewis. "It's not fair to her."

"It's Christmas Day and you've already told me off for talking about work," Lewis said, taking a corkscrew to another bottle of red wine.

"I'll allow that without an argument."

Lewis rolled his eyes dramatically. "I'm only staying at Johns Hopkins for another year then we're looking for a move up to New York or even Toronto. Although if you were offered the job then we'd have a good year together."

Starting somewhere new without knowing many people didn't scare me. I had enough confidence in myself to know I'd get along wherever I went. Yes, there'd always be bitches and people who wanted to drag you down but they were easily dealt with, as I'd learnt with Francis. "Let's see if the job becomes available and if I get it first," I said, taking a swig of the wine Clyde poured for me.

My phone vibrated and I itched to check it, but I didn't want to appear rude. The conversation diverted to British versus American Christmas traditions, and by default we started to educate Clyde about the history of the Christmas tree and yule logs. My phone vibrated another three times and I saw Clyde trying not to laugh.

"Just check it already, will you?" he said. "You keep mentioning this mysterious Max and I'm wondering if it's him."

I knew it would be him, or Seph or Vanessa. Since they'd left London to fly to Toronto I'd had regular messages from them and several photos: daft family ones with them all wearing pyjamas the day before Christmas Eve; one of Max scowling from Seph; Max and Jackson building a snowman which Seph and Payton destroyed minutes later.

Then there were ones from Max that were a little less family friendly: a photo of his fingers with a caption of 'guess where these would rather be' and more. I missed them. I missed Seph and his stupid grin and sensitive side where he would question himself on a regular basis. I missed Vanessa's friendliness and her attempts to draw me closer into having girlfriends—something that hadn't always been natural to me.

And I missed Max.

I pulled my phone out of my purse and saw more than the four messages I'd heard.

Max: Happy Christmas Day evening xo

Max: We've just opened presents. Seph excelled himself. He must've bought up the airport shops xo

Max: My parents have given us all shares in the winery, which kind of defeats the object. They also bought me and Jackson a really decent bottle of whisky which I'm now partaking of xo

Max: I expected bigger gifts because my family usually has no common sense and I didn't think they'd have considered suitcase space going home. I was wrong (this is unusual) so I might come to New York to buy some suits… xo

Max: Is your diary fully booked while you're there? Xo

There were separate messages from Seph, the first being a picture of Max that had been edited to put a party hat on him and changed his frown to a smile.

Seph: My brother misses you. Please get on a flight to Toronto and relieve us of his grumpy fuckwit self for a few days.

Seph: Someone to talk to with half a brain would also be welcomed.

Seph: And someone to talk to Vanessa and my mother about weddings as they're driving us mad.

> Seph: Payton's run off with the manager from a rival winery. She appeared briefly today, throwing stones at my bedroom window so I'd let her in at 5 this morning. She's just dived off again. My father is not happy unless she brings back 'top secret winery information'.

I had just finished reading when another message from Max appeared, this time a photo of a station masters' clock and informing me that his stepmother had found it at an antique's fair the weekend before.

> Me: Why are you sending me pictures of an old clock? Still, it's better than an old cock xx
>
> Max: Hilarious. You're an historian. I thought you'd appreciate something historical xo
>
> Me: I'd appreciate your cock more 8======>
>
> Max: You know where I am... (.)(.)

"I assume that's Max?" Lewis said. "The look on your face isn't one I recognise."

"And his brother."

"Kinky." Lewis raised his brows and smirked.

"It really isn't. I'm good friends with Seph. I think he's missing me," I said, wondering what Payton had got herself into. I'd met her several times, usually after work on a Friday when she'd torture the male population that she wasn't related to through flirting and being generally beautiful.

"How about Max? Is he missing you?" Lewis' voice was quiet and thoughtful.

"Some parts more than others, probably."

Lewis shook his head. "You shouldn't do yourself down, and if it's not that, then maybe you need to think about why you only want it to be about one thing."

"It's not just about one thing," I said defensively, although part of me was shocked that I said it. "He's a good guy. We get on really well." We did. He was the first person I called when something unusual happened, and he was the first person I wanted to see at the end of a busy day. He was fast becoming my best friend as well as my fuck-buddy, but that was all he was meant to be.

Lewis leaned over and topped up my glass. "How long have you been seeing him?"

"Just over three months. Not long."

"That's the longest you've ever been seeing the same person since I've known you."

"No," I said. "There was…" And there wasn't. Lewis was right. In the past four years I'd not seen the same man on a regular basis for more than about eight weeks, not that there had been many. The occasional one-night stand scratched an itch and there had been a couple of regular one-night stands, but that was it. "I suppose so. But this isn't the right time for this. And he's so career focused; I don't think he's interested in anything long term, which is fine, because I'm not either."

Lewis stood up and stretched, cracking his back and making me grimace. "Flights to Toronto are peanuts. Why don't you surprise him?"

I sat back, shocked. "Are you trying to get rid of me?"

He laughed loudly, causing Clyde to stick his head in from the bedroom. "Not in the slightest, but you've come all this way and you're here for a couple of weeks. Why not meet your man in Toronto, see his parents' winery, then bring him back here?

Clyde and I would like to meet him and you know we have to spend time at his parents for a couple of days."

That had been part of the reason for his change in plans when he said they were spending Christmas in New York. It was Clyde's sister's birthday and his family were gathering. Apparently there were loads of them and it was the first time Lewis had met most of them. I had been invited, but Lewis had suggested I made the most of my time with exploring and sightseeing rather than with Clyde's family, most of whom Lewis described as 'bizarre'.

"Bring him back for New Year."

It wasn't a bad idea and I didn't usually need much time to consider my actions.

"You're sure you don't mind?"

"As long as I get to meet him."

I pulled my phone out and opened my messages, going straight to Seph and texting him to see if he'd pick me up from the airport without telling Max. I figured if he was that fed up of his brother's moods—which, to be fair, could be fairly cranky—commandeering a car wouldn't be too much of an issue.

Almost an hour later I had a response and my eye on a flight the day after tomorrow.

Seph: That can be arranged. When?

Me: Tuesday? Landing at 13.05.

Seph: That's fine. I can borrow Dad's car. Are you really missing us all that much?

Seph: I knew you wouldn't be able to stay away. We're just magnetic.

Me: I'm more keen to sample the wine. Please let that be known. But not to Max.

Seph: As long as I can see his face when you turn up at the winery. And then ridicule him forever more. He's grumpy. Mum's already suggested it's because he's got blue balls.

Seph: That should give you fair warning of what mum's like, btw.

Me: I'll see you Tuesday at 13.30ish dependent on customs. I'm not discussing balls with you. That's wrong.

Seph: Just know that mine are better than his.

I decided not to contemplate that sentence and to concentrate on my wine instead.

———

Less than forty-eight hours later, Clyde dropped me off at JFK, picking up some distant relative at the same time who he was less than pleased to see.

"Enjoy yourself," he said. "Worth going up the CN Tower even if it's minus twenty-five. Get your man to keep you warm."

I'd given up arguing with them that he wasn't 'my man'. It was a pointless task as they just did it all the more.

"Enjoy your sister's birthday," I said, picking up my suitcase. I'd tried to fit everything into my hand luggage but the sweaters I'd packed to protect me against frostbite were too goddamn bulky.

He pulled his face. "Yeah. If I'm not here when you get back it's because I murdered Aunt Ivy and tried to dispose of her body in the Hudson. This is the sort of thing that murder stories are based on. Be glad you're escaping."

I stood on my tiptoes and kissed his smooth cheek. "You'll be fine. Lewis has the patience of a saint so he'll keep you sane."

He waved me off and I headed in to the airport, leaving him to navigate his way towards arrivals. I had questioned myself after booking the plane tickets: what if Max didn't want me there and this was all Seph seeing things that weren't there? What if I was intruding on his time with his family and he didn't want me to meet his parents? What if I ended up back in New York on an earlier flight and that was it, Max and I were over?

Practicality and rationality defeated doubts and insecurities in a battle that was over in the time it took for my plane to take off. If he didn't want me there, I'd stop in Toronto for a couple of nights, return to New York, shop the sales like a boss and indulge in lacy underwear and stupidly high heels. Then, I'dgo back to London no worse off. After all, I had a plan, and a man wasn't part of it.

Or so I told myself.

CHAPTER 17
MAXWELL

"This design would work well; given the themes you've chosen." I watched Vanessa work her magic with my dad the client, as opposed to her future father-in-law. She knew exactly what was needed for the branding for the winery and she would get him to make the right choice, all the time letting him believe it was all his idea. It was a skill I appreciated as I had never mastered it.

"What do you think, Maxwell?" His face looked less lined and his smile was genuine, something I'd not seen for years while he was working at the company. "Is that the one?"

Vanessa caught my eye, giving me a nod that told me if I didn't fucking agree she was going to extract my teeth and make me eat them, only she would be feeding them through another hole.

"I like how it's similar to the company's colours. And the font. It'll make it stand out."

"And the wine? Do you like the wine?"

I was holding a large glass of it and it was going down nicely. Getting back to the gym properly after the holidays was going to be fucking painful. I'd eaten and drank my bodyweight several times over in the past few days and was seriously considering checking myself into some sort of detox program.

"The wine's great. I've sampled enough of it."

"You need to have some shipped back for your girlfriend. Or ship her over here. It's been a long time since we've even heard about you seeing someone seriously. Marie's desperate to meet her." My father poured himself another glass.

I wondered if I needed to speak with Marie about arranging a six-monthly detox for him. There was definitely a bit of weight gain, which wasn't a bad thing as he'd worked himself gaunt at one point.

"Hold fire, Dad. Victoria and I get along really well, but she's got plans of moving over to America when she's finished her doctorate," I said. There'd be no hint from her that she was thinking of changing her mind, and that was becoming harder and harder to get my head around.

I hadn't seen her for a week. Seven long fucking nights of sleeping on my own and checking my phone more frequently than a normal person should to see if she'd sent me a picture or a message. I missed the feel of her skin against mine, whether it was her back from how she spooned into me or just her hand in mine; I missed her laugh and her fumbled words in the morning when she was just waking up; I missed our easy conversations and arguments. There was nothing I didn't miss.

"That's not a problem. You've passed the New York Bar. You can just come and run the office over here," my dad, ever the problem solver these days, suggested.

"He fucking well can't." Jackson said. "I need him in London. That's non-negotiable."

Jackson was right: my practice was back home. More importantly, my family was back there too. It had been bad enough Callum being away for so long, but now he was back I wanted to have the chance to be with my siblings for as long as they allowed.

My phone started to sound with a message, one that Seph had programmed in and I now referred to as 'the dick song'. It provided a good excuse to end the conversation so I read his message out loud. "Seph's on his way back. Apparently he's ninety minutes away and wants us to crack open the Champagne. Fuck knows. Does this place have Champagne, Dad?"

My father stood up and stretched having given approval to the design Vanessa was pushing for. "Damn right. Not from here, as it wouldn't be Champagne. I think there are four or five bottles in the fridge in the utility room. No point getting it yet though, if they're ninety minutes away."

"Who's they?" I asked. As far as I knew Seph had gone in to Toronto to pick up something he'd ordered.

Neither Jackson nor Vanessa said anything, just looked questioningly at Dad.

"Oh, for fuck's sake, who's Seph bringing over? It's not his ex, is it? He's been acting weird for the past couple of days." I had never liked the girl he had been with for several years. I'd thought she was a user and tried to control him. When they'd split up he'd been devastated and started drinking and partying too hard which had been worrying to watch.

"No, it's not her," Vanessa said. "I think it's an old friend of his from London. Shall we go and show Marie the designs?"

She linked her arm through my dad's, which he took graciously. I was in awe of the fact she'd fallen for someone like my brother, who was annoying at best.

"I thought this was meant to be a family thing. I really hope Seph's not going to spoil everything by bringing some friend and then drinking the house dry," I said, feeling riled.

Jackson laughed. "We're in a house on a wine estate. They'd struggled to get rid of it. Fancy spotting me on a chest press?"

The idea of lifting some iron appealed greatly. The heavier the weight, the more I managed to self-regulate. Dad and Marie had made sure there was an outhouse with a fully kitted out gym on the estate and all of us, apart from Payton, had spent a fair amount of time in there already. "Sounds good. I might see what I can deadlift."

———————

We spent the next hour discussing shit and training, and end with a sparring session that resulted in slight black eye for Jackson.

"You need to be quicker," I said, repeating the jab he'd failed to block. "If you're distracted, you will get hit."

"Then you shouldn't hit so hard, Maxwell!" Marie stood at the door, hands on her hips, glaring at me. "Go and get showered. Seph should be back in less than half an hour."

"What's the big deal with Seph and this friend of his?" I said. I was actually enjoying spending time with most of my family. Only Claire hadn't made it over, deciding instead to spend Christmas in Ireland with Killian's family.

Marie shook her head. "It's no big deal, but I'd prefer you looking fresh and smelling better than you do now."

Sometimes I think she thought I was fourteen instead of thirty-six, but my teenage years had taught me that arguing with Marie was a stupid idea because I'd never win. She'd been a lawyer—it was because of her I'd taken the New York Bar—and in court was far better than my father, although he was technically a better lawyer. Not that any of us told Marie that, least of all him.

"Fine," I said, pulling on a hoodie and heading over to the main house with a slight jog because it was fucking freezing. London would feel tropical when I got home.

Thinking of London made me think of Victoria and I wished I'd asked her to come for Christmas with me. I'd considered it a couple of days after I'd told her about her grandad's house, but I wasn't sure if it was too much, if it gave an illusion of something we weren't, something she said we couldn't be.

There were no messages on my phone from Victoria. She'd been quiet today; I'd had nothing since this morning when she told me she was heading out exploring. I felt apprehensive that something might've happened, or she'd gone cold on me.

Jumping in the shower, I tried to talk sense into myself and then pushed her out of my head completely, instead thinking about my PND case and England's chances of beating Australia in the cricket.

I'd just pulled a T-shirt on when there was banging on the bedroom door.

"Max, you're needed downstairs!" Payton yelled through the door, just as she had done when she was a pain in the ass four-teen-year-old.

"Why?" I said. "What is so fucking urgent about this friend of Seph's?"

There was no answer so I headed out of the room and down the stairs to the large entrance area.

I saw the top of the brown hair first and then, as she looked up, the doe eyes that were laced with excitement and worry. I nearly fell down the rest, battering down them with no pretence of being cool or calm.

"Fuck. I didn't think you were who Seph was picking up." And then I pulled her in and kissed her, not giving her time to speak, just needing to show her there was no reason to have worry in those eyes and every reason to have known I was glad she was here. "Best Christmas present ever. When do I get to unwrap you?"

I'd noticed that my family were strangely absent; they obviously all knew that she was coming.

"Probably after I've spent a reasonable amount of time being sociable with everyone. Are you sure you're okay with this? I kind of booked the flight without thinking and worried after. I have a hotel in Toronto picked out if this isn't good for you or it's too much because holy fuck, I'm forcing me on your parents. We weren't going to do that…"

"We've twenty minutes or so before they'll want to open the champagne as they've no concept of time. Come take your stuff up to my room." I saw the oversized suitcase standing near the door, probably put there in case she'd needed to take that hotel in Toronto. That wasn't going to happen. "I'll get your case, but I don't want to let you go."

She stood on her tiptoes and locked her mouth to mine, her hands holding onto my arms, her nails digging in. My cock recognised her, telling me that it had been too long since he'd last been inside her and that was where he needed to be. My hands were already under her sweater seeking soft skin. She pushed herself closer to me and the only part of my brain that was working told me to move before my father caught me heading towards second base with a girl for the first time since I was seventeen.

"Upstairs," I managed to say. "Bed and inside you." Not caring if anyone saw, I picked her up, making her yell then giggle loudly and took the stairs two at a time. Using my elbow to open the bedroom door, I strode over to the bed and placed her down with as much as my urgency could muster before leaning over and kissing her.

Counting the top ten English batsman of all time against Australia was the only thing I could do to stop myself from coming in my jeans. I pushed up her sweater to reveal her breasts, a sheer white bra doing nothing to hide the hard, pink nipples that screamed for my mouth.

"I've fucking miss this. I've missed you." The words rolled off my tongue before it found a peak, nipping and sucking. Her hands busied themselves undoing my fly and pushing my jeans and underwear down enough to release my dick which she started to palm.

I switched to the other nipple, pinching it hard enough to make her hips thrust against me. Then she squirmed beneath me and I lifted myself up to watchher pushing down her own jeans and kicking them off.

"Want you in me. I need to you to fuck me hard. Do you want to use a condom?"

She'd been on the pill for a couple of months but we'd kept using condoms, mainly because of my paranoia. But right now with her pussy giving off heat near my cock and feeling how wet she was with my fingers, I wanted all of that wrapped around me with nothing in the way and I didn't want to wait.

"You sure?" I said, the head of my cock at her entrance, her slickness leaking onto me.

"Fuck yes," she said in a half whimper, her hands on my ass and pulling me towards her.

She gasped as I thrusted into her hard, her tits bouncing with the force. I paused, grinning and letting her get used to my size. It had been a few days, a week, but unless I had recently fucked her she needed time to get used to my length and thickness.

"You feel so good in me. Need you to come in me."

I started to move, gradually increasing the pace and changing my angle so I grazed her clit. Any thoughts of anything but her were else-fucking-where, because right now, as she lay under me, she was the centre of the fucking universe. Her hands were setting wherever she touched on fire and her scent was taking over my head. The vision of her on the white sheets, her dark hair spread and her mouth open, murmuring my name were the beginning and the end of my everything.

She broke apart, her legs clutching my waist, my name on her lips and I joined her, erupting into her deeper than I'd been before. Andinstead of seeing stars I just saw her.

My movements slowed and I kept myself elevated on my arms, watching her as her breath became regulated. Her eyes stayed fixed on me and there was a look of wonder on her face.

Lowering myself, I kissed her softly, probably reverently, recognised the wetness where we were joined and reality began to nudge.

"I should say hello to your parents," she said. "Maybe get cleaned up first so I don't smell of sex."

"I like you smelling of sex," I said.

"You like me smelling of you because you think it acts as a deterrent to anyone else," she said, moving so we ended sitting up. "I've made a mess of the covers."

I shook my head, seeing the wet spot on the sheets. "We made a mess but it doesn't matter. Do you want to get a shower?"

"I should. Are you joining me?"

"I'd be a terrible host not to."

———

Half an hour later I led the way into the sitting room where my parents were lounging with Seph, Payton, Vanessa and Jackson. Ava and Callum had taken off skiing for a couple of days, which meant the greeting party wasn't quite as full on as it would've been. She'd told me that she was nervous; that she'd never met someone's parents before. What 'someone' meant I didn't ask, wanting to have that conversation when we were alone and had time.

"I'll get you some wine," I said loudly as we entered. "Pretend you like it, even if you don't. Dad's just spent a fortune buying it."

Marie laughed and my dad looked annoyed, wanting to say something but equally wanting to make a good impression on Victoria.

"This is Marie and my father, Grant. You know the rest, so you don't need to be polite to them."

They stood, edging towards her. Marie wrapped her in what I

knew would be a heavy hug while my father gave a light squeeze and a kiss to her cheek.

"It's lovely to meet you," Marie said, holding Victoria at arm's length and studying her intently.

My stepmother had long since been obsessed with Jackson, Claire and myself meeting someone and settling down. Since she'd found out about Victoria I knew she'd looked her up on Facebook and pulled information about her from Seph. She'd made not so obvious hints about how this was good for me, healthier than pouring my life into work so much that humanity was poured away with it. Although she hadn't given any direct comparisons to my father, they were there, unsaid.

"We've heard so much about you so I was over the moon when Seph told us you were coming to stay for a few nights. Now, what can I get you? As well as Champagne, of course."

"Let the poor girl get her breath back after you've just squeezed her like a cobra," my father said. "Have a seat, Victoria. You've seen your room and Max has taken your luggage up there?"

"I do have some manners," I said. "I was only dragged up by one uncivilised parent."

Grant's gaze was stony enough to make me laugh quietly. "If you're not careful, I'll find the photos we still have from when you were short and skinny."

"I think Victoria would love to see those," Seph said, topping up his glass of Champagne. "I know I'd enjoy watching you watch her look at them."

I shook my head and wondered what the improvement in the grapes would be if I buried his body somewhere on the winery.

Victoria looked amused, thankfully, Marie's arm tucked into hers. "I'd love a glass of Champagne," she said. "And a tour of the house. I've only seen Max's room so far, here and the entrance hall."

"Oh, I though Max had shown you round straight away, he

was so long in bringing you in here," Marie said, looking at me puzzled.

"I think he might've been showing her something else," Seph said with a straight face.

Again, I considered what quality of fertiliser he'd become.

"Have a glass and then I'll give you the tour," Marie said, gesturing for my father to pass Victoria a drink. "Not outside though, it's far too cold."

"That's what happens in Canada in winter," Jackson said. He was lounging on the sofa, Vanessa sitting in between his legs, lying on his chest. She looked relaxed and happy, one of my brother's hands resting on her hip. "I did suggest you bought a place in France or Italy where it was a bit warmer in the winter."

"We liked it here. Besides, the language barrier would have been an issue for your father. And it will be the summer when we're here more. This Christmas is an exception. How was New York, Victoria?"

"It's been great so far. Really good to see my friend Lewis and meet his partner," she replied, perching on the chair next to me. I put my hand on her hip, needing to touch her.

"I've done a little sightseeing too."

Marie nodded. "It was New York where I met Grant. I grew up there and first practiced law over there until this odd and intelligent English man somehow swept me off my feet and brought me to live with him and his four babies." She smiled around at us. "How quickly things changed. I had plans of owning a penthouse suite in New York and running my family's law practice there, making a name for myself."

My father laughed loudly and fully. "Marie, love, you managed all that and more. You still have a penthouse in New York, you've been involved in running a bigger version of your family's law practice and your name is enough to scare most other family law practitioners."

She shrugged. "True. And I'm going to be a grannie. We need

to make sure we appoint a really good manager for the winery because I don't know how frequently I'll be here this summer, after Claire's had the baby."

I saw Jackson's hands creep closer over Vanessa's stomach and wondered how long it would be before Claire's child had a cousin. My bet was on fairly soon.

Glancing at Victoria, I noticed her eyes looked glassy and raised my arm to pull her closer to me. "You okay?" I whispered into her ear. My parents, Seph and Jackson were discussing the list of potential candidates that had been shortlisted before Christmas. Before they flew back to England, my parents were interviewing to appoint someone to run the estate while they were away. "My family aren't that bad are they?"

"No." She shook her head. "I think I'm just tired and I'm happy for your sister, although the last I heard from her was a text about how huge she's going to be as one of Vanessa's bridesmaids."

"I doubt that's the way she phrased it: that sounds too polite."

"I don't know your parents well enough yet to swear that badly in front of them."

"Trust me, Claire learned any swear words she knows from Marie. And every insult. You sure you're okay?"

She nodded, turning her head to give me a lingering kiss on my beard. "I'm good. Thank you for worrying about me. I'm not used to that."

———

We spent the rest of the afternoon and evening alternating between showing Victoria around the house and nearby outbuildings, and eating and drinking. Seph monopolised her for an hour or so, desperately needing to show her something he'd been working on that he clearly didn't want to show any of us. As much as I plotted his death on a fairly regular basis, I was fond of my youngest brother, in a different way to Callum or Jackson. I'd noticed the way he looked at Victoria and I was undecided whether he thought of her as being a sister-type figure or whether he had a crush. The latter was my bet.

"I like her," my dad said when it was just the two of us in the kitchen. "She reminds me of Marie."

I almost dropped the whisky he'd poured for me; it was one of his better bottles. That gesture in itself had given me the head's up that he was about to impart his advice.

"She's nothing like Marie, Dad." I laughed.

"She doesn't look anything like her, but she's as feisty and argumentative as Marie. And as bossy and determined. Does she have a sister for Seph?"

My dad had already nursed a few whiskies this evening and I was convinced he wouldn't be having this conversation sober.

"She's only got an older half brother who's spoken for and a complete dick, so possibly Seph's type. I should go and check on him and Victoria. She's probably still too polite to not tell him to shut the fuck up yet," I said, feeling twitchy. Not for one minute did I think Seph would even try a move on my woman, but the lesser-developed part of my brain needed to go and claim her.

A phone rang in another room; Vanessa's laughter rang through the house and somewhere outside an owl hooted. Normal noises, sounds I was used to. What I wasn't used to was the fire that I felt inside me, the need I was developing for the woman three rooms away who was sitting with my youngest brother looking over some project he was too scared to show the rest of us. I wanted her to be mine.

I needed her to be mine.

"She can more than manage Joseph," my father said. "That's not what you should be considering. What you should be thinking about is whether she can manage you."

"What do you mean by that?" I hit the defensive, unsure as to what my father was insinuating. I had seen him at his best and his worse, and I saw myself in both sides. He had been critical of me more than any of the others, expecting the utmost in terms of achievements, probably because he saw himself in me too.

The kitchen door opened and Jackson entered, carrying a bottle of wine. "We're starting a poker tournament. You both in?"

I kept my eyes on my father, willing him to ask Jackson for a few minutes and elaborate on what he was saying, but instead he put down his glass and nodded. "Definitely. Who's joining us?"

"Me, Callum, Seph, you, Marie and Max," he said. "Victoria and Van have found the sauna and hot tub, so I think we've lost them for the night with a bottle of Champagne. We might need to check they've not drowned in an hour or so."

The reptilian part of my brain conjured up an image of Victoria in a bikini which had an instant effect on both my cock and my mouth. "I'll go check on them now. Make sure no one else is bothering them."

I pretended I didn't notice the look my father and Jackson shared as I left the room, and headed into the cold in just a T-shirt.

They were up to their chins in the hot tub which Marie had insisted had been installed for 'health reasons' and my father had never learnt to say no to my stepmother. Victoria's hair was piled high on top of her head and she looked utterly relaxed.

"How did you know to bring a bathing suit?" I asked, now needing to know the conversations she'd had with Seph in planning her visit here.

"I told Seph to tell her," Vanessa said, managing to just about keep her Champagne glass out of the bubbling water. "There was no way one of my tops would hold those babies." She nudged one of Victoria's tits under the water and giggled. "You got more than your fair share there, girl."

Jackson was more than likely going to have to carry Vanessa back to their room later.

"This is amazing, Max," Victoria said quietly, Vanessa now distracted by Jackson walking towards us. "Your family have been lovely and the views here…"

She looked away from me towards the slight valley in front of us. The winery was planted on a hillside, the reasons behind which had been explained to me by my father but I'd been more interested at the time in the photo Vanessa had sent me as it involved underwear I'd not met yet in person.

"They're pretty good, aren't they," I said, my frustration and hurt caused by my father subsiding with her smile. "I hope Seph wasn't being too demanding."

Those doe eyes gazed up at me and I wished I hadn't agreed to poker. "He was fine. We had a good chat. I'm helping him out with something but I can't say what."

"Yeah, well, as long as he keeps his hands and his eyes to himself."

"Maxwell Callaghan, you almost growled that!" She laughed, her tits bouncing up and down in the water.

I stifled a groan. The bikini top she had on looked black and covered enough for me to not worry about Seph coming out and seeing her but it didn't reduce the level of torture it was giving me.

"Yeah, well, I'm not happy with the idea of anyone else thinking you might be anything but mine." This time it was a growl.

Her wet arms came out of the water and reached for me, soaking my T-shirt. It was a cold night, but not the coldest and her body was warm from the water. "You need to let me know when that big brain of yours decided that I was yours."

I kissed and nipped the soft, delicate skin of her neck. "You were mine the day you argued with me over who was having that room to take seminars in. You just didn't know it."

She released her grip and slid back into the hot tub, ducking her shoulders right under. She was complicated and layered and I sometimes wished I had a map and a compass to be able to navigate my way through the depths of her.

"Where in all that law you've studied does it say you can own another person, handsome?"

"It doesn't," I stooped down to her neck again. "I read it somewhere else instead."

CHAPTER 18
VICTORIA

Two weeks into January and the time in the hot tub in Toronto and New Year's with Max in Times Square seemed like a decade ago. The sky over London remained just a single shade of grey and most of my colleagues' moods remained an uncolourful shade of black. Students returned from time with families or friends and launched themselves into all the work they'd neglected to do over Christmas, and with exams and deadlines looming, my admin job became more like an agony aunt's.

I'd spent four nights with Max in New York. He'd booked us a hotel suite near to Clyde and Lewis and we'd managed time with them as well as found chances to be by ourselves with no interruptions from work or friends or family. As much as I'd tried to keep what I was feeling in a neat compartmentalised box with the label of 'amazing sex' written prettily on the top, I knew I was failing miserably.

When we were alone, his professional, intelligent lawyer persona would now fall away completely and he'd turn into a teasing, playful man-beast who treated me as if I was his prized possession. And I let him.

I stuffed three student files back in the cabinet and locked it shut as my phone began ringing with the tone I'd allocated to Max. I'd handed my notice in two days ago, with the promise of staying on until they'd found a suitable replacement. My grandfather's legacy had been paid out and there was absolutely no reason not to solely focus on my doctorate, which is what he would've wanted more than anything else. I grabbed my phone and collapsed down in my seat.

"Good afternoon," I said quietly, not wanting Carol or the professor currently in her office to overhear. "And what can I do for my favourite flower-sending lawyer this grim London day?"

"Does that mean you want me to send you flowers?" he said, sounding surprised. "I hadn't thought of that. Shit. I'm sorry, Feisty, I've got a lot to learn about this sometimes."

Now I was confused. "You sent roses to my office this morning. Red ones with Baby's Breath mixed in."

I heard what I thought was a low growl. "They're not from me, Victoria. Where were they from?"

I looked for the card in the midst of the blooms. "Flores by Flora. Are you sure—no, stupid question. I'll move them. If they're not from you, I'm properly creeped out."

There was silence for a moment. "Take a photo of them and send it me. I know the florist—it's around the corner from the law department. I'll go in and see if I can find out who sent them. Then I'll have words with him."

"Okay," I said, starting to feel both concerned and needing a shower. "There's no note on the card apart from my name. Honestly, Max, I don't know who they're from."

His voice was low and like velvet. "Vic, you're beautiful and amazing and other men are going to notice you. That's never going to be something I'm going to be mad at so take that apologetic tone out of your voice. I'm not about to beat any one up, unless Seph has sent them, in which case his ass will be more than toast. I am going to take you out to lunch though."

I looked at the pile of filing that needed doing and the list of what needed uploading to the student area. It was potentially going to be a long working day but lunch with my mountain of a man sounded perfect.

My man.

I pushed consideration of the determiner back into the 'amazing sex' box and added to my to do list the need to potentially relabel it at some point in the near future because if I thought this was just amazing sex I was lying to myself and that was something I tried not to do.

"I'll let you," I said. "As long as it's brie, bacon and cranberry paninis from Jojo's. With a latte and possibly some banana bread."

Max had a low, delicious chuckle that made my girl parts turn to a liquid mess and my nipples resemble bullets. The sound of it almost caused me to change my demand to that of going back to his apartment for half an hour of quick satisfying sex but we'd done that yesterday and I was trying to control my addiction to his cock, even though he was more than happy to feed it.

"Just to let you know, I don't for one minute think I have any sort of power in this relationship."

"As long as you know your place," I said.

There was the chuckle again. "I have a few places." He was keeping his words deliberately quiet so I figured he was walking through reception. "On top, beneath, between your legs, behind you… tell me, Victoria, which place would you like me in now?"

"Maxwell?"

"Feisty?"

"I'd like your ass over here pronto because I'm fucking starving."

———

It took him half an hour to do a trip that was usually less than ten minutes, especially when he was on a mission. By the look on his face, I guessed he'd stopped at the florists on the way. He looked pissed and as soon as he laid eyes on me I felt the need he was emitting.

"Stop," I said, pulling on my coat and stepping from behind the desk to put my arms around him. My heels were a pair of my highest which brought my lips closer to his chin. "The flowers are in Carol's office. I'm here with you. So you can stop with the alpha one level of possession that you're radiating right now."

"It's your favourite student."

"Sorry?"

"Who sent you the flowers. I called in Flora's and spoke to Hayley who owns the place. It was a man who came in yesterday who paid cash. Tall, thin, glasses. Didn't speak much apart from to say that his girlfriend worked in admin in the law department and he needed to apologise for being away over Christmas," Max said, his hands spanning my waist and part of my ass.

"Sorry? Favourite student? You mean Peter Coffey?" I frowned and felt slightly nauseous.

"He fits Hayley's description, Vic. I don't like him: he gives off strange vibes," Max said, relaxing his hold and switching to guide me out of the office. "I know you're staying on till they've replaced you, but would you be able to work from home a bit more?"

I glanced up at him and saw the conflict on his face. He'd told me when we were in New York that he wasn't used to feeling possessive and jealous. It made me feel all sorts of special, especially as when we were in public or even with his family he hid his feelings to a large extent. He'd also soliloquised on how he was worried I'd find his alpha male tendencies a turn-off, given that I was as stubborn and strong-minded as he was.

Afterwards, when we were back in our hotel room, I'd tied him to the bed with my bikini tops and kept him on the brink of orgasm while I got myself off three times. Then I'd let him break free, unleashing the incredible hulk as he flipped me onto my front, held down my hands as he filled me with his cock. His words had been the dirtiest I'd heard and resulted in one of the hotel staff knocking on the door to ask us to keep the noise down.

"Max, it's okay to be concerned about me. I know that's why you asked that, so don't be so worried." I slipped my hand into his. "I may start doing that anyway, but the first thing I'm going to do is confront him. If he thinks I'm his girlfriend, I need to put him straight."

"Can I make a comment that you won't like and say make sure you have someone else with you when you do," Max said, pulling me closer into him.

It was cold and the wind was bitter.

"You can and know I was going to anyway. I'll probably ask him to come in to see Carol. She likes the flowers but she'll be more than a bit worried when she hears who sent them. Let's talk about something else."

We entered Jojo's and squashed onto the end of a table. I loved Amelie's café but I needed to go there when I had a couple of hours to spare, although I had taken to longer working lunches so I could pour over my thesis and drink her coffee. On days like today, the small greasy spoon we'd found worked well and the main waitress was rather keen on Max, so we tended to get preferential service.

"Something else," he said, his face relaxing. I nudged his leg with my foot, half wishing I'd made the suggestion to go back to his for a different sort of lunch. "It's Marie's birthday this weekend and she's asked us all round to their house in Oxford. She's explicitly mentioned you coming with me. Would you like to?"

"Would you have asked me if she hadn't 'explicitly mentioned' me?"

"You should've been a lawyer," he said.

I wanted to lean over the table and kiss away the stern look.

"Yes, I should have, but I also don't want to make you do something you don't want." Max watched me carefully. "Max," I said. "You know that would never happen. Yes, I'd like to come with you. I need a few more details for the weekend so I know what to pack."

"Clothes?" he said, looking boyishly puzzled. "There are hot tubs so a bikini, but one that covers you up so I don't have to punch Seph's lights out."

"Okay, clothes. Anything posh?"

"No. The only place we'll go to if we leave the house is the local pub, so you'll need something to wear on your feet down muddy paths. I'll buy you a pair of Hunters if you don't have any. Warm stuff. And that new underwear I caught sight of last week." His grin was now devilishly persuasive.

"I can do that. Why don't you stay with me tonight and I can give you a sneak preview?"

"Fuck, I have to visit the house after work and I promised Ava I'd buy her dinner. After that? Or why don't you pack tonight and take everything round to mine that you need for the next few days? I've offered to have poker night at mine tomorrow as Vanessa's gran's staying and last time she was there for poker night she pretty much cleaned up."

I started to laugh disbelievingly. "That's a joke. She didn't! You're just trying to make me laugh!"

He shook his head. "Seriously, she took the lot. Vanessa didn't tell Jackson beforehand that her gran was a known card shark in her local pub. I'm not sure Jackson's actually forgiven her for that. So we're hiding out at mine, if you can put up with us."

"Doesn't Seph usually sleep where he falls on poker nights?"

"I'll make sure he knows not to fall anywhere near you."

I put my hand on his and interlaced our fingers. We'd agreed that Seph possibly had a slight crush on me after he'd bought me his favourite ever book to read as a belated Christmas gift. I'd given him a chaste kiss and a big thank you and persuaded Max to one, not kill him and two, to not tell the rest of his siblings. Then I'd given him a blow job of pornographic proportions and so far Max had neither done nor said anything.

"I'll see you at yours then. Your spare room will probably be taken over with my stuff."

"Yeah, well, I don't see why you don't just start leaving your stuff there anyway." The look he gave was a cauldron full of emotions and feelings and now wasn't the time to go there—if there was ever going to be a time. I'd filled in my application for Johns Hopkins two days ago, as soon as Lewis had let me know that the vacancy was available. I hadn't told Max.

I didn't know how to.

———

"I'm not sure," Marie said, peering into the bag. "He must've had some help choosing this. I mean, in more than thirty years of being married he's never bought me underwear, so which one of you helped? For a start, he wouldn't have had a clue what size to get." She glared at the five of us, her hand in the Victoria's Secret bag as if she was about to pull out a gun. "If it's crotchless, I'm going to accuse one of the boys."

"Please, for the love of god, let it be crotchless," Claire said. "I need to experience watching them gain some insight into our parents' relationship and know that it involves crotchless panties. Or maybe edible?" She rested her hand on her growing belly. "Whoever helped Dad with this can have this child named after them."

Marie pulled the garments out of the bag and examined a

pretty underwear set that had definitely been well chosen. "It's even the right size," she said. "Confess. If one of you confesses, I'll go show the boys what he got me."

We exchanged looks, no words said. I had no idea who had done Grant's shopping for him, although I knew full well who had done Max's. He'd remembered on poker night that he'd not bought a present. Luckily, London shops rarely shut and I'd made a quick trip to Oxford Road with Max's credit card.

"It was kind of me," Payton said, running a hand through ridiculously gorgeous blonde hair. "But I didn't choose. I took Dad shopping although I needed an extra counselling session after going in Victoria's Secret with him. He might have made a few comments about the models needing to eat a few dinners or something like that."

Marie's eyes narrowed at her daughter. "Did you tell him my size?"

She shook her head rather like a chastised child. "No, but I told him to go in your underwear drawer and find out. Why men think they need to guess, I'll never know. I had one boyfriend who guessed once. He didn't last very long. But Dad chose this all by himself. I left him to it."

Marie nodded. "Good to know. Now how embarrassed would you like your brothers to be? Vanessa and Vic, feel free to sit this one out."

"Oh no," I said. "I take great enjoyment in seeing Maxwell feeling uncomfortable."

"Same," said Vanessa. "I just need to make sure I video it."

————

We headed into the lounge where the men were sitting around with beers watching sport on the huge TV which Grant had recently bought. It was a piece of equipment that had inspired over an hour's conversation during poker night yesterday, with various references to comparative TV's and which was superior, resulting in Max declaring that he was going to move so he had a wall big enough for one similar.

"Quick birthday speech," Marie said, standing in front of the screen, the bag held behind her back.

"Mum, it's a crucial point in the game," Seph said, gesturing wildly to move out of the way.

She smiled sweetly and didn't budge. "Firstly, thank you for coming here for the weekend. I know you're all busy working and playing hard, too hard in some cases, Callum, so I'm really glad you all gave up your time. Secondly, thank you for your lovely, thoughtful gifts and thanks to Claire for co-ordinating them. And thank you to Vanessa and Victoria, as I'm pretty sure they had something to do with Maxwell and Jackson's. Thirdly, I just thought I'd share with you what your dad got me…" She brought the bag round and put her hand in, loud cries of protest drowning out the commentary from the TV.

"Marie, I really think you shouldn't…"

"Mum, if I see what that is I will need to bleach my eyes…"

"Please don't do this to us!"

I started laughing, walking around to the back of the sofa where Max was sitting, covering his eyes with a cushion. I pulled the cushion away and he grabbed my hands instead. "Did you see what was in the bag?" he whispered conspiratorially.

"I did."

"Was it shit, or was it okay? I mean, it wasn't anything that could cause him to have a heart attack or something or something really—urgh, forget it; I don't want to know."

"If it helps, it was very sweet and I own nothing like it," I said, leaning over the back of the sofa enough so that my breasts brushed the back of his head. Everyone else's attention was still on the bag, although Claire's fiancé, Killian, had distracted himself with her bump and seemed to be talking to the baby, maybe trying to erase the noises it might have heard from its future uncles' protests.

It had a been a long day: we'd gone for a morning walk to get rid of any lingering hangovers from the night before, followed by a large pub lunch with lots of wine so no one had to cook and then a stroll back to the huge house owned by the Callaghans. I'd got used to the friendship offered by Claire and Vanessa over the previous months, finding it easier the more accustomed I became to having Max as a part of my life.

"I need to get you alone for a few hours," Max said, his head still resting into my breasts. His eyes were laced with desire, a combination of his closeness to my body and the comment about my underwear.

"I could live with that," I said. He stood up and headed for the door and I followed him like a stray puppy.

"Before you disappear, Max, I just wanted to mention something about the house and what we found there." Ava walked over to us, her blonde hair bobbing about down her back.

I'd spent a few evenings with her, looking at my grandfather's house and making a few suggestions around the kitchen and bathroom. It had already been altered beyond all recognition, a couple of walls removed, extra ones added, the plumbing for walk-in showers, a wet room and three en suites put in. Outside, an extension to what would be the kitchen and diner was taking place, the foundations firm already despite the miserable weather. It was exciting and sad at the same time. I was good to see the house being brought back to life for someone else to enjoy and I hoped they would be as happy there as I had—and that was why I was sad. That part of my life was over and I missed it, just as I missed my grandfather.

"Is everything okay?" Max said. "You know I wasn't keen on the electricians you brought in."

Ava shrugged. "They do a good job and do it thoroughly. I don't care whether you're keen on them or not. No, we found a box in the cellars that hadn't been cleared out. I don't know what's in it but I've brought it with me as I thought Vic would want it."

"Where was it?" I said, surprised that anything had been left.

"There was a small cupboard in one of the antechambers in the cellar. It was in there with a couple of books. I've kept those too, but figured you'd want the box sooner rather than later." Ava pulled her hair back and stretched, cat-like.

"Can you bring it to our room?" Max said and I realised he was supporting me around the waist enough to hold me up. I'd thought we had cleared everything from the house; everything I was aware of was accounted for. I had no idea what the box was or what might be in it.

Ava nodded. "Sure, I'll do it now."

Max guided me up the stairs, his arm reassuring rather than teasing. I knew I was leaning into him, taking what I needed from his warmth and strength, his biceps having a more practical purpose than just something pretty to look at.

"Any ideas what this box is?" he said as we got to the end of the long corridor.

Shaking my head, I sat down on the bed and pulled my socks off. "I honestly have no idea." My heart was racing and I tried to push all of my feelings and sadness back into a box that was already battered from everything trying to escape.

Max got on to the bed and sat behind me, pulling me into his chest and wrapping his arms around me. "It's not going to be anything bad, Victoria. It will be okay."

A light knock on the door sounded and then it opened. Ava entered with a wooden box that seemed familiar. It was carved and decorated with elephants. She handed it to me and I pulled off the lid immediately, hating the suspense, hating the surprise.

I put the wooden lid down next to me and looked at the contents: photographs, tiny wooden ornaments that looked African in origin like the box, and two rings. I held the rings in my hand with the box on my knee. Both were gold, one slimmer than the other and both were engraved on the inside.

"What do they say?" Max murmured and I looked up to see that Ava had gone, closing the door behind her.

My eyes swam with tears and try as I might, I couldn't force them not to fall. "William and Esme Davies. It's the same on both."

"Your great-grandparents: the soldier and the nurse," Max said, his voice silken and soft, tenderly wrapping me up in a myriad of feelings.

I nodded, trying Esme's ring on. It just about slipped onto my ring finger. I put William's ring on my thumb and took out the pictures. "Their wedding day," I said. "And with their first child. My grandfather was their youngest."

He took the photos, carefully holding them as I rummaged further through the box. There were a couple of old receipts, the ink too faded to see what for and more photos: my parents, an early one of my brother when he looked genuinely happy, me as a baby being cuddled by my grandmother and then a folded piece of thick paper. I opened it as if it might disintegrate in my hands or the ink would erase itself if it was accidently touched. There were names and lines, Esme's in the middle, names above hers, some with dates.

"It's your family tree," Max said then kissed my shoulder. "Your grandfather's left you the start of your family history. Look at your name."

My eyes shifted to where it read Victoria Esme Davies. Underneath, in his careful script, he had added my date of birth and a caption: 'my little historian'.

Max removed the paper from my hand and placed it back in the box with the photos. He held me into him and I buried my head into his chest, his familiar smell steadying the shakes that were trying to wrack my body.

"I can't believe this was missed when we moved everything."

"It doesn't matter: you have it now," he said, shifting us back onto the bed so we were lying down. "And you know you have the house if you want it."

I batted the tears away so I could look at him. "What? You'd sell me the house? I wouldn't be able to afford it—well, I could but…"

"There's time to think about it, Victoria. Just try to enjoy this little bit of your history that he left you," Max said.

My legs were entangled with his, his hand on my waist. His chest and his T-shirt were wet from my tears.

"Sorry," I said.

"What for?" There was amusement in his tone as if he had no idea what there was to apologise for.

"I've soaked your shirt," I mumbled, starting to feel steadier although still very raw. It was if someone had just taken a huge scab off my heart and now it had stopped stinging, I felt vulnerable.

He lifted himself up and pulled the T-shirt over his head, exposing ridges of muscle my fingers had committed to memory and the intricate patterns of his tattoos. If he was trying to distract me, it was working.

Something in the air changed and words fled out of the window. My hands went to his chest, fingers grazing over the pattern of hair that led to his jeans and over the peaks and valleys of his stomach. He let me roam, his eyes filled with feelings that didn't need to be said.

My fingers followed the outline of his tattoos: the hourglass, the owl, the Celtic patterns, all the way to his collar bone and neck, over his beard to his lips where I traced the soft skin. His tongue escaped and tasted my fingers. I entwined his hair around my fingers and pulled him down to me, slipping slowly onto my back. I needed him to take me and possess me, to fuck the pain away and replace it with the life I felt when he brought me to orgasm, when I was so full of him I forgot my name.

He pushed my arms away, his hands on my wrists, his legs weighing me to the mattress. I remembered who I was and why, and everything that had brought me here to this moment started to make sense. All of my history, all the fine particles of my past, began to clot together and that open wound ceased to sting.

Lips brushed mine, applying soft pressure and gentle strength. I pushed my hips towards his, encouraging him to go faster, but he didn't yield. Instead his mouth travelled down my body, softly biting the delicate skin of my neck to my chest. He undid the buttons of my shirt and found the front fastener of my bra, popping it open easily. I heard his sharp intake of breath as he looked at my breasts, my nipples hardening rapidly under his gaze, tightening with anticipation.

They didn't wait for long. He started to lick and bite and suck and pinch, taking pressure away when I needed it, adding it when I least expected, his hands back on my wrists, leaving my writhing under him.

"I want you in me," I said, trying to move my wrists so I could free his cock, impatient to feel it, to feel him. "Now."

He looked up from my breasts, the cool air reacting with the nipple he had been attending. "Patience," he said and my legs kicked out in frustration, making him grin. "I have other places to taste first."

My wrists were freed and I tried to touch him, but he moved down me, undoing my jeans and starting to wrestle them off, pulling the lace panties down at the same time.

And then his mouth was on me, his tongue straight onto my clit, giving it a delicate lick with the tip of his tongue. I ached and felt my pussy clench, wanting him in me and I moaned, needing more. He tasted me, lapping at the juice that I knew was coating the tops of my thighs and I heard him inhale deeply.

"Tell me how I taste," I said, the thin grasp I had on reality becoming like mist.

"Like salty honey and I can't get enough." Then his mouth

was on my clit and he sucked and I fractured into particles that only knew his name. At some point he lost his jeans and underwear, the sound of the zipper barely registering. My only functioning sense was touch as it was all I could cope with, all I needed. Him.

His hands came behind my knees and he pushed my legs high, his knees now further up the bed. One hand came down to shift my hips and then he held his cock and placed it at my entrance. Saying nothing, he entered me and I cried out at the perfect invasion, my muscles stretching around him and clasping his cock as he slowly started to thrust.

Something had changed in the room. The curtains were open, the crescent moon and stars uncovered by the glare of city lights, the only audience. The only sounds were our rapid breaths and gasps as he hit the spot deep inside me, turning me inside out and bare for him.

His pace increased and I knew he was close. My orgasm was building, a tsunami growing in power before it broke and my hands clutched his shoulders to steady myself as it climbed towards its peak.

Words were now completely out of the grasp of whatever brain cells I had still functioning. Instead, I held his eyes with mine, praying he could read what was behind them.

"You're going to come."

I whimpered and he altered his pace, increasing the force of his cock as it drove inside me.

"You're going to come all over my cock and milk it with your pussy."

With one hand he pushed my leg up to rest on his shoulder, increasing his depth and then I came with a scream, my hips leaving the bed and my body starting to shake.

He called my name seconds later and I felt the pulse of his cock as he came inside me, still pushing deeper. I clutched him, nails digging in and making my mark on his skin and then we started to slow, our breathing deepening as we chased oxygen, our hearts throbbing as our bodies started to regulate themselves.

I gripped still, my hands unwilling to break contact as he lowered himself onto me, his chest pressing against mine, using his hands to alleviate some of the weight. The kiss we shared had no finesse or tidiness, I nipped at his bottom lip and felt him chuckle into me, the vibrations softening the landing as reality began to come into focus.

"Come here," he said, rolling onto his side and pulling me into him. "You okay?"

I wrapped myself around him. "More than okay. Do we need to go back to your parents?"

"No. We can stay here all night now. I don't have any plans to move."

"Good. I don't want you to move."

———

We drifted in and out of sleep, at some point taking a shower which led to fast and furious and silent sex against the tiles, his finger discovering my ass and my ass discovering that gem brought an extra bite to my orgasm. I shouted his name as I came and he called something I couldn't translate. My particles had been rearranged and put back together, the open wound healing now everything around it was cemented in a solid foundation of my history and my present.

I slept deeply, Max's warmth encapsulating me. My phone made a brief noise just before Seph decided he was going to parade around the house singing and delivering coffee. Ignoring it, I woke into an easy Sunday where January seemed a little brighter and the world a little clearer.

It took until lunch for me to remember my phone. There was a text from a number I didn't recognise and no name. The message enough to change my expression and cause Vanessa to ask if I was okay.

Unknown: You know you're mine. You need to understand that you're mine. I don't know what will happen if you don't.

CHAPTER 19
MAXWELL

I agreed to stay for another couple of months."

The wine tasted acidic in my mouth as I processed her words. Staying permanently was good; staying in London would be the best news I'd had all week, possibly all year, but I knew she wasn't referring to that.

"Isn't it going to slow down your dissertation?" This again could be a good thing: if Victoria needed another year to complete it, that would be another year she would be in London, in my bed.

"It's going better than I thought. I'm reducing my hours and I'll do some of the work from the law department from home," she said, taking a bite of the entrée we were sharing.

"I thought they'd appointed someone?" I nabbed a larger piece of the pork belly. It was Valentine's Day and given that we'd managed to spend pretty much every night together since Marie's birthday, I hadn't actually asked her if she wanted to spend tonight with me too. In the past, I'd dismissed February fourteenth as a gimmick, an excuse to sell overpriced gifts and a day to propose on for those with a lack of imagination, but my opinions had been altered by the woman across the table from me who was trying to sneak the crispy bit without me noticing.

"They have, but she's on a three-month notice period, which is insane. It's fine: Carol's been so good to me and I enjoy working there so working fewer hours is the best scenario. It'll stop me from ending up a total history geek," she said, nibbling at the pork crackling. "You wanted this, didn't you?"

"I'd rather watch you eat it."

"We know you like watching me eat certain things." Her eyes twinkled, full of chocolate and warmth. We'd been at Claire's the evening before; she'd invited all of us round for supper, which turned out to be takeaway pizza. Victoria had created an emergency and dragged me into Claire's bathroom, telling me that the pizza had left a bad aftertaste and the only thing that would get rid of it was my cock in her mouth.

I'd been happy to oblige.

"I like your history geekiness," I said. She had a story about everywhere in London, from the Kings and Queens to Jack the Ripper. I had suggested she give up ideas of tenure and instead become a London tour guide. It was another way of trying to persuade her to stay.

"You just don't want me working in the office."

"True. Has the slimeball been back in since he sent that text?" I referred to Peter Coffey.

She offered me the last bite of the crackling, feeding me across the table. "He hasn't when I've been there. In fact, I think he's only been in twice, so he must be having withdrawal symptoms or something."

"No creepy Valentine's gifts?" She looked shifty and I knew there was something she wasn't telling me.

"Well, there was a bowl of hyacinths delivered this morning from someone…"

I'd figured roses were too obvious and she'd mentioned how much she loved the scent of hyacinths.

"And the underwear I noticed at your apartment. I assume that's for me?" she continued.

I chewed slowly and pondered her words. "What if it wasn't?"

Her eyes glowered. "Then my mouth won't be anywhere near your cock for the foreseeable."

"That would be a shame. My cock likes your mouth."

"Then the underwear had better be in my size, hadn't it?"

I chuckled quietly. "There might be one more gift for you too, but you'll have to be good to get it, so that might be difficult for you."

She tipped her head to one side and regarded me. "But sometimes you don't like it if I'm too good?"

I groaned, knowing what she was referring to and then applied what she'd determined to be my lawyer stare. "So there were no surprise Valentine's gifts delivered to your office?"

"Did Seph say he was sending one?"

I growled.

"Max, it doesn't matter. When Peter next comes in I'll set him straight and I'll make sure someone is there while I do it," she said, pouring more of the wine into her glass.

"So he did get you something?"

She sighed heavily. "There was a small bunch of roses with a copy of Edgar Allen Poe's The Tell-Tale Heart. I think we can file it under 'weird' at the very least."

I folded my arms across my chest, sittingback in my seat. "At which point will you agree to having someone from Killian's firm make sure you get back to mine safely after work?"

Her head tilted again. "He's harmless, Max. You've seen him. He has a crush."

"No, Vic. A crush is what Seph has when he follows you round like an excited puppy. He doesn't send you texts telling you you're his, or books by Edgar Allen Poe. If he'd sent you a book on the hospitals of the First World War I'd have been more understanding, but it's not about you, it's about him," I said, trying desperately to not reach for my club and bring out my pet dinosaur.

"I'll ask him to come into the department for a conversation with Carol. She knows what he's been doing."

"I know she does."

"Of course. You were the one who rang her up demanding security on the place whenever I was working. I believe your words were along the lines of 'if you want me to be back teaching next year, you'd better have eyes on who's coming in and out of this place,' correct me if I'm wrong?" I was eyed like a child who needed to sit on the naughty step and somehow managed to find it a turn-on.

"If you want a man who wears corduroys and can't lift a paperweight, then there's one sat over there at the bar." I turned my head towards him. "Oh look, he's drinking what looks like a margarita."

Her pointed glare turned into a badly covered laugh. "I'll go see what literature he's into. If it's Poe, I could be on to a winner. Although, I'm not sure my mouth would like his cock as much as yours."

"I bet it wouldn't," I said, keeping my voice low, my leg brushing against hers under the table. "I don't think your mouth would like any cock as much as this one. In fact, I'm willing to bet that it's been ruined for all other cocks it'll never get to taste."

She edged closer to me across the table, our hands entwining. "Max, I need to tell you something."

I sat up bolt straight, my heart rate leaving it's resting rate of around fifty-four to close to what felt like two hundred. *She's pregnant. She's pregnant,* my inner voice started to yell and I spanned between celebrating like a buffoon and needing to call Jackson as I had a meltdown. *She's drinking wine,* it then registered and I stilled myself.

"I've got an interview for the position at Johns Hopkins the day after tomorrow. I'm flying out tomorrow afternoon."

"Oh." It was all I could manage as nausea filled my throat and I tasted what hurt felt like. I knew this was coming; it was her dream and it hadn't changed, I hadn't made it change.

"It doesn't mean I'll get it," she said.

I tried to hide everything I was feeling right now.

"You will. There's no way you won't be offered the job. You're not just a stuffy historian, you're an amazing teacher and they'll need someone like you in the department," I said, focusing on this being her dream and wanting her to be happy.

"Thanks," she said almost looking shy. "I'm nervous. I suppose anyone would be. I don't know what the position will entail teaching or what their research focuses are, but those are things I'll find out at the interview."

Please let it be things she's not interested. Please let her hate the place. Please let it be minimal teaching as she'll hate that. "Write everything down beforehand; you'll look prepared and it'll stop you from forgetting if you're nervous. Not that you've got anything to be nervous about."

She said nothing, just smiled and sipped her wine, watching me with unreadable eyes. Gradually, our conversation drifted onto Vanessa and the wedding plans and the crabbiness of Claire who really did look like she was going to give birth to a baby elephant, although apparently I wasn't meant to make that comment to her face without expecting a severe beating with her purse.

We went back to mine and my mouth found hers and then every part of her that I liked to taste. And when I fucked her I tried to tell her with my body that I didn't want her to go.

I needed her to stay.

———

"When's she back?"

I only just missed Seph's jaw as he failed to block my fist. Boxing with my little brother was not a good idea. Most things hadn't been a good idea since Victoria had flown to Baltimore, including being awake at any point. I'd even slept on the sofa for the last five nights, the bed suddenly too big and cold. "Two days. Concentrate on my hands else you're going to get hurt."

"You're not quick enough," he added as a sharp jab came my way. I blocked it and threw him off balance. We sparred for a few more minutes, me shouting where to put his feet and trying to coach him at the same time as controlling the power behind my hits. I'd persuaded Jackson to join us later where I'd be able to let loose as Jacks was more than capable of holding his own against me.

"Time out!" Seph shouted, collapsing against the ropes. He was breathing rapidly and looked rather red in the face. I laughed.

"Fucking hell, Joseph, how do you keep a woman happy in bed with that level of fitness? You must pass out from exhaustion before you've got the job done."

He stuck two fingers up at me. "What are you going to do if she gets this job?"

I glared at him. "Be happy for her. If it's what she wants."

"Bullshit, Maxwell." Unfortunately, his breath had returned. "You've been fucking awful to be around since she went away. If she moves there permanently, maybe you should go with her."

I shook my head. "This was never a long term thing, Seph. I know you have it bad for her, but she always planned to work over in America. We said from the start it was just casual."

"You might've said that at the start but it's not the same now." He reached for a bottle of water. "If it was casual, you wouldn't be practically living together and you wouldn't have bought a house for her."

"I haven't bought a house for her. I've bought an investment property."

"That's crap and you know it. And you know you don't want her to leave," Seph said, tipping the rest of the water over his head. "And I don't have it bad for her. I really like her, far more than any girlfriend you've ever had, but I don't like her like that."

I eyed him suspiciously, calling horseshit.

"She's got the best rack I've ever seen, but please never tell her that. Besides, she's your woman."

I said nothing. Words failed me on both counts. One, the fact that Seph had not erased the image of her glorious tits from his brain as instructed, although, to be fair, they were unforgettable and two, because she was my woman. That was how I thought of her.

I wanted to be the one who took her to bed every night and made her come. I pretty much dedicated myself in the evenings to making sure she didn't remember ever having another lover and that no man who ever dared be in her future could ever match up to me. I wanted to be the person she woke up next to and shared her day with, tolerated disorganised family gatherings with my siblings and argued with me when I irked her by making random comments about the uselessness of history.

If she was my woman, I wanted to be her man.

But that was never our agreement.

"I thought I said to forget you ever saw that photo?" I growled at Seph and I swear I saw him wince. He was right; I had been in a foul mood since Victoria had flown off. Unfortunately, it was very easy to take my mood out on him.

"I tried. Seriously, if I ever think about how she looked… shit. I never want her to know I've seen that photo. She's like a kind of big sister; a bit like Claire would be if she wasn't so hormonal all the time. Please never tell Claire that either. I'd like to live a bit longer." Seph looked genuinely scared.

"If I ever need your share of your inheritance I'll be sure to pass on your views to Claire," I said. "Until then, I'll let you live."

"Have you told her you don't want her to go?"

"Who? Claire?"

He gave an irritated sigh. "No, Mr Fucking Difficult! Have you told Victoria you want her to stay?"

"There's no point."

"Why, exactly, is there no point?"

"Because if she chooses to stay I want her to do it because of her dreams, not because of me. If I asked her to stay, it'd put pressure on her. If things don't work out, I don't want her to blame me," I said, surprised at how easy it was to tell Seph that. Maybe my kid brother wasn't a complete ass after all.

"But that's only if things don't work out. And don't you think she deserves to know that you love her? Maybe that will be the thing she wants to stay for."

"I didn't say I love her." The word almost choked me.

"You don't?"

I said nothing, stepping back into the ring. "Get back in the ring and let me see if you can stop me from kicking your ass."

———

The father of my future niece or nephew looked even more like he was made of sheer muscle than ever. I was pretty sure he'd grown another half a foot since finding out he was going to be a dad, or that was just a defence mechanism to protect himself from an even-more-hormonal-than-usual Claire. Killian had been my best friend all the way through university and we'd kept close throughout his time in the Navy and since he'd left, joining his brother to set up a security firm. He also ran a decent PI side and could find out most things about most people.

"Your girl's student services, isn't she?"

I nodded, still enjoying any reference to Victoria being mine way too much. "That's part of what she does."

"Professor in training?" he said, a half hidden reference to my past where I'd tended to date women who were lecturers.

Vic had already received plenty of information about that, to the extent where she'd checked that I was interested in her body as much as her brain.

"Yes but let's move on."

He smirked. "This Peter Coffey you've asked me to look up —he's innocuous enough apart from one thing: he was advised to leave Cambridge after two complaints of stalking were made against him. The university investigated it and probably should've reported it to the police. Instead he was advised to continue his studies elsewhere and elsewhere became King's."

"What exactly did he do to stalk the women, assuming it was women?" I asked. Victoria was back in three hours—yes, I was counting—which gave me enough time to find him, murder him and dispose of the body.

Killian glanced at his iPad. "Presents, following them, messages. One woman he tried to kiss and grope and got quite handsy until someone else pulled him away. I had to do a bit of stalking myself to find that out. And maybe a bit of hacking."

"It's appreciated," I said. "I owe you a beer or five."

He shook his head. "Babysitting duty. And a cigar the day the baby's born."

"Damn right on the cigar front. Not sure about the babysitting duty—isn't that what grandmas are for?" I had no issue with looking after small people—I'd done it enough with Callum, the twins and Ava, but I had to try and act a bit manly.

"Who else will teach him about the rules of rugby?"

The door opened and a sharp gust of warm air blew into my office. "You're suggesting the baby's a boy." My sister waddled in and immediately sat down on a chair. "I'm sure it's twins. There's no way one baby can make you this fucking uncomfortable."

"Maybe it's time to go on maternity leave," Killian said, keeping a safe distance between him and Claire.

"Maybe it's time you grew a vagina and had the next baby yourself, then you'd understand about the lack of tolerance for fuckwit remarks like that!"

He gave me the look of a man whose patience had been severely tested.

"How about dinner at Padella?"

"How about you stop asking stupid questions and just take me there already?"

Killian stood up and gave me a brief nod. "Do you want me to arrange someone to keep an eye on him? Maybe do a bit more enquiring as to his hobbies?"

It was cryptic which suggested Claire knew nothing about Peter Coffey and Killian's research. If she did, she'd more than likely tell Victoria, who I suspected wouldn't be overly happy.

"Please. Then let me know what I owe you."

"You don't. Except babysitting and a cigar. And finding where Claire stored my balls."

"They've been frozen so you can never impregnate me again."

"That's not what you were saying last night."

I covered my ears. "Sister. Therefore, there's a lot I don't need to know."

Killian laughed and yanked Claire out of the chair, being treated to more verbal abuse for his efforts. "I'll see you tomorrow for poker. Enjoy your reunion and take my advice and wrap it up: that pill thing doesn't always work."

"Go. Go now." I said, both of them laughing as they left, Claire's arms around him as much as she could manage.

I checked the time, less than a couple of hours until Victoria returned. I still wasn't sure of what to say; Seph's idea about asking her to stay was still playing on my mind. I hadn't dismissed it yet, in fact I was considering it more, only the truth was, I didn't know the words to say.

CHAPTER 20
VICTORIA

It was a loud bang that caused me to move from the sitting room—that I had nicknamed the snug—into the kitchen. At points since Christmas, some of my belongings had made their way over to Maxwell's: a vase that had belonged to my grandmother, an art deco elephant my grandfather had picked up in New York when he was romancing my grandmother, a collection of books that had belonged to Virginia Woolf. The bang was followed by a few curses and I recognised Seph's voice above all the others.

"There is no logic in keeping chocolate in the fridge," Seph whined and I saw the hardened shrapnel from an Easter egg across the granite worktops. That had been the smash.

Callum reached over and grabbed a few of the pieces. I didn't know him as well as the rest of the other siblings; he was a veterinarian at London Zoo, a specialist in big cats, and when he wasn't on shift he was darting over to Europe or Africa to volunteer. I knew from Max that he had his own issues, predominantly with his father, but we were starting to see more of him, which could only be a good thing.

"Victoria prefers it refrigerated," Max said, obviously not

realising I was standing in the doorway. Poker night was well under way: at least a dozen bottles of Brew Dog had been polished off already and the whisky had been opened, just not poured.

"How does she take care of them then? A special box? Her underwear drawer? Or maybe where she keeps the knives?" Killian said, studying his cards and checking out Jackson's expression which was unsurprisingly blank.

Max eyed him over his beer. He was out of this round and was lounging on the wingback chair I'd forced him to buy and have re-covered when we'd spotted it at an antiques market we'd happened to find one Sunday afternoon. He moaned and grumbled about it, which was his usual response when it was something he was unsure of, but then he'd given in. It was now his favourite perching spot, unless he was on the sofa curled around me. "I'm assuming you're stating in a passive way that Victoria has my balls."

"Of course. You clearly don't own them anymore."

"Shall I ask my sister where she keeps yours?"

There was a general laugh and Seph lost a bit of chocolate from his mouth in the process.

"At the moment they're in her hospital bag." Killian leaned back, his T-shirt riding up exposing abs that Claire had spent almost the whole of one night obsessing over. "Three more weeks and they'll be shared between her and the baby." Killian looked a combination of worried, terrified and excited wrapped together. "I'm never getting them back."

Seph noticed me where he was still standing at the kitchen island, eating my chocolate. "So Vic, where do you keep Max's balls?"

"Where they'll do the most good," I said, fully entering. "When are you going to replace my chocolate?"

He at least had the decency to look sheepish. "Saturday. I'll replace it Saturday. In fact, I'll take you to breakfast and you can take me chocolate shopping."

I understood this to mean there was an arranged drinking session on Friday and Seph would be using the spare room.

"You're assuming Vic and I don't have plans for Saturday morning," Max said. He'd stood up and moved towards me. I felt his arms pull me into his chest and he stepped us back so I was on his knee as he sat in his chair. "And you're assuming that you're staying over, again."

Seph shrugged. He'd moved into yet another apartment, saying he needed a change but so far he'd spent more time staying with Max, Callum, Payton and Ava than at his new place. It would've been cheaper for him to have just rented storage.

"Yeah, well, we're going to the Baker's Vaults so this was the closest place." He sounded down.

"It's fine Seph. Max can take both of us for breakfast. Then I'm helping Vanessa with last minute wedding prep—I think I'm arranging the favours." Over the last couple of months, since coming back from my interview at Johns Hopkins, I'd become more involved with Vanessa and Claire in particular. We were of a similar age and all involved with men who could be grumpy and bossy and glarey as well as soft and tender, and when they were, they didn't know how to handle themselves. I hadn't heard from Johns Hopkins about the appointment, although Lewis had told me they were making a decision soon. I didn't know what I would do if I was offered the post; it was what I thought I'd always wanted, but now with Max and his family I had the beginnings of roots.

The beginnings.

We'd never had a conversation about us being anything more than temporary. Although he acted more and more like I was a permanent fixture, he'd never told me he felt any differently about what future we had. So I was aware that the beginnings of the roots were just that and may never grow any further.

"Yeah," Jackson said, sweeping a pile of cash from the table. "I think I'll be elsewhere on Saturday. Far too much oestrogen knocking about for my liking."

"The Bulls are looking for players on Saturday—an alumni team against the current second XI," Max said, his arms still around my waist. His cock was pressed against my ass and I figured he'd have to get it to calm down before going back to the table for the next round of poker. "Who's up for kicking some undergrad ass?"

There were several murmurs of agreement along with the sound of beers being opened.

"Shall we stay at Mum and Dad's?" Seph said. He'd given up with the rest of the Easter egg and had sat back down, leaving the chocolate on the worktop. He still needed house training.

Killian groaned. "I'll head back here unless I can persuade Claire to come over after the weddingy thing. I know there's three weeks to go, but every time my phone makes a noise it's like, fuck, it's time."

I pushed myself up off Max's knee and heard him make a quiet moan. He'd been complaining that everyone was coming round for poker night at least a dozen times this week, at one point listing all the things he would have done to me if we had been on our own. I'd almost cancelled the event myself.

"I'm going back to my work," I said, eyeing Seph. "Stay away from my chocolate. And if you decide to risk stealing it again, don't complain about it being in the fridge or just bring your own."

Seph held his hands up. "I'm more than happy to replace it with interest."

"I'll make sure you do. Happy playing." I left them to it, as the sound of card shuffling and clack of beer bottles on the wooden table top added to the jocular din of the kitchen.

———

It was early evening and it had only just gone dark outside. I knew we were running short of milk and I felt like stretching my legs before trying to finish off one of the last bits of my thesis. I grabbed my purse and headed out, briefly letting Max know. It was a calm night with spring in full flow and the temperature was mild for April.

The convenience store was only a five-minute walk away so I'd slipped on ballet flats and a light jacket, leaving my phone and headphones at Max's. A girl on a bicycle whizzed past me and a dog walker ambled by on the opposite side, but other than that it was quiet.

On the way back, I saw nobody and retreated to my own world of military hospitals and dressing stations, the focus of my dissertation. I was almost back at Max's when I noticed the sound of soft footsteps behind me and the rustle of bushes when there was barely any wind. I stopped, gripping my keys and heard my heart playing drums to a rock song.

Turning around, I caught sight of movement in the shadows and had an inkling as to who my follower was. "Peter?" I said. "If that's you, you need to come out and say hi." I was almost at Max's apartment, the lights flickering out on to the street.

A shadow moved; a shoe scraped.

"Peter?"

"Hi Victoria." He stood out in the open, looking dishevelled. "Sorry if I scared you. I was just making sure you got home safe. I do that sometimes."

"What?"

He shrugged. "If you're out late at night, I make sure you get home safe. Even if you're with him—Professor Callaghan. That's my job."

"Carol spoke to you, didn't she, about not sending me gifts?"

I wasn't sure how to have this conversation, but telling him to keep the fuck away from me felt like the wrong thing to do.

He looked at me, smiling as if he knew everything, and took a few steps closer. I itched to turn and run to the apartment, but I knew instinctively that he would run after me. I didn't want to argue with him or antagonise him as at this moment, everything in me was shouting to be careful.

"She said something about that. I thought she was jealous and I didn't want her to take it out on you. I've still been buying you gifts and saving them for you." He smiled nervously. "I know I need to wait until you've finished working at the department though. I won't make things bad for you."

"Peter," I said as kindly as I could muster. "I'm already in a relationship. I'm sorry if you think I've led you on, but I'm in… I'm seeing someone." The confession had nearly been one I hadn't yet made, even to myself.

"But that's only a cover. I know you're interested in me. I could tell how…" His words faltered and I was aware of a door slamming behind me.

"I think we need to talk."

I turned around and saw Max. He was wearing jeans and a T-shirt, but his feet were bare. Behind him was Killian, who at least had thought to put something on his feet. Both had crossed their arms over their chests where their T-shirts were tight enough to illustrate the power they had in their muscles.

Peter looked from Max to Killian and back and then to me. "Tell them, Victoria. Tell them about us."

"There is no 'us', Peter. I helped you because it's my job and I was kind to you because I felt sorry for you, not because I wanted a relationship." I felt Max's heat as he stood next to me. His jaw was clenched and his fists tight.

Killian was slightly more relaxed. "Look, we know that you were asked to leave Cambridge because you were accused of stalking two of the women there. Clearly you have a habit. So this is what's going to happen: you're going to stay the fuck away from Victoria, Max and her friends. You're not going to go into the office at the law school unless she's not there and I suspect most of your essays and shit can be sent electronically. I'm letting the law school know about your past and I'm going to advise them that you are a safety concern. And you're going to be watched."

Peter's eyes fixed on me and stared hard. "You don't want them to do this and if you say you do, I'll know it's because you're scared, that they're trying to control you—"

"Peter, I'm going to report you myself and put in a complaint. Something I should've done months ago. I also think you need help." A to do list was forming in my head: report Peter to the police, not that they could do anything apart from be aware; contact Student Services; check out his file with Carol; find out how Killian knew about the previous complaints about stalking because why the fuck hadn't Max told me?

He shook his head, turned around and started to walk away. I stood with Max's arm around me and Killian flanking my other side, watching him walk away. "So, gentlemen," I said. "Explanation?"

———

The explanation came later; Max had asked Killian to do a bit of PI work and the odd person had been dispatched to check on me when I had been working late as Max had been paranoid that Peter Coffey would try something more hostile—especially since he had form for it from when he'd been at Cambridge University. It was why he'd transferred.

"Why didn't you tell me?" I asked, after everyone had gone, leaving us with a bin full of beer bottles to take out to the recycling and several large pizza boxes.

Max shrugged. "Because I didn't want to worry you and I

also didn't want your response that I was being paranoid and there was no reason to check."

I thought for a moment before reacting, something I was working on doing. "You should've been honest with me. Yes, we would've argued about it because I would've thought you were being an overprotective weirdo with stalker tendencies yourself, but then you would've done what you were going to do anyway. And when Killian found out about his past in Cambridge I could've reported it through to Carol."

"She knows. I couldn't keep that information to myself. She spoke with him about it and he assured her he would keep his distance from you." Max was quiet and still, his hand on my thigh as we lay in bed, me dressed in one of his T-shirts, him in just his boxer briefs.

"Oh."

"He's on a warning. Him following you tonight will lead to disciplinary action. I agree with you though, he needs help."

"I'll do what I can to help him get it; although it will depend on him as to whether he accepts it," I said, turning so that both my legs lay over Max's. "Thank you for trying to look after me." My eyes felt wet and I did what I could to blink away tears. I was so used to looking after myself and every time he did something—even turning up at my office with lunch or texting me to remind me to eat or get a drink or go for a quick walk if I was swamped in work or my dissertation—I struggled to deal with it. Yet, I returned it without question, knowing that me turning up after work to surprise him would be appreciated or booking tickets to a gig or a performance at the theatre, or being in his bed naked. Max had been a learning curve; one I wasn't sure I wanted to end.

He laughed quietly, a hand on the small of my back. "The next time you have a stalker I'll let you know what I'm doing. Then you can shout at me for getting Killian involved and tell me I was right in the end."

"Is this the end?" I was still worried. There was no guarantee that Peter would leave me alone and I didn't want to spend the next however long looking over my shoulder.

"I don't know. I will look after you though."

Or if I move away. But I didn't want to say the words aloud.

"We received judgement on my PND case today." The words were said softly, quietly. I turned around and straddled him, his hands creeping up my T-shirt and touching my skin.

"What was the result?"

It had been a case that had emotionally drained him. Time wise, it hadn't been a consuming case, but for him, with what had happened to his mother, it had kept him awake at night and woken him up in the early hours, the bad night-fairy.

"His daughter is set for her future; she'll not accrue any debt if she goes to university and a deposit on a house won't be an issue for her. The compensation was what we hoped for. He's making a donation in his wife's name to a charity that supports women suffering from postnatal Depression too. He's a good man, Vic, and he tried to do everything he could but he was let down by a system that ultimately failed him, his wife and his daughter." Max pressed his forehead to mine.

I felt his need, his physical need to be close and I knew tonight I wouldn't try for dominance; I'd let him take what he needed and in turn he'd look after me.

"You've done what you could," I said. "Are you going to use the case to write an article?"

"Probably. There was no precedent set, but it's still key and highlights shortcomings in the system."

His lips found mine and he started to kiss me, hands pushing up my T-shirt before he broke the kiss and pulled it over my head. His eyes looked down at my chest. My breasts were moving with my breath and my nipples were already hard.

"Fucking beautiful," he said and his hands began to feel, to stroke and to pinch.

My back arched, pushing my breasts towards him. He took the hint well and dropped his head so he could suck one nipple, then the other. My hand went into his hair, gently pulling, my other hand splayed on him, feeling tense, taut muscle under tattooed skin.

"Lose your underwear," he demanded, releasing my breast from his mouth. I shifted back to give me space and pushed my panties down, leaving me exposed for him. I'd been waxed just a couple of days before and this was the first time he'd seen me properly since. His eyes fixed on my pussy. "Are you wet?"

"Yes." Wet and so very ready. All I needed was his hands or his mouth on my tits and I was primed and ready to come on his cock or his fingers or his tongue. Or all three.

"Spread your legs for me, I want to see."

I leaned back, using my hands to keep me upright and parted my legs, cooler air hitting my heat. He moved his hands up my legs towards my centre and licked his lips. I let out a breathy moan in anticipation and he gave me that small, quiet laugh that suggested more was going on in his head than he was letting on.

"Pinch your nipples," he said, his eyes still on my pussy. I used my stomach muscles to keep me upright so I could watch him and memorise the expression on his face as I did, electricity buzzing between them and my clit.

I expected him to touch me or go down on me, but instead it was a kiss, soft and undemanding. When he broke away he grinned, one hand heading towards my stomach and further south. I moved my hips to encourage him and he laughed, evilly. "Turn over, hands and knees."

I didn't argue, switching and spreading my legs so I was exposed to him. I heard his movements and waited for his touch, hands on my hips or a hand in my hair. I wasn't sure whether he would press his cock straight into me, going from subtle and nothing to hard and untamed or there would be something different.

And then I felt his tongue slide between my cheeks, pushing down to where I ached for him most. One hand grabbed my ass, the other pulled at a nipple and then his tongue dipped into me and his hand left my breast and and flicked my clit.

"Max," I gasped, his fingers working magic. My arms and legs felt wobbly as all my strength went into generating the oncoming force of the orgasm. He didn't respond, his mouth too busy on my pussy. "Fuck me, please."

I felt cold as he moved his face, his fingers still rhythmically strumming my clit. "I don't know if you're ready."

"I'm ready." I wasn't sure what he was referring to: his cock or something bigger?

I heard him move and then felt his cock against my ass cheeks, his fingers still rubbing me. The head of his cock pushed against my pussy, my hips automatically moving back to meet him, to make him enter.

"For fuck's sake, Victoria. I don't know if I'm going to be able to control myself."

"I don't care."

He pushed in hard, all the way in one go and I heard a scream that I knew was coming from me and then I came, the pinch of pain pushing me over the top of the rollercoaster and I started to contract around his cock, aware I was moving my hips, aware that his fingers had left my clit and his hand was in my hair, pulling my head backwards. I was aware that he was pummelling into me, telling me how tight I was, how wet I was, how hard he was fucking me, how I was his and no one else's, how hard he was going to come in me.

My head combusted with the sensations; his scent, his voice, the feel of him behind me, the feeling of being possessed so fucking thoroughly. All that there in the world at this minute was us. Nothing else existed; nothing else was. How could I ever leave?

One orgasm bled into another. He slapped my ass and bit my

shoulder, using a hand to pinch my nipples, ordering me to come again. I didn't need to be ordered. He growled at me, repeated my name and finally started to control my hips so my pussy fucked his cock as he moved deeper, harder, and I could tell he was close. I squeezed his cock with my muscles and heard him cry out as started to spill into me and I didn't have to squeeze those muscles anymore as they did it for themselves, a final orgasm.

All I could hear was our breathing. The sound of our breath filled the room as both of us tried to understand what had just happened because something had shifted. Max withdrew from inside me, leaving me bereft and, placing his hands on my shoulders, lifted me up. I shifted my legs so they stretched out in front of us and leaned back against his chest, his lips on my neck kissing me, nuzzling.

"I'm leaking," I said, because after that, stating the obvious was about all I could do. Anything profound was beyond my current capacity.

"I like it," he said. "I like knowing I've left something inside you." His hands went to my breasts and gently cupped them, his thumbs stroking my tender nipples. One hand left me and he reached for his phone that was on his bedside table. "Can I take a picture?"

We had never stopped with the photos. Even though he saw me naked most days I still sent him the odd tit pic or a mirror selfie so he could see my underwear. I had returns of various muscles, the occasional dick pic which was welcomed, sometimes, with his hand and a message telling me exactly where he wished his cock was.

He held up his phone, trying to get as much of my body in the picture as he could, his free hand still pinching my nipple. "You look amazing freshly fucked," he said.

And it was at that moment I had a realisation. "Shit," I said stiffening.

Max put his phone down quickly. "What is it?"

I turned to look at him, wishing I'd kept quiet because I had no idea how he would take the truth behind my sudden realisation. "I've forgotten my pill."

He paled, but didn't pull away. Instead, he moved me back to his chest and wrapped his hands around me. "Explain the medicine behind it. I'm a little in the dark."

"I have to take my pill within a twelve-hour window else I'm not protected. I've missed this morning's. It's unlikely I'll get pregnant, but there's more of a chance," I said. I took the progesterone-only pill, my migraines meaning the combined wasn't suitable.

"Do you need anything? I'm not sure what, but what can I do? I don't want you to worry—what's the worst that can happen?" I could feel his panic, but I didn't think it was because I had missed a pill, it was because he was worried about me.

"I could be pregnant. And given how deep you were and how much you've come..." I gestured down to the wet patch between my legs. At least it was on his side of the bed.

I felt his cock stiffen slightly and looked back over my shoulder at him.

"You being pregnant wouldn't be a problem," he said, starting to kiss my neck, one of his hands slipping back down to my clit. "Although showing any kid the picture we took after they were conceived might not be the best idea unless we want a huge counselling bill."

———

I pushed his response out of my mind until later when my muscles were sore and well used. The covers had been pushed off us, the room warm and Max acted like a blanket anyway. He curled round me, an arm possessively over me, a hand on my breast, his leg over mine. I'd push his leg away when I wanted to sleep, but for now I needed to think. He'd told me before that he didn't wanted children because of what happened to his mother, yet his response to me forgetting my pill was completely contradictory to that. And afterwards he'd fucked me again without a condom, coming inside me, knowing full well that I wasn't properly protected. Part of me understood that what I thought I was seeing in his responses to me was that this between us wasn't temporary anymore, that he wanted permanence.

But what did I want? Part of me hoped I wouldn't be offed the job at Johns Hopkins. Then the decision would be made by proxy; I'd be given a bye into the next round with Max. I fell asleep with his leg still over mine, his come still seeping out of me and his hand having slipped down from my breast to my stomach.

———

Coffee was a necessity after spending too much time last night orgasming instead of sleeping. Despite my pondering, I'd slept well, I just hadn't had enough of it.

We pottered about the kitchen, Max mixing a protein shake with oats in a blender and me downing coffee like it was my life source and debating whether to attempt to be healthy or not. Our mornings had turned into a pattern; we knew how the other moved around, how they got ready, what space they needed and it worked like a well-choreographed ballet, without the costumes or toe-murdering shoes.

My phoned pinged as it had done at least five times since I got out of the shower. It was a Friday, and Fridays were generally more relaxed with earlier finishes and less queries from students. I was on the verge of finishing my dissertation ahead of schedule and my tutor so far had been approving of it.

I checked my phone, inhaling deeply to prepare myself for what problems could be lining up and blinked at one of the notifications. "I've got an email from Johns Hopkins," I said, seeing the notification on my phone. I glanced up at Max who was now busying himself with the coffee machine. "This could be it."

I unlocked my screen and opened the email, scanning through the text. My heart pummelled through my rib cage into my mouth and I felt my arms and legs go weak and useless. "I've been offered the position. They want me." I reread the email. "My grandfather would've been over the moon right now."

The coffee machine began to grind, the only noise fracturing a silence that was now frozen. "Max," I said, looking over to him. "I've been offered the position."

"Congratulations," he said, barely glancing at me. "You've realised your grandfather's dreams. Have a good day."

He put a mug of black coffee in front of me and headed to the door, leaving me staring at his back, wondering what the hell had made him so foul tempered after an early morning with glorious, orgasm-ridden sex and good news. I hadn't had time to spit words at him or question his sudden mood swing, he'd just walked, leaving his bag on the sofa and the protein shake on the side. I wondered if me forgetting my pill was now playing on his mind, whether his reaction last night had been induced by orgasms and now reality had hit. I wondered if it was because of the news from Johns Hopkins—I hadn't said I was accepting. My mind was more unclear than ever as to whether I actually wanted to move.

I fought tears walking to the law department, blaming my emotional reaction on Peter Coffey and all the sex and me forgetting my pill, not how Max's sarcastic response had cut deep into me. Pushing thoughts of him away, I focused on my day, what I needed to get done and the conversation with Carol and student services about Peter. Anything but Max.

Two student traumas of not being able to meet deadlines for essays and a mix up on gradings weren't enough to take my mind of Max's mood any time before lunch. I hadn't heard from him, which was unusual in itself, even though I'd sent him a couple of silly texts and a quick picture of the thigh high stockings I was wearing today in the hope I'd initiate a response.

I'd gone through the whole story about Peter Coffey with Carol, who'd then contacted student services. There was nothing that could be done in the meantime, other than getting a restraining order against him, which was unlikely to be granted as he hadn't been threatening in any way. My mood was turning from elated that I'd been successful at interview to low and frustrated. My phone pinged as I was about to head out to source lunch; I checked it quickly, hoping it was Max.

It wasn't. Instead it was Seph's name on the screen.

Seph: What've you done to put Max in such a bad mood? His secretary's threatening to quit.

> Me: Nothing. He seemed a bit odd this morning when he left and I haven't heard from him since. I was hoping we'd go out for dinner to celebrate, but I'm not sure it's worth asking. Unless I take Jean out instead.

Seph: She's thrown a tennis ball at him after he snapped at her for absolutely no reason. He's now sitting in Jackson's office with an ice pack on his face. No one has any sympathy for him. What's the celebration?

> Me: Oh shit. Poor Jean. She should've hit him harder. I've been offered the post at Johns Hopkins.

Seph: In America?

> Me: Yes. It's to start September.

Silence resumed. No dots. No congratulations. Nothing. Seph was seemingly on mute. One of the professors came in, querying dates and asking for the details of how to log on to a database that he'd already been talked through at least three times.

Seph paced in just as Professor Fossman was collecting his pile of files and searching for his glasses. His tie was askew and hair rumpled. I fought the urge to tidy him up, especially as his expression was seriously not amused.

"So let me get this," he said, staring at me with eyes resembling pistols. "You tell my brother that you've been offered a job fuck knows how far away and you expect him to congratulate you?"

Standing up and folded my arms made me feel less like the target in an approaching verbal onslaught. "Why wouldn't he? He was adamant that this was a casual thing and our careers were the main priority for both of us. He knows how much this meant to my grandfather and I don't know—"

"Did your grandfather specify Johns Hopkins?" Seph said, presenting me with the lawyer instead of the little brother. "Or any American university?"

"No, but—"

"So you could stay here? Work at King's for example?"

I knew this line of questioning; it was one I'd been through myself, with Jacob too. "Yes, I could, but it's whether there's an opening."

Carol chose this moment to appear from her office, the door to which was open and I suspected she'd been listening all along, because that was Carol and how she got her rocks off. "There's an opening both here and at UCL. I was talking to your tutor this morning at some ridiculous breakfast meeting and he said the Richmonds had both decided to take retirement. He asked if you had heard from Johns Hopkins and was going to speak to you today some time about it. Not wanting to throw any spanners or anything." She took a handful of the sweets I kept on reception, smiled at me and chucked a sweet at Seph, before exiting stage right.

"Do you know why my brother is in such a horrific mood?" Seph said, putting the sweet on the counter rather than eating it, which emphasised the serious stance he currently had. Seph never passed on sweets.

"I'm thinking I have half an idea," I said, fighting back the tears that had stupidly filled my eyes, although why Max couldn't have fucking said I didn't understand.

"He doesn't want you to go to America. He wants you to stay here."

"Then why's he not said that? I can't read his fucking mind!" I said, frantically wiping my eyes. In around thirty seconds I'd have mascara all over my face if this continued.

"Because he's scared. He's fucking terrified, Vic. Max doesn't do relationships because he always said he doesn't want his own family after what his mum did. He's scared something will happen to the person he's chosen to love. And he thinks you'd rather move to America than have him because he's a little bit fucked up, even if he's decided that you're worth the risk." Seph's expression became that of the little brother I was used to, his blatant and obvious love for his oldest brother illuminated and underlined.

I didn't bother to wipe away the tears or the mascara. "He's never said anything, Seph. He needs to give me the words. I have almost nobody except my grandfather's dream; I can't throw that away based on Max's bad mood."

Seph looked at his feet. "I get that. I probably shouldn't have said anything. But my brother's sitting in his office looking like his world's ending and it isn't because I haven't done my time recording for the month. How would you feel if Max was moving away?"

I opened my mouth to speak but no words found their way out.

"Can I ask you one thing?" Seph said once he realised that I didn't have the capacity to respond.

"Sure," I managed.

"Before you accept, give him some time to ask you to stay. If he does, you have all the facts with which to make a decision," Seph said, his voice and demeanour now much calmer. "Especially as you now know there might be an opportunity here." He gave me a pained glance without an attempt at smile and headed out, his pace slower, shoulders sagging.

"Here." Carol emerged holding two glasses of wine. "It's past twelve and it's the decent stuff. Drink this, clean your face up and go over to the history department because he's right; before you can make a decision, you need all the information."

I took the glass and downed half of it in one gulp. "Do you always know everything?"

"Absolutely," she said, she said with a yawn. "How do you think I was so successful as a lawyer?"

———

King's had an opening. I was asked to apply. Asked. That meant there would be a very good chance I'd be offered the position. Bonnie Richmond, who was a piece of history herself, had handed in her resignation on the same day her husband had at University College London, making the decision to go travel the world while they still could. I saw her on my way in and she stepped up her pace to speak to me.

"Victoria! Have you heard? I'm going travelling—no more marking papers! Although I might write a book. They want you, you know." She gave me a quick, hard hug and tottered out of the building and I just about stopped myself from bursting into tears.

The storage unit I was renting was a forty-five minute tube ride out of London and I found myself there without really thinking about it. I signed in, producing ID which I thankfully had on me, and headed inside. It was a bit of an Aladdin's cave; intricately carved furniture and ornaments, some photographs and pictures that I couldn't bear to get rid of and in one of the drawers of the armoire was an unopened letter than my grandfather had composed a few weeks before he had died.

It was addressed to me, with the instructions to open it after he'd passed away, 'when I knew it was time'. If I needed his words ever, it was now. I opened the envelope with trembling fingers, thankful he'd chosen soft paper to avoid paper cuts, because those hurt like a bitch.

Dear Victoria Esme,

Firstly, I deeply hope you were all right after my death and that idiot Francis didn't wheedle any money out of you. Knowing him he will have tried, but fret not, because I will come back and haunt him. If he starts to complain about things in his house being moved, know it was me.

You, I will watch, so while you're reading this I'm possibly nearby, reading my words over your shoulder and watching your reaction. Your expressions always gave you away, my dear.

I've always had hopes and dreams for you: you were always my little historian but I worried you would live in the past too much and that your own past would stop you from finding a future you deserved. Travel, wealth, a job you enjoy and a family of your own. I had your grandmother and your father and you, and it was the most precious thing to me. I don't want you to be alone —I don't want you with some idiot who doesn't deserve you either—and I hope you do meet someone who makes the world—the present world—a better place for you and you for him. Or her. I'm open in that regard. As long as they make you happy.

Maybe by now you've finished your thesis and you're ready to move on to find tenure and teach and write those books you've always dreamed of. Or maybe you've already done this and you're now living in London or Manchester or Oxford or even abroad liked we once talked about. Or maybe you've done all that and you now have a family of your own. I have so much hope for you and I wish I could've seen more of your life and enjoyed it with you.

However, it was not to be. You were my greatest gift in my older years and know how proud you made me.

I wish you every happiness, my greatest (and only, but that's not the point!) granddaughter,

Your ever-loving grandfather,
Thomas Davies

I lost the plot enough and cried loudly enough for one of the workers to bring me a cup of tea and a couple of biscuits before scarpering as if I had truly gone mad. I remembered my grandfather writing the letter and noticed how his handwriting deteriorated towards the end when he must've been tired. There was no mention of Johns Hopkins or America or anything specific. Just of my happiness.

I bit back more tears, feeling spent and exhausted, but clearer. I would spend the night with Jacob—I needed to not be on my own tonight—unless I heard from Max, although I think we needed some space. If Seph was right anyway, Max needed to make his own mind up, or maybe, like me, he needed more information. My phone was on low battery and about to die so I typed rapidly.

Me: I might be offered a job at King's.

I pressed send and the screen went dark.

CHAPTER 21
MAXWELL

She could be pregnant. She probably isn't but she could be.

Would she stay if she was?

Would she stay for me?

Would I be the sort of dad my father was?

I might be offered a job at King's. Did this mean she was going to stay? Because she had a job she wanted or because of me?

I ran to up to the ball and kicked, my knee reminding me that I wasn't an undergraduate anymore and should probably be taking something for my joints. The ball sailed between the two white posts and Jackson and Maxwell jumped on me to celebrate, followed by Callum, Killian and Seph, plus Elijah Ward who was a salaried partner at Callaghan Green and ex-Oxford too. If my maths was correct, we'd just managed to beat the Oxford Second XI, or perhaps it was the third, but given that we were older and should be less fit, it was something to celebrate.

"Maybe we need to start a team from the firm," Eli said, clicking the cartilage in his nose. "I forget how much I like playing."

"You can organise it then," Jackson said, smacking him on the back. "Well played."

Eli had scored three tries and I'd been surprised as to how fast he'd been; given he was the same size as me.

"Are you staying with us?" I asked Eli. He'd joined us at the last minute, when other weekend plans had fallen through.

He shook his head. "No, but thanks for the offer. My girlfriend's down for the weekend. Her train gets in this evening so I need to get back to meet her."

"Long distance?"

He pulled a face. "Yeah. Not sure if it's working out. I moved down here and she talked about following, but then she got a promotion and she's stopped talking about it. Trust me when I say I'd rather be here with you lot downing beers and shots."

I wiped sweat off my forehead and fussed with my beard. "If you end up being a single man by Monday I'll take you out for a few beers to celebrate. You're coming to Jackson's wedding next weekend, aren't you?"

I still had a best man's speech to write. That would be one way of stopping me from thinking constantly about Victoria, and whether or not I was now a single man.

I'd acted like a fucking idiot on Friday. To walk out after just giving her a sarcastic response and not explain why was the stuff of ass-wipes and imbeciles—and if she thought about it, she'd probably realise she'd had a lucky escape.

"I'm there for the whole day. Doubt I'll be bringing a date," Eli said and I felt for the guy. I knew he'd been seeing his girlfriend for a few years and any change was hard to deal with, even when the change was probably for the best.

"I'd offer to hook you up with the bridesmaids but they're mainly my sisters," I said.

He laughed. "I'll probably just get shit-faced and fall asleep in a corner after practicing my dad dancing."

"You've got kids?"

He shook his head. "No, but according to my girlfriend, it's how I look on a dancefloor." He inhaled deeply. "This is probably going to be for the best."

"If that's what you're thinking, you're probably right." I gave him a slap on the back and headed to the showers where my brothers and Killian already were, taking the piss out of Seph for the amount of manscaping he'd been doing.

I eyed him weirdly, trying not to look. "Did you lose control of the clippers?" I asked, pulling off my top that already stunk of sweat before losing the rest of my rugby kit.

"Have you not watched any porn in the past decade?" Seph said.

Killian and Callum hooted crudely.

"Seph, you're not a porn star," Jackson said. "And if you've appeared in anything, however homemade, that's somewhere even a mile away from the internet then let me know so I can get a press release ready."

"It's okay," Callum said. "The only action he's been getting recently has been from his hand."

Seph looked ready to explode and there was a rugby ball far too close to his hand for him to aim at Callum; I knew Marie would rather her prettiest son stayed that way.

"Right, shut the fuck up the pair of you and finish tarting yourselves up. I've got a best man's speech to write so I need you thinking of how I can embarrass Jackson."

Jackson's eyes were now on me, digging in viciously, but Callum and Seph had stopped bickering like two old ladies. My thoughts had moved back to Victoria.

I hadn't replied to her text because I didn't have the words. I wanted her to stay, to move into her childhood home with me and make new memories there. I wanted what Jackson and Vanessa had, what my dad and Marie had and Claire and Killian. What even my two fuckwit youngest brothers would probably have if they could ever find people to put up with them.

My dad was waiting for us outside, ready to give us a lift back. There would be a debate about going to a bar afterwards and watching Leicester play Wasps in a proper rugby match, but Killian was continually worried about Claire and the baby coming early, so we'd opted to drain my father's drinks' cabinet instead.

"Good game, lads," Dad asked as we filed out, smelling better than we had done twenty minutes ago. "Where's Seph?"

"Still doing his hair," Callum replied, jumping in the front seat. "Like trying to put lipstick on a pig."

"I told you to fucking stop riling him up," I said, climbing in behind him. "Jacks, can you take Seph back?"

Jackson nodded, checking something on his phone. Possibly an update from Vanessa of what his balls were up to. I wondered what Victoria was doing to mine.

"All the girls are here," Dad said, getting in and starting the engine. "Except Victoria. We were expecting her. Don't tell me she's seen sense already?" He looked around at me and laughed.

"Don't, Dad," Callum said. I wasn't sure what he knew, only that he and Seph had managed a civil conversation over breakfast this morning and Seph had glanced over several times to check I wasn't listening.

"Oh well, it had to happen sometime! Don't worry, son, you'll meet someone else."

I felt the same anger burn that I had as a teenager and said nothing, trying to swallow the pain and fury back down.

The tension in the car was poisonous as no one said anything, Callum uncomfortable and not understanding in the slightest what he'd said.

"I'm sorry, Max, it was a joke. I'm sure she'll be back. Marie saw the way she looked at you the last time she saw you both and thought it wouldn't be that long before we'd be at your wedding," my father said, braking far too late at lights and jolting us forward.

"Leave it, Dad," I said and looked at my phone, at Victoria's text.

> Me: I'm sorry I was such a dick yesterday when you told me you'd been offered the job in the U.S. Congratulations.
>
> Me: And good news about the one at King's too. Choice is always good. Xo

I stared at my phone for five minutes, willing her to text back, but as we pulled up at my parents' house there was still nothing. I put my phone in my back pocket and headed inside, hoping that Marie was too occupied with the wedding and Claire's current state of about to give birth to a monster sized baby.

As usual after a rugby game, the drinking started immediately. Vanessa locked Ava, Payton and Claire in a room to fold boxes for the wedding favour—things which I didn't understand and I don't think Jackson did either, but neither of us asked for fear we'd receive a lecture on it. Callum fussed over the puppy Marie and my father had decided to get, a rescue mongrel who bounced all over the place before peeing on Seph's shoes.

"Shots," Jackson said, carrying a tray of glasses and a bottle of tequila into the room my father had chosen to place a huge TV in and had named his den. I grabbed a glass and knocked it back before Jackson had even put the tray down.

"So this speech," Seph said, sprawling out across the floor. At twenty-eight, he should've stopped growing, but I was convinced he'd still added a couple of inches so far this year. He'd also broadened out, needing to buy a whole new set of suits because the jackets looked like he'd stolen them from a thrift store and the trousers were starting to look indecent. "What sort of things are you including?"

Jackson stayed mute, checking his phone and pretending not to hear.

"The time he woke up in bed with twins?" Killian suggested. "And confessed that all he'd done was sleep."

I laughed. We'd teased him for weeks after that. "The time he locked himself out stark bollock naked after chasing Amy Smith down the road when she dumped him."

Jackson groaned. "No one wants to hear about Amy Smith."

"Wasn't there a time when you had to climb out of a second storey window and you ended up pulling down the drainpipe because you didn't want to get caught by the girl's father?" Callum said. "Or was that Max?"

"That was Max," Jackson said. "And just bear in mind that when it's your turn, it'll be me or Killian giving the speech and there will be plenty of jokes about the losing of virginities, vanilla sex and Ed Sheeran. Plus drainpipes."

I poured another shot of tequila and downed it. It burned my throat as it went down, the pain a sweet distraction from the agony in my chest.

"Victoria won't mind. She's already heard everything and worse," Seph said as he cleaned the freaking glasses that he didn't need.

The room went silent, no one knowing what to say.

Seph looked up, almost oblivious to the bomb he'd dropped. "Oh for fuck's sake. Van and Jackson broke up at one point because he was a dipshit and she overreacted. Max and Vic will get over this." He looked at me, glasses now in place. "Just tell her you want her to stay. Give her a reason to take the job at King's."

I stood up, knocking over Killian's beer. "What the fuck do you know about the King's job?"

Seph, at least, had the manners to look half-guilty. "I went to see her yesterday."

Even Jackson had put his phone down. Twenty seconds later Vanessa appeared with my sisters. Clearly he'd been giving her the head's up on the episode of Game of Thrones that was unfolding.

"What do you mean you went to see her yesterday?" I demanded. Killian passed me another shot. Probably not one of his better ideas.

Seph shrugged. "You were mad at the world and I figured it was because of her, so I texted her and she told me about the job offer. I went round to the department to speak to her, because, to be honest, I was mad at her for not realising what it would do to you if she moved." He was now a deeper shade of beet red, embarrassed and worried he'd ruined things. "While I was there Carol mentioned about someone retired from the History Department at King's and UCL and said the dean over there had mentioned to her about Victoria possibly being interested. That's how I know."

I sat back down, still holding the tequila. My hands suddenly became very interesting.

"I think Vic needs you to ask her to stay. She was going on about how you agreed it was just temporary and you weren't interested in a long term thing," Seph said, trying to squeeze his six foot four frame into the chair. I remembered him doing the same thing as a ten-year-old when he'd stolen my aftershave and used a load of it in an attempt to impress a girl in his class. He actually fit in the chair then, now he looked like a spider trying to escape a hungry bird.

"I probably shouldn't say anything because she's my friend and all that, but she's a wreck, Max. For someone you call Miss Feisty, she's not happy and she's not a pretty crier," Vanessa said, looking guilty.

I thought Victoria was a pretty crier, not that she'd cried

much since we'd been together. I didn't want her to be upset and now I felt even more like a shit than I did before, but she hadn't texted me back. I didn't know what else to say.

"Thanks for telling me," I said, not wanting to antagonise my future sister-in-law before she married Jackson. Her changing her mind was not an option. "Any other advice? Words of wisdom?" I held my glass up in a toast.

"Fuck yes," Claire said. I glanced at Killian who shrugged as if absolving himself of all responsibility. "Stop being a stupid dick and sort out whatever trauma you need to deal with in order to function like a normal human being, Maxwell. Because if you don't you're going to turn yourself in to Dad before Marie, and you're not our father. You practically brought me and Callum up until Marie came along, and I seem to remember you wiping dirty butts, prepping bottles, winding the little fuckers till they spewed on you and all the rest when these three were tiny. And still with Seph now when he's drunk."

"Cheers to the chief babysitter." Killian held up a shot glass and drank it quickly.

Claire glared. "Who's going to drive me to the hospital if I go into labour early?" she said, eyeing him and I hoped their child would inherit Killian's temperament rather than Claire's innate evilness.

"Marie's taken an online midwifery course so you'll be fine. Besides, you're three weeks away and if you're going to be early, it'll be at your brother's wedding," Killian said. "Now shut up and let me get drunk because this might be the last time for a while."

"It'd better not be at my wedding," Jackson said. "I don't want a repeat of my thirteenth birthday where you had to make sure you had all the attention on you."

"What did she do?" Killian said, looking happy to find some shit on my sister.

Jackson shrugged. "Did a strip tease on the bouncy castle

when we kept ignoring her. There's a film of it somewhere. It was the year Dad bought a video camera. I'm more than happy to dig it out."

"Fuck you, Jackson!" Claire said, giving him the finger and storming off.

Vanessa sipped her drink mildly, clearly used to my family, just as Victoria had become.

I checked my phone.

This time there were messages.

> Victoria: Thanks. Seph told me you didn't want me to go.

> Victoria: I need to know that from you. I'm not saying I'll make a decision based on that—the job at King's hasn't been offered yet. I have an interview on Tuesday. But if you want more than just something temporary then I could think about a compromise agreement.

Part of me wanted to give my man card up completely and ask Seph at the very least what I should respond, but I also knew I had to do this, it had to come from me even if I struggled to find the words.

> Me: I want more than temporary.

> Victoria: How much more?

And that was the problem: I didn't know how much I could give her.

———

I continued to drink through the afternoon and into the evening, my anger growing with each beer. Around five, Jackson refused to let me have any more and I noticed Killian had stopped completely, leaving just Callum and Seph—who had turned back into teenagers—and Ava and Payton, who were cooking something up on social media that I was trying to avoid being caught up in.

I knew I had to deal with my past and at the moment, my lack of control with the situation with Victoria was being placed on my father's desk. The clock struck six and in my half drunken state I decided that there was no time like the present to finally have it out with my old man, who had hidden behind Marie for too long, never giving any sort of apology for how he'd left Mum and us with the constant excuse of work.

I left my siblings and Marie to finish off the remains of the barbeque that we'd had and headed into my father's study, no longer trying to keep a lid on the monster that was screaming inside me.

My father looked up from his papers, initially unaware that I was in front of his desk, awaiting his attention, just like I had so many years before when my mother had died and I needed to know how to look after my siblings.

"Maxwell," he said, with a smile. "I'm glad you're here. How's things? How's Victoria? Seph said you'd heard from her."

"Why the fuck would you care?" I said, my blood now at boiling point and I knew I was about to spew word vomit all over his precious, orderly desk that matched my own in too many ways.

He stood up, eyes narrowed and stretched to his full height. "Why the fuck would I care about what?"

"Victoria. You made an insinuation at Marie's birthday that she couldn't manage me. Well, you'll be glad to know that, as usual, you were right." The words tasted as bitter as they sounded.

For a moment my father said nothing. His arms were folded across his chest and his glare was piercing, only there was nothing left of me to pierce.

"Hit me with it," he said, the quietness of his words surprising me. "Give me all you've got because whatever argument you've been brewing for the past twenty-five years clearly needs to be said. To be quite frank, Maxwell, I haven't a fucking clue what you're on about."

"You said you weren't sure whether she could manage me. Well, you were right. She's got the job in America and she's thinking about leaving, which is probably just as well given how I'm so fucking much like you I wouldn't want the guilt of fucking someone up just like you did mum. The fucking workaholic, that's all you did and you didn't give a fucking shit that we needed a father, that we needed you. Or even that Mum needed you." I felt wetness on my cheeks and I didn't care. "I don't deserve anyone like Victoria because I'll probably just fucking wreck her and any children we have. And she wanted that. She said. But I can't tell her I wanted the same because look what you did to mum, to us."

And then I was shaking with the sobs and my father's hands were on my shoulders shaking me.

"Maxwell," he said, that quiet voice which I never knew he had until Marie came. "You're not me. When I wasn't there for Claire and Jackson and Callum, you were. I remember you standing here, asking me for money for diapers and I wondered how the hell I'd buried myself in so much grief I forgot to live myself, that my seven-year-old son was looking after my children. How you can categorise yourself like that I don't understand."

"Because I work like you. I'm obsessed by it. I'm driven and I push myself and I forget that other people exist and that must be what Victoria saw." I felt the rage again, that spark of pure fight that I usually kept embedded in structured arguments and academia.

My father shook his head. "You're better than me. I had to work harder to be less excellent than you are. You spend time with your siblings and me and your friends and Victoria. I didn't until Marie. I didn't understand until then."

"But Mum. How did you not see? How did you not see she was sad? She was hurting, Dad. I could tell. She was never right with Callum and there were times when she looked at us like we weren't there. We ran wild that summer. Didn't you notice?" In my voice I heard the seven-year-old, the skinny boy with grazed knees and sunburnt arms.

"Max." His voice radiated pain. "I tried. I didn't do a good job because I was clueless, but I brought in doctors, I asked her to go to hospital. I wanted her to be happy. There are things you don't know, about us, and how we were and I probably should have told you but I didn't think it was my place. But if I knew how you tortured yourself, I'd have told you years ago." He sat down, his expression crippled in distress.

I had never seen my father cry. Only once, when Ava was poorly with a viral infection that could've been fatal, had he been close to it. Yet now he sat there broken.

The door shifted open and Marie appeared carrying a tray loaded with tea and a bottle of whisky.

"I couldn't wait outside any longer; I heard you shouting. I remind you that you're both lawyers and arguments that are planned and considered are far more productive, but sometimes a good old shit throwing competition is necessary too." She went straight for the whisky and I noticed she had a third glass for herself. "Maxwell, what you're saying about yourself is complete fucking bollocks. One, I knew how you looked after everyone before I arrived including making your father eat because you gave me clear instructions on exactly how everyone was to be fed and clothed and cleaned, so never doubt what sort of father you would make. Two, you had me and I was a fucking awesome stepmother so you learned from the best. Three, there's always a bigger picture and there are family secrets that you don't know and learning about them now is probably not the right time. You don't need to know them because, really, they serve no purpose. Four, and finally, what your father meant about Victoria is that she had her own issues to deal with before she could 'manage' you—which is a shit way of describing it, Grant. Does every expression you possess have to be to do with law or business?"

She glared at him and slapped him around the head gently. He caught her hand and held it against his cheek in an act so tender I felt a third-wheel simply watching.

And then I remembered a long dead vision of a man who was there in the afternoons, when Mum's door was shut and we played outside like the wild things we had become. It hadn't registered until now, because the main event of that summer was her death, not what came before it, other than she was sad. "She was having an affair, wasn't she?" I said quietly, calmly. "You knew."

My father nodded. "For some time. He ended it. She was going to leave me for him, but he ended it before she could."

I nodded. "Okay," I said. "Okay."

I stumbled to the chair near the window and half collapsed. Marie passed me a tumbler of whisky which I downed, the golden liquid burning my throat and reminding me that I existed and that this wasn't a dream.

"I'm sorry," I said. "What I said was what I thought as a

teenager. I've never managed to process the bigger picture. I'm still not sure I can."

For a moment my father said nothing, looking at the glass in his hand. "Maxwell, you were in a position that no child should be in and I didn't help. I can only apologise. But don't punish yourself for the mistakes others made. You made none. You looked after her as best you could and you looked after everyone else as well. I've never had a moment when I wasn't proud of you."

"Really?" I said, surprised as he'd never stopped pushing me to be the best I could.

"Except when you wrapped my car around that tree and wrote it off. The tree didn't murder you, but I almost did."

And then I laughed and he joined in, the noise dispelling the tension. I walked over to him, my legs still like overcooked spaghetti and opened my arms, stepping into his embrace and for the first time my father hugged me and the world was made better.

We spent the rest of the evening talking, just the two of us, with Marie coming in every so often to check the arguing hadn't started again. We talked about Mum and how young they were when they got married: Dad was still a student and Mum had never lived away from home before. They had me as soon as Dad started his training contract and he was focused on making a name for himself and not just relying on the fact it was his family's firm—something I understood too well.

"We started a family too soon," he said over coffee and the left-over ribs. "But your Mum was bored and wanted children young. We didn't think things through and if I'm honest, I resented your mum for that because I didn't have a clue what to do with you all and I wanted to focus on being a provider first. I don't regret having you now. I'll love your mum forever for giving me the four of you. I'm not sure I'll love Marie forever for giving me Seph though."

I laughed, knowing he was joking. "We never talked before."

My dad shook his head. "No, because neither of us are good with feelings and shit like that. Give it a few months and you'll probably want to shout again, but I'd rather you do that than bottle it up. That's not healthy. Marie taught you that."

"About what Mum did…"

"It doesn't matter."

"The others…"

"Don't need to know. They have her on a pedestal. Leave her there."

"I think they should know the whole story because it will change what they think of you," I said. "And it's you who's here."

My father looked at me in his considered way. "Maybe you're right. Maybe they should know the full story. Especially Callum. Especially Callum," he repeated it and I understood why. Callum blamed himself. None of the rest of us ever had; in fact, we'd loved him more because of what happened. "But not yet. Not while Claire's so pregnant or Jackson's wedding is approaching. Please give it a few months for everything to be calm again. Then if you think you want me to tell them, then I will. I don't want to force you to keep secrets from them. That's not fair."

I stood up, needing my bed and sleep and some headspace in which I could digest everything that had been said. "Thanks, Dad."

He stood too. "Maxwell," he said. "About Victoria."

"Yes?"

"Phone her now. Tell her everything now, or tomorrow. Don't bottle it up, Maxwell. That's what Marie taught me," he said. "And now I'm going to find her and say thank you."

I must've looked concerned at how he was going to do that.

"Don't worry, I'll keep it suitable for families," he said with a smirk that reminded me of Ava. "Until we get upstairs."

"Goodnight," I said, leaving him laughing hard.

————

I didn't phone Victoria before I went to sleep. Processing what I'd learned was going to take some time and I needed to understand it before I could explain it, but I did text her. I needed to respond to her when she'd asked how much more I wanted.

> Me: Everything. I want everything with you. I'm worried it won't be easy though.

> Victoria: Is anything worthwhile ever easy? See you tomorrow maybe?

> Me: I'll come straight to yours if you want?

> Victoria: That's fine. Message me when you're leaving your parents and I'll know when to be in. I'm staying at Jacob's.

> Me: Okay xo

For the first time in nearly forty-eight hours my heart rate subsided to something less than that of a hundred metre sprinter and I fell asleep easily, thinking of my mum and my dad and the past, but also of the now and the future. I felt hope.

————

Victoria was standing outside her apartment when I got there, looking at her front door like she was about to kick it in. "There's someone inside," she said. "I've been here about ten minutes and there's definitely someone inside."

I was surprised she hadn't gone storming in. The fact she was still outside, waiting for me, suggested that she was weirded out at the very least. She'd also not lost her shit; which Claire would've done on a huge scale. "How do you know?"

"I've seen shadows, movement. And only one lock's on. Someone's gone in with keys."

"Okay. I'm calling the police." Before she could tell me not to I was on the phone, putting the call through. And then I called Killian, who was already home having taken back a very cross and tired Claire. My sister hadn't slept, had bad indigestion and was probably about to murder one of us.

Luckily we didn't have to wait very long until two community support officers arrived, both looking serious and slightly dubious because there was no sign of a forced entry.

"Is there anyone who might want to enter your property for some reason?" one of them asked.

I glanced at Victoria, knowing fucking too well who would want want to be in there, going through her underwear and smelling her sheets.

"Possibly," she said, looking at me. "Peter Coffey. He's a student where I work."

She explained what had happened. I filled in the bits she deliberately skipped.

"Okay," the officer said. "Do you have your keys?"

Victoria handed them over. "You've my permission to enter. If it is Peter Coffey, he doesn't have permission."

They both entered, leaving us at the door watching. I wanted to barge past them and yank the bastard out myself and then use him to practice my right hook; however, my level of self-control was currently at 'good', so I let the police do their job.

Less than five minutes later, Peter Coffey was brought out in handcuffs, which were the main accessory to the jumper that he was wearing which was one of Victoria's and a pair of pyjama bottoms, which again, I recognised as being hers. I didn't want to think about what he had on underneath, but I expected we would be going shopping very soon.

"Is this the man who's been following you and sending you unwanted gifts?" one of the officers said.

Victoria nodded. "That's Peter Coffey."

"Have you been away from home for a few days?"

"A few nights."

"It seems like he's moved himself in, and he's added to the art work on your walls. We're going to take him down to the station and we'll need you to come down to make a statement." A police van pulled up and two more officers stepped out, taking hold of Peter.

"But you wanted me to live with you, Victoria," he shouted as he was dragged into the back of the van. "You wanted to be with me!"

She turned round to look at me. "Fuck," she said. "Fuck, fuck, *fuck*. I don't know if I want to go in there. Shit, he'll have touched all my stuff."

I pulled her into my chest and she clung to me and I clung back, needing to feel her against me after Friday, after thinking that we were finished. After finding out that Peter Coffey was in her house.

"We need to go in and look. Get an idea of what he's done because you'll need to explain to someone what he's changed or taken." I said, still holding her and not wanting to let go.

"I know," she said. "I know. And I know he'll have gone through clothes, what's there, and probably slept in my bed. I can deal with all that. It's what he'll have done with my grandfather's things. I can't replace those."

"Possibly nothing," I said. "Because they're not your things, they're not personal objects like your clothes. Let's go in and see."

It was clear that Coffey had made himself at home in the last few days. A collection of mugs was on the side table in the front room, one of her throws was crumpled on the sofa, dipping into a pizza box. The weirdest things were the photos: Victoria had a few pictures of her, her parents and her grandparents as well as a couple of Jacob. Coffey had added Photoshopped pictures of him and Victoria to the shelves and a couple of him by himself, one in a tacky heart shaped frame that was so not Victoria.

In her bedroom there was evidence of Coffey having slept in her bed, the blankets tossed back and a couple of dubious stains on the sheets. Clothes were neatly folded, both his and hers, and on her pillow was a selection of cheap lace panties and bras. I felt bile rise in my throat and was glad I'd stopped drinking when I had. It gave me time to sober up and avoid the thick head I would've otherwise had—and the vomit that would no doubt spewed everywhere.

"I think it's safe to say I won't be staying here again," she said, remarkably composed, using her phone to take photos. "I also don't think he's bothered with my books or knick-knacks. I'll get them out today and back into storage."

"Just bring them to mine. I'll drive my car round after we've been to the police station and you can load it up," I said. There wasn't that much other stuff, and unless she'd been round to mine to pack her belongings, she had plenty of clothes and bits there already.

"Thank you," she said. "Thank you, Max."

———

It was evening before we sat down in my lounge with two large glasses of malbec, music playing quietly. Victoria sat with her legs folded under her, wearing a fitted T-shirt, baggy pyjama bottoms and no bra. The last bit was important because I had to try my goddamn hardest to not stare at her tits which were still as perfect as ever; I didn't think I'd ever get bored with them.

The sex we'd had on Thursday had been different and things

had shifted again. She'd given me what I'd needed and she'd taken whatever I'd given her. When she'd told me about the missed pill I knew that it upped the chances of her being pregnant by me, but those chances were still small. I still had my worries, one evening with my dad wasn't going to change those, but I felt braver and more like me, not some reincarnation of Grant Callaghan.

"Where do we start?" she said, sipping the wine.

"Twenty-eight years ago?"

Her doe eyes widened and I began the story, leaving nothing out. The words came easier than I thought and when I stumbled, she asked questions, never afraid of any answer that might come out.

"So you're going to tell your siblings?" she said, pouring from the second bottle that we'd opened.

"At some point. Not yet. I need to talk to Dad again when I'm calmer. Yesterday was heightened and not the right time for the conversation really. I shouldn't have stormed in the way I did," I said, not quite sure of how to even start untangling my feelings about my parents. Victoria was the focus right now: I needed to get my present and future right first.

Victoria shrugged. "I'm not sure. You've bottled everything up for so long, it needed something major to pop the cork so it could fizz out. If you were calm, I doubt you'd have instigated the conversation."

"You're right."

"So where does this leave us?"

I topped up my own glass. "I don't want this to be temporary. I want more. I want to ask you to stay, but I also know that if the best opportunity for you is to work at Johns Hopkins, then you need to take that and we'd find some way to make it work long distance."

"Long distance would be hard. And expensive," she said. "But I could put a limit on how long I'd be out there so we'd know it wasn't forever." She stared at her hands and I noticed she didn't seem as enthused about the idea of going to America. "I have the interview at King's on Tuesday. I need a job, well, I need a job for my sanity and it's what I've always wanted to do so I'll weigh up the pros and cons."

We looked at each other, the only light that from the buildings outside. My apartment was on the third floor so I needed little privacy, the glass being privacy glass so leaving the curtains open was always an option.

"Is me wanting you to stay a factor?" I said, needing to know even though I sounded like a complete wuss.

She laughed. "Yes. I don't want this to be temporary either. I found a letter from my grandad. It was more about wanting me to be happy rather than pursuing some of the things he talked about. I think when we discussed me working at a college in America he was trying to expand my horizons and make me think that anything was possible."

"You've been offered a post there, Vic, it is possible. It just depends on what will make you happiest."

She put her glass down and came over to me, straddling my lap. "Are you okay with me staying with you until I know what I'm doing? I can't go back to my apartment."

"More than okay. I'd feel better with you being here too," I said, my hands going to her ass and moving her closer. I was only wearing sweatpants and a vest and her closeness and the shape of her tits through her top and the way I could see her nipples through the fabric was enough to make me hard. My sweatpants did nothing to hide it.

"What if you're pregnant?" I said, my voice almost too quiet to be heard.

She lifted her hand to my face and cupped my cheek, her thumb toying with my beard. "Then I'll be turning Johns Hopkins down regardless and you'll be a wonderful dad."

"What if you're not?"

"Then I make my decision after I hear back from King's and at some point in the future we'll choose when we have kids and you'll still be a wonderful dad. How's that for an agreement?"

I pushed her top over her head, exposing her tits, her nipples hard and begging to be touched. "Our babies are the only people ever allowed to even look at these other than me," I said, although even I'd admit to it coming out more like a growl. "Unless I let someone else see them." I liked the power of the ownership and of the shared intimacy. She had a wild side that brought out mine and made me fearless—possibly stupid too.

The tips of her nipples puckered even more and I felt my balls tighten. My hand went into her hair and pulled it back, making her chest rise. "Stand up and take your clothes off."

She did, pushing the bottoms and her underwear down and stepping out naked. I lost my sweatpants, my erection jutting out hard and impatient to get inside of her. Stepping behind her, I put my hands on her hips and guided her over to the large floor to ceiling window. A neighbour on the same level or the one above would be able to see us, not clearly, but certainly the shapes of us. "Put your hands on the window and press your tits to the glass. Keep your hips back."

She moaned as the coldness stung her nipples. I kept one hand on her hips and moved my other round to the front, using a knee to encourage her to spread her legs. My fingers landed on her clit that was already slick with her want and I started to work it, two fingers going round in circles; medium pressure was the surest way to make her come quickly. I pressed my cock against her back, wanting her to know how hard I was for her, how she made me.

"Is anyone watching, feisty girl? Is anyone seeing how I own this body?"

She canted her hips back further, hands positioned, tits still against the glass. "There's someone on the balcony, over there," she gasped out, unable to point. I looked about and saw him, standing, no lights on behind him and I couldn't tell if he was watching us or not. Probably not as we were too far away, but the idea of having her and showing the world she was mine was heady.

"Do you like him watching you like this? All spread out for me and about to come. Seeing your tits pressed against the glass and my fingers on your clit, in your pussy?" I slipped one finger inside briefly and elicited an almost agonised moan from her lips.

"Yes," she said. "I like him watching you do this to me."

"Are you going to like him watching you take my cock and seeing you come all over it?"

Her response was to break apart on my fingers, my other hand holding her up, her tits away from the window and bouncing with each pulse of her pussy.

I didn't give her time to recover, putting her hands back on the window and guiding my cock straight into her slick centre, filling her with one thrust that made her slam against the glass. Her legs were spread wide and I could see our voyeur watching us still, his hand in his trousers. This was stupid after what had happened with Peter Coffey and part of my brain was telling me that. But he wouldn't be able to make out our faces or identify us and the idea of being watched as I took her, as I claimed her as mine was enough for me to ignore that sensible part of my head.

"Are you going to come on my cock, feisty girl?"

"Fuck me harder."

I did as she asked pressing her into the glass and hearing her cry out loudly. Her pussy began to contract and squeeze around me and I bit the side of her neck as I came myself, deep into her, making her mine.

And me hers.

CHAPTER 22
VANESSA

"When are you going to tell him?"

I opened one eye and stared at Jacob who was sprawled on a chaise longue, admiring his manicured nails. I switched eyes so the make-up artist, who was a friend of Jacob's, could blend the eyeshadow on the other lid. "Today at some point. As soon as I get chance, really."

I hadn't seen Max since Friday morning when we'd both left for work. He was staying at the hotel where Vanessa and Jackson were getting married, supposedly to help Jackson calm his nerves the night before the big day, but we all knew it was to make sure the rest of his siblings were hangover and black-eye-free.

I'd been pulled into the Dean of the History department's office at the close of play on Friday, giving me the outcome from the interview and texting or phoning Maxwell seemed like the wrong thing to do: I needed to tell him in person.

And now there were two things to tell him. A message just wouldn't suffice.

I wasn't pregnant. My period had started this morning when

I'd walked around Max's apartment making coffee. I'd taken two pregnancy tests to be certain and they'd come up negative, so I was pretty sure that we weren't going to be parents in nine months' time. I wasn't sure he'd be pleased by that, given his response last week, and I hadn't decided how I felt about it either. The negative result didn't have me jumping for joy, which illustrated that it wouldn't have been a huge catastrophe if I was been pregnant.

"How are you going to tell him?" Jacob said. "You need to balance her left eye more. Her right lid is a little lazy and on photos looks like it's sagging slightly. If you use a bit of high-lighter there," he pointed to a spot on my face, "it'll prevent it."

"Thanks for pointing out my imperfections," I said, glaring at him.

"You're more than welcome. Now, let's talk what you're wearing. Please tell me you've changed your mind from the black disaster?"

I sighed and prayed for patience. I adored Jacob and all his personalities but today when I was nervous enough about attending a wedding of rather huge size and proportions and telling Max a couple of things that would impact on his future, I needed the calm, non-soap opera side.

"The blue off the shoulder number should be what you go with. With the nude heels. It showcases your waist and those boobs. You do have the decent strapless bra, don't you? That idiot didn't try it on or something?" Jacob passed the make-up artist a pot of eye shimmer or something.

The idiot, also known as Peter Coffey, was with his parents in Stevenage, hopefully getting some form of help. He'd been charged with breaking and entering, damaging property and a couple of other offenses. There was now a restraining order against him which meant I could sleep at night. My apartment had been cleared out, some furniture put back in storage, my oddities and ornaments brought to Max's and the clothes he'd touched or even potentially touched, incinerated.

"I've got a new strapless bra that does a good job of holding up my boobs," I said. "Although they do a good job of staying up on their own."

"They do, but given that your nipples harden every time Max come anywhere near, the bra stops you looking totally obvious," Jacob said. He'd brought himself round for dinner on Tuesday under the guise of checking I was okay, which may have been half-true. The other half of it was that he wanted to see what Max's apartment was like.

"Fair point. Or should it be points?" A mascara wand was waved in front of my face with the order to look down. I hated having my make-up done, but I wanted to look different to how I normally did and as I only knew one way to apply everything, Jacob had insisted he get one of his friends in to do it for me. One of his drag queen friends. I had no idea how I was going to end up looking but really didn't have time to reapply everything if I looked more queen than princess.

"Just lips now," the artist said, inspecting my choice of lipsticks. "Let's go with this. Part your lips slightly."

"She's good at that."

Luckily my mouth was too occupied to swear at him.

The hopefully miracle worker stepped away and Jacob held a mirror out so I could inspect. I had no complaints: my eyes were smoky, there was some subtle sculpting of cheekbones and high-lighting and my skin looked even and clear. It was better than I could do, but I still looked like me. "Thank you," I said. "You've done a great job."

"It was no problem. And now Jacob owes me a favour which I shall be cashing in later." My make-up artist gave Jacob a smouldering look and started to pack away his tools. I decided not to ask. It would be safer for all.

"The blue dress," Jacob said. "Not the red and definitely not the black. You want to have his eyes on you from the word go."

I smiled, pulling off my robe. I already had the strapless bra on and Jacob had seen me in my underwear plenty of times. I had a sudden recollection of Sunday night when Max had pushed me against the window and fucked me in front of an anonymous neighbour. It had felt dirty and erotic and I wanted it to be repeated, even without anyone looking. We'd spent a lot of time the last week in bed, and out of it. He'd taken a liking to positioning us so he could watch what he was doing to me and his obsession with my breasts seemed to be growing if that was possible.

"Pass me the blue one."

Jacob unzipped the side and handed it over. Then he helped me into it. It was a clingy, form fitting dress with a split up the side and a Bardot neckline. I'd bought it months ago when it was in the sale for a university ball and I loved the colour.

"Let me curl your hair and you'll just about do." Jacob attacked me with his straighteners which he'd somehow learned to curl with, despite having short hair himself. "You look stunning." It was a whisper, so he meant it. "I bet you have sex before the reception starts."

―――――

Vanessa and Jackson's wedding was an all day and all night event at the Soho Hotel, a venue I'd attended once before with Jacob and his father. Max had sent me a message to say that he was in the bar with Jackson, if I wanted to get there a little earlier and have a drink, and luckily, I wasn't running behind time.

The four brothers and Killian were propping up the bar and nursing whisky while Grant eyed them suspiciously. My jaw only semi-dropped as I had developed a little resistance by now to the way they looked, especially when they were in tuxes and bow ties, beards and stubble freshly tidied.

My eyes found Max without trying, fixing on him. He'd let his beard grow a little longer this week, although his hair had been trimmed and style. His tux had been made to measure to cover his broad shoulders and narrow waist and I had to bite my lips together before I came out with something completely inappropriate in front of his brothers and father.

He put his glass down on the bar and stepped over to me, long legs covering the space between us in four strides. "You look amazing," he said, his eyes all over me. His voice was low so no one else could hear. "I think you need to change."

I wrapped my arms around his neck, an easier feat than usual due to the height of my heels. "I think you need to stop growling. How's Jackson?"

Max nuzzled into my neck, his signature greeting. "Nervous, excited. It took him twenty minutes to style his man bun. We've stopped telling him Van won't turn up because he was starting to believe us. Have I told you that you're beautiful?"

"You have, but not today."

"Because I haven't seen you today. Have you heard?"

"Heard what?" I said coyly, knowing full well what he was referring to.

"From King's. About the job?"

"Yes. I've heard."

He stepped back, his hands on my hips and I felt the tension charging down his arms. "I need to know."

I gave him a half smile and wondered how cruel it was to keep him in suspense, but it was his brother's wedding and he had to give a speech and socialise and not be grumpy, which was hard enough for him when he wasn't considering what his future would be.

"What's it worth?"

He started to smile and I figured he knew what the answer was if I was playing games.

"You can have an orgasm later. Maybe two."

"I can do that myself. Up your offer."

"I'll let you live with me."

"That's more of a treat for you than me."

He groaned. "Vic. For the love of all that is historical, fucking tell me. I spent last night desperate for you to phone me and all I got were pictures of you playing with your tits and pussy."

"That was way too loud!" I was pretty sure Seph overheard, given the look on his face that I'd caught sight of.

"Then put me out of my misery. Am I spending half my life for the next couple of years somewhere over the Atlantic or inside you?" His voice was in my ear now and he was pressed up against me, his hands straying just above my ass

"I got the job at King's," I said, his eyes on mine. I saw the hope in them and felt his heart rate rise. "And I've accepted it."

My Max was usually underwhelmed and calm, accept when he was angry. His excitement when his team won or he had a successful case was muted and relaxed, but right now it was as if I'd made all his dreams come true. He lifted me up and twirled me round, laughing loudly. I heard my giggle mix with his along with my demands to be put down as my shoes had been thrown off and I was aware of the eyes of the bartender and he didn't look impressed.

"I take it Victoria's staying in London?" Grant said, his face beaming.

"I am," I said, my feet finally down on the ground although my height had shrunk four inches. Seph passed over my shoes and enveloped me in a huge hug which only ended when I heard Max telling him to 'get the fuck off her.'

Jackson asked the bartender for a bottle of Champagne and popped it himself. Max kept his arm round me and looked concerned again and I knew what his next question was and what had prompted it.

"I can drink Champagne," I said quietly, definitely not wanting Seph to overhear that. "There's no risk. Maybe in another year, if we want that."

He nodded and I saw feelings swimming in his eyes that made me want to find our hotel room and deposit him on the bed for at least an hour. "Definitely. I'm not relieved, by the way."

I stroked his beard softly, listening to the teasing comments from Killian and Jackson behind me. "Me neither. Although I think it's something I'd like to plan. And practice. Lots of practice."

He kissed me softly. "That can always be arranged."

"Champagne for both of you," Jackson said, bringing two glasses. "We're all glad you're staying. Van will be thrilled too."

I broke away from Max to turn to Jackson, who leaned forward and kissed my cheek. "Thank you. I'll stop distracting your best man now."

Jackson shook his head. "He'll be distracted no matter what; he has been since he met you. And that's a good thing by the way. Congratulations on the job. King's have got lucky."

We took the Champagne and gathered back with his brothers, Killian and Grant. Seph began to tease again and we let him, while Jackson pretended that he wasn't getting nervous.

It was twenty to three when the bride walked down the aisle, a grand total of ten minutes late—ten minutes in which Jackson started to increase in his pallor and begin to clench and unclench his fists while Max, Seph and Callum pointed out all the reasons why Vanessa might've changed her mind. Everyone in the congregation was amused: it was just Jackson who struggled to see the humour. His expression only altered when the music changed and the doors opened to reveal the bridesmaids with his bride behind.

Jackson's gaze didn't wander from Vanessa as she walked up the aisle; his sisters were ignored and there was no one else in the room. I glanced at Max who was smiling at his brother and I managed to catch his eye. His grin widened and his shoulders seemed to broaden. Then Vanessa was with her soon-to-be husband and our gaze broke as we sat down.

The service was simple and short, the only exception being their first kiss when the celebrant had to tap Jackson's shoulder to encourage him to end it and continue with the ceremony. Vanessa's eyes shone as she and Jackson led everyone outside into a large, beautifully decorated room, for the start of the reception.

"More Champagne," Max said, heading over to me after being stopped by several people. As best man I knew his time would be taken by various others during the course of the afternoon and evening, but his eyes kept on finding me and searching me out. "I need to keep an eye on Seph and Callum. Whoever decided that a free bar was a good idea didn't consider those two. Throw Ava and Payton into that mix too," he mumbled and I noticed that his drink looked suspiciously non-alcoholic.

"You're staying sober?"

"At least until I've done this speech. And maybe longer." He wrapped his arms around me and pulled me into the side of him. "I know this is my brother's wedding but I wish I could slip off with you for an hour so we could be on our own."

I turned so we were facing each other, my arms going around his back and I felt the hard muscle beneath his suit as I pressed in close. "It's one day, Max. We've got plenty of time after that."

His expression was happy and hopeful. "I would've flown across to you whenever I could, you know; if you'd decided to take the job at Johns Hopkins I wouldn't have wanted to give you up. We'd have made it work."

"But you don't have to invest in an air company. I'm staying. King's was a better offer with the salary and also what they were looking for me to specialise in. And I didn't want to leave you."

He bent down to kiss me, the noise in the room quietening as it no longer needed to exist. There was a promise to his touch, and a need and my body softened into his.

"You two need to get a room." A hand touched my shoulder and I pulled away from Max to turn and see Vanessa.

"Congratulations," I said. "You look beautiful." She did, her gown an elaborate mix of silk and lace and pearls, fitted to show off her toned figure. She loved the gym as much as I hated it; she'd kept threatening to drag me along and change my mind.

"Thank you. And congratulations to you too. Jackson said you're staying in London, thank god." She started to touch her hair then remembered not to.

Max's fingers pressed into my waist.

"Yeah, King's made me an offer I couldn't refuse. And I didn't want to chance a long distance thing," I said, giving him a quick glance. He was still beaming.

Vanessa leaned up and kissed Max on the cheek and then did the same to me. "I'm so pleased. You seem to make each other happy."

"Vanessa!" Payton shouted and then gesticulated wildly from the bar, blonde hair now completely escaped from the up do it had been in for the ceremony. "Shots!"

The bride laughed and turned around. "Do you know where Jackson is? I really don't want to start doing shots. I haven't had anything to eat since a really early breakfast."

"He's in the other bar with Killian and Eli," Max said. "And I think they are doing shots."

She eyed his drink. "I take it you're on putting to bed duty?"

Max laughed. "Only till after the speeches."

Vanessa rolled her eyes and headed off, Payton clambering over guests to ply her with something that looked like a lemon drop.

"Are you sure?" I asked when we were left on our own.

We walked towards the patio where the sea of strangers had parted. "Sure of what?"

"Us. This."

He laughed, holding me at arm's length and looked at me. "I've never been more sure of anything. Come, let me introduce you."

CHAPTER 23
MAXWELL

"Where are we going?"

I turned left and then immediately right, trying my best to throw her off track completely. We'd spent the week since Jackson's wedding talking and making plans. I'd left work early one evening to have a look at the furniture she had in storage and we'd had a heated debate about where to put it and if any bits would fit in my apartment. I said yes; she said no. On this occasion, Victoria won.

"You'll find out when we get there."

"Maxwell, you know I don't like surprises."

I squeezed her leg. "You'll like this one."

"I'd like it better if it wasn't a surprise."

Ava's car was parked outside already and she was standing on the doorstep with Payton and Seph. I'd tried to persuade them to leave us in private for this, as I wasn't entirely sure what Victoria's reaction was going to be and if I was going to be rejected, I'd prefer it to not be in front of my siblings.

I parked the car. "Can I take this off now?"

"No. Leave it for another few seconds. I'll come round and

get you," I said, wanting to be able to see her face when she saw it.

We'd decided we'd live together. For two people who had been so resistant to a relationship in the first place, we were doing a good job of throwing ourselves into it, and so far I hadn't struggled to find the words I'd needed to explain my fears and concerns and wants. There was just one more thing left to say.

I opened her door and took both her hands in mine to guide her out, walking her down a newly laid driveway with a carefully tended garden. "Stop there and keep your hands by your sides." She was facing the house, her grandfather's house, which was now my house and what I hoped would be our home. "Before I take the blindfold off I need to tell you a few things."

Turning around I gestured wildly to my siblings, pointing to the back of the house and flicking them the bird. Seph shook his head and was then dragged away by Ava. Payton gave me two thumbs up and followed, leaving us on our own.

"Victoria Esme Davies, I've told you countless times this week I want to make a future with you and for some reason, you seem to want the same thing. I want our future to start here. If you think it's weird or you'd rather be somewhere else, then I understand. If you want to start here on your own and I'll join you in the future that's fine too. But," my voice had started to wobble and I realised that I was flying by the seat of my pants with this more than anything ever in my life. "I want you to know that I love you, I'm madly in love with you and…"

"Just take the blindfold off already," she said, then grabbed my hands before I could untie the knot. "One second. I think I know what you're about to show me. Before you do, I need to tell you that I love you as well. Next time you tell me can I not have a blindfold on so I can see your face?"

I undid the knot and let the material fall away to the floor, stepping to the side so I wasn't blocking her view.

Her expression was everything I'd hoped it would be: excitement, joy, happiness and I felt I'd managed to do something very, very right.

"Holy fuck, Max," she said, starting to walk towards the house. "It looks incredible."

The casement windows had been replaced, keeping the same style but with a grey stained wood. The front door was now like the one the house would've originally had and the lawn and flower beds had been tidied with new shrubs added. The driveway was completely new, grey stone that Ava had insisted we have. She'd been right, as she had about so much.

"I'm glad you like it. I was worried it would be too different."

Victoria shook her head. "No. It's different, but it's still the house I grew up in. It just now looks like what it should." She took my hand in hers and we walked over the drive to the front door that was slightly ajar. Ava had even managed to get some planters out which added some colour.

Inside had been completely revamped. The floor had been replaced with grey-stained wooden boards, walls had come down, fireplaces had been reinstated, everywhere had been rewired, replastered and painted. Wallpaper that had been expensive enough to make my credit card cry had been hung and there were a few soft furnishings, but Ava had refused to add more, saying that Victoria needed to choose her own. The kitchen had been extended into a kitchen diner with bi-fold doors and Velux windows. The fitted units were the ones Ava had managed to trick Victoria into picking.

"What do you think?" Ava appeared through one of the open doors, a huge grin covering her face. My youngest sister had been glowing for the past week at what she had done and had gone as far as to ask if she could have the property herself if Victoria decided she didn't like it. "Do you like it? Is it what you thought it could be like?"

"Give her a chance to see the rest of it, Ava," I said, watching Vic's reaction. She was mesmerised, her eyes everywhere.

"It's incredible. You've done an amazing job." She turned to me. "This must've cost a fortune, Max. Why did you spend so much?"

"It was probably less than you think. Remember I get mate's rates from Ava." My tone was gruff and quiet. I was still nervous. "Let's go see upstairs."

She followed me to the hallway and the wide staircase that was now carpeted, the banister sanded and painted to match the rest of the house. "It's stunning," she said, her shoes discarded at the bottom of the stairs. "It's... fuck, it's just incredible."

She saw the master bedroom, the thick carpet underneath her feet, the ensuite wet room and the master bathroom with a bath in the centre of the large space. Ava had suggested making the room into another bedroom and partitioning another room in two, but the house was already six beds and I didn't envisage having that many children, so we'd kept it.

"What do you think?"

"I think this is where I'll be spending poker nights when you're downstairs with the rest of the boys."

I heard her words and my heart began to ping electricity through me at the implications. We saw the rest of the floor and the one above, the fireplaces that had been in each room now uncovered and restored or replaced with similar ones. Some were even working, such as the one in the bathroom—something Ava was inextricably proud of.

We headed down to the cellars that were now kitted out with gym equipment in one chamber and a huge screen and projector in the other.

"A man cave," she said shaking her head. "I got bathrooms, you got a man cave. Is there a bed down here for Seph?"

"I'm allowed to move in?" the boy behind us said. He'd been

quiet, watching Victoria's reactions also, examining the fireplaces and new fittings.

"No, Seph," I said. "We might let you stay once in a while when you're too drunk to get home, but you're not moving in."

"I could have my own room. I'd be no trouble. Or even that summerhouse in the garden. There's even WiFi down there," he sounded enthusiastic and I knew one of us needed to have a chat with him about his current phobia of living alone.

"Summerhouse?" Victoria said. "Is there anything you didn't include?" She looked between me and Ava.

Ava nodded. "You need to furnish it. Max told me about the furniture you have in storage and it'll obviously fit with the period of the house, but I'd suggest having it repainted. Same with soft furnishings. I have a friend who will do your curtains and blinds, and you'll need rugs but I can help you shop for them. I still have Max's credit card."

Victoria nodded, biting her bottom lip which I knew by now meant she was was thinking of how to phrase what she wanted to say. Panic knotted through me and I felt my hands start to become clammy.

"Thank you," she said to Ava. "You've done an amazing job. I love it, I absolutely love it."

"That means you're going to move in? With Max?" Ava said, her hands clapping together as they had done since she was a little girl whenever she was excited.

Victoria looked at me, her eyes soft. "Can you three give us a minute? Then we'll order pizza and I hope someone had the sense to bring Champagne."

There was a burst of noise, Seph saying something about taking up residence in the summerhouse and then we were left in the quiet.

"Is it too much? Did I go over the top? I don't want to scare you—"

She stood up on her tiptoes and silenced me with a kiss. "Yes, it's too much; yes, it's over the top. You bought me a house months ago when we were only temporary. Am I cross or mad or scared? No. I love it, but I love you more."

This time, I kissed her. Our hands roamed as if we had new territory to discover, although I knew her body as well as I knew my own. When we broke apart it was because of the noise outside and I recognised Callum and Claire's voices, then Killian's laugh.

"I wanted us to be permanent back then," I said. "I just didn't think I could."

"Now you know you can."

I nodded. "Am I allowed to live here with you?"

Her laugh sounded like music. "Yes. Hell yes. Try not and see how far you get."

"That sounds almost like something a stalker would say," I said, my hands on her ass, needing her badly, accept most of my family was cock blocking me. "By the way, security is in place."

She smiled. "I didn't doubt it. Shall we go tell everyone we're moving in together?"

"Do you think they don't already know?"

"Were we that obvious?" She tipped her head to one side and looked at me curiously.

"To everyone but ourselves, yes, I suppose so." There was some comfort in knowing that my family knew me better than I did myself.

"Then let's go tell them that they were right."

EPILOGUE

VICTORIA

"**S**eph, you need to bend your legs! Like you would for a deadlift, not with a straight back!"

I sipped my coffee and watched the carnage before me, feeling surprisingly calm as members of Max's family, plus a couple of friends and colleagues, carried in various pieces of furniture.

"I still think that would look better in the snug," I heard Callum say, pointing to a chaise lounge that had been recently reupholstered and was now sitting prettily in the kitchen-slash-diner. "I'd sit on that while reading a thriller and drinking a martini."

"Good to know what circles you move in, brother," Jackson said, frowning. He spent a lot of time frowning, unless Vanessa was there, in which case he didn't frown at all because all he could focus on was her.

"Can someone come help with this desk?" Max yelled down the hallway. I watched as Seph and Callum immediately looked down towards him, their bodies half in and half out as if working out exactly how they could get out of lifting something else.

"For fuck's sake, get your asses out there and help!" Claire said, her baby girl strapped to her chest in a sling that I would need a video guide to use. "There are five more big pieces of furniture to come in, plus two more beds and a pool table. Find your man cards and help. Pussies."

"Vic, where do you want these going?" Killian walked down the hallway with a chair in each hand.

"The study," I said, pointing him in the right direction. "There a beer in there as well."

He smiled and nodded, heading away from the rabble that Seph and Callum were causing over the desk. I was pretty sure he'd enjoy the beer before coming back out again.

Killian and the rest of them hadn't stopped, emptying delivery vans and the two vans we'd hired to clear Max's apartment and my storage unit. We'd started at seven am and we're still going strong twelve hours later, but the end was in sight. Marie had commandeered the kitchen, Claire had taken over the role of sergeant major and Max had very quietly and efficiently project managed, knowing where things were meant to go and checking with me when he thought they wouldn't work. I'd sorted it out room by room with Ava and Payton, unpacking as quickly as we could, unwrapping pictures and antiques and we had some semblance of a home, just one where every door was open as things were still being brought in.

"Bring that bed in here!" I heard Grant holler, followed by a curse from Eli, one of Max's partners at Callaghan Green.

"Can we make sure that gets put together tonight?" Seph's voice called. "I'm sleeping there."

Max's eye caught mine as he walked down the stairs and he shook his head. We'd officially adopted Seph. He was moving in temporarily, and yes, the agreement had named a date when he would be moving out. I didn't mind; he reminded me of Tigger from Winnie the Pooh: continually bouncing round annoying everyone but completely harmless. He'd asked us two days after we'd told everyone, a genuine and heartfelt request that had Max walking off to the bottom of the garden and me mixing a margarita.

We'd said yes and considered it good practise for when we had children of our own and from our conversations, it wouldn't be that long if all went well. A year of working at King's and we'd see what happened, although I would be surprised if we lasted that long waiting to try.

"Mattress coming up, Dad. Get ready at the top," Max yelled and I went back to unpacking the box of antiquities to go into what had been deemed the snug and would, in fact, be my office.

Three hours later and people had either left or were dozing in a chair with a glass of wine or a beer. Ava was deep in conversation with Eli about property, wine clearly fuelling their ideas. Seph had found an old guitar and was in the midst of a fantasy where he could actually play. Marie and Grant had found a loveseat to collapse into, one that desperately needed reupholstering and was on the list for the following week and Max was lounging on a sofa, acting as my cushion as I lay back into him with a very large glass of malbec, my eyelids drooping.

"It's been a productive day," I said, watching Callum talking to Payton, both of them animated and impassioned about whatever they were discussing. "We just need tomorrow to be as smooth."

"It'll be easier," he said. "Jackson and my dad will make sure everything's assembled and where it should be; Marie will sort the kitchen out and Claire and Vanessa will do the bedrooms. All you'll need to do is over see things." He started to move, knocking me away from him. "There's something to see in the summerhouse."

I followed him across the garden where I'd played as a child, a new tyre swing now hanging from the large oak tree that Seph and Ava had hung that evening. He flicked the lights on in the summer house and everything was as it should be, a tidy area with a log burner and a faux sheepskin rug with two comfy weather-worn leather chairs and a small table. Nothing as it hadn't been a couple of days ago.

I stifled a yawn and sat down on the rug. I'd quite happily sleep here tonight as long as Max was with me. In fact, we'd get more privacy out here, unless Seph discovered where we were.

"Vic," he said, sitting opposite me.

"Maxwell," I muttered tiredly. It had been a long and exhausting day, but not one I would change for the world. I'd spent it with the people I was coming to regards as family, helping me to settle in to our new place and caring about us.

"Will you marry me?"

I sat bolt upright, suddenly very awake and my heart pounding as if I was about to skydive from a great height. "Sorry?" I said, unsure as to whether I'd heard right.

"Will you marry me?"

He was nervous, his face pale and he kept biting his lips together. One hand held a diamond solitaire, the other was stroking his beard.

I blinked. My words had evaporated as I stared at the ring.

"Victoria?"

I blinked again, my mouth not working.

"I love you. I want a family with you. I saw how long it took Van and Jackson to sort a wedding so I want to give you time to plan the wedding you want…"

"What about the wedding you want?"

"I just want to be married to you. We can get married in Vegas if that's what you'd like. As long as you end up being my wife," he said, half way between nervous and considered.

"Yes."

"What?"

"Yes, I'll marry you."

"Are you sure? You don't need longer to think about it?"

"I'm sure that I'll marry you. And no, I don't need longer to think about it. Decision made." I'd known he would ask; we'd kind of mentioned it but I'd thought it would've been in a few months, not just two weeks after I'd confirmed I'd be staying in London.

"Good. Shall we go in and tell everyone?"

I smiled and reached for him, letting him pull me into his arms, the place where I felt most at home. "Tomorrow," I said. "Why don't we stay here a little while and enjoy the quiet?"

"Good plan."

So we did, and we'd continue, making the most of the compromise every single day.

The End

Maxwell and Victoria have a second wee story that's available when you sign up for my newsletter - grab Compromising Positions FREE! https://dl.bookfunnel.com/b3vyfgqnot

READY FOR YOUR NEXT BOOK BOYFRIEND?

Want some more time with the Callaghans? Let me help you make your mind up with where to go next.

Could there be anything better than a book boyfriend who owns a bookstore? Payton Callaghan isn't sure; although giving up relationships when she might've just met The One is a dilemma she's facing in Between Cases, a meet-cute that'll have you swooning over Owen Anders.

Is Enemies to Lovers your jam? If it is, take yourself up north to Manchester and meet the Manchester Athletic squad in Penalty Kiss.

Or, do you fancy a change of scenery and want to take a trip to a small town? Visit Severton, in Sleighed; this friends-to-lovers romantic suspense will capture your heart as much as Sorrell Slater steals Zack Maynard's.

Still not sure? Then turn the page and find a little peak into each!

NEXT IN THE SERIES

He's the plot twist she wasn't planning on…

Workaholic? Check.

Poor choice in men? Check.

Debatably losing the plot? Check.

Payton Callaghan has had enough. She needs time away from her stressful job, time away from her disaster of a love life and what she really doesn't need is a hot bookshop owner trying to verbally outwit her in the middle of his store.

Owen Anders believes in creating his own plot. Successful businessman, talented musician and book nerd, he hadn't accounted for Payton and her wrath at the exact moment his well-constructed world was hitting an unplanned crisis. However, he needs a lawyer and he thinks she needs him.

With Payton insistent that a relationship is not in an upcoming chapter, can Owen persuade her to change her plot and ensure her happily ever after stars him?

Find out here and read on for a preview: Between Cases

BETWEEN CASES

Payton Callaghan is up next in the fourth book in the Callaghan Green series.

And here's a quick peak!

———

CHAPTER ONE - PAYTON

If he didn't take at least two steps backwards he was going to find his balls spewing out of his throat and his penis retracting into his bladder. I was officially done with this shit.

"Excuse me," I said, trying to slip past him even though he was midsentence on some topic that was 'All About Him'. I had no idea why I was being polite.

"Shall I come with you?"

He grabbed my arm. He grabbed my fucking arm. I resisted the temptation to knee him hard in the testicles and make all my fantasies come true.

The bar was loud enough to make me raise my voice. "No thanks. I'm going to find my friends." Who were at the bar.

Together. Drinking margaritas. Together. While yet again, I was being hit on by a totally douche.

"But I thought we had a thing going here. You know, I've bought you a drink and we were mid-conversation about the choices I'm having to make about my career and…"

I exhaled deeply and tried to seek my inner calm. Unfortunately, the bitch that was my inner calm had decided she was taking a vacation in Hawaii and had left her cousins Tired and Stressed in her place. "Actually, I put my drink and your drink on my tab. You're telling me about you, and haven't asked me a single thing about me yet and you're way too close into my personal space considering you've known me all of twenty minutes." I could've been worse. To be fair, that was pretty tame for me.

He looked shocked, his overly large mouth gaping slightly open and his eyes wide. "I thought—"

"Look, Ed, I think this was never going anywhere. If you want to score here on a Friday evening you need to get a bit more creative. You know, ask a few questions, listen to her answers, at least pretend you're interested in what she has to say and you never know, she might be drunk enough to go home with you," I said, almost applying the cruelty filter. "Good luck in your search."

He started to speak but I managed to find enough room to turn around and walk towards the door where my sister, Ava, was waiting for me, along with two of the girls I worked with at my law firm, Callaghan Green, where I was a commercial litigator—a commercial litigator who had endured an incredibly stressful and busy week ending in a huge win for my client.

The end of a case always depressed me somewhat. I liked the busyness of a big case with a lot at stake. I enjoyed the adrenaline rush and the deadlines, the battle of wits with the opposition. But when it was over I felt a huge sense of loss and something my counsellor had equated to grief. I wasn't quite sure it went that far, but I would always get a little bit more tense than usual until the next client came along. I was aware I wasn't quite sane.

"Do we need to let the bar staff know where you're leaving his balls?" Ava said, her long blonde hair hanging in a curly mess. She was my youngest sibling, the baby of the seven of us, and looked the part of princess, a role she had always been given by our four older brothers, although Seph, my twin, was only just older than me.

I shook my head. "I left them attached. It was too much effort." We headed outside into the spring London night. It was just about warm enough to be able to wear a jacket rather than a coat and I was dreaming of evenings sitting by the Thames with a cool beer and the warm sun on my shoulders. Those sorts of evenings were still a couple of months away, which made me feel even more like going home and burying myself in a good book and having a hot bath. "Where are we heading?"

Ava gestured to a side street. "Silvia's. Unless you want to go pick up another mansplaining arsehole to insult for the evening."

My sister was surprisingly sober. "I'm giving up on men," I said, feeling better now the confession had met the air. "I'm done. I'm all about the job and my family and my friends."

Ava raised her brows disbelievingly. "You said this about ten years ago and decided you were into girls instead."

This was true. I had an experimental phase around the start of university as my boyfriend had been a cheat and an idiot. It had lasted about nine months, during which time my parents hadn't raised a single eyebrow and had welcomed the single girlfriend I'd brought home with the same open arms they'd shown everyone else. "No. No relationships. No dating apps. No men. I've had enough with picking up wankers in bars."

"Stop picking up wankers in bars then. Other places are available as are other sorts of men. Join a book club or go to the gym with someone who isn't one of our brothers and therefore doesn't look like a bodyguard. Ask Callum to set you up with one of his colleagues at the zoo." Callum was our brother who wasn't a lawyer. Instead he was a vet, one with his own YouTube channel and a very popular Instagram feed.

"Callum would probably try to set me up with a gorilla and video it to get a few thousand likes," I said as we entered Silvia's. "Besides, I don't see you setting the dating world on fire." Ava had been dateless for at least four weeks; I hadn't even seen her on-again, off-again bed warmer Antonio about.

"The gorilla would probably have better grooming techniques than most of the men you've dated in the past twelve months, Payts. Regroup, consider what you want and then set about it the right way; not picking up dicks in bars when you're both half-drunk. But joining the nearest nunnery is not going to make you happy. Decent sex and a few good orgasms should be mandatory," Ava said, heading straight to the bar and ordering two margaritas.

Silvia's was a small, very boutique-style, cocktail and bottled beer bar that was most popular straight after work or for a liquid lunch. It was quieter as it was later on and we perched on the barstools, accepting the small plate of stuffed vine leaves and a bowl of olives. It had a Greek theme and we knew the owner—who wasn't called Silvia—well enough to be fed whatever bar snacks she hadn't sold at lunch.

I stared at my sister, my two colleagues and a friend of Ava's now in the bar with us. "Since when did you become an expert on decent sex and few good orgasms? I thought Antonio was yesterday's headline?"

"He wasn't much of a headline," she said. "He had a good-enough sized cock that filled a hole but he really didn't know what else to do with it."

"Don't let our brothers hear you say that," I said, taking a sip from my margarita. "Else they'll fill his hole. With cement."

Ava laughed. "They've heard much worse from Claire. Have you heard from her today?"

Claire was our other sister, a few years older and currently very pregnant, which meant she was more argumentative than normal. The only person able to handle her was her soon-to-be-husband, Killian, and even he was looking slightly fraught. "A text this morning wishing me luck for when we received judgement and another letting me know that sex does not induce labour. I didn't ask for details."

"We should go see her tomorrow. At least try to be supportive while she has the world's longest pregnancy. And it'll give Killian a break from trying not to kill her," I said, biting into a stuffed vine leaf. It tasted divine: all glorious carbs and flavour.

Ava groaned. "I need to go shopping for a house warming gift for Max tomorrow. Fuck knows what to get the couple who have everything." Max was our eldest sibling and had just moved into a newly renovated house with his girlfriend, Victoria. "Let's not have too many of these and we can go early."

I raised an eyebrow. "Why do you want an early start on a Saturday morning?" My sister was a notorious late riser on the weekends. She flipped houses for a living and spent Monday to Friday on job sites, bossing about construction workers which meant starts earlier than seven am a lot of the time.

"I'm viewing a few houses tomorrow afternoon," she said, knocking back the margarita and gesturing to the bartender for another two. "Time for a few new projects."

I finished my own drink and felt slightly less cranky. Ava felt the same way I did when a project was finished. "Why can neither of us accept when we're between jobs and just relax like normal people?"

"Because we're not normal people," Ava said. "We're Callaghans."

———

Despite having invested in the biggest bed I could find, I woke up each morning tucked onto one side, as if leaving room for an imaginary boyfriend. It had been a long time since anyone had been on that side on a regular basis: my last boyfriend had been booted nearly three years ago, and although I'd had a few casual relationships since then, no one had been under my sheets for more than three separate occasions. I'd been burnt, and not just when I was a teenager, but since. There had been Matt, who was an investment banker: charming, intelligent and charismatic, he'd treated me like a princess and in my head I'd picked out the names of our children and where we'd hold our wedding reception. In his head, he already had a wife and a piece on the side, which happened to be me. I'd found out when I'd met Claire for a meal in an upmarket restaurant and he'd been gazing into his wife's eyes instead of mine. Somehow, I'd not lost the plot. Instead, I'd taken a photograph and sent it to him and then watched him finish his meal absolutely petrified that I was about to come over and cause a scene.

Then there'd been Gary. He'd healed my heart and promised me the world for two years. For a few months we'd even lived together. He was a teacher and played soccer every Saturday afternoon, taking me out for lunch on a Sunday and tolerating my twin brother, Seph. One evening I'd come home from work to an apartment empty of all his belongings and a note apologising, telling me he'd met someone else and wanted to end it before anything physical happened. And that had been three years ago and there had only been men worthy of up to three nights since.

I stretched out across the mattress, enjoying the coolness of the sheets and the space. We'd left Silvia's early last night, avoiding any more wankers and I'd strolled home to a hot chocolate with a dash of whisky and my book, the latest in a series set in an interesting club in Seattle. It was making me wonder if such clubs existed in London and how to discover one without alerting my siblings. Lazily, I checked my phone, knowing there would be a couple of messages from Seph at least. My twin was still struggling to find himself since splitting from his very long-term girlfriend and needed frequent mollycoddled. He had managed to move in with Max and his girlfriend, Victoria, but given that they had six bedrooms and countless reception rooms I didn't feel too sorry for them.

Callum: Is it tonight Max is having this house party?

Claire: Yes. I sent an invite that you should've accepted and it should be in your calendar on your phone. I say should because you keep ignoring me.

Callum: Shouldn't you be giving birth to my niece or nephew round about now?

Claire: Yes, but I'm not. He or she has inherited your DNA for being late, clearly.

Callum: Does the diary entry have something in it about bringing a gift?

Claire: This is a lot of questions for Friday evening. Shouldn't you be getting laid?

Callum: Who says I'm not?

Seph: You're messaging us about a house warming party. If you're anywhere in the process of getting laid you definitely won't be seeing her again. If it is a her.

There was a break in the timeline while Callum clearly went back to whatever he was, or rather who, he was doing and Claire no doubt continued pacing around the house in the hope it would induce labour. I skimmed down the rest of the messages, enjoying not having to rush out of bed to get to work or a meeting, or god forbid, a gym class.

Callum: What sort of gift am I meant to get for a fucking house warming present? This sort of shit needs to come with instructions.

Claire: For fuck's sake, Callum. A plant? A bottle of wine or Champagne? You could go with something more personal but not, and if I could underline NOT I would, a pet or any form of animal.

Callum: But what if we all turn up with the same present?

Seph: If we all turn up with whisky Max'll probably have a freaking orgasm.

Payton: And what about your future sister-in-law? Do you think she'll appreciate the whisky?

Seph: Get her a bottle of really decent merlot or malbec. Then they'll both be happy. Did they get engaged too?

Claire: No, but it's only a matter of time. Like this baby making an appearance. Hopefully. I think it wants me to be pregnant forever.

Seph: None of us want that. Seriously. You were bad tempered before, now you're just unpleasant. We've nominated Killian for a sainthood.

Payton: Claire, what've you bought them?

Claire: A set of red wine glasses and a bottle of merlot. Hopefully to be used later for wetting the baby's head.

Payton: Keep wishing. Ava was nearly three weeks late. Anyone heard from her this morning?

Seph: Weren't you with her last night?

Payton: Only till about 9. It wasn't a late one.

Seph: Maybe she's just sleeping in.

Payton: Apparently she's checking out some houses this afternoon so she wanted to go shopping early on. Although it is only 8.30. I wish I could sleep in longer.

Callum: Back to presents, people.

Claire: How about passes to the zoo? Or an adopt an animal thing—as in one you get newsletters about, not an actual animal. I don't see Max homing a friendly alligator or something.

Callum: That's me sorted. Cheers.

Claire: And you couldn't have come up with that yourself. Lazy.

Seph: I have no idea either.

Claire: Which is ridiculous seeing as you live with them. How about a voucher for a meal out so they can get away from you?

Seph: Somewhat harsh but I'll take that and run with it. See you later.

I hit the home button and left the conversation, wondering what Ava's plans were given that she wanted to be done early afternoon. She answered her phone just as I was about to hang up, sounding predictably groggy.

"What time is it?" she said, muffling a groan.

"Quarter to nine. What time are we meeting?" I said, still sprawled out in bed.

There was a low groan and a muffled voice that sounded distinctly male and familiar, but I couldn't place it.

"Eleven?"

"I thought you were busy this afternoon?" I said, now highly suspicious that my little sister wasn't alone and when she said she was going home yesterday, she had lied.

"I can push the viewings back till later. Meet me at eleven at Walsingham's on Thayer Street. I think I'm going to get them this set of cushions and throws I've seen that'll be perfect in the snug," she said, still sounding half asleep. "Actually, make it midday." There was definitely stifled laughter in her voice.

"That's fine," I said. "But when we meet, you're going to tell me who you're with and you're not going to lie to me."

"Gotcha," she said, and hung up, leaving me feeling more than a little bit lonely in my bed on my own.

PENALTY KISS

ROWAN - CHAPTER ONE

Nothing could turn a warm, summery Mancunian morning into a shit-tastic fuckery of a mess like a nine o'clock meeting.

With my manager. And agent. Plus, no hint of what this meeting was about, although I could guess. It wouldn't take a genius to work out exactly which parts of the last two weeks they were pissed about, and it wasn't the photos of me doing extra training on the beach where two of the lads and I had been on holiday.

Oh no. There would be no pats on the back for that, or the fact I'd had more goal assists than anyone else last season, or sold more shirts with my name on than anyone else at Manchester Athletic, including Nate Fleming, who was the team's golden boy.

I was about to be torn a new asshole, and then have it rammed without lube.

Nothing good came of Monday morning meetings when you were still meant to be on holiday, enjoying a leisurely morning dreaming up how to spend the rest of the day without being bored. A trip to the gym maybe, or a dip in the indoor pool to stretch a few muscles. Perhaps lunch somewhere given that my usual rigid diet plan was slightly less rigid with just another few days to go before pre-season training started. Didn't mean I could go completely rogue with carbs and sugar, just that I was less likely to get a rollocking off from our chief meal spoiler, also known as the club's nutritionist.

We never asked her out for team meals, or to parties, but I don't think she cared. I wasn't entirely sure what she cared about.

The stadium was the shining diamond in the campus Manchester Athletic's new owners had built when they took over half a decade ago, investing money into an area that needed to be developed. It was now the place I spent most of my time, enough to wonder why I didn't just live in one of the suites at the hotel there.

I nodded at Mandy, the woman who ran the reception at the entrance to part of the building dedicated to offices and the business side. She didn't like footballers, despite her job existing because of the football team, but then I didn't think she liked most people. Still, I was never rude to her when I saw her on the few occasions I came in this part. In fact, I made a point of being especially friendly to her, because I figured that pissed her off even more.

The team's manager, Guy Babin, had an office on the second floor, with a meeting room next to it. I'd been here exactly four times before: the day I came for talks about joining the team, the day I signed, two days after I scored my first hat trick for the club, and after I ended up in the media for being thrown out of a bar for fighting. That last time was admittedly the most uncomfortable – the fight was with a bloke who just happened to support our main rivals, and it looked bad.

In reality, that fight had nothing to do with what team I played for and everything to do with how he was speaking to his girlfriend. Unfortunately, that wasn't the take the press had, especially after he sold his story to a Sunday tabloid.

The door to the meeting room was open revealing Guy and my agent, sitting opposite each other, a huge, polished rosewood desk in between them. They were both laughing.

Until they saw me come in.

"Rowan. Good of you to be on time."

Only Guy Babin could make being on time sound like you were late.

I looked at Rhys, the man I paid to have my back. He folded his arms and sat back in his chair, expression grim. He had a suit on too, which made me take a deep inhalation. A cleansing breath, something our yoga instructor would be proud of.

Shit was about to hit the fan, and that fan was about to spread it all over me.

I sat down next to Rhys, bracing myself, not sure what to say. There was no point going on the defensive – that would just make me sound guilty. Or more guilty than I actually was.

"We have a problem." Guy didn't sit back. He didn't look relaxed, but he did look tanned.

I fucking hoped he hadn't come back off his holiday to wherever it was just to deal with this.

The door opened again, and Genevieve Casson, our Head of Player Support waltzed in, looking like she'd just stepped out of a modelling shoot. "So sorry I'm late. I had to deal with a call from the press." She sent a look my way. Something that was obviously my fault.

"Not an issue."

Clearly Guy didn't have the same standards about tardiness with her.

I glanced at Rhys again, who just shook his head, opened his mouth a few times and then closed it, as if he didn't have the words to express how utterly I'd disappointed him.

If we'd been elsewhere, I'd have laughed – Rhys was only a

couple of years older than me. We'd played on the same football team back when we were kids in Newcastle, only he'd ended up shattering his knee coming off a skateboard, so he'd found another way to be involved in the game.

Guy's gaze was back on me, his eyes piercing. "Rowan, the last two days have been something of a shit-show. Since Saturday morning, I've had phone calls and emails asking me for comments about the story in the press, and the photos of you in the pool with the young lady have added an additional layer of difficulty. We have to look at how this situation is managed."

He wasn't wrong, apart from the young lady part. There had been nothing lady-like about the girl in the pool, whose name I'd only found out when I'd seen the picture on social media, but she had been all woman.

I didn't smile at the memory. I wished it hadn't happened.

"I had no idea Jade was going to go to the press." Which was the truth. We'd split at the end of the season when I'd gotten tired of her being so fame hungry. There were more photos of me on her Instagram than there were on mine, and the pressure from her to spend all of my free time doing stuff that involved being seen.

"I did warn you." Rhys always liked to say *I told you so*, usually with a big shit-eating grin on his ugly face, which he was managing to hide right now under the pretence of being professional.

There was no point responding. Jade had made up a story to sell, painting herself in the light she wanted to be seen in, casting me as the villain. I'd read it at stupid o'clock this morning, when I'd been woken by Rhys' assistant telling me I had to get to the stadium ground for this meeting. When I'd asked why, she'd told me to Google myself.

I'd ignored the media while we were on holiday. I hired someone to manage my social media accounts, adding the odd post when it was something more personal, and even though my season had been a hundred-percenter, after ten years as a professional footballer, I'd learned not to read pundits' opinions in the press.

Which meant this morning had been a bit of a surprise.

"Rowan's solicitor is involved already. We're researching if we can sue Ms Young. The timing of the other photos are unfortunate." Rhys reached under the table and pinched what he could of the skin on my thigh hard – a sign to shut the fuck up.

I had no idea my solicitor was involved, clearly something else Rhys was taking care of.

Rhys continued without missing a beat, "But this is all solvable, and we can use it to our advantage."

He was trying to gloss over it.

Guy stared at me in a way that made me feel he was analysing my soul. "You should pursue it with Ms Young and the paper. You do need to defend your image on this one, Rowan. Goals and assists aren't going to be enough to clear up the image you now have." His accent sounded even more French than usual. "Genevieve, where are you up to with the media?"

Pretty green eyes looked up from the tablet in front of her. "The party line is that Rowan was single – Jade doing a tell-all has actually helped in that case – and entitled to enjoy himself, and that he's also entitled to his privacy." Her eyes narrowed. "Having sex with a woman on a sun lounger in full view probably wasn't your wisest move though."

I rubbed my forehead. "It was a private party. I didn't know her friend was going to take photos and post them."

"That's the problem, Rowan, you can never know when someone's going to do that. You were our record signing, you're on our record wages. We've taught you to always think the worst of people who you don't know well, or can't be vouched for, until you know them better. You're not stupid, but the holiday photos are damaging to your image, as is Jade's interview. We have damage control to do." Guy's jaw stiffened and his eyes had that dark gleam to them that usually made me want to stay well away.

I shrugged. "I understand what you've said – I have shit taste in women and I didn't make a good choice at the party." No point in trying to bullshit my way through that.

Genevieve shook her head. "How can you have sex in front of other people? Never mind, you're a footballer. Therefore, you have a whole different set of rules."

She was right. Money, fame and adoration were a toxic combination. When you heard fans chanting your name in the stadium, saw your name on banners and shirts, encountered women making themselves available for you when you wanted, you couldn't be untouched by it. For a kid who grew up playing footy on the fields of Newcastle, whose mam couldn't afford to buy him new boots, it was a lot.

"I apologise on behalf of all footballers. What damage has been done?" I had the sense not to argue with her. You didn't argue with Genevieve.

"There's questions in the press whether you can handle the pressure of your price tag – but that's been on and off since you joined us." She checked her tablet. "A lot of backlash from fans about your behaviour on holiday – 'you're paid to be an example', which you are." She looked up at me, still glaring. "And a lot of negativity from women's groups following on from Jade's interview and the photographs. That's not what you need. Or what the club needs."

I took another deep breath. She was right. Manchester Athletic portrayed itself as being family friendly and a community-based club. Rory Baines, the owner, had invested not only in the campus, but the surrounding area, regenerating what had been a run-down, historically industrial area of the city, only the industry wasn't there anymore. Families were encouraged, the club had a ton of junior football schools for kids too.

"We have a few weeks until the season starts…"

That wasn't a sentence I was going to let Genevieve finish. "We have one week until pre-season training starts. You know how intensive that gets. Whatever you're about to say, keep that in mind."

Rhys' hand patted my back. "I'm sure Genevieve has taken all that into consideration. We all have an interest in how you're perceived – just like your sponsors."

I wanted to tell Rhys that I didn't give a shit about my sponsors, but that wasn't true. My mam had brought me up on her own – me, my little brother, and our younger sister. My wages and the income from sponsorships made sure the life we'd lived back then was just a bad dream, and the future, especially my sister's, was comfortable. She had severe learning difficulties and required round the clock support. While our mam was heavily involved, she couldn't manage on her own, so the first thing my income did was provide for them. I had no intention of their quality of life changing, unless it was for the better.

I swallowed again. "What's your plan?"

Genevieve glanced at Guy. She'd probably not had chance to run this past him yet. "There are two options. You lie low and keep out of the media, hoping it blows over, go legal with Jade. But that will take longer and after the issue with the fight last season, where we used that tactic, it's going to leave you open to a lot more speculation and scrutiny. We've already had journos digging for comments on your sister, and your ex before Jade." Genny had always managed to stop the media from digging into my family's background. I had no idea how. Maybe she baked them cakes or sent choirs round to serenade them; I didn't know how. I was just grateful.

"What's the second option?" Rhys leaned forward.

She glanced again at Guy. "We work proactively. Get Rowan in front of the cameras but in situations that promote the image we all want him to have. I do know how intensive pre-season training can be and we won't be looking at cutting into any of that."

Guy nodded. "And if you're busy with this, you won't have a chance to get in any more trouble."

"What do you want me to do?"

The look Genevieve gave Rhys did not fill me with joy.

"The answer's no."

Rhys laughed. "You don't have an answer to give. You're doing it. End of. And I think it's a great idea."

"Because you'll have something to take the piss out of me about for the next five years."

"I've already got plenty of things to take the piss out of, Ro. This is just extra."

He helped himself to coffee from the machine in my kitchen that I'd never learned to work. Rhys was an expert at using it. Adding the beans, knowing which setting to use for the perfect coffee, and just the right amount, so he could squeeze his milk in. Precision. Very Rhys.

"I'm not doing it. Anything – I can do the kids football school by myself, and the hospital stuff. Jones doesn't need to be involved." I swore this was a punishment.

Rhys sat down at the table that came with the house. Since I'd transferred to Athletic, I'd been living in one of the properties the club owned, renting it off them while I found my own place. My contract was five years, with various options to extend, so buying somewhere was at the top of my to do list and probably something I should be doing this week before pre-season started.

I was about to get a new housemate too. Ryan O'Connell had signed for us last week from Arsenal, and I'd been told he was moving in here since security and all that shit was at its best.

I'd played against him plenty of times but didn't know him. We'd both been capped by England, but never in the same squad. With the World Cup next summer, we'd both be looking to be involved, so playing together at club level would hopefully boost us both.

Rhys had been my agent since I was twenty-one, and my previous one had tried shafting me with a contract that even a nursery kid would've known was corrupt. Rhys had been twenty-three and an apprentice agent. I'd been his first big name. But unlike the first guy, he had more than money as his motivation – he'd spent more time growing up at my house than his own.

Right now, Rhys was far too fucking amused for his own good.

"It's one week coaching kids, which you're good at. You never know, you might actually get along this time." He sniggered, reminding me of the fourteen-year-old version of him who caught me kissing a girl round the back of the garages.

"Dee Jones hates me." I took a mouthful of the protein smoothie I'd made myself, thinking about the not-so-lovely Dee. "She thinks she's Miss Perfect, so she's going to fucking love me being in trouble."

Dee was captain of Manchester Athletic's Women's Team. We played the same position – attacking midfield – and we both wore the number ten shirt.

No love was lost between us.

Rhys grinned. I could almost see the thought bubbles bursting from his head. He'd been there a few months back when Miss Dee and I had exchanged a few words about her parking in my space.

"I'll remember to wear ear plugs. And bring a first aid kit for after she's finished chewing you up." Rhys finished his coffee, which must've been hot enough to take off a layer of his mouth. "What did you do to piss her off? Have you figured it out yet?"

I had no idea what I'd done to earn the wrath of Dee Jones. I hadn't slept with her, I'd never said anything negative about women's football – I actually thought it was more skilful than men's football most of the time – and I hadn't done anything to any of her teammates that I was aware of.

It wasn't the parking incident. She'd been unimpressed with me before that, a little like a raincloud that liked to piss on my parade whenever I had something to celebrate, to mix my metaphors.

I scored a brace, she'd get a hattrick. I won man of the match, she ended up in team of the week. I bought a new car; she did an interview where she discussed how cars were killing furry animals.

"I was born."

Rhys banged down his coffee cup and headed back to the machine, choking on a laugh. "She's a nice person. We've got her as a client now."

"Really?"

He shook his head at me, turning on the coffee machine again and then heading to the fridge for more milk. "We do take on female clients, you know."

"I didn't mean that. Just – *her*. She probably bathes in hand sanitiser to keep herself so squeaky clean." I finished the rest of my shake. "And you know I'd rather focus on pre-season than have to do all these appearances."

I saw his sigh, his chest rising, nose flaring slightly. "Rowan, you've fucked up. I know Jade was a bitch to go to the press, and I know half of what she said wasn't true – you didn't cheat, and you weren't partying all the time, but you did pretty much ignore her rather than just break up with her…"

"Until I did break it off."

"Yeah, well. She was desperate to be a WAG. Next time, listen to what I say and don't go there with women who're just after one thing. Men are so much more straight forward." He found a jug I didn't know I owned, filled it with milk and stuck it in the microwave. Clearly we were feeling classy today.

Rhys had come out when he was eighteen, not that he'd

needed to. He'd never had a girlfriend, despite being scouted by a modelling agency, and had politely turned down every girl that had asked him out.

My mum inquired one day if he was going to ever go on a date with a girl called Katy, who lived across the road from us, and was always hanging around in the hope that Rhys would ask her out.

His response? *I'm actually interested in her brother.*

And that was that. Nothing more was said. And Rhys did end up dating her brother for about eighteen months.

"And Mexico – what the fuck were you thinking, Ro? I get you were on holiday, but you've been too much in the media. You've had your face everywhere. Fucking a girl on a sun lounger isn't classy, mate."

The microwave pinged.

I pushed the glass away. He had a point. The media loved a story about WAGs, footballers wives and girlfriends. Some magazines would devote whole pages to them.

"Please tell me only alcohol was involved."

"Only alcohol was involved. I still don't touch anything else. You know that." Rhys' dad had been a user. Coke had been his drug of choice.

He nodded. "Good. I just needed to hear it." He sat back down, coffee to his liking. "You need to manage your mouth with Dee. There's been a ton of shit about how you treat women after what Jade said, and those photos."

"I know. I will."

Somehow.

Maybe with superglue.

SLEIGHED

Take a trip to Severton, with this small town, romantic suspense - you'll never want to leave!

———

Zack Maynard rubbed at the thick stubble that had accumulated since that morning and debated which incompetence he should yell about first. He was spoilt for choice given that one of his staff had failed to lock a door that should be kept locked and bolted at all times, and a resident had gone exploring. His cousin, Jake, had delivered a truck full of alpacas to the field next to Severton Sunlight Care and Nursing Home and had neglected to tell his farmhand to ensure the gate was shut. And the world's slowest builders had seemingly been employed to take as much time as possible to erect the extension to the dementia care unit and entertainment hall, and the words coming out of the site manager's mouth were not the ones he wanted to hear.

"We're looking at mid-January."

Zack stuffed his hands in his coat pockets. "I'm sorry. Can you repeat that?"

"It's unlikely to be finished before mid-Jan. I realise that's a bit of a pain…"

His accent was broad, thickly Northern and Zack knew he needed to be careful not to mimic it.

"You realise there's a clause in the contract if the building wasn't fit for purpose on December twentieth so we can use it for Christmas dinner?" He managed to ignore an alpaca that was lingering nearby. He was going to kill his fucking cousin.

Jez Hammond, site manager non-extraordinaire, nodded and made a noise that could be interpreted as an agreement. "I realise that, as does the company. However, there was some issues with laying the foundations that's slowed us down and we've encountered a problem with labour."

Zack looked at the site, the half-finished shell of a building and the surrounding rubble. "What's the issue with labour?" He could see maybe four men at work and even though he wasn't an expert on construction, even he knew that this wasn't enough.

"The usual shortage. Contractors, you know?"

The alpaca made an odd snorting noise and edged closer, its mouth slightly hung open, displaying large teeth.

Jake was going to die.

And then possibly be used as alpaca food.

"I don't know. I manage a care home for the elderly. Working with builders, electricians, plasterers, plumbers—*that* isn't my speciality. It's what I'm paying *you* for. And right now, I can count the number of people working on this project on *one* hand."

The alpaca came closer. It nudged Jez's arm and made a strange sound again. A rather excited sound. One Zack was wary of. He was going to fucking kill Jake, even if it would upset his aunt.

"I'm doing what I can, son. We were running behind, but we should've been done in time for Christmas so you could use the hall for your do, but the lass at the hotel on the hill has paid over the odds for labourers so we're down. If these bloody schools would stop encouraging kids to go to university to study bleeding Harry Potter and get them in proper work instead, we wouldn't be so far behind." Jez patted his shapely beer belly.

Zack's words froze in his mouth. Not because the temperature was skating lower than normal for this time of year, but because the alpaca's expression had turned to one of sheer delight as it started to sink its teeth into the thick fleece of the site manager's coat. It was an action Zack could only attribute to fate.

"Holy fuck!" Jez yelled, yanking his arm away. But the alpaca's teeth were firmly sunk into the material. "Get this bastard animal off my bleeding arm? I thought this was a care home, not a freaking petting zoo with sadistic fucking beasts." He carried on pulling his arm away from the set jaws of the alpaca.

"I'm going to feed Jake limb by limb to his new fucking pets," Zack muttered under his breath, trying to entice the alpaca away.

He saw Lee Barnes, Jake's farmhand trying to round up the rest of the escaped animals and shouted him over. Lee strode over, taking his own sweet time. He was dressed in just a T-shirt and ripped jeans, oblivious to the cold.

"We have a situation." Zack pointed at the animal. "Please let my cousin know he's going to be in a situation later. Where the hell have these creatures come from? And why?"

Lee shrugged. He was a man of few words at the best of times, preferring to communicate through the set of drums he hit most weekends. He leaned over to the creature and blew at its nose. The alpaca gave a gentle snort and released its death chomp.

"Sorry about that." Lee didn't look that sorry. "I'll get rounding them up."

"Make sure you do." Zack turned back towards Jez. "Why

can't you stop your contractors from working on the hotel and get them back down here?"

Jez rubbed at his arm. "We don't have the budget to pay them what the lass up there has agreed to. And they'll only be a couple of weeks, then they'll come back down here and finish off. I'm sorry, Zack, but there ain't much more I can do."

"I'll see about upping the budget." Zack rubbed his face. He hadn't slept well the night before, which wasn't unusual, but he could do with climbing into bed in one of the unoccupied rooms —or hell, even May Pearson's room because she didn't move from her sofa in front of the TV—and collapsing for an hour or six. "Find out how much more she's paying them and let me know."

Jez shook his head. "But then you'll be stuck paying that rate until the job's done. It's not just extra cash over two weeks, you'll end up going right over. If I were you, I'd hang on till the lass has had her work done. It's only an extension and from what I hear it's pretty straightforward." He looked to where Lee was herding the alpacas, apparently turning into the animal whisperer. "How do you think those animals taste?"

"Not as good as revenge will when I get hold of Jake."

ALSO BY ANNIE DYER

Simone Wood is a restaurant owner who loves to dance, she's just never found the right partner until her head chef Jack starts to teach her his rhythm. Problem is, someone's not happy with Simone, and their dance could be over before they've learned the steps.

Mythical Creatures

The enigmatic Callum Callaghan heads to Africa with the only woman who came close to taming his heart, in this steamy second-chance romance. Contains a beautifully broken alpha and some divinely gorgeous scenery in this tale that will make you both cry and laugh. HEA guaranteed.

Melted Hearts

Hot rock star? Enemies to lovers? Fake engagement? All of these ingredients are in this Callaghan Green novel. Sophie Slater is a businesswoman through and through but makes a pact with the devil – also known as Liam Rossi, newly retired Rockstar – to get the property she wants - one that just happens to be in Iceland. Northern lights, a Callaghan bachelor party, and a quickly picked engagement ring are key notes in this hot springs heated romance.

Evergreen

Christmas wouldn't be Christmas without any presents, and that's what's going to happen if Seph Callaghan doesn't get his act together. The Callaghan clan are together for Christmas, along with a positive pregnancy test from someone and several more surprises!

The Partnership

Seph Callaghan finally gets his HEA in this office romance. Babies, exes and a whole lot of smoulder!

The English Gent Romances

The Wedding Agreement

Imogen Green doesn't do anything without thinking it through, and that includes offering to marry her old - very attractive - school friend, Noah Soames, who needs a wedding. The only problem is, their fauxmance might not be so fake, after all…

The Atelier Assignment

Dealing with musty paintings is Catrin Green's job. Dealing with a hot Lord who happens to be grumpy AF isn't. But that's what she's stuck with for three months. Zeke's daughter is the only light in her days, until she finds a way to make Zeke smile. Only this wasn't part of the assignment.

The Romance Rehearsal

Maven Green has managed to avoid her childhood sweetheart for more than a decade, but now he's cast as her leading man in the play she's directing. Anthony was the boy who had all her firsts; will he be her last as well?

The Imperfect Proposal

Shay Green doesn't expect his new colleague to walk in on him when he's mid-kiss in a stockroom. He also doesn't expect his new colleague to be his wife. The wife he married over a decade ago in Vegas and hasn't seen since

Puffin Bay Series

Puffin Bay

Amelie started a new life on a small Welsh island, finding peace and new beginnings. What wasn't in the plan was the man buying the building over the road. She was used to dealing with arrogant tourists, but this city boy was enough to have her want to put her hands around his neck, on his chest, and maybe somewhere else too...

Wild Tides

Being a runaway bride and escaping her wedding wasn't what Fleur intended when she said yes to the dress. That dress is now sodden in the water of the Menai Strait and she needs saving - by none other than lighthouse keeper Thane. She needs a man to get under to get over the one she left at the altar - but that might come with a little surprise in a few months time…

Lovers Heights

Serious gin distiller Finn Holland needs a distraction from what he's trying to leave behind in the city. That distraction comes in the form of Ruby, who's moved to the island to escape drama of her own. Neither planned on a fake relationship, especially one that led to a marriage that might not be that fake at all…

Manchester Athletic FC

Penalty Kiss

Manchester Athletic's bad boy needs taming, else his football career could be on the line. Pitched with women's football's role model pin up, he has pre-season to sort out his game - on and off the field.

Hollywood Ball

One night. It didn't matter who she was, or who he was, because tomorrow they'd both go back to their lives. Only hers wasn't that ordinary.

What she didn't know, was neither was his.

Heart Keeper

Single dad. Recent widow. Star goal keeper.

Manchester Athletic's physio should keep her hands to herself outside of her treatment room, but that's proving tough. What else is tough is finding two lines on that pregnancy test…

Target Man

Jesse Sullivan is Manchester Athletic's Captain Marvel. He keeps his private life handcuffed to his bed, locked behind a non-disclosure agreement. Jesse doesn't do relationships – not until he meets his teammate's – and best friend's – sister.

Red Heart Card

She wants a baby. He's offering. The trouble is, he's soccer's golden boy and he's ten years younger. The last time they tried this, she broke is heart. Will hearts be left intact this time around?

Severton Search and Rescue

Sleighed

Have a change of scenery and take a trip to a small town. Visit Severton, in Sleighed; this friends-to-lovers romantic suspense will capture your heart as much as Sorrell Slater steals Zack Maynard's.

Stirred

If enemies-to-lovers is your manna, then you'll want to stay in Severton for Stirred. Keren Leigh and Scott Maynard have been at daggers drawn for years, until their one-night ceasefire changes the course of their lives forever.

Smoldered

Want to be saved by a hot firefighter? Rayah Maynard's lusted over Jonny Graham ever since she came back to town. Jonny's prioritised his three children over his own love life since his wife died, but now Rayah's teaching more than just his daughter – she's teaching him just how hot their flames can burn.

Shaken

Abby Walker doesn't exist. Hiding from a gang she suspects is involved in the disappearance of her sister, Severton is where she's taken refuge. Along with her secrets, she's hiding her huge crush on local cop, Alex Maynard. But she isn't the only one with secrets. Alex can keep her safe, but can he also take care of her heart?

Sweetened

Enemies? Friends? Could be lovers? All Jake Maynard knows is that Lainey Green is driving him mad, and he really doesn't like that she managed to buy the farm he coveted from under his nose. All's fair in love and war, until events in Severton take a sinister turn.

Standalone Romance

Love Rises

Two broken souls, one hot summer. Anya returns to her childhood island home after experiencing a painful loss. Gabe escapes to the same place, needing to leave his life behind, drowning in guilt. Neither are planning on meeting the other, but when they do, from their grief, love rises. Only can it be more than a summer long?

Bartender

The White Island, home of hedonism, heat and holidays. Jameson returns to her family's holiday home on Ibiza, but doesn't expect to charmed by a a bartender, a man with an agenda other than just seduction.

Tarnished Crowns Trilogy

Lovers. Liars. Traitors. Thieves. We were all of these. Political intrigue, suspense and seduction mingle together in this intricate and steamy royal romance trilogy.

Chandelier

Grenade

Emeralds

Crime Fiction

We Were Never Alone

How Far Away the Stars (Novella)

Printed in Great Britain
by Amazon

37956047R00202